BLOOD CRUISE

BLOOD CRUISE

MATS STRANDBERG

Jo Fletcher
BOOKS

First published in Great Britain in 2018 by

Jo Fletcher Books
an imprint of
Quercus Editions Ltd
Carmelite House
50 Victoria Embankment
London EC4Y 0DZ

An Hachette UK company

A CIP catalogue record for this book is available
from the British Library

HB ISBN 978 1 78648 780 3
TPB 978 1 78648 779 7
EPUB ISBN 978 1 78648 778 0

10 9 8 7 6 5 4 3 2 1

Typeset by Jouve (UK), Milton Keynes

Printed and bound in Great Britain by Clays Ltd, Elcograf S.p.A.

*This book is dedicated to my mother,
who taught me how to read and always
encouraged me to write. I love you and I miss you.*

Marianne

Almost an hour to go before the ship departs. She can still change her mind. She can still grab her bag and leave, pull it through the terminal building and back up the pier, head down into the underground, go to Stockholm Central Station, travel all the way back home to Enköping. She can try to forget this utterly foolish idea. Maybe at some point she will even be able to have a good chuckle about last night, when she was sitting in her kitchen, where the voices from the radio were unable to fully drown out the ticking of the clock on the wall. After knocking back one too many glasses of Rioja, she decided enough was enough. She downed one more glass and decided to do something about it. Seize the day. Seize adventure.

Sure, at some point she might be able to laugh about it. But Marianne doubts it. It is very hard to laugh at yourself when there is no one to laugh along with you.

What was this whim in aid of anyway? She had seen the advertisement on TV earlier that evening – people in evening wear who looked just like regular people, only a bit happier – but that is hardly sufficient explanation. This isn't like her.

She quickly booked the ticket before she could change her mind. She was so excited she could barely fall asleep, even after all that wine. And the feeling had lingered all morning while she dyed her hair, all afternoon while she packed, all the way here. As though an adventure was already unfolding. As though she could actually escape herself by escaping her everyday life. But now her reflection is staring back at her and her head is pounding and regret has caught up with her, like a hangover on top of her hangover.

Marianne leans forward and rubs at some wayward mascara. In the blueish fluorescent light of the terminal building's ladies' room, the bags under her eyes look grotesque. She backs up. Runs her fingers through her sensible bob haircut. She can still detect a faint whiff of hair dye. She digs a lipstick out of her purse and tops up her makeup with the smooth movements of habit, smacking her lips at her reflection. Pushes down the dark cloud that wants to swell up inside her, swallow her whole.

A toilet flushes in one of the stalls behind her and the door unlocks. Marianne straightens up, smoothing her blouse down. Get a grip, she has to get a grip. A dark-haired young woman in a sleeveless hot-pink blouse emerges from the stall and walks to the sink next to Marianne's. Marianne furtively studies the smooth skin of her arms, the muscles that can be sensed underneath as she washes her hands and reaches for a towel. She is too skinny. Her features are so angular they look virtually mannish. Still, Marianne assumes a lot of people would call her beautiful. Sexy, at least. A tiny diamond twinkles on one of her front teeth. Pink rhinestones on the back pockets of her jeans. Marianne catches herself staring and quickly turns away. But the girl disappears out into the terminal without giving her so much as a glance.

She is invisible. And she wonders if it can really be true that she was ever that young.

It was so long ago. A different time, a different city. She was married then, to a man who loved her as best he could. The children were little and still believed she was some sort of demi-god. She had a job that gave her validation every day. And her neighbours had always been happy to have her over for a cup of coffee when she could spare the time.

Imagine: there had been days when Marianne had dreamed of being alone. A couple of hours in her own company, so she could hear her own thoughts properly, seemed like the height of luxury.

If that was the case, she is swimming in luxury these days. In fact, luxury is all she has left.

Marianne checks her teeth for lipstick. Looks down at the trolley bag next to her, a gift from the book club she is a member of.

She folds her down coat over her arm, resolutely grabs her bag and leaves the bathroom.

There is an excited din in the terminal building. A few people are already queuing by the barriers, waiting to be let on. She glances around, realising that her pink blouse and knee-length skirt are much too formal. Most of the other women in their sixties are either dressed like teenagers, in jeans and hoodies, or have gone the opposite way, hiding under shapeless tunics and tent-like dresses. Marianne doesn't fit in with either group. She looks like an uptight, retired medical secretary. Which is exactly what she is, of course. She tries to force herself to acknowledge that many of them are older than her, uglier than her. She has a right to be here too.

Marianne sets her course for the bar at the other end of the terminal. The wheels of her trolley bag make it sound like she is pulling a steamroller across the stone floor.

Once she reaches the counter she scans the gleaming bottles

and beer taps. Prices are listed in chalk on blackboards. Marianne orders a coffee with Baileys and hopes drinks are cheaper on board. Are the bars tax-free too? She should have checked. Why didn't she check? Her drink is served in a highball Duralex glass by a girl with gleaming scraps of metal in her lips and eyebrows. She doesn't look at Marianne, which eases her conscience about not leaving a tip.

There is a free table at the far end of the glassed-in seating area. Marianne carefully picks her way between the tables with her noisy bag and the coat that seems as big as a duvet. The glass is burning her fingers. Her purse strap slides off her shoulder, landing in the crook of her arm. But at long last she reaches the table. Puts the glass down. Pulls the strap back up and miraculously squeezes through the narrow gap between the tables, coat and all, without knocking down a single thing. When she collapses onto the chair she feels completely drained. She gingerly takes a sip; the beverage is not nearly as warm as the glass so she drinks more greedily. Feels alcohol, sugar and caffeine slowly spread through her body.

Marianne looks up at the mirrored ceiling. Straightens up a little. From the bird's-eye perspective, you can't see the wrinkles on her neck, and the tightness of the skin around her jaw makes it look chiselled. Perhaps it is because the glass is tinted, but her eyes are alert in a face that could almost pass for tanned. She runs her fingers along her jawline until she realises she's preening in public. She deflates in her chair, takes another sip. Wonders how far she is from becoming a bona fide eccentric. One time she made it all the way to the bus stop before noticing she was still wearing pyjama bottoms.

The black cloud threatens to well up again. Marianne closes

her eyes, hearing laughter and talking all around her. There is a loud slurping noise. When she turns that way she sees a small Asian boy examining a glass with nothing but ice cubes left in it. His red-faced father has his phone glued to his ear; he appears to hate the whole world.

Marianne wishes she still smoked, that she could step out onto the pier and have a cigarette, just to have something to do. But at least she is here now. Surrounded by sound. And she makes her mind up. No, this isn't her. But she is so sick of being herself.

She can't go back home. She spent the whole summer cooped up in her flat, listening to laughter and voices and music from the other flats in the building, from the balconies, from the street outside her kitchen. The sounds of life happening everywhere. Back home, that damn kitchen clock is ticking away right now, and the calendar with pictures of grandchildren she has barely met is counting down the days until Christmas. If she were to go home now, she would be trapped in solitude for ever. She would never attempt anything like this again.

Marianne suddenly notices one of the men at the next table smiling warmly at her, trying to catch her eye. She pretends to look for something in her purse. The man's eyes are large in his gaunt, drawn face. His hair is much too long for her taste. She should have brought a book. For lack of a better option, she pulls out her boarding pass and possibly makes too big a show of carefully scrutinising it. The shipping company's logo in the top right corner: a nondescript white bird with a pipe and a captain's hat.

'Hey, love. You here all alone?'

Sheer reflex makes Marianne glance up. The man's eyes meet hers. She forces herself not to look away.

Yes, he's a bit worse for wear. And his light-blue denim waistcoat is filthy. But he must have been gorgeous at some point. She can see it, underneath the face he wears now. Just like she hopes someone will see the same underneath hers.

'Yes,' she says, and clears her throat. 'I was supposed to be going with a friend, but she was confused about the dates; I just found out. She thought it was next Thursday and I . . . I thought that since I had the ticket anyway, I might as well . . .'

She breaks off and concludes with a shrug she hopes comes off as nonchalant. Her voice sounds creaky, as though her vocal cords have dried up. She hasn't used them in several days. And the lie, which she prepared so meticulously the night before, in case of exactly this kind of situation, suddenly sounds laughably transparent. But the man just smiles at her.

'Then squeeze in with us – you need someone to toast with!' he says.

He already seems a bit tipsy. And one quick glance around his table is enough to confirm that his friends are in even worse shape. There was a time when Marianne would never have considered an offer from the likes of this man.

If I say yes, I'll turn into one of them, she thinks to herself. *But I can hardly afford to be picky any more, can I? And besides, isn't 'pickiness' just cowardice by any other name?*

It is only twenty-four hours, she reminds herself. Then the ship will be back in Stockholm. If this turns out to be a mistake, she can bury the memory of it where she has buried so many other things, like the opposite of a treasure chest.

'Sure,' she says. 'Yes. Thank you. That would be nice.'

Her chair scrapes loudly against the floor when she moves over to their table.

'Name's Göran,' he offers.

'Marianne.'

'Marianne,' he says, and smacks his lips a little. 'Yes, that actually suits you. You're as sweet as the Marianne mints.'

Luckily, there is no need for her to respond to that. He starts introducing her to the others. She nods at them, one after the other, forgetting their names as soon as she hears them. They are strangely similar-looking. The same guts bulging under the same chequered shirts. She wonders if they have known each other since they were young. If Göran was always the handsome one, the one who lured girls into the group.

Her coffee is cold and stale by now, but before she has time to gulp it down regardless, one of Göran's friends returns with beer for everyone, her included. Marianne doesn't say much, but no one seems to mind. They drink, and she stops thinking so damn much, starts feeling a tingling of anticipation again. It builds and builds, until she has to stop herself from abruptly laughing out loud like some kind of village idiot. When one of Göran's friends tells a lame joke, she seizes the opportunity. Her laugh is riotous and too loud.

It is sad, really, how much she has missed something as simple as sitting around a table with people. Belonging. Being invited, and not out of obligation.

Göran leans in closer.

'That thing with your friend is unlucky for you, but pretty darn lucky for me,' he says, and his breath his hot and moist in her ear.

Albin

Albin is sitting with his head in his hands, chewing his straw. He sucks melted ice water from the bottom of his glass with a loud slurping sound. There is only the faintest trace of Coke flavour left. Like drinking cold saliva from someone who had a Coke fifteen minutes ago. He giggles. Lo would like that joke. But Lo isn't here yet.

He stares through the glass partition at all the strangers moving around the terminal. One guy is wearing old-lady clothes and has lipstick smeared across half his face. A cardboard sign around his neck reads KISSES FOR SALE. 5 KRONOR. His friends film him with their phones, but you can tell from the way they're laughing they're not really having fun. Albin slurps on his straw again.

'Abbe,' his mum says. 'Please don't.'

She gives him that look that means Dad is already annoyed enough. Don't make it worse. Albin leans back in his chair. Tries to sit still.

He hears a laugh that sounds almost like a dog barking. Looks over that way and spots a couple of overweight girls a few tables away. The one who is laughing is wearing pigtails and something pink around her neck. She tilts her head back and crams a handful of peanuts in her mouth. A few land between her breasts, which are bigger than any he has ever seen in real life. And her skirt is so short he can't even see it when she is sitting down.

'Why does she even have a mobile when it's always switched off?' his dad exclaims and puts his own phone down on the table with a bang. 'Classic fucking Linda.'

'Calm down, Mårten,' his mum soothes. 'We don't even know why they're late.'

'And that's what I'm saying. You would have thought my sister could have called so we didn't have to sit here wondering where the hell they've got to. It's so fucking disrespectful.' His dad turns to him. 'Are you sure you don't have Lo's number?'

'Yes, I told you already.'

It hurts having to admit it again. Lo hasn't been in touch to give him her new number. They haven't spoken in almost a year. They have barely written to each other since she moved to Eskilstuna. He is worried Lo might be angry with him for some reason, a reason that must be a misunderstanding, but his mum keeps telling him Lo is probably just very busy with school because studying doesn't come as easily to her as it does to him, and now that they are in sixth grade, things just keep getting more difficult. When Mum says that, she sounds like when she tries to persuade Albin that the kids bullying him at school are just jealous.

Albin knows better. There is no reason for anyone to be jealous of him. He might have been cute when he was little, but not any more. He is the shortest person in his class, his voice is still high and squeaky and he is not good at sports or anything boys need to be good at to be popular. That is a fact. Just like it is a fact that Lo wouldn't have stopped talking to him unless something had happened.

Lo isn't just his cousin. She was his best friend while she still lived in Skultuna. Then all of a sudden Aunt Linda decided they had to move and Lo had no choice but to go.

Lo, who could make him laugh like no one else, laugh so hard he almost panicked because it felt like the laughing would never stop. Lo, who told him the truth about how Grandma died. They cried together because suicide is so sad, but the secret, shameful thing about it was that he *liked* crying with Lo; it felt good. Finally there was something obviously sad, something they could share, unlike the other stuff, which he can't even talk to Lo about.

'No, Stella,' a man's strained voice exclaims somewhere behind Albin. 'Stop that. Do you want to go straight to bed when we get on board? Do you, Stella?'

His questions are met with furious howling.

'Then stop that right now. It's not funny, Stella. I said no! No, Stella, don't do that. Please, Stella, come on.'

Stella lets out another shriek and a glass shatters. Albin can feel his dad getting more and more agitated and his mum getting more and more nervous about him *causing a scene*. Out of the corner of his eye, Albin notices that familiar movement. The jerk of his dad's head as he empties his pint. His face is even redder now.

'Maybe they're stuck in traffic,' his mum says. 'It's rush hour; lots of people trying to get home from work.'

Albin wonders why she bothers. When his dad is in this mood, there is no way to calm him down. He just gets more worked up when you try.

'We should have picked them up on the way,' he says. 'But then Linda would probably have made sure none of us made it on time.'

He rolls his glass back and forth between his palms. His voice is already sort of fuzzy around the edges and seems to sit further back in his throat.

'I'm sure she'll be here,' his mum says with a glance at her watch. 'She wouldn't want to disappoint Lo.'

His dad just snorts. His mum stops talking, but it is too late now. The silence between them makes the air thick and hard to breathe. If they had been at home, this is the point where Albin would have gone to his room. He is just about to say he needs to go to the bathroom when his dad pushes back his chair and stands up.

'Abbe, another Coke?'

Albin shakes his head; his dad moves off in the direction of the bar.

His mum clears her throat as though she is about to say something. Maybe about last night. That his dad was just really tired. Work stuff. And that with her needing so much help, he never gets to rest. But Albin doesn't want to hear it. *Tired*. He hates the word *tired*, their code word for the unspeakable. His dad is always like this, especially when they are going somewhere or doing something that *should* be fun. He ruins everything.

Albin pointedly pulls his history textbook out of his backpack, which is slung over the back of his chair, and finds the section they have a test on next week. Frowns. Tries to look properly absorbed by scorched-earth tactics, even though he already knows it practically by heart.

'So fitting that you're studying the Swedish Empire when we're crossing the Baltic,' his mum says.

But Albin doesn't respond. He has made himself completely unapproachable to punish her, because he is even angrier at her.

Mum could get a divorce so they wouldn't have to live with him. But she doesn't want to. And he knows why. She thinks she needs Dad.

Sometimes he wishes they had never adopted him. He would have done better in the orphanage in Vietnam. Or he could have ended up anywhere in the world. With another family.

'Look who I found,' his dad says, and Albin turns around.

His dad is holding another beer; Albin can tell from the white foam climbing up the side of the glass he has already started in on it. Next to him is Linda, her blonde hair falling loose over her shoulders. Her jacket is fluffy and pink like spat-out gum. She bends down and hugs Albin. Her cold cheek presses against his.

But where is Lo?

Albin doesn't spot her until Linda moves around the table to hug his mum. He hears his mum make the same old joke she always does – *Apologies for not getting up* – and Linda chuckle like she has never heard it before. But the world around Lo seems to fade until she is the only thing he can make out clearly.

It is Lo, but it is not Lo, not the Lo he knows, anyway. He can't stop staring. She is wearing mascara, which makes her eyes look bigger and paler. Her hair has grown long and it is a bit darker, the colour of honey. Her legs look impossibly long in the tight jeans she is wearing, which end in a pair of leopard-print trainers. She removes her scarf and leather jacket. Underneath, she is wearing a grey jumper that has slipped off one of her shoulders, revealing a black bra strap.

Lo looks like those girls in his school who would never in a million years say hi to him.

This is much worse than a misunderstanding. A misunderstanding could have been rectified.

'Hey,' he says, tentatively, hearing in that short syllable how childish his voice sounds.

'Big shock to find you hovering over a book,' she says.

She's wearing a perfume that smells like caramel and vanilla, and when she speaks he catches intermittent puffs of sweet mint from the gum she is chewing. She gives him a quick hug and he can feel her breasts pressing against him. Albin is almost afraid to look at her when she straightens back up, but her new, adult face has already turned away. She pushes a strand of hair behind her ear. Her nails are painted black.

'Oh my, Lo, how you've grown,' his mum says. 'You look really pretty.'

'Thanks, Aunt Cilla,' Lo says, and gives her a hug as well, a much longer one than the one she gave Albin.

Mum reaches up to get her arms all the way around Lo's back.

'But you're bloody skinny these days,' his dad says.

'Well, she's growing,' his mum replies.

'I hope that's the only reason,' his dad says. 'Boys like a little something to hold on to, you know.'

Albin just wants his dad to shut up, right now.

'Thanks for the info,' Lo says. 'My number one goal in life is to make guys like me.'

The silence that follows lasts half a beat too long, then his dad laughs.

Linda launches into an interminable monologue about which route they took from Eskilstuna and exactly what the traffic was like every single inch of the way. Dad drinks his beer in silence, passive, while Mum tries her best to look fascinated by Linda's narrative. Lo rolls her eyes deep into her skull and pulls out her phone; Albin seizes the opportunity to study her furtively. At length, Linda gets to how hard a time they had finding a parking spot near the terminal and then she is finally done.

'Still, you made it; that's what matters,' his mum says with a glance at his dad.

'Maybe we should go join the queue,' he replies, and empties his glass.

Linda's eyes follow the glass as he sets it down on the table. Albin gets up, puts his history textbook in his backpack and pulls it on.

The queue on the other side of the glass partition is growing and Albin notices that it has started moving forward. He checks the clock on the wall. Only fifteen minutes until departure. People sitting at the tables are getting their things together, finishing their drinks.

Mum checks over her shoulder and starts reversing in her wheelchair, apologising all the while. The people behind her have to push their table aside to let her to pass. She toggles the joystick on the armrest back and forth.

'It's like parallel parking, this,' she says in that slightly too cheerful tone of voice that means she is stressed.

'Are you all right?' Lo says, and his mum replies, 'Of course, sweetheart,' in that same forced-cheery voice.

'Are you looking forward to the cruise?' Linda asks, ruffling Albin's hair.

'Yes,' he replies automatically.

'I'm glad somebody is,' Linda says. 'I thought I was going to have to chain Lo to the car to get her here.'

Lo turns to them and Albin tries not to show how hurt he is. She hasn't looked forward to seeing him at all.

'You didn't want to come?' he says.

'Yeah right. Going on a cruise to Finland is my number one advice to the general public.' She doesn't even talk the same any more. There's a new whiff of mint as she sighs. 'Mum refuses to let me stay home alone.'

'This isn't the time for that discussion, Lo,' Linda says, and stares at his mum and dad. 'You should be happy boys hit puberty later. This is what you have to look forward to.'

Lo rolls her eyes again, but somehow also looks pleased.

'Not necessarily,' his dad says. 'All children are different. And it depends on how much they feel a need to rebel.'

Linda doesn't respond, but after he turns his back she shakes her head.

They start moving towards the exit. His mum goes first, and Albin hears her say *beep-beep* a few times when tables are too close together or suitcases block her way. He looks away. Through the glass partition at the ticket barriers two guards study the people passing through the gates.

'Isn't it heartbreaking that she thought she could pull off a miniskirt?' Lo whispers far too loudly when they pass the girl with the pink feathers around her neck.

'Lo,' Aunt Linda admonishes.

'Maybe if we're lucky the boat'll sink when those two waddle aboard. Then this nightmare would be over.'

The *Baltic Charisma*

The *Baltic Charisma* was built in 1989, in Split, Croatia. She is 560 feet long, 92 feet across and has a carrying capacity of more than 2,000 passengers. But it has been a long time since the Swedish-registered cruiseferry was fully booked. Today is Thursday, and only about twelve hundred passengers are pouring in through the doors. Very few of them are children. It is early November; the half-term break is over. In the summer, the sun deck is crammed with deck chairs, but now it is empty aside from some of the passengers who came on board this morning, in Finland. They gaze out across a cold Stockholm, chilly despite the last rays of the setting autumn sun. Some are waiting impatiently for the *Charisma* to leave port so the bars can reopen.

The woman called Marianne is among the last in the flood of people who slowly stream across the gangway high above the parking lot. The long-haired man has put his arm around her. On the other side of the glass, the sun hangs low in the sky. Its slanted, golden light softens their faces. The tunnel turns sharply left, and now Marianne sees the ship. She is stunned by its size. It is taller than the block of flats she lives in. Storey upon storey of white-and-yellow painted metal. *It should not float.* She notices the bow is open, an enormous, ravenous mouth feeding on rows of vehicles. She wonders if that is the bow visor and the floor suddenly sways under her feet, as if she is already at sea. She thinks about the cabin she booked. The cheapest one available, underneath the car deck. Below the waterline. No windows. The ship seems to grow with every step she takes. The name BALTIC CHARISMA is written on its side in curlicue, the letters several feet tall. The pipe-smoking bird gives her a gargantuan smile. She wants to turn around, run back into the terminal. But she can hear the sound of a kitchen clock ticking in an empty flat, so she keeps on walking. Tries to ignore the sudden notion that they are animals, passively trudging through the corral on their way to the abattoir.

Andreas, the general manager, is standing by the entrance, advertising the karaoke night and the offers available in the tax-free shop, smiling as warmly as he can. The cruise director should rightfully be doing this, but he called in sick this morning. It's the second time since the end of the summer. Andreas is well aware the cruise director has developed a drinking problem since he started working here.

The *Charisma*'s commander, Captain Berggren, is on the bridge, ticking off the boxes on the departure checklist with his staff. Soon, they will pilot the ferry away from the pier with the aid of the navigating officer and the lookout. They are intimately familiar with all the thousands of rocks and skerries and shoals in the Stockholm and Åbo archipelagos. Once the *Charisma* is out of the harbour, she runs on autopilot, and the captain hands control to his staff captain.

*

There is feverish activity in the staff quarters. The employees whose ten-day shifts start tonight have collected their uniforms and changed. Waiters are scurrying from the galley – the *Charisma*'s enormous, steaming kitchen, which supplies food to all the on-board restaurants – with enormous platters destined for the serving tables at Charisma Buffet. Some of them are still hungover after a night of partying. They gossip about who was called to the infirmary to have their blood alcohol levels checked that morning, and who didn't come out of that so well. In the tax-free shop, Antti is conducting a run-through with his staff. When they open back up, half an hour after departure, an impatient line of customers will be waiting outside.

The water is perfectly still in the spa's big, round hot tub. The surface reflects the clouds and sky outside the panorama windows. The massage benches are unoccupied. The heater in the sauna is quietly creaking away.

Down in the engine room, the engines are given a last once-over. If the bridge is the *Charisma*'s brain, the engine room is her beating heart. Chief Engineer Wiklund has just put in a call to the bridge, informing them that refuelling is complete and the fuel line safely disconnected. He studies his engineers through the window of the control room. Finishes his coffee and puts his cup down, looks at the orange doors of the crew lift. As soon as the *Charisma* has made it safely out of harbour and is striking out on its familiar route towards Åbo the staff chief engineer will take over and Wiklund can leave. He doesn't need to come back until they are approaching Åland; he is planning to take a big nap.

*

The *Charisma* has pretty much seen it all. In the no-man's-land of the Baltic Sea, inhibitions are lowered, and not only by cheap booze. It is as though time and space warp, as though the usual rules cease to apply. And the whole thing is monitored by four security guards, who are busy preparing for nightfall, each in their own way. Four people, tasked with maintaining order in the utter chaos that can be wreaked by twelve hundred people, most of them drunk, crammed into an enclosed space they can't leave.

Outside the engine room, on the car deck, members of staff are giving passengers instructions in Swedish, Finnish and English. They have guided lorries, cars, caravans and two coaches to their designated places. Everything is carefully calibrated to ensure the ship's stability. The air down here, where the sun never shines, is cool and smells strongly of petrol and exhaust fumes. Tired lorry drivers and road-tripping families move towards the lifts and stairs. Soon the car deck will be sealed, not to be opened again to passengers until right before docking on Åland. The big lorries are brooding silently in the dark like sleeping animals, tethered to the steel floor with heavy chains.

Everything is routine. The *Baltic Charisma* travels the same route, day after day, year round. She stops at Åland just before midnight. Reaches Åbo in Finland around 7 a.m., at which time most of the Swedish passengers will be sound asleep. In twenty-three hours, the *Charisma* will be docking in Stockholm once more. But on this particular cruise, there are two passengers unlike any the ship has ever seen.

A small blond boy, around five years old, and a dark-haired, heavily made-up woman have just climbed out of their caravan.

They seem tired, gaze almost longingly at the harshly lit lift, but choose the poky stairs instead.

They both keep their eyes carefully lowered, meeting no one's gaze. The thick layer of makeup can't quite hide that there's something wrong with the woman's furrowed face. The boy has pulled up his hood, clutching the straps of his Winnie the Pooh backpack. They smell of lilacs and menthol and something else, something strange yet familiar, and people seem to have noticed, glancing furtively at them. The woman fiddles with an oval gold locket on a thin chain around her neck. Aside from the locket and a gold ring on her left ring finger, she wears no other jewellery. Her right hand is hidden in her coat pocket. She looks at the little creature next to her. His shoes slap against the vinyl carpet. The climb is much steeper for his tiny legs. There is so much love in her eyes. So much grief. But she is afraid of him too: afraid of losing him. Afraid that he is close to the edge, and afraid of what might happen if he steps over it.

Up on the glass-walled gangway, Marianne and the man called Göran walk through a plywood archway decorated with brightly coloured flowers. A woman with dark, frizzy hair points a camera at them; Göran smiles at the lens. The shutter clicks and Marianne wants to ask her to take another one – she wasn't ready – but the woman is already pointing the camera at Göran's friends. And then they step on board. Maroon carpet under their feet. The brass railings, the wood panel and faux marble walls and the smoked glass of the lift doors gleam in the warm lighting. An army of cleaners disembark. Grey uniforms, not a white face among them. Marianne barely listens to what the general manager has to say about the evening's offerings, doesn't recognise the name of the celebrity leading the karaoke.

Overwhelmed with impressions, Marianne's fear melts away, leaving no trace whatsoever. Only anticipation remains. *How is a person supposed to experience it all in just twenty-four hours?* She is here now. And Göran's arm around her tightens. *Let the adventure begin.*

Dan

Dan Appelgren runs and runs, but is getting nowhere. It is a perfect metaphor for his fucking turd of a life. To make it worse, he is running on this cruise ship travelling back and forth, back and forth, along the same route, day after day, night after night. He feels like a mythological ferryman, doomed to travel the same godforsaken waters until the end of time.

He hears the signal indicating the *Baltic Charisma* is leaving port. Warning smaller boats to make way for the monster.

Dan turns up the speed of the staff gym treadmill. The whine it emits rises in pitch. His feet hit the worn rubber harder and faster. He is dripping with sweat; it burns his eyes. The smell is distinctly sour. Chemical residue being squeezed out through his skin. He can taste blood now and his pulse is pounding in his ears. It would be pretty fucking undignified to have a heart attack right now. EUROVISION STAR DIES ON FINLAND BOOZE CRUISE.

He touches his stomach through his soaked vest top. Not too shabby for a forty-five-year-old, but he can't help pinching the thin layer of fat between his skin and what used to be his six-pack. He turns the speed up higher. Just because he's a fucking loser doesn't mean he has to look like one.

The slapping of his soles against the treadmill is the only

rhythm he runs to. He can't handle music in his earphones any more. Being aboard the *Charisma* every night is one long music overdose. Hour after hour in the karaoke bar, where he shepherds the drunks through their caterwauling, cheering them on, pretending he thinks they are hilarious, pretending he hasn't seen and heard it all before. The same songs. The same people, just with new faces. He needs a bloody avalanche of coke to get through it. And to help him sleep he drinks copiously in one of the clubs afterwards. The music is everywhere: a thumping, ear-numbing inferno that kills his soul. Hell's waiting room, where the same bands and the same DJs play the same songs over and over again. Give the mob what it wants.

This fucking boat.

The *Charisma*'s got him. Nothing awaits him on dry land. Not even the gay clubs book him any more. He has nowhere to live and the friends who are willing to open their doors to him have become few and far between. What is he going to do once he has nowhere to go at all? Where is he going to get money? It's not as if he knows how to do anything else, and it's not like he's planning on getting behind the till at McDonald's. On the ship room and board are included, but he spends all the money he makes on trying to forget that this is his life now. Forgetting is expensive, so he is stuck here until he dies, or until the ship is scrapped. Whichever comes first. The race is on: the *Charisma* is a pathetic old eighties behemoth and he has heard the rumours, is aware of the staff's ever-present fear of losing their jobs.

Dan is getting light-headed, as though he has used up all the oxygen in the windowless gym. He slows the treadmill to a walk. Sweat gushes out of him in waves, dripping onto the rubber, evaporating from his hot skin. Eventually, he turns the machine off and steps onto the floor. His legs are shaking. A new wave of dizziness hits while his body tries to come to grips with the fact that the floor isn't moving.

But then it is never truly still either, of course. The vibrations from the ship's engines are always there. His body reverberates with them even when he is on shore leave. He wakes up at night thinking he is still on board, because he can feel the vibrations in every cell, like phantom pains.

His sopping vest top is cold now. Clinging to his skin. Dan drinks greedily from his water bottle and pulls on his sweatshirt. He quickly steps out into the corridor and walks past the common room and the mess, where the staff are having their evening meal, neatly divided into cliques, as always. It is just like school. Plastic potted plants and chequered tablecloths on scuffed old wooden tables. Bread and deli meats and fruit have been set out on a counter. Baskets of ketchup and HP sauce. He spots Jenny and the flabby guys in her dorky little *dansband*. She looks away when she notices him. Hatred bubbles up inside him when unwelcome memories from his first night on board resurface. Jenny is right. He is a has-been. But she is a wannabe wasting her time on never-gonna-bes. And there is absolutely no reason for her to think herself above him. For her to pretend that she has integrity when she works on a fucking cruiseferry. What a fucking joke. At least he knows what he is.

The ship is full of people who would be nobodies on land, but here they live like they're the kings of the world. Like that security guard Pär, who loves his uniform so fucking much it is painfully obvious he must be thoroughly browbeaten in real life, probably by a frigid wife and nasty-looking kids. Or take the captain himself, Berggren, and his posse. They even have a separate officers' mess, so they don't have to eat with the rest of the staff. It isn't even nicer. Just smaller. And with real plants. Everyone on board is obsessed with the pecking order, with the number of stripes on their shoulder bars. Berggren is the lord of the floating manor, of course, and everyone treats him like royalty. But the king of something as pathetic as the *Charisma* is not someone Dan's ever going to kowtow to.

He heads down a flight of stairs to deck nine and turns along a corridor. His cabin is small, but at least it has a window, unlike the staff cabins on deck ten. Jenny's, for example.

Twenty years ago they would have given him the ship's only luxury suite. They would have laid on free dinners in the real restaurants upstairs, allowed him to invite guests on the cruises. And he would probably still have declined. 'Like Fever in My Heart' was at the top of the charts and it would have been beneath him to work on a fucking booze cruise.

Dan removes his sweatshirt. His vest top hits the floor with a smack. He kicks off his shoes, pulls off his socks. The blue vinyl is cold under his feet. When he removes his shorts, the musty smell of old sex wafts from his crotch. What was her name? Everyone he fucks on board the *Charisma* seems to be called Anna, Maria, Marie, Linda, Petra, Åsa. But this girl was younger. Elsa? She said she had adored 'Like Fever in My Heart' when she was in preschool. It simultaneously made him uneasy and got his cock so hard it practically dribbled pre-cum. And she had known exactly what to do with it. Some of the girls born in the nineties are porn-damaged. They turn the bed into an ADD circus show. No position can last more than a few minutes. They want to be held down, have their hair pulled, be strangled. He always has the feeling the attention is the only thing they truly enjoy, and the hope of making an indelible impression.

He scrubs all traces of Elsa off in the shower. Gets a half-boner while trimming his pubes. His cock feels big and heavy. He wonders what Elsa did the rest of the day, after he left the cabin she shared with a friend he never met. Did she roam the ship looking for him? Did she tell her friend everything about what it was like having sex with Dan Appelgren? She might be home by now, wherever home might be. The ship has spat her out and devoured a fresh set of bodies. And soon it will all start up again.

Filip

His coffee went cold while he sorted out the till, but he downs the last of it anyway, hoping the caffeine can help cut through the soupy fog in his head. The *Charisma*'s engines make the glasses hanging above the bar clink softly against each other. He considers doing a shot of Fernet, but picks up a rag and wipes the counter instead.

Filip is doing his eighth consecutive day behind the bar at the *dansband* club Charisma Starlight and he is beyond tired. He feels worn out in the truest sense, as though his body has been put through the wringer and every muscle is torn. He should probably be more worried about how long his body can keep this up. He had a few hours of kip while the ship was docked. When he lay down, his back was so stiff and numb he could barely feel the mattress underneath him. The bar opens again in half an hour, and he will be here until five tomorrow morning.

He gets to go home in a couple of days. Finally catch up on his sleep. Sometimes he is virtually comatose for days on end, only leaving his bed to slump on the sofa in front of the TV. Right now, that sounds like heaven. And yet he knows he will miss the *Charisma* after a week's shore leave. He will be restlessly counting the days until it is time to embark once more.

Marisol comes up behind him, picks up his empty glass and disappears into the staff room. Filip's spine cracks when he straightens up. In the ceiling beyond the bar twinkle the constellations of lights for which Charisma Starlight was named. When he turns around, Marisol is back. She is looking at her phone. The screen illuminates her dimly from below. She smiles as her thumbs dart about the screen.

Filip walks to the stack of drinks crates and starts restocking the fridges with Bacardi Breezers.

'When are you going to stop being so nauseatingly in love?' he says, and laughs.

Marisol slips the phone back into her apron pocket and gathers her long, dark hair into a ponytail. The hair band makes a snapping sound when she twists it into place.

'Well, I'm away from home half the time so I reckon we're allowed twice as long as normal people, no?'

She has lived in Sweden all her life, but there are traces of her Chilean parents' pronunciation in her speech.

'I might forgive you if you'd ever come out partying,' he says. 'You've been proper boring since the two of you got together.'

Marisol grins at him.

He wonders how she makes it work with her new boyfriend. In all his years working aboard the *Charisma* he has never managed to build a relationship with a land-dweller. It becomes unsustainable in the long term. The hurried chats, crowbarred in between shifts and insufficient sleep. His efforts to collect stories, to remember everything that happens on board so he'll have something to talk about when he gets home. But once he's back on dry land, the stories always feel pointless. They have lost their sparkle. It is difficult to bring the two worlds together. Lots of crew members lead double lives. They have one relationship on land and one at sea.

Filip and Marisol work for a while in companionable silence. He enjoys the daily routines with Marisol before the bar opens. It is peaceful, but there is something to get on with. Filip closes the fridge doors and carries the empty crates out to the store room.

'Speaking of lovebirds,' he says when he comes back out, 'I wonder how Calle's doing?'

'Have you heard anything?' Marisol mechanically slices lemons, throwing them into one of the plastic tubs under the counter.

'No, not yet,' he replies, washing his hands and placing a handful of limes on a cutting board.

The wet sound of the knives slicing through fruit fills the silence. The glasses keep on clinking.

'I feel like it was just yesterday Calle worked here,' he says. 'Time bloody flies. It's mental.'

'Yeah, old men tend to think so,' Marisol snipes, and shoots him a sweet smile.

It stings more than he cares to admit.

'You'll be my side of forty in just a couple more years.'

'Are you sure you want to bring that up when I'm holding a knife?' she asks. 'Did you say you've met this new boyfriend?'

'No, I've barely even seen Calle since he quit and moved down south to study. I should have kept in touch but . . . you know how it goes.'

Marisol nods agreement, and Filip realises he might be saying something similar about her one day. To her, the *Charisma* is just a job. To him, the ship is his life, his home. The only place, in fact, where he has ever felt at home. He can't imagine working anywhere else. Yet another thing he should probably be more worried about. Especially now there are rumours the *Charisma*'s days are numbered.

'What did he become?' she asks. 'I mean, what did he study?'

'Garden architect,' Filip replies, 'or something along those lines. Shit, I should really know that, shouldn't I?'

'Probably.'

He hopes Pia knows so he won't have to ask Calle directly.

Marisol is just about to say something else when the steel security grille at the entrance jangles. They exchange a look.

'It's your turn,' she says.

But when Filip walks to the grille, it turns out not to be an impatient passenger trying to get into the bar, but Pia, standing there with a paper bag in her hand, rocking back and forth in her boots.

'I had a text from Calle,' she says. 'They just sat down for dinner at Poseidon.'

'Give me a minute,' he says, and goes back to the bar to hang up his apron. 'It should be quick. But I might not make it back to open.'

'I think I can manage for a bit,' Marisol replies.

There is a loud rattling as Filip fills a Plexiglas bucket with ice. Marisol takes down two champagne glasses and hands them to him when he has finished burying the bottle in the ice.

She walks him to the grille. It sticks in the usual place about three feet off the floor. He can feel Pia and Marisol grinning at each other when he curses. Every goddamn day he has to stand here tugging at this bloody grille. He shakes it, jiggles it, pushes it with his hip while he pulls and finally it rolls all the way up with a deafening clatter.

Albin

Stockholm's archipelago is slowly gliding by outside the windows behind his mum and dad. The last rays of the setting sun set the treetops ablaze. Albin gazes at the wooden villas peeking out between the trees, the gazebos down by the water. He wonders what it would feel like to sit on one of those jetties and watch the big cruiseferries pass. His dad has told him those houses cost at least ten times as much as the terraced house they live in.

His mum says money doesn't buy happiness, but Albin can't imagine anyone being unhappy in one of those houses. Especially if it were on its very own island, which no one could find their way to unless he wanted them to.

'Those idiots in purchasing are clueless,' his dad says. 'The left hand doesn't know what the right hand is doing. And I'm bloody tired of always being the one who has to clean up after them.'

He claims he loves his job, but it never seems that way when he talks about it. It is all problems all the time, problems of other people's making. He is always blameless and everyone else is either stupid or lazy.

When Albin was little, he thought his dad was the best at everything. His dad told him stories where the whole world was under threat from fire-breathing dragons and massive earthquakes, and then he would swoop in and save everyone. But the best stories were the ones about when they picked up Albin from the orphanage in Vietnam. About how he knew instantly that Albin was their little boy, and how they stayed for several months so Albin could get to know them before they brought him back to Sweden. Albin had thought his dad could do anything, knew everything. But now he knows better. Everything that comes out of his dad's mouth is just a story.

Last night, he was talking about Grandma again. Those are always the worst nights.

Maybe I should do what Mum did. Then you'd all be happy, wouldn't you? His voice was really thick and gross.

I've been such a fucking idiot, thinking I was worthy of love.

You would have left me a long time ago if you thought anyone else would have you. You and Abbe just want to get rid of me.

Albin lay awake, listening to his dad pacing downstairs. He wanted to be ready if he heard him coming. His dad's tread on the stairs is like a language unto itself. You can tell if the dad coming is angry dad or the dad who can't stop crying. They are like two completely different dads, even though they say practically the same things. And both dads are scary, because it is as if neither one of them listens or even understands what you are saying. Sometimes, he disappears in the middle of the night. That is when he says he is going to do *it*, that he can't take it any more.

I want you to know that if I can't take it any more, it's not your fault, Abbe. Never think that.

A handful of seagulls fly past the windows. Their beaks open and close, but the screeches can't be heard from inside the Charisma Buffet. All you can hear in here is cutlery clattering against plates and loud voices. If Lo had been here, and if Lo had still been Lo, he would have told her that in the olden days people thought seagulls were the souls of dead sailors. And he would have told her there were tons of shipwrecks everywhere in the Baltic. Tons of dead sailors who were never found.

But Lo isn't here yet. They have started without her.

Lo, who didn't want to come on the cruise with them._

Albin looks at his plate. Potato gratin, meatballs, mini hotdogs, gravlax, egg halves with shrimp. He is hungry and yet there is no room in his stomach. His thoughts are taking up all the available space, like a big lump of cement. Last time he saw Lo was the previous summer. His mum and dad and Linda had rented a cottage in Grisslehamn. It rained almost every day that week; he and Lo read in their bunk beds. He was on the top and sometimes he couldn't stop himself from peering over the edge to watch Lo's face. It had moved unconsciously, so he could tell from her expression what kind of scene she was reading. Every evening they ate soft-serve with mint sprinkles down in the harbour, despite the rain. Lo had seen lots of horror movies and at night she told Albin about all the scariest parts. Sometimes they were so terrified he had to sleep in her bed. They lay awake together, watching the shadows in the corners and the trees moving outside the windows. It was like accidentally peeking behind a curtain they didn't even know existed, glimpsing another world behind the regular one. A bottomless world where anything could be lurking. Albin was so afraid it felt like the fear itself became a magnet that attracted the very thing he was afraid of. And yet those were the best moments of that whole vacation, lying under the blankets with Lo, fear rushing between their bodies, consumed by hysterical laughter they couldn't stop.

'So how's sixth grade treating you, Abbe?' Linda says, and puts a glistening piece of pickled herring in her mouth.

33

'All right, I guess,' Albin replies.

'Are you still doing well?'

'Best in his class,' his dad says. 'His teacher even gives him extra assignments so he won't be bored.'

Albin puts his cutlery down. 'Not for maths. Loads of people are better than me at maths.'

'I hated maths in school,' Linda says. 'That's probably why I've forgotten it all. I can barely help Lo with her homework any more.'

'Abbe just has to learn how to study,' his dad says. 'He's never had to put any effort in before.'

'What's your favourite subject?' Linda asks.

Albin looks at Linda. Braces himself. His aunt is nice. But she is the kind of grown-up who always asks the same boring questions, just for the sake of asking something.

'English and Swedish, I think,' he says.

'I see,' Linda says. 'Well, you did always like reading and making up stories. Lo was the same, but now it's all about makeup and boys.'

The cement in his stomach gets even heavier.

'Have you decided what you want to be when you grow up?' Linda continues, just like Albin knew she would.

He can feel his dad watching him expectantly, but he stubbornly keeps his mouth shut.

'He's going to be a programmer. That's the future,' his dad says. 'He's at least as creative as those guys who came up with Spotify and *Minecraft*. Right, Abbe?'

Albin hates him. That is his dad's idea, but he has managed to persuade himself it is what Albin wants. Albin has no idea what he wants, except that he can't wait to change schools after this year.

'That's exciting,' Linda says. 'Just don't forget us when you're a multi-millionaire.'

Albin tries to smile.

'And what about Lo?' his mum asks.

'She's got it in her head she wants to be an actress,' Linda says with a laugh. 'And, granted, she's definitely a drama queen. I can't deny that.'

It sounds rehearsed; Albin senses it is not the first time Linda has used that line. It's mean to Lo, but his mum just nods and smiles.

'I'm surprised you let her walk around dressed like that,' his dad says.

'Dressed how exactly?'

'She looks pretty grown-up now, with the makeup and everything. I don't know if that sends the right signals.'

His mum eyes him nervously. 'I think Lo looks lovely,' she says. 'I suppose that's how they dress now.'

'Aren't you concerned about Lo growing up too fast?' his dad says, his eyes fixed on Linda. 'She doesn't have a male role model at home.'

The table goes dead silent. All the unspoken things weigh so heavily on Albin he can barely keep upright on his chair. He glances out of the windows again. The gloom is already several shades darker.

'All I'm saying is that there are a lot of nutters out there,' his dad says.

'Thanks,' Linda retorts. 'I'm aware of that.'

His mum clears her throat. 'She's started talking funny,' she says. 'Is that something they do in Eskilstuna, or . . .?'

'No,' Linda says, almost looking like Lo when she rolls her eyes, 'that's just Lo and her friends. It drives me up the wall.'

His dad gets up and Albin watches him. He tops his wine glass up to the brim from one of the taps by the buffet tables.

'How's he doing?' Linda says.

'Just fine,' his mum replies, glancing at Albin as if it is important to keep certain things from him. As if he doesn't already know.

Linda sighs and checks her watch when his dad returns to the table.

'No, you know what, I'm calling Lo,' she says. 'She has to get here soon if she wants to have time to eat.'

'I suppose she learned timekeeping from her mother,' his dad replies. He has that look on his face he always has when he pretends to be kidding but actually means it.

'I'll go and get her,' Albin says, and gets up before anyone has time to object.

He needs to get out of here.

Dan

He jogs down the white-painted staff stairwell to the seventh floor. Cuts through the general manager's depressing, windowless office. Posters of old sea maps on the walls, row after row of binders on the shelves. The general manager himself, Andreas, doesn't seem much livelier. He barely looks up when Dan walks past him and opens the door to the public areas. The din and music hit him like a wall. He stares down at the maroon carpet, trying to look stressed and busy while he walks the few feet to the information desk. *Do not disturb.*

Someone tugs at his elbow.

'Aren't you Dan Appelgren?'

He plasters a big smile on his face and turns to face a short-haired woman. Blue-and-white-striped top. He wonders if all the old hags in blue-and-white-striped jumpers wear them all the time or just when they are on a cruise. Do they imagine they have something of a *maritime air* about them?

'Guilty,' he says with a winning chuckle.

'I knew it!' the woman says, as if she deserves a standing ovation.

She is probably his age, but she has really let herself go. Smoking wrinkles line her top lip. There are grey roots in her hair. Her top is tight enough to reveal the rolls of fat above her bra strap.

'My husband and I fell in love to "Like Fever in My Heart",' she says.

'That's nice to hear,' Dan replies.

'Yes, well, he's my ex-husband now. But I still like the song.'

He laughs politely. Reckons the ex-husband hasn't regretted ditching her for one second.

'It should have gone through to the Eurovision finale,' she presses on. 'But I suppose people tell you that all the time.'

'I never tire of hearing it,' Dan says, and winks at her.

No, he thinks to himself, *I never tire of being reminded of my failure. Of the fact that even when I was a winner, I was a loser.*

'I just wanted to tell you that,' the woman says.

But she doesn't walk away. She is clearly expecting something.

'Thank you,' Dan says. 'That means a lot.'

She finally nods and starts walking towards the tax-free shop. Dan goes to the information desk and Mika wordlessly hands him the microphone. He looks long-suffering, as ever. He is the only one who seems to hate the *Charisma* as much as Dan does.

Dan clears his throat and pushes the ON button.

'Dear passengers! This is Dan Appelgren and I am hoping to see as many of you as possible in the karaoke bar tonight!'

A few passengers stop to watch curiously. A small Asian boy holds up his phone; Dan fires off a smile, holding it until he hears the shutter click.

He turns back to the microphone, mustering all his energy to get through the usual litany and putting exclamation points at the end of every single sentence. 'We have everything from golden oldies to the hottest hits of the day! There is something for everyone, and remember: everyone is a singer! And, of course, we have special offers on beer, wine and cocktails! The party starts at nine in the karaoke bar, which is located at the bow end of deck seven! See you there!'

The *Baltic Charisma*

The ship glides through the archipelago at the leisurely pace of fifteen knots. The light from her lanterns and myriad windows sparkles in the dark water.

Up on the bridge, all is calm. Captain Berggren has gone to bed in his quarters. The lookout is scanning the waves for small vessels the radar might have missed, and the on-duty officer makes sure they stay within the speed limit.

In the galley on deck eight, these are the most stressful hours of the day. Cooks and servers call out to each other. There is sizzling and steaming from the ranges and deep fryers, clattering and rattling from the big crates of dirty dishes that are pushed through the wheezing dishwashers; the sound of rapid-fire knives against cutting boards is like a drumming of woodpeckers.

In the spa, a middle-aged couple are soaking in the hot tub. They are holding hands under the surface, gazing out through the large, arched windows. Below them is the bow deck, where people have gathered to look at the last band of islets and skerries before the ship reaches the open sea. The sun has set, but the sky is not yet completely dark.

*

Pia and Filip have just set out an ice bucket with champagne on the upper floor of the split-level suite; now they are putting up a large banner together above the bed.

General Manager Andreas is at his desk; he watches Dan Appelgren walk past again. He opens a binder. Despair overwhelms him when he thinks about all the bills that have to be paid, about the owners who want him to make staff cuts.

The boy called Albin is standing at the foot of the stairs on deck six, studying a deck plan. He finds the red dot telling him where he is and searches the long rows of tiny, numbered squares. There are so many of them. And there are blind spots here and there that remind him of an unfinished jigsaw puzzle. Albin wonders what might be hiding in those white areas. He finds numbers 6512 and 6510 all the way at the other end of the ship. He runs down the portside hallway. The plan made it look long. In reality, it seems endless. A couple of older ladies watch him fondly as he dashes past.

Pre-parties are under way in several cabins, aided by purchases from the tax-free shop. Anticipation is building in lockstep with the temperature and volume. There is a stag do in one of the cabins on deck five. The groom is wearing a white veil. They are singing a drinking song.

The dark-haired woman with the heavy makeup can hear them. She is standing in front of a mirror in a cabin just a few feet away. Applying yet another thick layer of powder. Her breasts dangle like empty skin flaps on her chest; she is wearing a dark cardigan over her black dress. She buttons it all the way up, imagining the day when she will look like this permanently: when *she* will be one of the Old Ones. The thought fills her with horror, but the alternative, not living long enough, is just as frightening. She looks out of the window, rubbing her hands together as if for warmth. Her flesh moves strangely under her skin, as if it is too loosely attached to her bones and sinews. Two fingers are missing from her right hand, severed above the first knuckle.

'It'll be dark soon,' she says, turning to the boy who is tucked into the double bed. He doesn't meet her eye. 'I'll be quick,' she adds and brushes lilac-scented oil on her neck. Her unharmed right index finger traces the chain of her necklace, stops at the locket. She attempts a smile. Her teeth are yellow. The enamel of some of them is chipped. The boy makes no answer; the woman's smile fades.

She bows her head and steps out into the corridor, shoves her hands into her cardigan pockets, glances anxiously at the strong lights and quickens her pace. Her shoes murmur against the maroon carpet as she passes door after door after door, all identical. Voices seep out from behind some of them. A group of lads bellowing something that might be a football chant. A woman laughing. Loud music. The woman is nervous. She is thinking that it is too risky to do this on board, but she won't make it further into Finland if she doesn't. Exhaustion has turned every bone in her body to stone. It saturates her flesh, boring all the way into her soul. *If I still have one.*

A door is thrown open in front of her and a handful of young men in their twenties tumble out; she quickly turns towards the nearest door, pretending to search her pockets for a key card. Once they have moved off, she carries on down the corridor, discreetly sniffing the air. The smell of them is overpowering in the narrow hallway: cheap aftershave, warm skin fresh from the shower, wet hair. Beer, tar-flavoured lozenges, brushed teeth. But the strongest smells of all emanate from their bodies: their anticipation and blissful intoxication. The feelings make their blood pump faster, closer to the surface. The smells are so strong she can almost taste them. She fights to maintain her self-control.

She reaches a side passage leading towards the main stairs. There are more people here. She keeps her eyes fixed on the carpet as she lets the flow of people carry her upwards, trying to focus, to fend off the hundreds of synthetic smells assaulting her nostrils. Underneath there is sweat, blood, hormones, urine. The sharp metallic hint of dried semen on someone's skin. Scalp grease. Her hunger is growing ever more ravenous. It crowds out her doubts.

The woman's son leaves the bed and peers out of the cabin door. He squints at the corridor. Light falls on him, revealing a face that is dry and wrinkly like paper. He wonders how much time he has before she is back.

Albin

He jumps when a door opens with a bang behind him and turns around. A couple about the same age as his mum and dad practically fall out of their cabin. The woman leans against the man while he locks the door, and Albin notices a line of sweat running down his shirt, between his shoulder blades.

'That buffet is going to be so fricking good,' the man exclaims, too loudly, as though the woman were far away rather than right next to him. 'I've been dreaming about it for, like, a bloody week now, you know?'

The woman nods. Her eyelids are heavy. She reminds Albin of a doll Lo had. It was supposed to close its eyes when you laid it on its back, but the eyelids were stuck in an in-between position, neither awake nor asleep.

Neither one of them notices Albin as they walk off in the direction he came from. He continues down the corridor, unsuccessfully trying to figure out where the unmarked areas on the plan might be. A door opens in one of the side corridors as he passes and two gaunt women in sparkly dresses step out. Both have long, narrow faces and dark-red lipstick on their extremely thin lips, which makes it look like someone slashed their faces open.

'Tonight's going to be amazing, Mum,' one of them says. 'So fucking *amazing*!'

'Watch out, boys, here we come!'

Their raucous laughter echoes down the hallway behind him.

When he finally reaches door 6510, almost at the very end of the hallway, he taps it gingerly. As he waits, he notices the vibrations in the floor, hears other doors opening and closing. He knocks again.

'Stellar job of stressing me out!' Lo shouts from inside, and then the door is thrown open.

Lo has put her hair up and her face has been transformed yet again. Her skin looks like impenetrable plastic. Her lips glisten, her eyelids shimmer. She looks relieved to see it is him. She retreats back into the cabin; he hesitates for a moment before following her.

'I saw Dan Appelgren,' Albin says, and holds up his phone. 'I took a picture.'

'Super,' Lo says without turning. 'He is my number one entertainer in the world.'

Albin doesn't respond, wishing he hadn't said anything. Lo gets down on all fours next to the double bed. The smell of her perfume is everywhere. A jumble of clothes and a pink toiletry bag are scattered across the bed. Makeup and jewellery litter the tiny desk. A big round hairbrush and a hairdryer have been discarded on the floor. The dryer is still plugged in. It's like a tsunami of girlishness has swept through the cabin, leaving wreckage on every surface.

'Are they totally bitter about me being late?'

'You won't have time to eat if you don't hurry,' Albin says, perching on the edge of the bed.

'That's heartbreaking,' Lo says, and sits back up on her knees. 'I always wanted to get food poisoning from that place.'

She has pulled out a miniature vodka bottle, a brand he recognises. If it had been regular-sized, Lo would have been a giant. She unscrews the top, purses her glistening lips around the neck and drinks. She gags and her eyes tear up, but then she giggles and holds the bottle out to him.

'Do you want some or what?' Lo asks, and grins when he shakes his head. 'There's a couple more if you change your mind.'

'But what if Linda finds them?'

'Then I'll tell her the cleaners must've missed them,' she replies, and gets to her feet.

'You told me you'd never start drinking.'

Lo looks at him with something bordering on pity. 'We were, like, ten,' she says. 'Kinda seems like you still are.'

'No, I'm not.' He sounds so childish. He should shut up. He doesn't know how to talk to this Lo. He doesn't even know who she is. 'Where did you get the bottles?' he says.

'That's why I'm late. The tax-free shop just opened.'

'But children can't buy alcohol.' He gets it as soon as he says it. Lo shoplifted the vodka.

She finishes off the bottle and rolls it under the bed. 'Thanks for the info,' she says, taking a piece of gum out of her jacket pocket and putting it in her mouth. 'I guess we'd better head out, then.'

Madde

A warm, damp fog that smells sweet and fruity fills the tiny bathroom. She has washed her hair, lathered up her whole body, scrubbed her face. She is standing under the hot jet, letting it unknit her shoulders and back, rinse away the drab, the everyday, the so-called 'reality'. She looks down at the drain at her feet, imagining the water disappearing down it and out into the Baltic Sea.

Madde had the exact right number of drinks at the terminal. She is going to the buffet with her best friend, and she is going dancing and then, who knows? Anything can happen on a cruise-ferry. And she can be whoever she wants. Or rather, she can be who she really is.

She has taken tomorrow off work. When her colleagues are on the subway out to Kista, she and Zandra will be starting their day with a champagne breakfast.

She is going to have a lot of fucking time off soon, probably for a long fucking time, but that is the last thing she is going to think about tonight. She is not going to think about her boss, who tilted his head and looked so sorry about it all. Like she doesn't know he will likely get a fat bonus in return for the money he saves by getting rid of the admin assistants.

She is glad she didn't cancel this trip. It is exactly what she needs.

'Are you dead in there, or what?' Zandra calls from the other side of the door. 'It's like a greenhouse in here!'

'Coming!'

Madde reluctantly turns the shower off and pulls the white curtain aside. Wraps a towel around her head like a turban. Wipes the condensation from the mirror above the sink, but only catches a fleeting glimpse of her glowing red face before it fogs back up.

She grabs another towel, the perfect level of rough, and rubs herself dry. The intro to 'Livin' on a Prayer' starts playing on the other side of the door. Madde smiles and throws the towel on the floor. How many times have the two of them listened to this song? It was one of the first albums Madde bought: they lived on Solgatan in Boden, they had just started fourth grade and they had just discovered makeup. Zandra still spelled her name with an S; they were both in love with Jon Bon Jovi and they both thought the song was about living on a prairie.

Zandra opens the door without knocking and hands her a bottle of super-strength beer. 'I saw those four Italian guys again,' she says. 'In the tax-free. God, they're so fit, even though they're so short.'

'If they're too small, just grab 'em all,' Madde says, and takes a swig from her bottle. After the sweet strawberry cocktails at the terminal the beer tastes bitter and boozy.

'So long as they're not too small where it counts,' Zandra replies, and holds out her own bottle. 'Cheers, you old slut.'

'Cheers, you toothless slag.'

The bottles clink and Madde pours more beer down her throat.

'I'm, like, drunk already,' Zandra says, leaning against the doorpost.

'Then slow it down. We have to last all night.'

'We will, don't worry. We're not *that* old.'

'No, but you know how it goes sometimes,' Madde says, and puts deodorant under her arms. 'We don't want to peak too soon.'

'Sure thing, Mum,' Zandra replies with a grin.

'Oh my God, I need to have fun tonight. Otherwise I'll go out of my mind.'

'You know we're going to have fun. We always do, right?'

Madde starts rubbing on body lotion. The specks of gold in it make her skin shimmer faintly.

Zandra disappears from the doorway and Madde turns to the mirror. Her reflection slowly emerges from the glass, like a ghost out of mist. She takes a few more swigs of beer. The glugging of the bottle is very satisfying. The roar of the hairdryer drowns out the music, but she still sings along while the smell of conditioner and warm hair fills the cramped space. She sprays her blonde curls into place, finishing them off with a second spray that also contains gold glitter, until it looks like her hair is made of spun gold. She does her makeup as quickly as she is able. She kills the bottle once her eye shadow is in place. She has already started sweating again after the shower.

'I need a smoke,' Zandra calls.

'Me too,' Madde says. 'I'll be done in a second.'

'Hurry up. I'm going stir-crazy just sitting here staring at the walls.'

Madde refrains from reminding Zandra that she was the one who booked a cabin with no window. Their cabin is on deck nine, off the central hallway. A tiny shoe box, jammed in between other shoe boxes. But Zandra had pointed out that the only time they would be in their cabin was when they were sleeping. If then. And Madde had reminded herself that she had to get better at saving, on account of the thing she isn't supposed to be thinking tonight.

'Go on ahead if it's so bloody awful,' Madde calls, and studies her face in the mirror.

Every part of her glints and sparkles. The soon-to-be-unemployed admin assistant has been completely erased.

When she steps out into the cabin she bursts out laughing. Zandra has put up a string of bright plastic flowers around the mirror by the desk. Inside each flower is a little light.

'You've made it so pretty,' she says.

Zandra turns the TV on. Switches channels until they can see the Club Charisma dance floor. Still empty. But not for long. Madde feels a fluttering of anticipation.

'Here,' Zandra says and hands her a shot of Minttu.

The smell of mint in Madde's nostrils is refreshing.

'Cheers to tonight,' Zandra intones solemnly. 'May it end any which way.'

'Any which way!' Madde echoes, and downs the shot.

The cruise is officially under way.

She squats down next to her suitcase, rummages through the clothes inside and pulls out her short black dress, which is so transparent it is barely there.

When she is dressed and has put in her big gold hoop earrings, she sprays a dense cloud of perfume in the air in front of her and does a little pirouette to help the scent get to every part of her. Zandra coughs theatrically.

'How do I look?' Madde asks.

'Fat but hot,' Zandra replies, and disconnects the speaker from her phone. 'Just like me. Now let's go.'

Madde stuffs the essential makeup things into her purse. Zandra wraps her feather boa around her neck and adjusts her tits in her bra. They step into the corridor. The door proves difficult; it refuses to lock until they slam it shut with a loud bang. An old man who is closing the door to his own cabin studies them, amused. His eyes wander up and down their bodies.

'Did you forget to put clothes on, girls?' he says slimily.

'No,' Madde replies. 'We forgot to take them off.'

Zandra giggles and takes her hand.

Marianne

Marianne reaches the eighth floor and steps into a spacious hallway with floor-to-ceiling windows running along its left-hand side. The lighting is warm and not too bright. It is flattering to the people moving about. A young couple passes, hand in hand, beaming with infatuation. A group of women her own age laugh loudly. Marianne walks on. Passes Poseidon, a restaurant with white linen tablecloths. She walks past a café and a pub, turns around and spots the restaurant she has been looking for at the end of the hallway, right next to the stairs she just came up. Charisma Buffet's large, smoked-glass doors are open. But no Göran. Didn't they say to meet outside?

Marianne takes up position by the windows. The dusk has sucked the last juicy morsel out of the dying day. She pretends to gaze out across the water, but in reality she is studying her spectral reflection. She could really do with a glass of wine. She runs her fingers through her hair. Sniffs her wrist discreetly and wonders whether she poured on too much perfume before leaving her cabin.

People pass behind her; she studies them in the window. Everyone seems to know exactly what they want, where to go. She has no idea.

She runs her fingers through her hair again, suddenly feeling a creeping sense of unease, like ants under the skin of her back.

She realises she feels watched. Marianne furtively glances this way and that. No sign of Göran. But the feeling is growing more intense. She becomes aware of the piano music trickling out from Poseidon. Vaguely Irish rock music from the pub.

Further down the hallway, a couple of dishevelled old men have parked themselves in front of some kind of games machines with large screens. Beyond them, in a little booth, she spots the woman who took their picture when they boarded. Marianne peers into the pub, which is depressingly dark. There are shamrocks on the mirrors behind the bar, adverts for the kind of dark beers that taste like wet bread. A green neon sign informs her the place is called McCharisma. The clientele is predominantly male, and none of the guests is Göran. The only woman is sitting at the far back. Her hair is dark, dull. She has wrapped a cardigan around her and looks cold. Despite the gloom, the furrows underneath her heavy makeup are clearly visible. Her eyes lie in shadow. A glass of beer sits untouched on the table in front of her.

The ants under Marianne's skin multiply and march up to her scalp. Suddenly she is sure the woman in the pub is the one watching her.

There is something about the woman's face: something wrong. *It's not as it should be.*

It must be a trick of the light, she tells herself. The unfortunate makeup reminds Marianne of that old film with Bette Davis. *And why would she be sitting there staring at me, of all people?*

Two men with babies strapped to their chests pass her. Marianne glances at the infants, the plump cheeks, the kicking legs, the happy, toothless mouths.

'There you are! My little mint sweet!'

Göran is hurrying towards her. He takes her by the arm like it is the most natural thing in the world and leads her to the buffet restaurant. She shoots McCharisma one last look. The woman is studying the table top. Her hair is hiding her face. Now all Marianne sees is a vaguely tragic character, alone. Not unlike herself.

Göran's friends are waiting outside Charisma Buffet. The man behind the pulpit inside the glass doors gives them a business-like smile and shows them where their table is located on a stencilled seating chart.

'Are you hungry?' Göran asks as they proceed inside.

The wall of voices and clattering cutlery nearly overwhelms Marianne, as though she is on the brink of dissolving into atoms and disappearing. She realises she has to give Göran some kind of answer. The smell of warm food fills her nostrils. She nods. And then she spots the buffet tables. Row after row of different dishes.

'Oh my goodness,' she hears herself exclaim. 'Where do you even start?'

Göran chuckles, pleased by her surprise. She looks at him and is unexpectedly struck by the crazy notion that by the time they disembark, she might be in love.

Calle

Unobtrusive piano versions of Frank Sinatra hits provide the acoustic backdrop at Poseidon. There are only a few guests, and it is still early enough for most of them to be talking quietly.

Calle and Vincent's eyes meet across the enormous shellfish platter that has just been set down on the white tablecloth: a mountain of lobster, langoustine, crayfish, fresh prawn, smoked prawn, clams and crab claws on glittering ice.

'Bon appétit!' says the server, whose gel-infused spiky hair has been meticulously combed every which way.

'This is actually kind of sick,' Vincent opines with a laugh once they are alone again.

'I told you,' Calle says, and raises his champagne flute. 'Cheers.'

'Yes,' Vincent replies, 'cheers to me finally seeing this part of your life.'

They both sip their drinks. Calle is so nervous he can barely get his down. He looks at his hand, surprised it is steady.

He was on the brink of outright panic when they changed for dinner. He stared at the outfits he had packed. Whatever happens, they are both going to remember tonight, and he wants to look as good as possible in Vincent's memories. He settled on a black jacket and a white T-shirt, his oxblood Dr Martens.

'So how does it feel to be back?' Vincent asks. 'Does it look the same?'

Calle nods. It does. When they boarded, the smells that somehow always clung to the ship hit him. The sweet, sickly hangovers and old beer, the vinegary carpet cleaner. It was like being thrown eight years back in time. But it wasn't just the memories from the *Charisma* that resurfaced, it was the memory of who he was back then. He hadn't seen that coming. That was when he realised this might not be such a good idea after all.

'It's a lot more run-down,' he says. 'And there are fewer people. I guess the *Charisma*'s not quite keeping up with the competition these days. The new ships are bigger and have more bling.' He tries to sound casual, but he had been sad to see the wear and tear. Or maybe he was simply seeing her with fresh eyes.

'Our suite's pretty damn swanky, though,' Vincent says with a grin.

'That's because it's almost always empty,' Calle replies. 'Not a lot of people are eager to spend that much for one night on a cruiseferry.'

'How much is it then?'

'No idea. Filip sorted me out with a discount.'

Filip, who might be in the suite with Pia right now.

He watches Vincent reach for a crab claw and break it open.

'Are you not having anything?' Vincent says, and dips the meat in aioli before shoving it in his mouth.

'Yeah, sure,' Calle says, doing his best imitation of someone who is not about to have a nervous breakdown. 'I'm just not that hungry.'

'You can't leave me with all this,' Vincent says.

Calle picks up a prawn and clumsily peels it. It tastes rubbery; he focuses on chewing.

'It's so gorgeous out there it's almost ridiculous,' Vincent says, gazing out of the window. 'We have to go outside and have a look later.'

The skerries are darker shadows in the blue-tinted gloom. Here and there, lights twinkle between the trees. Calle murmurs agreement, studying Vincent's profile: his slightly bumpy nose, his dark hair, his superhero chin. His moustache accentuates the full middle part of his lips. The blue of his eyes always seems to shift with the light, just like water. His face is so alive. How many times has he looked at Vincent and felt like it is the first time he sees him?

'It's hard to believe the Baltic is so polluted when you see it like this,' Vincent says.

'Yes,' Calle agrees and stares at the shellfish, none of them fished from the waters outside the window. 'If Poseidon were real he'd probably have moved away.'

Vincent laughs, picks up a prawn and peels it.

It has been five years since their first date and it took Calle a long time to get past the feeling of not deserving Vincent, not deserving that kind of blessing. They are settling into their new flat and every morning Calle wakes up in their bedroom with its tall white walls, wondering how it all came to be. It is still hard to believe sometimes that he and Vincent finally found their way home.

And now he is about to ask for an even bigger blessing.

'Where did you go?' Vincent says.

Calle shakes his head. 'It's just so weird being back on the *Charisma*.'

He spots a woman wearing a security officer's uniform approaching their table. Her dark hair is tied in a bun in exactly the same way as always. But there are grey roots in it now, which give the impression that it is thinning. Her uniform is a few sizes larger than last time he saw her. And she looks tired, despite the big smile on her face.

'Calle!' she says. 'I heard tell you might be sailing with us today! It's so good to see you!'

Her voice sounds the same: raspy and warm and close to laughter. A voice with a magical ability to calm drunk and disorderly passengers. A voice that can take on a steely edge when required. How many laps around the promenade deck have they walked together, just talking, talking, talking?

'Hi, you,' he says, and gets to his feet. 'You look the same.'

'And you're still a bad liar,' she replies, giving him a warm hug. 'But *you* look so handsome these days!' Pia takes a step back, looking him up and down, then runs her hand over his shaved head and grins. 'I think success suits you,' she says. 'And the beard does too.'

'This is Vincent,' Calle says. 'My boyfriend.'

Vincent gets up, shakes Pia's hand. They eye each other curiously.

'Sweet ink,' she says, nodding to the tattoos covering his arms. Classic Japanese style but with Swedish motifs. Cloudberries and elks. Salmon instead of koi.

'It's nice to meet you,' he says, sitting back down. 'Maybe you can tell me about what Calle was like eight years ago?'

'Lost,' Calle says, too quickly, and smiles, too big.

'He wasn't that lost,' Pia says. 'They would have made him retail manager if he hadn't quit.' She looks almost proud as she says that.

'Pia's on-board security,' Calle adds.

'I gathered from the uniform,' Vincent says with a smile. 'So, good gig?'

'Well,' she says, 'something's keeping me here. I suppose it's because I like the people I work with. Most of them anyway. There are almost two hundred crew members on the ship every time we set out.'

Vincent gives a low whistle.

'But the passengers'll drive you insane,' Pia continues. 'Sometimes I feel like I'm working at a big playgroup for adults.'

Vincent laughs. 'Things look surprisingly serene to me,' he says. 'These boats are pretty infamous, after all.'

'We'll see how you feel when we're closer to midnight,' Pia says, looking at Calle. 'But it might be quite a calm night. It's almost fifty-fifty.'

'Fifty-fifty?' Vincent asks. 'Of what?'

'It's pretty common to have a disproportionate amount of men,' Calle explains. 'And that almost always means a lot of fighting.'

'Yep. If they can't get laid, they need something else to do,' Pia says, and puts a hand on Calle's shoulder. 'But tell me, what do you actually do these days?'

Calle looks at her and thinks what a good actor she is, but then he realises she really doesn't know. They never got that far on the phone. They had mostly talked about Vincent, and about what Calle has come here to do.

'I'm a landscape architect now,' Calle replies.

The title makes him hesitate; he still isn't used to it. He feels like a fraud every morning when he steps into the plush office by Skanstull.

'So you do flowers and stuff?' Pia asks.

'No, not quite,' he says. 'I guess you could say a landscape architect does the same kinds of things a normal architect does, apart from the actual buildings.'

Something in his tone jars. Does he sound like he thinks he is better than her?

'I see,' she says slowly.

'You design landscapes,' he continues. 'Everything from which trees to plant in a park to how to plan a city square . . .'

'It never occurred to me that that's someone's job,' Pia says.

'Well, that's not unusual – most people don't realise,' Calle says. 'It's the kind of job where, you know, if a landscape architect is good at their job, you never even notice.'

He wonders if what he said makes any kind of sense, because he feels muddled.

'That sounds really cool,' Pia says. 'I always knew you'd make something of yourself.'

'And you? How are you?' he asks to change the subject. 'Your kids must be grown now.'

'Twenty and twenty-one,' she says.

Calle shakes his head incredulously. He met them once, when he spent a few nights at Pia's house on Åland. They had both been mid-puberty and it was like something from a poor version of *The Exorcist*, all slamming doors, stomping and deranged shrieking. And Pia had just got divorced. But she still found the energy to listen to his problems. God, he had been so young then.

'Do you have any plans while you're on board?' Pia asks.

'I'm counting on getting a guided tour tonight,' Vincent says. 'And Calle has booked us spa treatments tomorrow.'

'Nice,' Pia says, and turns to Calle. 'But, hey, if you *really* want to show Vincent something special, we should take him up to the bridge when you're done eating.'

She makes it sound so natural, like she only just thought of it. Calle gives her a grateful look.

'Do you think that would be okay?' he asks.

'Sure. Berggren's in charge tonight, and you know him, right?' she says. She looks at Vincent again. 'After 9/11, we're not really supposed to let people up there, but I'm sure the captain will make an exception for you two.'

'That would be awesome,' Vincent says. 'But only if we're not in the way.'

'I'm sure it's fine,' Pia says. 'I'll come and get you at the end of this sitting. I can probably get away for a bit around then.'

'Thanks,' Calle says.

'No problem,' Pia says, and winks at him. 'Filip says hi, by the way.'

After she leaves, Calle knocks back his champagne, and Vincent tops up both their glasses.

'She seems cool,' he says.

'She is,' Calle replies. 'She was the one who gave me the courage to quit and go back to school.' *And I thanked her by disappearing from her life*, he adds to himself.

'What did you mean about being lost?' Vincent says, and grabs a langoustine. 'Lots of partying or what?'

'That's putting it mildly. I was drunk almost every night after work.'

A few times he'd been caught with elevated blood alcohol levels the next morning. Nurse Raili, who was in charge of the breathalyser, had been sorry to have to report him. He had been brought in for a talk with Captain Berggren and the general manager, told this was his last chance. He'd promised not to drink again, but of course he did.

'It wasn't just that,' he says. 'It's hard to explain.'

'Try. I'm curious.'

'Well, I thought this gig was just temporary. But time kept passing. It was like . . . I made more money than I could have dreamed of at that age. With all the add-ons, I netted almost twenty-five thousand kronor a month. Plus tips. And you spend hardly any of it, except on alcohol, and they sold that to us at a discount. There's this thing called the slop ration; it's like a ration you can buy for your own private consumption for practically nothing. And my friend Filip used to give me free drinks in the bar where he works.'

He breaks off, pausing to think. How to explain what it was like? 'This bizarre world is like a bubble and anything outside the bubble starts feeling a bit unreal after a while.'

'Don't you ever miss them?' Vincent asks.

Calle ponders the question, playing for time by picking the meat off a lobster tail. He can't remember ever having a better time than on this ship. Pia and Filip were the best friends he has ever had. But he always knew he had to move on before he got stuck. He just didn't know how.

And there had been things he couldn't stand. But it was only afterwards, when he returned to the normal world, that he realised how much he had grown accustomed to it. The extreme macho culture on board. The Finns who claimed all Swedes were gay. And the Swedes who did everything to prove the Finns wrong. The casual racism. Their shop manager, who with a significant look might say that *it was looking 'dark' on the gangway today.* Or Lill, who was in charge of the perfume section and openly complained that *it's actually really difficult to find a scent that suits the Africans, because they smell so different.* The persistent myth that Arabs brought their own camp stoves to cook in their cabins, because they were too cheap to eat in the restaurants. And Calle hates himself for not having put his foot down more often. More forcefully. For not asking who it was who had seen all these Arabs with their camp stoves. But he had been too young, too much of a coward.

Instead, his strategy had been to assume the role of the 'fun gay guy'. He took every opportunity to score cheap points with gay jokes before someone else could beat him to it. He made himself completely harmless to the macho guys. Slipped into the role of the girls' finger-snapping, bitchy gay friend. It was so easy. Too easy. In the end, he barely knew who he was underneath it all. Only Pia and Filip saw other sides of him.

And then there had been his own cynicism, which had grown more intense the longer he stayed on board. Seeing all that drunkenness. Spending all day every day with people in their most primitive state. And worst of all had been the ones who went on a booze cruise as an ironic gimmick, like some kind of common-people safari, pointing and laughing.

He would have lost all faith in humanity if he had stayed.

Thinking about how genuinely happy Pia had been to see him makes the lobster turn to ash in his mouth. Why did he ever stop calling her?

Well, first it was the years of studying in Alnarp. That had been a new bubble, and every time he went up to Stockholm, he had just wanted to see Vincent. They had realised they were not an exception to the rule of long-distance relationships being hard. Then he got a job – a new bubble – and it had been easy to forget

Pia and Filip, to tell himself all they had shared was the job. The job and the partying.

Now he realises Vincent is waiting for an answer. Does he miss them?

'We've been in touch a bit on Facebook,' he says, chewing, 'but it's hard. You know how it is.'

His phone beeps. Calle carefully wipes his hands on the linen napkin on his lap and makes sure the phone is angled away from Vincent so he can't see the screen as he reads the text.

HE'S A PERFECT TEN! ☺ EVERYTHING READY IN THE SUITE, SEE YOU SOON / PIA.

Madde

Dan Appelgren is looking at Madde from the laminated poster next to the stairs. He is wearing a dapper, Mafia-style suit and is laughing with one hand behind his neck, almost as if he is embarrassed in front of the camera, despite being so fucking fit. He is so fucking *sexy*. Dan definitely looks like he knows how to fuck. Like he knows what he wants and how to take it.

'Mummy misses you too,' Zandra coos into her phone. 'Lots and lots.'

Dan is somewhere on this ship right now, and the thought makes Madde's stomach flip. She checks the corridor they came from. She knows there is a split-level suite up here on deck nine. Maybe that is where he is staying. He might have been taking a shower at the same time as her, just a few feet away. Madde shoots him one last quick glance before starting down the stairs.

'And tomorrow night, around this time, I'll come pick you up from Daddy's,' Zandra says.

Madde had hoped to get Zandra to come out with her tomorrow night. They could have partied all the way back from Finland and then hit the town. Zandra claims her ex refuses to swap days, but Madde isn't convinced Zandra really tried to talk him around. Everyone is so old and boring these days. Everyone has children and everything has to fit around them. Sometimes they are too tired to go out even when they are free. Like pensioners. And Madde wonders what things will be like when she is unemployed, when she doesn't even have a social life during the day.

Don't think about it, she admonishes herself. *Don't ruin tonight, the time we actually do have together, before it even starts.*

'You're going to have a lovely night, aren't you?' Zandra continues, and Madde wishes she would wrap it up already.

They reach deck eight, right by the entrance to Charisma Buffet.

'Say hi to Daddy,' Zandra says. 'I probably won't be able to call tonight, but I promise I'll think about you when I go to bed. Of course, sweetheart. Don't be sad. Lots of kisses. I love you. Bye. Lots of kisses. It'll be all right. Love you, bye.'

'What's up?' Madde asks as they pass through the open doors.

'I think I managed to calm her down,' Zandra says. 'She had a bad dream about me.'

Madde only half listens. A blond, skinny guy with bulging eyes greets them. Madde has never seen him before.

'You're late,' he says testily after crossing them off the list. 'You only have an hour and fifteen minutes before the next sitting.'

'So?' Madde says. 'What's it to you?'

'Table twenty-five,' he says, pointing to a plan. 'It's one of the tables on the right, near the windows.'

'I know,' Madde says impatiently. 'We're *regulars*.'

'Oh my God, what a grumpy little fucker,' Zandra says as they make their way between the tables.

'Right? It's not like we're late for the Nobel dinner.'

But she actually doesn't give a toss about the bovine maître d'. Lovely smells are reaching her from the long buffet tables and the room is packed.

Anticipation fizzes inside her like the bubbles in a glass of champagne.

Madde grabs a tray and a plate, expertly piles it high with gratins and sauces and ham, egg halves and gravlax and shrimp, using the space on her plate as efficiently as possible, as though she is playing buffet *Tetris*. She skips the potatoes, bread, anything that is just filler. They walk to the taps, take two glasses each, filling all four to the brim with white wine, and toast as soon as they sit down. The wine is sweet and just the right temperature. She takes a picture of her food, manages to upload it on the second attempt. She digs in. So fucking delicious. It always is.

Madde must have gone on the *Charisma* at least twenty times over the years. She was only little the first time. Her family had taken a trip down to Stockholm and rounded their vacation off with a cruise. Madde loved it. She sat here at Charisma Buffet, thinking this must be what it felt like to be as rich as the people on *Falcon Crest*. It was her first proper glimpse of another world beyond Boden, and the first time she realised she could be part of it. She just had to seek it out. In a way, it was because of the *Charisma* she moved to Stockholm. And Zandra had come with her, thank God.

By now, Madde obviously knows that people who are properly rich would never be caught dead on a booze cruise to Finland. But it doesn't matter. She can still get the same childish thrill from taking off like this. It is like giving everyday life the slip. A twenty-four-hour escape into a parallel universe.

Zandra looks amazing tonight. She has put her hair up in pigtails; the hair ties have pink feathers on them, like her boa, and they make her look like the Zandra Madde got to know almost thirty years ago. The one who was bullied for her lisp and had overprotective parents, who already considered Madde a bad influence on their daughter.

'I want another toast,' Madde says, and notices to her surprise that she is already slurring her words. 'To us. For being so fucking awesome.'

Zandra raises her glass. 'Hear, fucking hear,' she exclaims, and downs the contents.

Madde follows her lead. 'You're still my best friend, you know that, right?'

'Of course I know,' Zandra says with a giggle. 'Who else would put up with you?'

'Bitch,' Madde replies, and takes a sip from her second glass of wine.

Zandra lets out another giggle. One of her front teeth overlaps the other; Madde loves that snaggletooth. My God, she must be well on her way to being hammered if she is already getting sentimental.

'And that thing about your job,' Zandra is saying. 'It's going to be all right, right?'

Madde takes another sip. 'We have to go check out the karaoke later,' she says.

'Sure,' Zandra replies. 'I wouldn't mind being Dan's groupie.'

'No, I already called dibs. Why don't you snog those four Italians of yours instead?'

'I don't think I'd turn down a Quattro Stagioni,' Zandra retorts.

'I hope they'll hold the cheese.'

Zandra laughs like only she can: throws her head back, her large breasts jiggling in her cleavage, her tongue sticking out. It is impossible not to join in.

And somehow the second glass of wine is suddenly empty too. But there is more where that came from. For almost a whole hour still they can eat and drink as much as they please. To be honest, Madde is full already, but there are so many more things to try. She pushes her plate aside when she gets up for more. The plates are like the towels: you can always get another. Someone will get rid of the used one.

Albin

His dad is telling a story about Irma, one of the carers who look after Albin's mum when he is at work. Instead of doing her job, she always just sits at the kitchen table, smoking and flipping through magazines while going on and on about her dog or her love problems. Anecdotes involving her normally make Dad angry, but tonight he is in a good mood. They morph into funny stories; his mum and Aunt Linda laugh a lot.

This is his dad at his best. He does a perfect impression of the carer, and he really paints a picture, telling the story. But he is constantly topping up his wine from the taps, apparently not noticing that Mum and Aunt Linda have barely touched their glasses.

Why does he carry on drinking? Surely he knows how it ends?

And why don't Mum and Aunt Linda ever tell him off properly, instead of first egging him on with laughter and then reaching for the snarky comments and veiled looks once it is already too late?

'She reminds me a bit of that woman we lived next to as children,' Linda says. 'That Jonsson or Johansson lady.'

'Who?' his dad says.

'Oh, you know. The one whose son was in my class. The boy who always wore the same clothes. I think he played bandy.'

'I can hardly be expected to remember everyone you went to school with; I barely remember the ones in my class.'

'No, I know,' Linda agrees. 'I'm just trying to help you remember the old lady next door. Well, maybe not an *old* lady, I guess. She was probably no older than we are now.'

She tries to laugh at herself, but his dad is glaring at her impatiently. Albin feels sorry for her.

'Her dog injured its hind leg one time and she wheeled it around in a pram all summer,' Linda continues.

'Right,' his dad says. '*That* I remember. Maybe you should have led with that if you wanted to jog my memory.'

Linda looks dejected.

'So what about her?' his dad wants to know.

'That's it,' Linda says. 'That was the whole thing. That she wheeled the dog around like a baby. I bet your carer would have done the same.'

His dad takes a big gulp of wine. His face is expressionless.

'Oh dear,' his mum says. 'Some people really do go crazy for their pets. But I guess they rather become part of the family.'

She clears her throat and puts a piece of chocolate cake in her mouth. Albin picks up a piece of his own, dips it in cream. The edges are just the right level of chewy.

'I love the stellar reception here,' Lo exclaims, shaking her phone.

The couple at the next table turn around to look at her.

'Would you put that away?' Linda snaps. 'It wouldn't hurt you to spend a bit of time with us, you know.'

Lo narrows her eyes at Linda, but she does put her phone away. 'I guess I don't have much of a choice,' she says.

Linda heaves a sigh and turns to Albin's mum and dad.

'Sometimes I think Lo's phone has grown attached to her hand. She's completely addicted to social media.'

'Well, we don't let Albin do any of that,' his dad says. 'He has to wait until he's fifteen.'

'I'm not exactly much better, but still,' Linda says. 'It's like the more ways of communicating we get, the less we actually *communicate*.'

'I love that you have such incredibly original opinions, Mum. Really.' Lo's eyes roll so far back Albin worries about them spinning all the way around.

'But it's true,' Linda says. 'You just sit there fiddling with your phone.'

'*Fiddling?*' A soundless little giggle escapes Lo.

'Yes,' Linda says. 'Seems to me it's all you're interested in.'

'Sorry if I forgot to take notes about all the fascinating things you're saying.'

'Lo, that's enough!' Linda is almost shouting. 'I'm so fucking tired of your attitude! I'm taking your phone if you don't cut it out right now!'

'I already put it away,' Lo mutters.

The couple at the next table are watching the scene unfold, apparently finding it hilarious.

'Isn't the chocolate cake just delicious though?' his mum says with a pleading look at Albin. 'Do you remember that summer when you and Lo wouldn't stop baking them?'

Albin nods. They had been eight. They ate until their whole mouths tasted of chocolate, lying on the sofa together, watching film after film on the laptop.

His mum had still been able to walk back then. She'd had long hair that she used to brush every night before going to bed. His dad's hair had been more blond than grey. And his grandma had still been alive, even if Albin had never thought about her, because he had never met her. It was only after she died that his dad started talking about her when he had been drinking.

'The two of you were unbelievable,' his mum continues. 'Between you, you could scarf down a whole cake. And you drank so much milk!'

'Drinking milk is my number one advice to the general public. It's, like, a *bodily fluid*.' Lo is looking straight at Albin when she says that and, for the first time, he detects a hint of the old Lo.

He giggles. Pulls his fork through the whipped cream and puts it in his mouth. Smacks his lips.

Lo giggles too. 'From a dirty old cow teat,' Lo says.

'Delicious,' Albin retorts.

Mum looks disappointed.

If the grown-ups hadn't been around, Albin would have reminded Lo that she used to suck on her mum's boob when she was little. He laughs out loud as a shiver of revulsion runs down his spine.

'Or eggs,' Lo says, and nods at the leftovers on Linda's plate. 'It's like menstruation, except it comes out the bum.'

'That's enough,' his dad says.

'Yes, please,' Linda adds.

Imagine if Lo knew his mum keeps a peeing bucket next to her bed. She stands over it when she doesn't have time to make it to the bathroom in the night.

Sometimes Albin has had to help her in the bathroom as well. Her toilet seat rinses her bum, so he doesn't need to do anything *down there*, but she needs someone to hold on to while she shuffles the few paces back to her wheelchair.

A few tables away, those girls from the terminal are laughing again. Lo glares at them. 'I love middle-aged people with pigtails,' she says. 'Isn't it heartbreaking that she looks like the world's fattest five-year-old?'

Albin giggles again; the grown-ups pretend not to have heard.

'But then again, maybe that's what she's *going for*,' Lo presses on. 'Maybe that was her big goal in life. If that's the case I shouldn't feel sorry for her, because she *made all her dreams come—*'

'Enough now,' Linda breaks in. 'Wait until you get older; you'll see it's not so easy to look perfect all the time.'

'At least she has a lovely laugh,' Lo says, smirking. 'I'm done. Can Albin and I go and have a look around?'

His dad opens his mouth to object as she starts pushing her chair out.

'Please,' Albin puts in quickly. 'I haven't seen Lo for so long.'

'I don't know if I think it's such a good idea,' his dad says in that way that means he knows exactly.

'It's fine with me if it's fine with you,' Linda interjects, glancing at Lo. 'It might be a relief for all of us.'

His dad looks imploringly at his mum, but he has already been voted down. Albin has to force himself not to bounce up and down on his chair impatiently.

'You have to be in bed by eleven,' Linda says, and Lo smirks again. 'I don't want you running around out here on your own once people are getting tipsy.'

'One of us will stop by the cabin to check on you,' his dad adds. 'At eleven sharp.'

'We promise,' Albin says.

'Don't talk to grown-ups you don't know—'

'But *Dad*,' Albin tries to cut him off. 'We know.'

'—and if you need us and you can't get a signal, ask a member of the crew for help. Or go to the information desk and have them call us over the speakers. And don't lean out over the railings if you go outside, because if you fall in—'

'Don't get worked up, Mårten,' his mum says with a quick laugh. 'We're not sending the kids to war, we're just letting them have some fun on their own for a bit.'

'People have actually been known to disappear on these boats,' his dad says.

'I know,' Lo replies, and turns to him. 'I have a friend whose mum used to work on a cruiseferry. But the people who disappear are the ones who are so drunk they're oblivious, or they jump overboard to kill themselves. And we're not going to drink and we're not like Grandma . . .'

Albin can feel rather than see his dad stiffen.

'Lo!' Linda gasps.

'Sorry,' Lo says quickly, still looking at his dad. 'All I'm saying is, it's fine. We'll be good. I just want to check out the tax-free shop and buy some sweets and then we'll go and watch a film in the cabin. Right, Abbe?'

He nods fervently.

'It's fine, Mårten,' Linda says. 'It's hard to believe sometimes, but Lo has good judgement where it counts.'

'Eleven o'clock,' his dad says. 'At the latest.'

Albin and Lo get up from the table.

'I'm finished too,' Linda says. 'What do you think? Should we go and have a look around as well?'

His mum picks up the napkin from her lap and places it on her smeared plate. His dad gets to his feet, swaying slightly, and asks the family at the table behind them to move to allow Mum to get past in her wheelchair. A small blonde girl studies Mum curiously.

'Are you a baby?' she asks.

'Do you think I look like one?' his mum says with a laugh.

'No. But you're in a pram.'

The girl's parents look mortified.

'Stella, leave them alone,' the dad says, and Albin recognises his voice from the terminal.

'But she's a really weird baby,' Stella insists, clearly surprised her dad doesn't see it.

His mum laughs again, and her laugh is perfectly genuine.

'They're so lovely at that age. If only they could stay that way for ever,' Linda says.

'Was that for me?' Lo asks, but when Linda looks caught, she just giggles.

'Come on, Stella, stop staring,' Stella's dad says.

'It's all right,' his mum says as she navigates between the chairs. 'It's only natural to be curious.'

She smiles at Stella and her parents to reassure them, while struggling with her joystick. And just then, Albin's heart breaks a little. He loves her so much, he forgets that sometimes, but in this moment the feeling is so strong it overwhelms him; it kind of catches him unaware and he almost starts crying.

'Let's go,' Lo says.

Calle

Calle and Vincent have just got up from their table when a group of men in ill-fitting suits pour into Poseidon. Conference guests with corporate cards; Calle could spot them a mile away. One of the men has removed his tie and is spanking the bottom of the only woman in the group with it. He is definitely the most intoxicated, but the others are not far behind. The woman snatches the tie from his hands and barks furiously at him in Finnish. He just laughs. The others laugh with him. Maybe he is their boss.

Vincent tries to take Calle's hand, but he pretends not to notice, looks around for Pia. How ironic is this? He is about to propose to Vincent, but he doesn't even want to hold his hand. Doesn't want to provoke anyone. He knows how quickly fights can erupt on the *Charisma*.

They exit into the long hallway that runs the length of the ship. At the other end, by the stern, is Charisma Starlight. Filip is probably tending bar right now. Calle examines the booth where they sell the photographs they take of everyone as they board. He is surprised it still exists. Who buys those pictures now that everyone has a camera phone?

There is anticipation in the air. Raucous laughter and drunken voices. Many of the passengers will have looked forward to this cruise for a long time. Eating, drinking and dancing in the no-man's-land that is the Baltic. He is suddenly seized by a desire to protect them from certain types of gazes.

Many of his colleagues at the architecture firm would consider this the most exotic experience of their lives. And isn't that exactly the angle he has exploited in his tales about working aboard the *Charisma*? He's told some of his war stories so many times they have become classics: the lady who grabbed a whole side of salmon from the buffet and shoved it in her purse; the bloke with tribal tattoos who threw a tantrum because there was no McDonald's on board. The older, leathery woman who blew a group of young men in her cabin, after which they ran out into Club Charisma in nothing but their underwear, flashing V-signs at their friends. The man who tried to climb up a chimney. The girl with the word HARDER tattooed on her lower back. The woman who travelled with them at least three times a week, all year round, and talked about how she would love to live aboard the *Charisma* permanently. All the people having sex in the hallways, on the weather decks, the dance floors and the ball pit in the children's area, without realising every inch of the ship is covered by CCTV.

He has distanced himself by acting like his life on board was nothing more than an anthropological field study.

'There she is,' Vincent says, pointing towards the stairs.

Pia has spotted them too. She says something to her colleague, Jarno, whom Calle has barely met. He is short, good-looking in a bland way; seems nice but shy. The only thing Calle knows about him as a person is that he is married to Raili, the on-board nurse. He waves to Calle before disappearing up the stairs.

Pia stops for a moment in the hallway, seizing a turquoise aluminium can of gin and tonic from a couple of middle-aged women with short, spiky hair.

'You'll have to go to one of the bars if you want to drink,' Pia says.

'Oh come on!' one of them protests loudly. She puts her hands on her hips and stares at Pia. The rhinestones across the front of her hoodie spell out SEXY BITCH.

'I'm sorry, those are the rules,' Pia says.

'So screw the rules. What do you care?'

'Sorry, girls. Just doing my job.'

'That's what the Nazis said.'

The woman's voice has risen an entire octave. Passers-by stare curiously.

'Fucking Nazi cunt,' her friend mutters, and Pia chuckles.

'Wow,' she says. 'It's the first time someone's called me that. On this cruise at least.'

'Can I have my drink back so I can at least take it to my cabin?'

Pia calmly shakes her head.

'That's practically stealing,' the woman says threateningly. 'We should fucking report you. You're probably planning on drinking it yourself.'

'If you want to report me you should head to the information counter by the tax-free shop. They'll be happy to assist you. I have to move on now, but I think you should have a few glasses of water. The evening has only just started, after all.'

'What a goddamn nanny state this is,' the woman says, and swans off with her friend in tow.

'Just another workday, eh?' Calle says when Pia reaches them.

'I'll bet you don't miss the *Charisma* quite as much after seeing that.' She grins. 'Ready to go?'

A new wave of anxiety washes over Calle. It is almost time. The little box in his jacket pocket suddenly feels like it is made out of lead.

But Vincent is going to say yes. He is. They have talked about this, after all, about getting married someday.

'My God, they were such jerks,' Vincent says.

'You have to try to bear in mind that most of them are actually good people,' Pia says, leading them towards the lifts.

'And those who aren't? What do you do with them?'

'More often than not they can be talked down,' Pia says, and pushes the lift button. 'If they're too wasted we stick them in a drunk tank. And if it's really bad we kick them off the boat first chance we get and let the police handle it.'

The lift doors *ding* and slide open. A tall woman with heavy features and a chequered shirt exits, smiling when she spots Pia's uniform.

'What kind of trouble have you been causing, boys?' she says in a rough-whisky voice, and smiles suggestively at Vincent.

'You don't want to know,' Pia replies with a smile, and steps into the lift.

'I can help you cuff them,' the woman calls out after them, and Vincent laughs.

'Don't you ever get scared?' he asks as the doors close.

'Once or twice. But there are four of us on the boat and we almost never patrol alone. I'm meeting up with my colleague again as soon as I've taken you to the bridge.'

'Do you carry weapons?'

The lift rises towards the tenth floor. Calle is so nervous pit stains are forming on his jacket. He looks at Vincent and Pia. It feels surreal that his two worlds are meeting.

'Just my nightstick,' Pia says. 'We don't want any peashooters on the boat, you know; it could end really badly.'

She steps off the lift ahead of them. Everything is calm and quiet up here. Just the stairs leading down, dark conference rooms with glass walls that make them look like terrariums, the doors to the promenade deck and a wood-panelled wall. Pia swipes her pass through the reader on the wall and punches in a code. Four shrill beeps, then she pushes a cleverly concealed door open.

Calle's heart is pounding. He can barely wrap his head around the fact that this really is it. He has been planning this for so long, imagined it so many times, it feels like déjà vu. They are on their way. Captain Berggren is waiting for them.

Tomas

'What do you want?' Åse says. 'Do you even know why you're calling?'

He catches himself squinting, as if that might make her words on the other end of the line clearer. She is at home in Norrköping, but she might as well be on the other side of the planet.

Tomas takes his phone from his ear to look at the screen. One bar of reception left.

'I just wanted to see how you're doing,' he says.

The lift doors in front of him open and he steps in and pushes the button. The smoked glass covering the lift walls reflects him from every angle, the reflections reduplicating again and again, endlessly. His ginger hair is tousled and damp.

Why doesn't Åse say anything?

'Don't you get it? I miss you,' he says, hating that he can't keep from slurring. 'Everyone's asking about you. Don't you get what it feels like to be at Stefan's stag do and not be able to tell them we're getting divorced?'

The doors open and he steps out on deck five. Just stands there, realising he doesn't know the way to his cabin. Where are all the signs?

Åse laughs gruffly. 'It's so like you to pretend to want to know how I'm doing when you actually called to tell me how *you're* doing.'

Tomas squeezes the phone harder. She sounds so cold, so fucking cold. She could make the whole Baltic freeze over.

Calling her was a mistake: a big, fat mistake. But he knew that. And he did it anyway.

'Well, excuse me for finding this fucking difficult,' he exclaims.

Two women coming down the stairs giggle at him.

'Excuse me for having feelings,' he adds, as much to them as to Åse.

He heads down one of the corridors. He is just getting a pack of smokes from his cabin. He should have waited to call until after a few drags; smoking makes it so much easier to think clearly. But he doesn't want Åse to hear him puffing away. He still cares what she thinks, even though it is none of her business what he gets up to any more. It is just that the cartons in the tax-free shop were so damn cheap and he does have the best goddamn excuse ever to start smoking again.

If things had been normal, he would have told her they got Stefan completely hammered before they even left the bus from Norrköping, and that Peo and Lasse are trying to pull every piece of white trash they can find. He wants to hear Åse laugh. Laugh for real. He would like to tell her how annoyed he is with Peo and Lasse, who expect him to pay for his share of the drinks they are buying for all those girls, and he wants to hear Åse agree with him. He wants her to know he isn't trying to pick anyone up. That no one compares to her.

'Say something,' he says, 'please. You have no idea how much I miss you.'

'I do, actually,' she says. 'I do know.'

'Don't you miss me at all?' He makes a face, hearing how pathetic he sounds. He pulls out the bottle of beer he stashed in

82

the inside pocket of his jacket and takes a big swig. Lukewarm and flat. Looks around. Where is he and where the hell is cabin 5314?

5134 . . . 5136 . . . 5138 . . . So he is not even in the right corridor. How the fuck is anyone supposed to find their way when everything looks the same? The same carpet on the floor, the same fucking doors with tiny silver numbers.

He is like a rat in a maze, a ridiculously drunk rat at that, and he is never going to find his way out.

'I do miss you,' she says, 'but it doesn't matter any more.'

He stops mid-step, a fragile hope bubbling up inside him. *She misses him*. If he can find the exact right thing to say right now, he might be able to turn this around.

'Hey,' he says, 'if we're missing each other, then that's all that matters—'

'No.' She cuts him off. 'It doesn't matter. It's too late.' The frost has crept back into her voice.

'Fuck you,' he says. 'You're such a fucking bitch.' It feels good to say it, but he regrets it instantly.

'I'm not the one who cheated,' she replies.

That sets him off again. It must feel pretty good to be so morally superior, to be able to throw that in his face whenever she pleases.

'Maybe I wouldn't have if you hadn't been such a bitch,' he hears himself say.

The regret is significantly more intense and even more immediate this time. He turns, walks back up the corridor, waiting for a reply, but none comes. He looks at the screen again. The one bar of reception is still there. The seconds tick by, aggravatingly large on the screen. The call has lasted three minutes and twenty-seven seconds. He stops by a short, narrow hallway that turns right. He must have just passed it, but he doesn't recall seeing it before.

'Are you still there?' he asks. 'Can you hear me?'

'. . . not even 9 p.m.,' Åse is saying. 'How much . . . been drinking anyway?'

She says something else, but she is breaking up and he can't make out the words. It makes him irrationally angry with her, as if it is her fault.

'Never fucking mind,' he says. 'It's none of your business any more. Not since you dumped me.'

'I'd love to not mind,' Åse retorts. 'But you're making it my business . . . calling even though . . . asked you not to . . .'

They are cut off, and for a moment he is convinced she hung up on him. But when he looks at his screen the reception is gone. He curses loudly and takes another big swig of his tepid beer. Turning right down yet another short hallway, he glances at the cabin doors as he passes: *5139 . . . 5137 . . .* Suddenly the numbers jump to *5327 . . . 5329 . . .* The corridor branches off again up ahead. But at least the numbers are starting to look more promising. He turns left.

This corridor is identical to the one he started from: long and narrow, low ceiling. For a split second, the perspective shifts abruptly, as though he is staring down a deep, square well, about to fall helplessly into it. Tomas' innards do a somersault. He leans against a wall until the dizziness passes and the corridor becomes just a corridor once more.

Tomas checks his phone and notices the reception is back. He redials the last number he called. He doesn't hear any signals, but suddenly the seconds start ticking by again on the screen.

'Hello?' he says. 'Can you hear me?'

Silence. The line is completely dead, but the large digits keep ticking by. Two girls come out of a cabin. He would guess Syrian. They are so good-looking he can't help staring. But they don't even notice him.

'Hello?' he says into the phone. 'Are you there? I can't hear you but . . . but if you can hear me, then . . .'

He looks after the girls until they disappear around a corner.

The realisation slams into him. He is single. He is alone. And he knows what Åse is like. Once she has made her mind up, there is no going back.

'Please,' he snivels. 'Please. I'm so goddamn sorry about everything.'

He has circled back to the stairs he came down. He studies the cabin numbers. *5318* . . . *5316* . . . and then he spots the door to the cabin he shares with Peo.

'I'm so fucking lonely,' he says. 'I don't want to be this lonely and I don't want to be this miserable.'

Tomas pulls his key card from his back pocket. Glances at the phone. The call has ended. No reception. He shoves it back in his pocket. Puts his key card in the door just as another door opens further down the corridor.

'Hello?' a small voice calls.

A child. Tomas looks around the corridor, but it's empty.

'I need help,' the voice says. 'Please, can you help me?'

The voice is melodic and crystal-clear, strangely old-fashioned, like a puppy in a Disney animation, or one of the children in some ancient feature film.

Tomas pulls his key card out and the lock beeps. He hesitates. Puts his hand on the handle. Just wants to pick up his cigarettes and get back out there, drink himself senseless, forget everything.

'I'm scared,' the child says.

Tomas lets go of the handle and walks towards the open door.

Calle

'Wow,' Vincent exclaims when they step onto the bridge, and Calle is inclined to agree. He has only been here a few times but every time it has taken his breath away.

The view is almost the same as from their suite, but it is different seeing it from the *Charisma*'s control room. Countless screens illuminate the gloom: electronic sea charts and the classically green radar. The consoles are covered in what appear to be thousands of buttons and dials.

The half-moon hangs white in the sky outside the big windows. The dark sea reflects its pale light. It is so beautiful. It is perfect.

'I've brought a couple of VIPs,' Pia says.

Captain Berggren gets up. Normally, he wouldn't be on the bridge at this hour, but Vincent doesn't know that.

'Good to see you, Calle,' Berggren says. 'It's been a long time.'

There is an amused glint in his eye. He has clearly been looking forward to this. The staff captain eyes them curiously.

'Too long,' Calle says, extending his hand, apologising inwardly for its clammy state.

Berggren is broad-shouldered in his uniform, and his handshake is as warm and steady as you would expect from a ship's captain. But he has grown older too. His chin has all but disappeared; it is little more than a speed bump between his face and his wide neck. They don't know each other very well. The longest conversation they ever had was probably the one that followed Calle's second failed breathalyser test. But Berggren is well liked and respected by the crew because he never hesitates to take their side in conflicts with the owners.

'This is incredible,' Vincent says as he shakes everyone's hands. 'Thanks for letting us visit.'

He asks questions, which Berggren answers enthusiastically. Calle hears every word but he is not listening, would probably not understand if he tried right now; his only focus is disentangling the box from the lining of his inside pocket.

Pia smiles at him, holds up her camera phone and gives him a tiny nod.

He gets the box out. His pocket turns inside out. The lining hangs out like a lolling tongue; he fumbles it back in.

'I'm so glad you brought me here,' Vincent says, his back to him.

'I'm so glad you came,' Calle says. 'I'm so glad you exist, Vincent. You know that, right?'

It is time. He squeezes the box hard and gets down on one knee. Hears the click from Pia's phone. Vincent turns around.

Tomas

Tomas is standing in the harshly lit corridor, peering into the gloom on the other side of the open cabin door. It smells weird in there: like menthol and lilacs and something musty, rotting.

A group of young men push past him on their way down the corridor.

'What's the matter?' Tomas asks hesitantly, stepping across the threshold.

'I am scared,' the child says again, sobbing. 'I am sick and my mother was supposed to get me food, but she has been gone for such a long time.'

The voice really does remind Tomas of old movies.

Darkness envelops him when he shuts the door behind him. The smells grow more intense. There must be a problem with the plumbing in here. The toilet door is ajar on his left, but the smell isn't coming from in there, he realises as he moves past it.

Only one bedside lamp is lit. It is angled inwards, away from the room. Its beam strains halfway up the wall, almost touching the ceiling. The child is on the other side of the double bed, his back to Tomas.

A small backpack sits on the desk by the foot of the bed. On it, a smiling Winnie the Pooh digs into a jar of honey. A black wheelie bag sits on the floor below it. Next to the bag is a pair of high-heeled boots.

It would almost have been better if the bedside lamp were switched off. The angle of the light makes every shadow in the room droop downwards. The effect is depressing, as if gravity is so strong in here even shadows are weighed down. Tomas feels increasingly uneasy. His scrotum contracts.

'Do you mind if I turn on the overhead light?' he says, and reaches for the switch.

'Don't,' the child pleads immediately. 'I'm sick; the light hurts my eyes.'

Tomas lets his hand fall and reluctantly takes another step into the cabin, starting when he sees movement out of the corner of his eye. He realises it is his own reflection in the mirror above the desk and feels stupid, and yet the fear rumbles on inside him. The strange smell becomes more noticeable when he approaches the child's side of the bed.

'What's your name?' he asks, noticing he's slurring.

The child doesn't answer. He looks like a boy. His white, straight hair has fallen across his face. Tomas realises he is not even wearing a T-shirt. His thin, pointed shoulders stick up above the duvet, bare. What kind of mother would leave her child like this? Her sick child. And hasn't he been taught not to let strangers into the cabin? Tomas shudders to think what could have happened here.

He sits down on the edge of the bed, right next to the boy.

'Do you want me to ask them to call out for your mother over the speakers?' he asks, focusing on keeping his tongue fully under control this time.

'No. Mother might be cross. Can't you just stay here with me until she comes?'

Tomas glances down at the high-heeled boots and doesn't want to meet the woman who owns them. She might be a properly mental nut job. Someone who wonders what the fuck he's doing in here, sitting on the bed with her son.

But how can he leave the boy here, alone and afraid?

The smell is pushing into his sinuses. 'What's your name?' he asks again.

'I'm not going to tell you if you're going to make them call it out over the speakers. Mum would be cross. She's always so cross.'

Tomas reaches for the boy's shoulder. His skin is cold, rubbery somehow, under Tomas' fingers. He wonders if the boy is contagious, and has to resist an urge to snatch his hand away. 'I still think that would be best,' he says. 'I'm sure she won't be cross. And I can wait here with you until—'

'You can't leave,' the boy declares.

Dips have formed in the skin of his shoulder where Tomas' hand is resting, as if the flesh is loose underneath.

Tomas' scalp feels like it's shrinking. There is an internal telephone on the desk. He could use it to call the information desk. But he wants to get out of here. He wants to get out now.

'I'll be right back,' he says. 'Don't open the door again, unless it's me or your mum.'

He gets up, relieved not to be in contact with the boy's skin any more. He wants to wash his hands.

In the mirror, he can see the boy sitting up in the bed behind him. The single light illuminates his hair from behind. It glows like a halo around his head.

There is something wrong with him: something very, *very* wrong.

'Wait here,' Tomas says.

He has almost made it to the door when he feels a small hand tugging at his jacket.

'Stay,' the boy says. 'I need you.'

'I'll be back,' Tomas replies, and realises he is lying. He has no intention of returning.

The boy lets go of his jacket and there is silence behind Tomas.

There is a tingling sensation around his coccyx; his entire skin seems to be shrinking now, tightening around his body.

He reaches for the door handle.

Suddenly there are arms wrapped around his neck. Kneecaps digging in between his shoulder blades. The boy has jumped onto his back and is clinging to him like a monkey.

The tiny arms press against his Adam's apple. Tomas can't breathe. He yanks at the boy's forearms, trying to loosen his iron grip. His fingertips sink into the boy's skin, the flesh parting until he can feel bone.

The boy's skinny legs encircle his waist.

'Let me go,' Tomas wheezes on his last breath. The world is going dark. He can hear a snapping sound next to his ear.

He pitches forward, tries to throw the boy off, tries to tear free of those damn little arms. But he can't shake him – the boy must be insane; that must be where he gets his strength from – and his throat hurts, hurts, hurts. It feels like his head is going to explode, and what is that horrible snapping sound, like a big fuck-off pair of scissors, a fucking *hedge trimmer* . . .

Tomas slams back against the wall as hard as he can. Squeezed between Tomas' body and the wall, the boy's grip slackens. Tomas wrenches his arms apart, forces his legs open, hears him crash onto the floor behind him.

His Adam's apple aches. He greedily sucks in air; the pain is unbelievable. He forces himself to take another breath. The black smoke clouding his field of vision is dissipating.

A rapid patter of feet next to him, and suddenly the boy is between him and the cabin door. He is blocking the way out with his body, which is so pale it is practically fluorescent in the gloom.

Tomas reaches for the switch and light floods the room. The boy puts a hand over his eyes and lets out a yelp.

An involuntary moan escapes Tomas' lips.

The boy is no bigger than a five-year-old, but his chest sags like an old man's. His skin is baggy, as if it is a few sizes too big for his body. And his face: the bony cheeks; the grey skin; the flesh that dimples oddly when he winces at the light.

Does he have that disease that makes children age prematurely – what's it called? Could it have messed up his brain?

'You can't leave,' the boy says, lowering his hand. His unnaturally large eyes blink at the light. The boy

the creature

looks so small, so pitiful and frail, and yet Tomas is terrified of him.

He glances at the toilet door on his right, trying to think clearly, to formulate a plan. There is nowhere to run from the bathroom. But he could lock himself in. The mobile reception has to come back at some point, right? He can bang on the walls. Someone passing by outside will hear him. The boy's mother might eventually return.

Where has she really got to?

He is convinced the woman who owns the shoes is in the bath-room, has been lurking there the whole time, letting the boy play a part in her sick game.

Tomas reaches out and pushes the bathroom door open. The light falls in across the same peach plastic vinyl that covers his and Peo's bathroom floor, the same white shower curtain. It's half drawn, but he can see there is no one behind it.

He hurls himself towards the bathroom, but the boy is faster. Hands grab his shirt collar and legs wrap themselves around his waist again, from the front this time. The horrifying face is so close to his now. A foetid stench of decay wafts from the boy's mouth. Tomas staggers back into the room, stumbles and falls flat on his back on the floor. His head misses the edge of the bed by a hair's breadth. The boy straddles his stomach. Pins his arms to the floor. Leans forward.

The bottle in Tomas' inside pocket is leaking, wet and tepid in his armpit. He barely notices. The synapses in his brain crackle, relaying information about what his eyes see. Every detail is crystal-clear. It is as if time has stopped.

The boy's eyes flash like blue fire, but the thin skin around them is saggy and lifeless. He opens his mouth and pulls back his chapped, broken lips; reveals yellowed teeth and gums that are grey with darker spots.

What's wrong with him? What does this to a child? Could it be rabies? No, that's a ridiculous thought, isn't it?

The boy's tongue slides out between his teeth like a grey, meaty slug. His mouth comes closer.

This isn't happening, this isn't happening, this isn't happening.

Tomas tries to squirm, to arch his body to throw the boy off.

He shouldn't be this strong; it should be impossible.

The dry flakes on the boy's lips touch the skin on the side of Tomas' neck. Tickle the hyper-sensitised nerve endings. Then he feels the teeth, small and pointed. He shakes his head wildly, trying to get away.

The teeth bite through his skin. The pain almost makes him black out again. And the sound, *the sound*. He can feel the boy's tongue darting along the edges of the wound. It laps at them gingerly, almost playfully. Gets slippery and wet with his blood.

Madde

She looks into her own eyes in the screen of her phone, trying to make her arm as long as possible while keeping her head tilted at the right angle. The wind on the afterdeck tears at her hair; she and Zandra laugh and raise their glasses in a toast to everyone who is going to see the picture. The waves in the wake of the cruise ship form the backdrop, a white fan set against the black. She presses the camera symbol with her thumb, testing a different pose with each click.

A group of guys is standing further down the deck. One of them is wearing a bridal veil: clearly a stag do. Madde can sense them watching her and Zandra, so she works the camera harder. Really gives them something to look at.

Zandra lights them a cigarette each while Madde studies the results. Quickly deletes any picture that doesn't do her justice before Zandra has a chance to persuade her to post them because she happens to look good in them. But then she gets to the picture that blows the other ones out of the water, and Madde knows there is not going to be a debate. Zandra is smiling with parted lips in the picture, with eyes like she has just spotted something really sexy; one end of her feather boa has been snatched up by the wind and is soaring in the darkness behind her. Madde's head is tilted back, her eyes half closed and her mouth pouting for a kiss.

She chooses a filter that makes everything soft and golden and turns the contrast up high to make their eyes and cheekbones pop. Zandra hands her a cigarette, and when shown the picture, nods contently.

'No wonder those blokes can't stop staring at us,' she says.

Madde takes a few deep drags and dances to the music thumping out from Club Charisma while she attempts to upload the picture. No reception. There is supposed to be Wi-Fi on board, but it never works right.

She slips her phone into her purse, takes a deep swig of vodka Red Bull, leans back against the railing and takes a slow drag on her cigarette, pretending not to notice the stag-do lads staring at them.

Zandra grins. Obviously knows exactly what she is up to.

But, in all honesty, Madde doesn't care about those guys. They are just practice. She is going to make Dan Appelgren notice her tonight.

Dan

Dan is sitting on the unmade bed in his cabin, studying the four lines neatly spaced out on the mirror he has placed across his knees. The ritual itself is so comforting he already feels better. He bends over, sticks a cut-off straw up one nostril, meets his own eyes in the glass. Inhales one line. Swaps nostrils. Snorts up line number two. Pinches his nose. Feels the chemical flavour all the way at the back of his throat. Clears his throat. Swallows. Repeats the procedure. Then he wipes the last of the white dust from the glass with his finger, rubs it onto his gums. Digs around the plastic bag with his wetted finger to get the last remnants out of the corners.

His gums grow numb immediately. This is good shit. He puts another bag in his pocket along with a few Xanax, hangs the mirror back up. Studies himself carefully. Tilts his head back to make sure there are no tell-tale snowballs stuck in his nose hair.

Dan turns his head. His hair is freshly dyed, no traces of grey at the temples. He pulls his shirt up. Slaps his belly hard. No jiggle. Most guys in their twenties could only dream of looking this fit.

The soles of his patent leather shoes slap loudly against the floor when he energetically starts jumping up and down. He throws a few jabs at his reflection.

He puts on his silver rings. He is ready.

Tomas

He manages to buck the boy and sits up quickly. They get to their feet at the same time.

His neck is throbbing. The sound of teeth tearing through skin echoes in his head.

He stares at the boy's terrifying face. The blood smeared on his chin. The slack skin of his body, the almost concave chest.

Every cell in Tomas' body is screaming at him to get out, but the boy is blocking the exit again.

Tomas pulls the beer bottle from his inside pocket, seeing his reflection mimicking his movements out of the corner of his eye. He clutches the neck of the bottle, afraid it might slip through his sweaty fingers. He smacks it against the edge of the desk. Nothing happens. He strikes again, harder; the glass shatters.

The sharp edges glint in the dim light.

Tomas waves the broken bottle about in front of him. A loose shard falls onto the carpet. He moves closer to the boy. *Must get out. Nothing else matters.*

'I don't want to hurt you,' he says.

His heart is pounding faster and faster; the pain from the gash in his throat throbs to its beat. The boy doesn't reply. Tomas can't even hear him breathing.

Thoughts flash through his head. Peo and the others are at

Club Charisma now. They have no idea where he is. They are probably going to assume he passed out somewhere. Or possibly hooked up with someone. They won't start wondering in earnest until tomorrow morning.

Tomas takes another small step forward; they are no more than three feet apart.

'Please,' he says. 'I won't tell your mum, or *anyone*, if you just let me go.'

The boy's mouth opens and closes. That snapping sound.

'But if you're not careful, I might—'

The boy rushes him, arms outstretched, teeth biting the air. Tomas swings the broken bottle in an arc in front of him and watches, horrified, as the sharp edges slice into the skin right below the boy's collarbone and sink further into his flesh. It is so easy. *Too easy.*

He pulls his hand back, lets go of the bottleneck. 'I'm sorry,' he whimpers. 'I'm sorry, I didn't want to . . .'

The boy looks at him, almost reproachful. He touches the torn, ragged edges of the cuts with an air of disbelief. Tomas can see how deep they are, but there is no blood. Only grey flesh underneath, which shimmers faintly in sickly hues. Like mince left sitting in the fridge too long. And the smell is so strong now, it fills the cabin. Like ammonia and sweet, rotting fruit.

This is impossible, this is impossible, I must be dreaming, I need to wake up.

The boy climbs on top of him again, clings to him like a parody of a terrified child seeking comfort from an adult. His teeth sink into Tomas' neck; he presses his mouth against the opening, sucks as though the blood isn't coming out fast enough.

Tomas staggers backwards, only managing a couple of steps before his legs give out. He sits down on the floor between the bed and the desk with a thud, tries to push the boy away, but the shock is so overpowering it has made him weak.

The skin of the boy's back is losing its grey pallor, turning pink and healthy as the blood fills him. Tomas watches without understanding. And then the child clamps down on Tomas' neck again. Knocks him onto his back. The shard of broken glass on the floor cuts through his jacket and shirt. Blood starts trickling out of the boy's wound. Tomas' own blood is dripping back onto him in a perverse circulatory system.

Black clouds are blooming in his field of vision, growing into one another.

If he faints now, he won't survive. And a part of him wants to simply accept it. It is so tempting to let the darkness dancing in front of his eyes swallow him, to let himself fall into the unknown, escape the pain. It would be no harder than drifting off to sleep on the sofa in front of the telly at home.

But he doesn't want to die.

The boy is sucking slower now, like a nursing infant starting to feel full.

This can't be how it works.

This can't be how it ends.

He has to try.

Tomas raises his right hand, takes a few quick breaths and lands a blow with his right hand on the side of the boy's head, smacking it into the edge of the desk.

The boy hisses at him like an animal. There is blood
my blood
on his teeth, glistening on his lips, chin, slowly seeping out of the wound below his collarbone. The flesh there is pink and healthy now. His face looks like that of a real boy.

His teeth snap in mid-air. Tomas strikes the side of his head again. The boy's eyes roll back into his head. He collapses on top of him. Tomas' scream bounces back at him from the walls of the cabin. The body is so little. So light.

He almost vomits as he struggles to get up off the floor. The cabin is swaying, as if the ship has sailed into an unexpected storm, and maybe it has. He doesn't know; he no longer has any sense of what might be reasonable. The room is spinning faster and faster. Pulling him down into the dark.

Albin

Glass clinks against glass on the shelves Albin passes on his way to the tills. The tax-free shop is bathed in white light. Perfume bottles and liquor bottles glint and glitter, the gilded parts of the Marlboro multipacks and giant Toblerone bars sparkle. Albin has put a jar of liquorice in his basket. His mum and dad have given him two hundred kronor to spend on board, but it was hard to choose when there were so many options.

A woman with dead-straight, peach-coloured hair and red lips watches him from the perfume section when he joins the queue. It makes him nervous; he wonders if she has noticed that he is with Lo and knows Lo shoplifted here earlier.

But nothing happens. When he exits the shop, Lo is waiting for him, impatiently chewing her gum.

'Way to be quick about it,' she says, starting to walk before he even reaches her.

He follows, glancing at the information desk and the man standing behind it looking bored. They take the stairs and end up outside Charisma Buffet again, then walk sternwards, past a restaurant, a café and a place called McCharisma, where a number of men in overcoats are drinking beer. They pass big arcade games, where a handful of little kids are pressing buttons without understanding how they work. It is completely dark outside the windows; the only things Albin can see in the glass are his and Lo's reflections.

'Abbe!' Lo calls.

She has set her course for a stand displaying shiny photographs on a board covered in black fabric. When Albin catches up, he recognises the girl standing there: she's the one who took their picture when they first boarded.

'Those are just display copies,' she says in a heavy regional accent when their eyes meet. 'You can have a look at today's pictures right here. It's forty-nine kronor for a paper copy, and you can pick it up in an hour.'

She holds out an iPad. Lo snatches it from her and quickly swipes through the pictures while chewing her gum hard. Sometimes she stops, commenting on something: *Isn't it heartbreaking that no one has told her about conditioner? Pulling your jeans all the way up to your armpits really is my number one advice. I wonder if he knows his parents are siblings?* It almost makes Albin dizzy to see all the unfamiliar faces flash past on the screen. He is looking for something to comment on too, but Lo always beats him to the punch.

'Look, it's us,' she says.

The image appears so suddenly it feels like he is looking at yet another group of strangers. Everyone is so blond. Everyone but him.

He had just spotted the camera and was trying to smile, but now he can see the smile was only half formed on his lips; it mostly looks like a weird grimace. His white trainers are dirty. His jeans have baggy knees. He wonders what Lo would have said about him if he were one of the strangers.

'I always love it when I look like a retarded sleepwalker,' Lo says.

The Lo in the picture has her eyes closed mid-step, but she is still pretty. Linda has put a hand on her shoulder and is smiling professionally. Dad's face is a bit shiny, but he is smiling at the camera too. It's almost like he and Linda are the married couple. Mum is in her wheelchair, looking diffidently up at the camera. Albin knows how much she hates having her picture taken. It makes her stiff and weird whenever anyone holds up their phone. She always begs off or turns her head away the moment you take the photo. Albin has never managed to take a good picture of her. He wishes she could have looked nice in this one. Then he would have bought it and shown her.

He looks back at his dad, trying to imagine that the man with the confident smile is the same dad as last night.

Maybe I should do what Mum did. Then you'd all be happy, wouldn't you?

'What a lovely family,' the girl says.

'I wish,' Lo says, and pulls Albin away.

They walk past a room with dark walls and a sign that reads CASINO. A girl is standing behind a table covered in green felt. A few people are slumped on bar stools in front of flashing fruit machines, pulling levers and pressing buttons. He and Lo keep walking until the hallway ends. *Dansband* music is being played at a high volume. Lo's ponytail swings back and forth like a pendulum with every step she takes, caressing her shoulder blades. Albin would like to touch it, feel the hair between his fingers.

They enter a bar with a big dance floor. CHARISMA STARLIGHT is written in florid letters above the bar; the ceiling is decorated with little white lights meant to look like constellations. Multicoloured lights are flashing on the dance floor, making patterns on the hardwood floor and the closed red, curtains in front of the stage. An old couple are holding each other, taking tiny, shuffling steps from side to side, back and forth, not even remotely to the beat. It is as though they are in their own world. They look like they're in love. Next to them a barefoot woman is jumping up and down, clapping her hands from time to time with a big, ecstatic smile on her face.

'If only I could have a fun and bubbly personality like that,' Lo says, looking grave. 'You know, it's all about choosing happiness.'

They walk among the tables between the bar and the dance floor. Lo reaches for a half-empty bottle of beer someone left behind. The blond bartender shakes his head at her. He doesn't look angry – actually, he is grinning – but Albin wants to leave now.

'Isn't it heartbreaking that he took fashion advice from a traffic light?' Lo says, nodding towards a bald man a bit further on.

The man is wearing a red shirt tucked into green jeans. His gut is jutting straight out over his belt, defying gravity. He actually does look like a traffic light. Albin bursts out laughing.

The barefoot woman is circling the older couple. They watch her for a bit. A group of muscle guys in tight T-shirts walk up to the dance floor. One of them glances at Lo and Albin while he drinks beer straight from the bottle. Albin wonders if it looks like they are together. He moves closer to her.

'Was that true about knowing someone whose mum works on a cruiseferry?' he asks.

'Mmm,' Lo replies. 'My friend told me all kinds of gross things. The people who clean have, like, the most disgusting job in the world. I mean, imagine. But at least they get a five-hundred-kronor bonus every time they have to clean up someone's sick. And loads of people throw up, especially in their cabins. They can, like, make a fortune from vomit.'

Albin looks around. Everything is so clean here: the brass railing with the smoke-coloured glass around the dance floor; the gleaming tables and bar counter. He peers at the maroon carpet. Can't see any stains, but the room is fairly dark.

'The best thing is when someone hurls in a urinal, because then all they have to do is hose it down the drain. Five hundred kronor, just like *that*.'

Lo snaps her fingers. Albin tries to imagine having a job where you have to deal with other people's vomit every day.

'There's all kinds of other gross things,' Lo says, lowering her voice. 'Loads of girls get raped in the cabins. But the police can't do anything. They can't collect any evidence because there are so many different *DNA samples* in the cabins.'

She looks expectantly at Albin, as if she has already told him the punchline. But if she did, he missed it completely.

'Don't you get it?' Lo says. 'I'm talking about sperm. There's old sperm on the walls and the floor and everything because everyone's doing it everywhere. It's so incredibly gross.'

Lo squeals and waves her hands about as though they are covered in sticky stuff. Her eyes are alight with revulsion.

Albin doesn't know what to say. He turns back to the dance floor. That guy is still eyeing Lo, but she doesn't seem to notice, or she doesn't care. She pulls her ponytail over one shoulder, combing it with her fingers.

'Do your parents still have sex?' she says. 'Can your mum even do it?'

'Stop it,' Albin says.

He doesn't want to think about it. His mum's ribs feel so fragile when he hugs her. His dad would be able to break them without even trying, wrench something out of joint, even if he was attempting to be careful.

'What about Aunt Linda?' he says.

He doesn't really want to know, but anything is better than talking about his mum and dad.

'I heard her once,' Lo replies. 'With her latest boyfriend. Though it was mostly him making noise.'

She sticks her fingers down her throat and pretends to gag. At least Albin is fairly certain she is pretending.

'I bet she's super-boring in bed, since she's such a super-boring person in general. She probably doesn't even know what a blow-job is.'

Lo rolls her eyes. Albin doesn't know what to say now either. The word *blowjob* hangs in the air between them. Imagine if Lo knew how much time he spends thinking about sex these days. Imagine if she knew what he looks up online sometimes. How it makes him feel. Scared and aroused and grossed out all at once.

Sex is like a parallel universe where people who seem normal suddenly turn out to be something else. Almost like the monsters in his nightmares. They can look like anyone, seem like they belong in the normal world, until you peek behind the curtain.

Is Lo one of them now? Has she done it with someone?

'Wanna leave?' Albin says, and tries to smile.

'Yeah,' Lo says. 'But you have something stuck in your teeth that I'm really tired of looking at.'

Albin lags behind when she heads for the exit, picking his front teeth with the nail of his index finger until he dislodges a small, green speck. When he puts it back in his mouth, it tastes hot and spicy.

He wipes his finger on his jeans and runs after Lo.

Madde

Madde is jumping up and down on the spot, one arm in the air, barely noticing how much her feet hurt in her high heels. Sweat is pouring down her face, trickling between her breasts, which are threatening to pop out of her top at any moment. The teeny-tiny gold flakes on her skin are shimmering like thousands of stars under the strobing lights of Club Charisma. Her fist is pumping to the beat until it feels like she is controlling the music. Her other hand is clutching her drink; vodka Red Bull is spilling over the edge of the glass, making her skin sweet and sticky.

There aren't a lot of people here yet, but they are staring at her and Zandra. Madde loves it. Their attention charges her like a bloody battery. As long as they keep staring, she will never get tired. She is going to give them something to talk about. And Zandra feels the same way, Madde knows she does; she can see it in her eyes. Zandra comes over, letting her feather boa slip down her shoulder like a stripper. She tosses the boa around Madde's neck, pulls her close as though she has caught her. The feathers are warm and wet against Madde's skin. Madde giggles, takes a big swig from her glass. Zandra's grip on the boa tightens and she starts grinding her hips, goes all the way down into a squat. Her miniskirt rides up her hips; her white lace panties are practically fluorescent.

And then Zandra wobbles and falls on her bum without letting go of the boa. Madde's head is yanked forward and she very nearly goes down too. Her drink is sent flying. Zandra finally lets go and lies down on the floor, feet kicking, arms flapping every which way. Her laughter cuts through the music. And Madde is laughing so hard she can't breathe; it saps her muscles of strength, so she can barely stand up. She leans forward, gasping, with Zandra's shrieking ringing in her ears. Drool is dripping from Madde's mouth; when she notices, it makes her laugh even harder.

Filip

It is always twilight in Charisma Starlight, which can make it easy to lose track of time, but Filip doesn't need to check to know it is just coming up to nine. The guests arriving after the first sitting in the restaurants are on their second round of drinks. Filip and Marisol mix gin and tonics, pour beer and wine and Jägermeister, open bottles of cider, alcopops and special-discount sparkling wine. They keep an eye on two old men, leaning heavily against the counter, bickering loudly.

'You can't bloody well claim it counts as an international vacation,' one of them says. 'We're only in Finland for one hour.'

'That's exactly right. Finland's a different country, isn't it, or maybe it belongs to Sweden?' the other one retorts obstinately, in a tone that could drive anyone up the wall.

'Just about.'

Filip scans the room while he pulls a couple of pints from the taps. The barefoot woman on the dance floor is showing no sign of tiring. She has been joined by more dancing couples. A skinny woman standing in the dark next to them is making Filip uneasy, even though he can only see her as a silhouette against the flashing lights. She is standing much too still – it's almost as though she isn't real, a badly executed photomontage. Sometimes the lights briefly skim across her face; he can tell she is emaciated, furrowed, wearing far too much makeup.

'If it's not international travel, how would they be able to sell things tax-free?' one of the old geezers says, looking smug.

'But that's not the point. We don't even set foot on land there.'

'And that's exactly it: we're not in Sweden either, so we're abroad.'

Filip keeps scanning the room. The seating between the bar and dance floor is filling up. A family has sat down on one of the sofas. The two younger children are climbing over the back of the sofa, throwing themselves between armchairs, but the eldest, a girl of about seven with thick glasses, watches her parents drinking their beer in silence. They look well on their way to getting plastered. There is a determination to their drinking he never used to see much on the *Charisma* before. He doesn't know when it started, but it feels like it's an unstoppable spiral. The passengers looking for a calmer, more family-friendly cruise only need to do a simple Google search to realise they should pick a different ship. Filip has seen the comments. Other ships entice patrons with themed cruises and famous DJs and much bigger guest acts than Dan Appelgren. The *Charisma* is the ship that was left behind, its only real draw cheap booze. It makes him sad sometimes. Filip hates seeing children with parents who can barely keep themselves upright; he remembers all too well what it felt like to hear the clinking from his own parents' bags full of liquor bottles. He thinks about that a lot; how ironic it is that he works with alcohol all day every day now.

He hands back the change for the pints and takes the next order. And the next. And the next. He enters the zone where he is like a machine, just doing the job. Banters, fires off smiles, winks when he senses it might generate extra tips, but he isn't thinking. His mind is completely blank.

Marisol has tried to get him to meditate. He can't imagine anything more stressful than sitting completely stock-still. But what Marisol describes when she tries to convince him – the quieting of the thoughts, the sense of being present – reminds him of this flow-state. Work is his meditation.

'Four Cosmopolitans,' a girl says, and he nods at her, making a mental note of her sharply drawn-on eyebrows. There is always some little detail to help him remember who is waiting for what.

Filip pours ice into Martini glasses to chill them. Vodka, Cointreau, ice and cranberry juice in the shiny shaker. He spots Jenny, who has taken a seat in Marisol's section of the bar. She is wearing her red stage dress and there is a glass of vodka soda in front of her, the same drink as every night. Red lipstick stains the edge of the glass. She looks like a star from a bygone era, her blonde hair in glossy curls. She is about to go on. He has heard her run through more or less the same repertoire all year and still he is going to miss her husky, smoky voice, which somehow makes him believe the insipid *dansband* lyrics. The day after tomorrow is her last night on board, and to be completely honest, it is not only her voice he is going to miss.

Filip puts the drinks down in front of the girl with the eyebrows, takes her credit card and swipes it through the card reader.

'You all right?' he calls out to Jenny, who smiles.

'Absolutely,' she calls back. 'Aside from the fact that, yet again, there's no cruise director.'

He tries to give her an encouraging smile. He knows how much she hates having to take on the cruise director's duty of leading the singing of 'Happy Birthday' to the people in the audience whose birthday it is. It makes her noticeably uncomfortable to engage with the audience that way.

Someone shrieks: the old men at the bar have started fighting. Marisol has already picked up the phone to call the information desk to request security.

Filip walks around the bar to place himself between the old men, hands on their chests to keep them apart. Luckily, they are so drunk they don't put up much of a fight. They're more pre-occupied with staying on their feet.

Pia and Jarno arrive in less than thirty seconds.

'All right, gents,' Pia says, and Filip backs away to give her space. 'What's going on here then?'

'Yes, my name is Hans-Jörgen and I want to report this bastard for assault,' says the obstinate old man, spitting saliva.

'Then I'm reporting you right back!' the other one bellows. 'I didn't start it; all these people are my witnesses.'

'I think it would be a good idea if the two of you were to come with us and have a nap,' Pia says. 'Then we can talk some more when you've sobered up a bit.'

Surprisingly, neither man objects. They just glower at each other.

'How did it work out for Calle?' Filip asks, while Pia and Jarno put handcuffs on the two old men.

'All done with the proposing,' Pia replies. 'And let me tell you, the guy had no clue. He looked pretty shaken.'

Filip laughs. 'I hope they stop by,' he says. 'I wouldn't want to miss Mr Perfect.'

'I wouldn't count on them leaving their suite tonight,' Pia says with a smile. The handcuffs jangle. 'I was thinking we could go for a walk with them on the promenade deck tomorrow, before your shift.'

'Absolutely,' Filip says.

Impatient looks from several people at the bar. It is time to go back to work.

'You haven't seen anything I should be keeping my eye on?' Pia says.

Filip had almost forgotten about the emaciated woman by the dance floor, but now his eyes turn that way of their own accord. The silhouette is gone. For some reason, that makes him even more uneasy.

He shakes his head, attempting to rid himself of the feeling.

'Nothing worse than a couple of kids trying to swipe leftover beer. A boy and a girl. He was about twelve, from Thailand or thereabouts would be my guess. She was blonde, could have been anything between twelve and seventeen.'

'All right,' Pia says. 'See you later.'

She and Jarno each put an arm around one of the old men and guide them towards the exit.

Filip goes back in behind the bar and thinks to himself, not for the first time, that everyone working aboard the *Charisma* is lucky they have Pia. He knows the security guards on many of the other ships only handle what they absolutely have to and pretend not to see the rest. They leave people passed out in hallways, look the other way when drunk parents drag their three-year-olds around the dance floor long after midnight. It is largely thanks to Pia things aren't more out of hand than they are. Filip knows that if the owners had their way, they would push the alcohol even harder, serve people who are too drunk to order. The cruiseferries aren't bound by the same laws and regulations as bars on dry land, and the *Charisma* has to start turning more of a profit if she wants to keep afloat. But Pia would never allow it and her attitude rubs off on the rest of the security staff, and that in turn persuades everyone working in the bars to think twice.

Filip takes the next order: five pints for a man with blond dreads and a Green Party pin on the collar of his denim jacket.

'Did things work out okay for your friend?' Marisol calls to him, and Filip nods happily, giving her a thumbs-up.

The next order is for two glasses of red and a bowl of peanuts. An older couple. The man has a cluster of age spots by his hairline. Then two more pints. Two guys in striped polo shirts.

Calle

They walk down the ninth-deck corridor to the suite. Calle's body feels light. His soul has swelled, expanded like an entire universe. It almost overflows when he looks at Vincent, sees how overwhelmed he is.

'Don't forget to breathe,' Calle says, and laughs.

'I think I need a drink,' Vincent tells him, his voice thick. 'Let's head to the bar where your friend works, okay?'

'I want to spend some time alone with you first.'

Calle manages not to let it slip that he has one more surprise in store. They reach their door at the end of the hall. Calle inserts the key card and gives Vincent a quick kiss before opening it and stepping in.

Vincent freezes in the doorway. Stares at the rose petals scattered across the hallway floor. Calle turns the lights on and Vincent's eyes grow wider.

'How . . . ?' he says. 'How did you—? But we were just here?'

Calle takes his hand, stares at the beaten white-gold ring on Vincent's finger identical to the one on his own. Same size, even.

They walk into the large room on the lower floor, grinding rose petals into the carpet. There's a bowl of pink jelly hearts on the coffee table. Clutches of pink streamers hang from the banister of the staircase leading up to the bedroom. Soft rain patters against the large windows. As they walk past them, Calle glances down at the bow deck. The white railings, sharply lit against the dark water, meet in a rounded point: an arrow pointing straight out to sea. The deck is crowded, despite the drizzle.

They go upstairs. A champagne bucket is sitting on one of the nightstands. Pia and Filip have scattered rose petals on the bed as well. A big banner above the headboard reads CONGRATULA-TIONS! written in rounded letters using red and hot-pink felt tips.

'My God, they're nuts,' Calle says with a laugh. 'All that's missing now is a couple of pink teddy bears or something.'

But he is touched. He sits down on the bed and picks up a petal. It is soft and silky against his fingertips.

'Come here,' he says.

Vincent stays where he is on the top step of the staircase. He stares at the banner as if he doesn't understand what it says. 'You must have been planning this for ages,' he says.

'You really didn't know?'

Vincent shakes his head.

'Really? I was so nervous . . .' Calle starts saying, but cuts himself off when their eyes meet.

Something is wrong. Vincent is not just overwhelmed. He looks *sad*.

'Are you okay?' Calle asks.

'I just need the loo,' Vincent replies, and walks back downstairs.

The tap starts running in the bathroom after he locks the door behind him. Calle slaps his knees, drumming out a nervous beat. He is imagining it. He needs to stop imagining things.

Vincent said yes. They are getting married. He and Vincent are *getting married*! Of course that is a lot to take in. He has been thinking about it for months, planning the whole thing.

Calle studies the ring on his finger, turning it this way and that. He stands up. His jacket is too tight. He removes it and pulls at the neck of his T-shirt, which suddenly feels like it is throttling him.

He walks to the railing and looks down at the room below. He can't see the bathroom door from where he is, but he can still hear the tap running.

Calle grabs the champagne bottle from its bucket; the ice rattles loudly. Melted water drips from the bottom. He peels off the foil and rotates the cork until it comes out with a pop. Should he have waited until Vincent came back up? Too late now. He pours champagne into the two flutes, waits for the foam to settle, tops them up. Hesitates for no more than a split second before taking a couple of deep swigs, then pours himself a second glass. He wishes he had some candles to light, but there are none to be had on the ship, on account of the fire hazard.

The bathroom door opens downstairs. Calle takes a glass in each hand and sits down on the bed. Waits. Hears footsteps.

Vincent's head appears. He stops halfway up. 'I can't. I'm so fucking sorry, but I can't.'

'What do you mean?' Calle asks, even though he knows already.

'I can't marry you,' Vincent says.

Calle has a sinking feeling, strong enough to pull the *Charisma* into the abyss. 'But you said . . . you said yes,' is the only thing he can think to say.

'What was I supposed to do, in front of all those people? What was I supposed to say?' Vincent sounds almost accusatory.

Calle gets up off the bed. A handful of petals flutter to the carpet. 'I just don't understand.'

'I'm sorry,' Vincent says. 'I didn't mean . . . I just didn't know what to do . . . What the best thing would be . . .'

His eyes look so sad, like a beaten dog: as if Calle has put him through an ordeal. Calle has no idea what to do now. He holds out a flute, but Vincent shakes his head.

The letters on the banner beam at them mockingly. Calle downs a glass of champagne in one go. The foam swells in his mouth. He has to turn away to swallow it while putting the glasses down.

'But why?' he says without looking at Vincent. 'We've been talking about getting married.'

'I know,' Vincent says. 'But that was a long time ago and . . .'

'A long time ago?' Calle cuts him off. 'We talked about it this summer . . . that we were going to do it after we moved . . .'

'I know.'

'Right. So what the fuck has changed since then?'

'I don't know. I wish I could tell you.'

Calle turns around. Vincent looks more miserable than ever.

'I don't know why I don't want to,' he says. 'It doesn't feel right.'

'Have you met someone else?'

Vincent shakes his head firmly.

'Then what is it?' Calle demands.

Silence.

'Do you even want to be with me at all?'

Vincent hesitates a second too long. 'Yes,' he says.

But he has already averted his eyes.

Calle wants to hate him for doing this. For destroying everything. 'How long have you felt this way?'

'What do you mean *felt this way*? I don't even know how I feel.'

'Ambivalent,' Calle says. 'Isn't that what this feeling is called?' His voice sounds cold and detached. Good. 'Were you already feeling this way when we bought the flat? When we took out that massive mortgage?'

'I'm sorry,' Vincent says. 'I'm sorry. I thought it would pass. I thought it was one of those things that just come and go . . .'

'That *come and go*?'

'Yes! It happens. You've never had doubts?'

'No,' Calle says. 'I haven't.'

They look at each other. The distance between them feels vaster than the whole of the Baltic Sea.

Maybe our relationship is like the sea out there, Calle thinks to himself, *beautiful and glittering on the surface, but full of dead zones, so damaged nothing can live there. And I had no idea.*

He thinks about their flat. The newly sanded floors. The paintings that are finally all in the right place. The extra loan just to finance the renovation of the kitchen. The fucking ordeal of moving in Stockholm. The stress of the sale, the charade of the home staging, the surreal sums of money they had played with when they signed their souls over to the bank. Had Vincent already known he wasn't sure then?

'I know things have been difficult for a while,' Calle says. 'Or maybe for a long time. But that's behind us now. And maybe you're just nervous because things suddenly turned serious . . .'

He stops talking. He can't humiliate himself by trying to persuade Vincent, even though it is all he wants to do. *It's supposed to be us. It's supposed to be you and me. I can't be wrong about that, can I?*

'I don't know what happened,' Vincent says, 'but I can't marry you until I've figured it out.'

'And how are you going to figure it out?' Calle asks. 'By sleeping around a bit to see if you can find someone better?'

He doesn't even know what he is saying any more. Can't find a thought or a feeling to hold on to.

'Cut it out,' Vincent says. 'It's not about that.'

Then what is it about? Calle wants to scream.

'What do we do now then?' he says. 'What the fuck do we do now?'

Vincent says nothing.

'I can't be with you if you don't know how you feel,' Calle says. 'You get that, don't you? It won't work. I can't walk around and be all ... *see, being with me is amazing.*'

'I realise I can't ask that of you,' Vincent replies.

'So this is it? I guess it must be.'

Suddenly, dead silence inside him. His feelings have stopped pulling in every direction. They have simply vanished. And his mind is no longer racing. It is laser-sharp, starting to organise things into a to-do list.

They need to move again. Neither one of them will be able to afford to stay in the flat on their own. They are going to have to bring in an estate agent, have another valuation done. Talk to the bank lady with the big hair who looked so happy for them. He has to find a new flat, pack all his things in the moving boxes that are still sitting in their attic storage space.

But first he has to get off this damn ship. He has to survive tonight and tomorrow, figure out where to go once they disembark.

He realises Vincent is crying on the stairs and his first impulse is to console him.

'I need to get out of here,' Calle says.

'We can go somewhere to talk.'

'No,' Calle says, 'I don't want to talk. Stay here. Or do whatever you want. But I can't be anywhere near you right now.'

He pushes past Vincent on the stairs, trying not to look at the banner, the petals on the floor. The bunches of streamers hanging from the banister whisper softly in the draught as he passes. He finally reaches the cabin door, steps out into the hallway and closes it behind him. His breathing is heavy and laboured.

Luckily, no one is around. He pushes down the tears trying to escape. He needs to hold on to this clarity of mind.

He can hear Vincent moving about behind the door, so he starts jogging down the corridor towards the stairs.

Tomas

He stares at the ceiling, then looks around, bewildered, before remembering where he is. Becomes aware of the stench in the cramped space. Sees the bloody

my blood

little body lying on its side next to him on the floor. Tries to understand what just happened.

He needs to lean heavily on the edge of the bed to get to his feet. The adrenalin has dissipated; now his entire body is shaking.

This is too easy, he thinks to himself. The boy was so strong. He is just playing possum. Any moment, he is going to open his eyes. The hand, so limp now, is going to grab him, quick like a cobra. His eyes are going to open and it is going to start again . . .

The boy's body has firmed up. His skin has acquired a pale but healthy glow from the blood-filled flesh underneath it; his cheeks are rosy.

Suddenly Tomas' perspective shifts. He sees the scene from the outside. He sees what everyone else would see. And he breaks down in tears.

How is he going to explain that this tiny child terrified him, scared him beyond all reasonable limits, so that he was barely aware of what he was doing when he *killed him, I killed him, oh my God.*

The wound on his neck is throbbing dully. He turns to the mirror above the desk. Sees his own wildly staring eyes, the eyes of a madman. Blood is no longer trickling from the puncture wounds that form a perfect imprint of the boy's teeth.

Self-defence. They are going to think the boy bit him in self-defence.

But what about the blood? The blood inside the boy's body is *his*; the boy had none of his own. They have to be able to prove that . . . tests . . .

Tomas tries to imagine how he is going to tell the on-board security about this. He can't even believe it himself.

He dashes into the bathroom and throws up into the sink, liquid vomit consisting only of curdling beer and stomach juices. The saliva continues to dribble out of the corners of his mouth while it dawns on him just how insane it all is.

So insane it can't actually be true, so insane I must have imagined the whole thing because I AM insane. I was seeing things, I was drunk and worked up and my psyche snapped like a dry twig and now I've murdered an innocent CHILD and I'm stuck on this boat—

The boy had clearly not been well, but there must have been a way to help him.

Instead of killing him.

Tomas spits, but the string of saliva is so thick he has to pinch it off with his fingers. He watches it slowly disappear down the drain. He knows he is not crazy. He knows what he saw.

But isn't that what all crazy people think?

He forces himself to peek out of the bathroom door.

The body on the floor is motionless. The blond hair gleams.

No one saw me go into this cabin. I can leave now, pretend like everything's fine. No, there are security cameras everywhere. They're going to find the recording.

He has to get out of here. His head is spinning; he leans against the sink until it passes. He washes his hands, but the blood has found its way under his nails. Tomas splashes freezing water on his face, trying to clear his head.

The blood is practically invisible on his black shirt and jacket. He wets a towel, wipes off a sticky stain from his chest. The blood that dripped from the boy's wound. The wound he made with a broken bottle.

Tomas almost vomits again. He pulls out his phone. No reception, but he wouldn't know who to call anyway. It is only just past nine o'clock. How is that possible? How can everything change so quickly?

Suddenly, he remembers the high-heeled boots in the cabin. Somewhere on the ship is a woman who could show up at any moment.

I killed her child.

Tomas wipes down the tap and sink with loo roll and staggers out of the bathroom, picks the bottleneck up from the floor and wipes it clean with the edge of his shirt. Where else might he have left fingerprints?

The body is still completely motionless.

He walks to the door, takes a deep breath and opens it. There is no one in the corridor.

He needs to find one of his boys. Peo, maybe. He has to talk to someone he can trust, before informing security.

Or you keep your mouth shut until the ship docks in Åland, a voice inside him says. *Get off there. Get away. Escape on a different ship.*

It is a tempting idea, but this is not some fucking American action flick. There is no Mexican border to make a run for. He has nowhere to go, no hidden stash of cash.

The wound on his neck is throbbing and burning. His back is soaked with sweat. He has to lean against the wall to walk. A couple of long-haired blokes come out of a cabin, glancing at him briefly before moving on. Tomas watches them. Wonders if he just looks like a drunk, any old drunk, or if you can tell what has happened, if they are going to go and alert security. Maybe they even heard something through the wall?

He needs to get far away from this corridor. He needs to find a place where he can think in peace.

Dan

'Ladies and gentlemen, welcome to Charisma Karaoke! My name is Dan Appelgren and I will be your host tonight!'

Scattered applause. It is still early. Mostly old people are slumping on the sofas. One geezer has fallen asleep with his pint glass resting on his enormous gut.

Dan is sweating in the spotlight. His senses are sharpened by the coke: it makes him more present, while at the same time sheltering him from the hideousness that surrounds him. He can see it, but it doesn't bother him.

'Who knows, we might discover a new star here tonight!' he says.

A few people giggle. An old woman playfully nudges her husband's arm. Dan can tell who wants to sing but is too scared. They are the ones glancing around at everyone else. And they are the ones who will never want to stop later, who will get off the stage and march straight over to Johan's booth to sign up for another song.

'I figured I might warm you up with something I think you'll recognise,' Dan says with a wink. 'Sing along now, everybody! And if you need help with the words, the lyrics are up there!' He points to the widescreen television on the wall. The screen is an empty blue that tints the old faces closest to it, making them look like wrinkly Smurfs.

'Are you ready?' Dan says, throwing the microphone in the air and letting it spin a few times before catching it. He looks at Johan. 'Then *let's go!*'

The spotlights go brighter. Hotter. He closes his eyes. Plants his feet wide apart. Turns his head to one side. His hand clutches the microphone.

And then the strings fade in to the song he sings at least twice a night on board the *Charisma*. The song he once sang to millions of viewers in a sold-out arena during the grand final of the Swedish Eurovision competition.

One of the old people in the audience coughs, wet and phlegmy. The bartender drops a bottle. The drum machine kicks in. Someone starts clapping along. Someone else joins in. The strings build to a crescendo. Dan raises the microphone to his mouth, opens his eyes and stares straight ahead. Lets the spotlights blind him.

For a moment or two, all he sees is light.

'*Like fever in my heart, your love has got me burning. I'm dying when we're apart, on fever clouds of yearning.*'

Two older ladies smile at him. Some people are whispering and giggling to each other. The old man with the big belly twitches and looks around drowsily.

'*Your body is so hot. Your smile sets me on fire,*' Dan continues, working up to the chorus. '*There's no cure for what I've got, I'm burning on your pyre.*'

The text scrolls across the screen, yellow capitals against a backdrop of people splashing each other with water on a beach, swinging in a sunny playground, trying on zany hats at a fair.

'Come on now! Everybody sing along! I know you know this one!'

A couple of the old biddies obey him, bellowing out the lyrics that have netted the fucking faggot who wrote them millions in royalties. The bald little bastard likes to brag about how it only took him fifteen minutes to write 'Like Fever in My Heart'. Dan has been stuck with it for twenty years, singing it thousands upon thousands of times at company functions and in gay clubs and small-town city squares, and he no longer even has a savings account.

'Don't want no doctor, don't want to be healed. You are my malady, the fever I feel. Like fever in my heart, you know you are my fire. I'm burning for you, baby, your love can take me higher.'

New verse, chorus, modulation and chorus, and the song is finally done. Dan smiles from ear to ear, bows deeply from the waist. The old people clap politely.

'Amazing! Loving it! For those of you who want more, you can buy my latest album at the bar and in the tax-free shop!'

Five more hours to go. He looks at Johan, who gives him a tired nod.

'And now I think Johan has had his first request of the night,' Dan says. 'Who is brave enough to be the first one on stage?'

An ancient fatso in tight-fitting clothes comes waddling across the room like something out of *Jurassic Park*. She smiles nervously at Dan, who holds out an arm for support when she steps onto the stage.

'Hey there,' Dan says with all the enthusiasm he can muster. 'And what is this young lady's name?'

Scattered laughs.

'Birgitta,' the woman says quietly in a sing-song regional accent. 'Birgitta Gudmundsson.'

'And where are you from, Birgitta?'

She squirms. She is clearly so nervous she can barely hear him. He is just about to ask again when she opens her mouth.

'Grycksbo.'

'A lovely place, from what I hear.'

It is a miracle she doesn't catch the sarcasm. Where the fuck is Grycksbo?

Her face has taken on a deep shade of red that matches her dress. Dan can almost feel the heat from her blushing cheeks.

'Well, yes,' Birgitta says. 'We like it there. We do.'

'Is there a special someone you will be singing for tonight?'

'That would be my man.'

Birgitta lights up when she turns to a deflated, desiccated thing in a shirt and sweater-vest. The man beams back at her. No wonder he looks so malnourished: Birgitta probably scarfs down all the food they have at home.

'And what are you going to sing for him tonight?' Dan asks.

'Well, it's going to be "Jolene" by Dolly Parton. It brings back a lot of wonderful memories.'

'How long have you been married?'

'Forty years,' Birgitta replies proudly. 'We're here to celebrate our ruby wedding and all.'

'Is that right? Well, then I think we should all give Birgitta and her very lucky husband a warm round of applause,' Dan says.

Birgitta laughs nervously while the applause rings out. Dan can't help noticing that they sound a lot more enthusiastic now than after his performance.

Marianne

It is already past ten and at Charisma Starlight they are doing the four-step under the flashing lights. In the thick and humid air they bump into other bodies as warm as their own. Marianne is covered in a thin film of perspiration that makes her blouse cling to her skin. The hair at her temples is dripping. She has no clue how many glasses of white wine she drank at dinner. At the buffet, you could just top up your glass from a tap; she guzzled it like squash without it slaking her thirst one bit. It was much too sweet for her taste, but she didn't want to switch to red wine and have to discover later on that her teeth were blue.

Göran holds her hands in a firm grip and his eyes lock on hers. It no longer makes her uncomfortable. Quite the opposite. His gaze seems to make her less invisible. More real. Almost beautiful.

She feels free for the first time in years: free from the other Marianne, the one who always hovers by her shoulder, judging her.

Göran only knows the most basic steps, but he leads with confidence nonetheless. From time to time, they improvise together. When Marianne stumbles, he makes sure she doesn't fall.

The singer of the band is beautiful in her red dress. The red velvet curtain behind her hangs in heavy folds.

Marianne dances this way and that, glimpsing snapshots of other couples whenever a coloured light illuminates them, hands resting on backs, caressing waists and bums, wrapped around a partner's neck. Eyes closed in pleasure, eyes looking around as though they want to leave. Mouths unabashedly kissing one another, laughing, shouting something in someone's ear. So much life happening. And Marianne is in the midst of it.

Göran pulls her closer; suddenly, they are in an embrace. His neck is wet against her cheek. The song ends and a new one starts, but they stay where they are, completely still. Everything is so overwhelming.

'I know what you want,' he whispers in her ear.

Marianne is about to reply that he can't possibly know that, because she doesn't know herself. But that would probably be a lie by now, and not a very convincing one either.

'And what might that be?' she says.

She holds her breath and waits to hear what he will say next.

'A beer, of course.' He relaxes his grip enough so he can look at her and smile mischievously. 'What did you think I meant?'

Marianne looks away, embarrassed.

Göran is constantly on the verge of turning the whole thing tawdry. But she likes how he makes everything seem so easy. He is leading her through this game she has long since forgotten how to play.

'Come on,' he says.

They walk across the dance floor, hand in hand. Other couples bumble into them from every direction, drunkenly staggering into their path. An elbow hits Marianne between the shoulder blades, almost knocking the wind out of her.

She takes up position next to the dance floor while Göran goes to buy them a pint each. She studies the seething cauldron of dancing couples. A lonely middle-aged man is swaying back and forth with his arms above his head, his eyes closed under the brim of his cowboy hat like he is in a trance.

A big group of people are sitting at one of the tables close to Marianne, talking in Finnish. She glances furtively at them, unable to judge their mood on account of their strange language. She thinks about the old factory town she grew up in, all the Finns who came there in the sixties to work. They were the only immigrants the town had ever seen and there was no end to the talk about how strange the Finns were, how loud they were and how ugly their language sounded, how much they drank and how uninterested they were in getting to know any Swedes. People said the Finns bought new cars every time they went back to Finland, so they could brag to their families back home. It seems so long ago now. Almost picturesque. Yet at the same time, people don't appear to have changed at all.

Marianne realises the band on stage are singing yet another song and she starts wondering what is taking Göran so long. She turns around and is relieved to spot his back. He is standing calmly at the bar, holding up a couple of hundred-kronor notes to show he is both ready and of means.

A man in a suit reeking of sweat sidles up to her. She reluctantly glances at him. His round face has big, heavy jowls and his head is crowned with flimsy tufts of hair. He looks like an oversized baby. A baby that moves in close until his body is pressing against hers. She steps to the side, staring intently at the dance floor. She just wants him to leave. Can't he see that?

But no, he is pressing against her again, moving his pelvis back and forth.

'Pardon me,' she says, and turns on her heel, striding off in the direction of the bar and Göran's back.

'Place is full of dried-up cunt tonight,' the man shouts after her.

She stiffens.

'Come on, dance with me,' the man demands, catching up to her, grabbing her.

Marianne shakes her head and stares at the floor.

Göran is finally by her side. The baby-man mutters something and slouches off.

'Already making new friends?' Göran says with a grin. 'What did he say?'

'It doesn't matter.' Her voice is trembling.

But Göran just shrugs, hands her a pint and points to a couple of armchairs that have just opened up near the bar. 'I think I need a quick breather,' he says. 'God knows I'm not as young as I used to be.'

'Yes,' Marianne says, 'God does know.'

She looks around while they walk. The baby-man is nowhere to be seen. They sit down in the upholstered armchairs and she takes several big swigs. It is wonderfully refreshing. The bubbles scratch away the thirst from her parched throat. Göran was right: a beer was exactly what she wanted.

'Have you seen your friends around?' She shouts to make herself heard over a group of girls who have started screeching along to the music with their arms around each other's shoulders.

'No, but who cares about them?' Göran says. 'I'm here with you now.'

Filip

The group of girls is going to give him tinnitus. Filip has to lean across the counter to catch the other patrons' orders. He wipes his brow with a paper napkin. A bit of sweat has found its way into his eyes, making them sting. It is at times like these he wonders how he ever put up with his first bartending job, back when smoking was still allowed in bars and cigarette smoke infused his hair and clothes, made his eyes and lungs burn.

He meets a pair of eyes across the bar. A woman with red metal glasses: two Malibu and Diet Cokes. He serves the drinks. Wipes his forehead again, takes the next order. An older man whose eyebrows are so bushy several hairs hang down into his eyes. He pays for his beer with crumpled notes. One of the members of the shrill gaggle of girls orders a bottle of bubbly and five glasses.

A bearded guy in a white T-shirt is standing next to the bar, staring intensely at Filip; when their eyes meet, Filip is stunned. It is hard to believe it is him; he looks so different.

Calle.

It is suddenly brought home to him just how long it's been since they last saw each other, and how much he has missed him.

Filip gives him a big hug. Calle smells of fresh air and the out-side. His beard is soft but cool. He stands stock-still.

'Congratulations, man!' Filip says. 'Pia told me you nailed it! I'm so bloody chuffed for you!'

Calle

Calle lets himself be hugged, have his back slapped a few times. Not even that shakes him out of this dreamlike state.

'So you decided to come out and celebrate after all?' Filip says, releasing him. He is glancing around, clearly searching for the husband-to-be.

Filip's uniform is the same: white shirt under a red waistcoat, small brass name tag on his chest. His hair hasn't changed either, though the light-brown tangle is thinner.

The dark-haired girl working the other end of the bar gives Calle a happy wave. 'Congratulations!' she mouths.

Filip looks back at Calle, grinning like a lunatic.

Calle seriously contemplates not telling him, to not have to hear himself say the words.

'So, where's the fiancé?' Filip asks.

Calle shakes his head. 'I think he's in our cabin,' he says. 'My God. Nothing's changed here.'

'Except us, I guess,' Filip retorts.

Calle tries to smile.

The singer on stage starts in on an old ABBA song. The group of girls by the bar squeal in unison, top up their glasses and dash headlong towards the dance floor. Calle watches them go.

'Is everything okay?' Filip asks.

'I don't know,' Calle replies. 'No.'

'What happened?'

'I don't know,' he repeats. 'I don't know shit any more.'

Filip nods, a bit perplexed. Calle is acutely aware of the heat and the crowding and the looks from the impatient patrons and the volume you have to speak unnaturally loudly to be heard over.

'I can't go back to the suite,' he says. 'I don't know what to do.'

'You can stay with me tonight if you want,' Filip offers.

'Thanks.'

'Want to borrow my pass? I'll come up for a chat as soon as I can.'

Calle shakes his head. The pre-parties are probably just getting started up in the staff quarters. He doesn't want to go there by himself. Not yet. And definitely not sober. But his old colleagues could turn up here too at any time. There is nowhere to hide.

'They're a lot stricter now than when you worked here, so the staff don't tend to be out partying among the passengers much these days,' Filip says, as though he can hear Calle's thoughts.

And Calle has to fight back the tears again. 'I need a drink,' he says. 'Something strong.'

'At least we have plenty of that. Your usual, or—?'

And Calle nods. Yes. His usual.

Tomas

He is cold.

He managed to get up to the tenth floor, as far as the lift would take him, and staggered out onto the promenade deck. He'd intended to go to the sun deck, which covers the entire top of the ship, but had made it only a few feet.

Now he is curled up on a bench, shaking. There is a roof above him, but rain is being carried in on the wind. He has turned to face the wall. He hears people passing by, groups of them laughing and shouting at one another, far too loud in their inebriated state. There are too many impressions; he can't process them. And it is getting worse. There is nowhere to go. He can't go back inside the ship, with its chaos of voices and music and flashing lights and ringing fruit machines and the smells that are more overwhelming to him than anything else: cleaning products, perfumes, food, hand soap, body odour, buttery skin lotions, alcohol, cigarette smoke. He even thought he was able to smell the warm coins in people's pockets. But the strongest smell of all made all the others pale in comparison, made his head roar. The smell of menstruation. It lingered in the air outside the lift. He could sense it, like a shark senses blood in the water from a mile away. He wanted to find the woman, bury his face between her legs. Go straight to the source. Tear her flesh open to get more, faster.

He turns his head and vomits. The buffet food is coming back up, heavy and caustic. Luckily, he hadn't managed to eat much.

Åse. He had been thinking about Åse, that was why he had barely been able to get anything down. He knows that. But when he thinks about the name Åse now, there are barely any feelings attached to it. Only the memory of the blood smell makes him feel anything at all.

He is going crazy, properly crazy. And the roof of his mouth aches, all the way up to his sinuses. When he runs his tongue over his palate, it is taut and rigid.

The only thing he can do is to try to focus on the deep, monotonous rumbling from the belly of the ship, the almost imperceptible vibrations of the bench. The *Baltic Charisma* is singing to him, soothing him with her basso profundo, helping him shut out all the other things.

He wants to cry, but can't get the tears to come.

'Stellar,' a child's voice says somewhere nearby.

He yelps in terror, certain it must be the boy from the cabin. He has found him again, come to exact his revenge. Tomas reluctantly turns his head and sees two kids standing there staring at him.

They smell so strongly. He can almost see the swirls of particles around them. The girl is wearing a lotion with a sweet chemical smell. Under that is her blood, her young, vital blood, healthy and warm in her veins.

The roof of his mouth tightens. He can feel his face twisting into a grimace; when the children take a step back, he realises he must look frightening.

Like a child-killer.

'I'm sorry,' he says. 'I'm all right. Just resting for a second.'

His voice sounds thick and strange. He just wants them to leave now, afraid of what might happen if they stay. The girl has put on a deliberate air of jaded boredom. He can tell from her breath she has been drinking.

The smell of their blood is so strong. His stomach contracts, his body rolls up into a foetal position. There's nothing but bile coming up now.

'Really, really stellar,' the girl says, and pulls the boy away.

A few seconds later he hears them giggling with revulsion.

He turns back to the wall. His skull is pounding and aching, but his body feels cleansed, purified. His stomach is an empty black hole.

A new jolt of pain shoots up from the roof of his mouth, through his nose and straight into his head; this time, his eyes tear up.

Albin

'That was, like, the number one most disgusting thing ever,' Lo says when they reach the white-painted steel stairs to the sun deck.

Albin nods and shivers, thinking about the man on the bench, how his whole body tensed up when he hurled.

'Maybe we should tell someone,' he says. 'He wasn't even wearing a coat.'

'That's his problem. People who are middle-aged should have figured out how to drink normally.'

Albin thinks about his dad. 'But still,' he says, 'he didn't exactly seem to be feeling well.'

They step out onto the roof of the ship. The deck is vast and covered in a green non-slip material that makes it look like a football field. There are little cranes along the side railings, and round, grey skips he knows contain life rafts.

'It's good to throw up after you drink too much,' Lo says. 'That's why they put emetics in all alcohol in Sweden, so people don't get alcohol poisoning as easily.'

Albin looks around. Some of the people on the sun deck have definitely had too much to drink. They move oddly, their eyes empty, like zombies.

'Speaking of disgusting things,' Lo says, nodding at a guy wearing a T-shirt with a SWEDEN IS FOR SWEDES print.

Another set of stairs leads up to an observation platform. Albin follows Lo up, hugs himself to keep the wind out when he reaches the top. This is the ship's highest point. Albin almost feels dizzy when they walk to the railing. Diagonally below them, several storeys down, is the bow deck. Ahead of them is nothing but the wind and the sea and the black sky. Not a light in sight. No stars. The fine drizzle has settled on his face. Somewhere out there is Finland, and they must be close to Åland by now. On a map, the Baltic Sea is puny, but from here it might as well be endless.

His vertigo subsides, turning into a rather pleasant feeling in the pit of his stomach instead. As though he is flying. He stretches his arms out, closing his eyes against the wind and rain, then hesitates. If Lo hasn't seen the film, she is going to think he's some kind of weirdo.

'I'm the king of the world!' he calls out, but not too loudly.

'You realise the *Titanic* sank, don't you? Maybe I'm not exactly loving the reminder at this particular moment.' But she still giggles. 'Come on,' she says, and starts walking down the stairs. 'We have to find some place where we can be alone.'

Lo checks around when they get down, before slipping in under the stairs. Albin walks to the railing and looks at the water far below. He almost thinks he can make out the roaring of the froth along the hull. It is so white against the rest of the water, slick and black like oil. He moves in behind the stairs and sits down next to Lo. She has opened one of the tiny vodka bottles. She drinks a mouthful and holds it out to him.

He sips cautiously, having to fight back a grimace. It is so gross, like what petrol must taste like. Lo laughs. He hands the bottle back to her. Putting his hand on the cold metal floor between them, he feels the vibrations of the ship.

'You don't want more?' she asks.

He shakes his head.

Lo shrugs. She has draped her scarf over her head to keep the rain off. He pulls up his hood from under his jacket.

People are passing by, but no one turns in their direction. It is like they are invisible.

'Have you ever been in love?' Lo asks, and turns to him.

'I don't think so.'

'You would know if you had.'

'There are some people I like,' he says.

It is not an outright lie, but it is also not entirely true. There are girls in his class who are prettier than the others, but does he actually *like* them? He can't imagine trying to get together with one of them. Albin doesn't even know what he would do if he succeeded, what would be expected of him.

'But they're not interested, or what?' Lo asks.

Albin pulls the sleeves of his jacket down over his hands, which are getting chilly in the wind. He feels more childish than ever. He ponders what to say in order to conceal just how inexperienced he is, but Lo beats him to the punch.

'It's fine with me if you're gay, you know that, right? I mean, you could tell me.'

He wonders if she has been talking to some of her old classmates, who still go to the same school as him. He knows there is a rumour about him being gay. He can never seem to manage to be like the other boys, at least not like the popular, loud ones who say mean things as a joke and squeeze the girls' breasts until they scream.

But if Lo is in touch with people from her old class, why won't she ever talk to *him*?

Four guys have taken up position further down the railing. They are smoking and talking loudly in a language Albin thinks might be Italian.

'You could be pretty good-looking if you were more confident,' Lo says.

Albin shrugs again. 'Maybe,' he says, not wanting Lo to see how happy that makes him. At least Lo doesn't think he is ugly. Then maybe there are others who don't either. But how do you get more confident? People say you just have to be yourself, and then everything will turn out great, just great. Yet another lie.

Sometimes he fantasises about coming back to school and finding everything changed. He would still be weird and different, but in a *good* way, a way that made him mysterious and exciting. And everyone would realise they had been underestimating him all along. 'What about you?' he says. 'Are you in love with someone?'

Lo nods. Her lips smack against the bottle when she empties it.

'Are you together?' Albin asks.

'No, because unfortunately he doesn't know I exist.'

She is quiet for a long time. Albin glances furtively at her. How could anyone overlook Lo's existence? How could anyone miss it?

'He's in the seventh grade. We don't even go to the same school any more. At least before, I got to see him every day.'

Albin can tell from her voice that she is close to tears. He hesitates for a second before moving closer. Timidly, he puts an arm around her back. It starts shaking quietly.

'What's his name?'

'Soran,' Lo says, wiping her nose.

'Is he cute?'

'No, he's *beautiful*. But he doesn't know it. You can tell. That's what makes him so amazing.'

146

'But doesn't that mean he's not confident?'

'It's not the same thing,' Lo says.

He is afraid to ask her what she means.

'I could show you a picture of him if this crappy boat had any reception,' Lo says, wiping the tears from her cheeks. 'And he's a good person too. He's always posting links about human rights and environmental stuff. He cares about things that actually matter.'

Albin glances at the railing. The Italians flick their smouldering cigarettes into the darkness and walk away.

'Can't you just tell him the truth?'

'That's a real stellar idea,' Lo says. 'Number one advice.'

'I think he'd like it. I would.'

'You would?' Lo clears her throat. 'Seriously? If it were me? And I wasn't your cousin, obviously.'

Having her ask him for advice feels surreal. As if he actually knows anything about guys like Soran, or girls like Lo.

'Yes,' Albin says, trying to look as dead certain as he can.

Lo wipes her eyes and pulls a powder compact out of her purse. She studies herself in the mirror on the inside of the lid.

'We have to go back to the cabin soon,' Albin says.

'Mmm,' Lo says. 'And *turn in*.' She rolls her eyes as she mimics Linda's favourite expression. 'I wonder who first started calling it *turning in*? Turning into *what*, exactly?'

'Imagine if that's what actually happened,' Albin puts in. 'That you turned into something.'

Lo lowers her powder compact and bursts out laughing. It is so sudden Albin is caught off guard, and then he starts laughing too. He can just picture it, how someone would get into bed and turn into something completely different the moment they nodded off.

'Super-awkward if you turned into something embarrassing,' Lo howls. 'And if you fell asleep on, like, a train, the guard would have to wake you up so you'd change back into a human . . .'

Albin can barely breathe. He gasps for air while trying to explain the image that just popped into his head of a dormitory full of random inanimate objects snoring away in their beds.

They take it further and further, because they both want to be the one who comes up with the last and best image of sleeping people turning into random things. And when it is done, Albin feels physically exhausted and his head is empty of thoughts and he is completely calm.

'That, like, gave me a headache,' Lo says.

'And my stomach hurts,' Albin says.

'I'm just going to try to make myself look vaguely human,' Lo says, and pulls her powder case out again. 'It's, like, so my top tip to go out in public looking like this.'

Albin studies her while she adds another layer, and it strikes him that the makeup and all the rest of it is like an exoskeleton. A hard shell that encases everything gooey and sensitive inside Lo, hides it so no one can get at it.

But now he knows it is there.

He wishes he had something to hide behind too, when he needs it.

Madde

Lasse is snub-nosed, to the point where Madde can actually see up his nostrils a bit, even though he is facing her head-on. The fact that his face is pink with sunburn makes him look even more like a pig. Tiny flakes of skin are peeling off around his nose. And Madde feels fucking offended. Why does it have to be the ugliest of the stag-doers who is hitting on her? She may not be the most beautiful woman in the world, but how the fuck can someone like *him* think he has a chance with *her*? And his provincial accent is hardly helping matters either.

At least he is done droning on about his job and his trip to Sri Lanka, which apparently is *the new Thailand, you simply have to go before the tourists catch on.* As though he becomes a native wherever he goes.

'Poor Stefan,' he says with a nod to his friend.

The grimy veil hangs askew on the groom-to-be's head. One of his boobs has deflated under the floral dress. He is draped over some of the guys in their group; otherwise he would probably be unable to stay upright, even if he *weren't* in heels. It is a miracle he hasn't fractured his ankles yet. Madde has a distinct feeling Stefan is going to be hobbling down the aisle on crutches.

'It wasn't my idea to hit a booze cruise,' Lasse says.

Madde reluctantly leans closer to hear him over the thumping music at Club Charisma. The floor is swaying under her feet; she can't be sure if it is the rolling of the ship or her intoxication.

'I suggested we do something that would be fun for everyone,' he continues. 'Like, first do some kind of action thing together and then have dinner at Riche. Do you go there a lot?'

Madde shakes her head and searches for Zandra, hoping against hope that she will come back from the dance floor, where she is sucking face with one of Lasse's mates. Peo, or whatever his name is.

'The lads voted me down,' Lasse continues, and when she turns back to him he looks sad in a way that feels like a pose. 'We don't hang out that much any more. I suppose we've grown apart. That's how it goes. Sad, but true, you know.'

Madde finishes her gin and tonic. Shakes a couple of ice cubes into her mouth and chews them, making a loud crunching sound in her head. Like a rock crusher working to the beat of the music.

'Wanna dance?' he says.

'Zandra and I were going to head to the karaoke in a bit.'

She regrets saying it when he lights up.

'Sounds like a riot,' he says.

'Mmm.'

'I do a mean Spice Girls,' Lasse says, and watches her expectantly, apparently waiting for some kind of reaction.

He is actually truly repulsively ugly.

'Neat,' she says.

'Do you want another drink in the meantime? If you don't mind me asking? I don't want you to think I'm expecting anything in return.'

150

She hesitates. Zandra had better not make her wait much longer. One more drink, then she is leaving without her.

'Fine,' she says. 'I'll have another G&T, I guess.'

Lasse nods and turns to face the bar. Madde's feet are numb in her shoes. She leans back against the counter, spotting an attractive bloke, but he doesn't even look at her. No one is going to look at her while Pig Face is standing right next to her, acting like he has called dibs.

'Here,' he says, and hands her a foggy glass.

'Wow,' she says, surprised, 'that was quick.'

'I always make sure I tip well the first time I order,' he says, clearly pleased with himself. 'That way you get good service all night.'

She giggles. The little piggy is falling over himself to impress her.

'What's so funny?' he asks with a smile.

'Nothing.'

Someone pushes at her arm and she turns around, annoyed. A balding man in a suit that reeks of sweat glares back at her.

'Would you mind pulling your tits in so people can get past?' he shouts.

'God, calm down, will you?' Madde tells him.

'Yeah, calm down,' Lasse says.

'It's not my fucking fault she's so fat her tits take up half the bar,' the man bellows.

Madde bursts out laughing, spilling her new drink. 'Why are you so bloody obsessed with my boobs? Is it because you know you're never going to touch them in a million years?'

She can sense Lasse watching them nervously.

'You're just begging to get slapped about, aren't you?' the man says. The stench coming from his jacket almost suffocates her.

'I never beg,' she replies.

'Are you telling me you'd hit a girl?' Lasse manages behind her.

The man's eyes narrow and Madde is suddenly scared. Lasse is trying to make out like he is going to defend her honour, but she senses he wouldn't think twice about using her as a human shield.

'She's not fucking worth it,' the man hisses.

Madde shrugs. 'That's what cowards tend to say,' she calls after him as he lumbers off. She leans back against the bar, sucking hard on her straws.

'I hope he didn't upset you,' Lasse coos in her ear.

'Why would I be upset?'

He hesitates. 'Because he called you . . . fat.'

Madde runs a hand through her hair. 'Well, I am,' she says without looking at him.

'Maybe according to current norms,' he says. 'But that's only because we have twisted notions about the female form.'

She swallows another mouthful, feeling his hesitation. Little Piggy is rooting around the dirt for the right words.

'You're really . . . wow,' he says finally. 'You really stand up for who you are.'

'And who am I?' she says. 'I mean, according to you?'

He licks his front teeth. 'You are who you are, you know. You don't apologise. You wear sexy clothes and demand respect; you're kind of like, *Take me the way I am or get lost.* You really own your body. Know what I mean? You don't apologise.'

He looks like he has just bestowed a marvellous gift and can't comprehend why she isn't over the moon. But she doesn't need validation from Pig Face. She needs to have fun, and she bloody well isn't having fun any more. Madde puts her glass down and pulls the strap of her purse up over her shoulder.

She is just about to announce that she is leaving when Zandra appears with her face sucker in tow.

'Let's all go and do karaoke!' she squeals.

The whole stag-do gang cheers, Pig Face too, and Madde realises that if she wants to see Dan Appelgren tonight, she won't be able to shake him.

Tomas

He notices that the people walking by the bench he is on are keeping as far away as possible, virtually pressing themselves against the railing as they pass. He doesn't look at them. Doesn't want to be looked at. He just hears their footsteps, hears their conversations die when they draw level with him.

He can't move. Can't scream. His body has shut down. The only thing left is his heart, pounding against the bench underneath his chest, and a crunching sound that fills his head. Hard things that crack as other hard things push up beneath. Soft parts that are torn apart with a wet sound. It hurts. So bad. Like needles, no, like awls, drilling through his skull. He tongues the roof of his mouth; the surface is hard now, like cartilage.

His teeth shift when the tip of his tongue touches them, wobbling back and forth in their sockets. He can't keep from touching them again. One of his front teeth falls out. A trickle of warm blood seeps from the hole in his gums and down his throat.

More teeth come loose. Some are cracked; they fill his mouth like sticky gravel. He sucks the blood and pulp off before opening his mouth, letting the teeth fall out. They land on the wooden bench with a hollow rattle. Some fall onto the floor below.

The molars are the last to go. They take with them clumps of mangled gums that he swallows along with the blood. When he spits them out, it sounds like he has thrown a handful of dice.

Blood. So much blood. It is threatening to start leaking out of his mouth, even though he keeps swallowing it down. The tip of his tongue roves across his gums, touching the even rows of deep holes. He sucks harder. Suckles the blood out.

Something sharp in one of the holes nicks the tip of his tongue. Just a splinter, a tooth fragment? No. The sharp thing is moving. Growing. And now he can feel it in several places: new teeth, replacing the old. Every corner of his skull is creaking, but the worst of the noise has subsided. The path is clear in his gums.

And then everything is quiet.

He can still hear people at a distance. The deep sound of the ship's engines is ever-present; it feels like a part of him now. But inside him, it is quiet, quieter than it has ever been.

He swallows, but there is barely any blood coming out now.

He can no longer hear his own pulse in his ears. And he suddenly realises what the silence means. The blood has stopped pumping through his veins.

His heart isn't beating.

What an emptiness they have left in his chest, his heartbeats.

The thought is distant. Fascinated.

And then the next wave of pain crashes over him as his body begins to die.

Calle

The tiny vibrations in the floor, the familiar sensation in the pit of his stomach when the *Charisma* changes course are reminders that they are not on dry land. Soon they will reach Åland.

The whisky no longer burns Calle's throat but slides down like soft, liquid velvet. He closes his eyes, tries to focus on the sounds to keep from thinking about what Vincent might be doing at this moment, somewhere on the ship. He hears a glass shatter, the laughter coming from the dance floor, the singer who is making a painfully corny *dansband* classic sound like something from a film noir despite the jaunty accompaniment, the clattering of a cleaner clearing glasses from a table.

Calle opens his eyes and downs the last of his whisky. The beams of light flash across the dance floor in the same patterns as always. Even the voices around sound the same. And behind the bar Filip is pulling pints with the well-practised movements Calle knows so well.

It is as though he just imagined quitting his job on the ship. As though everything that has happened since was a dream. He is suddenly struck by a crazy feeling that the *Charisma* has sucked him back into his old life. He managed to get away from her once, but the ship lured him back with the moronic idea of proposing here, and he stepped right into the trap.

Calle raises the glass to his lips before realising it is empty. Filip gave him at least a triple. His second one of the evening.

He looks at the dance floor. The group of girls who were in the bar before have formed a circle and are singing along with gusto. A couple are necking gratuitously, open-mouthed, violently kneading each other's buttocks. A bloke in a cowboy hat is standing alone with his arms raised, rocking like a child who has just learned to stand up unsupported. Calle hasn't seen any of them before, yet he has seen them all.

'Why are you sitting here all by yourself?' someone with a Finnish accent shouts in his ear, making him jump.

When he turns, a woman is standing right next to him. She is wearing a sparkly top that ends just above her bellybutton. Her white-blonde hair falls in soft curls around a cute face with a pointy nose. She looks like someone who has lived a hard life, but there is something regal about her. It is the woman who always used to say she wanted to live aboard the *Charisma*, one of his classic anecdotes.

But she doesn't recognise him.

'Come on, let's dance!' she shouts, snatching up his hand. 'I love this song!'

'No thanks,' Calle replies, 'not tonight.'

'What do you mean, "not tonight"? All we have is tonight!'

She grins, but he knows she can turn at any moment, become aggressive. He shakes his head.

'I can't,' he says.

'Sure you can,' she says, pulling on him so hard he almost falls out of his armchair. She bursts out laughing. 'Oops! Come on then!'

'Just leave me alone!' Calle says, and immediately regrets it. 'I'm sorry, but—'

'Why the fuck are you here if you don't want to dance?'

'I've had a really bad night,' he says, trying to look apologetic.

'I can make it better. I promise.'

Her grip around his arm tightens. Her nails are chewed down to the quick.

'Thanks,' Calle says, 'but no thanks.'

'Oh come on now, don't be so bloody boring!'

He pulls his hand, which is getting sweaty, back from her.

'Not happening,' he says. 'I think you should walk away.'

A long tirade in Finnish. He recognises a handful of the curse words.

'You think you're better than me, is that it?' she says finally.

He doesn't have it in him to try to get through to her again. She is so drunk she is nothing but a jumble of emotions and no impulse control. She collapses heavily into the chair next to his; he can't be sure if she fell or meant to sit down.

'No,' Calle says wearily, 'believe me, there's no one I feel better than right now.'

'So what's wrong with me then?' she says in an accusatory tone, tossing her hair. 'You can tell me, I can take it.'

Calle doesn't know what to say to that. And what difference does it make? She won't remember this tomorrow anyway. He spreads his hands.

'Fine, suit yourself, your fucking loss,' she says. 'You don't know what you're missing.'

She shakes her head derisively at him and looks away. Calle is just about to leave when he spots Vincent at the bar.

Calle can only see his neck, a glimpse of a shoulder, but that is enough.

Vincent says something to Filip, who shakes his head, looking consolatory, just like he promised he would.

Calle stands up and realises that he is drunker than he thought. He moves behind an octagonal column covered in mirrors reflecting the dance floor spotlights. It is a pathetic hiding place. *He* is pathetic. He is standing here, hiding from the man he thought he was going to marry.

The woman who wants to live aboard the *Charisma* has nodded off in her chair.

Madde

'How are you doing, ladies?' Dan Appelgren says. 'Are you having a lovely cruise so far?'

The spotlights are hot on Madde's face. Beyond them, the room is a dark haze. And Dan has put his arms around her. He smells so good, just the way she imagined: spicy perfume and warm skin. An undertone of sweat. He smells like sex. Like the morning after sex. Before more sex. And his body is so hard against her soft one. His muscles feel like they are bolted tight to all the right places. The top few buttons of his shirt are unbuttoned; she can see soft little hairs climbing up his chest. She wants to feel them against her fingertips. She wants to sniff his neck.

'Wonderful,' Zandra replies.

As always when she feels stressed, her accent is more pronounced.

'Great, great,' Dan says. 'And where are you from?'

'Boden originally,' Zandra says, and someone howls in solidarity in the dark. 'But now we live in Stockholm.'

'Excellent. So what are you going to sing for us tonight, ladies?'

'"You're the One That I Want",' Madde says.

'Blimey,' Dan says, and winks at her. 'Is that a come-on?'

Madde can hear laughing in the audience but it takes her a moment to get the joke. Zandra giggles shrilly, on the verge of turning into the screeching seagull.

'Maybe,' Madde replies.

Dan gives her a warm smile. 'Which one of you is doing Sandy then? And who is doing Danny?'

Zandra looks hesitantly at Madde. They have sung the song lots of times, ever since there was a bit of a *Grease* revival when they were in secondary school. But they have never divided the song up between them. They have both sung both parts.

'Zandra can do Sandy,' Madde says. 'She's the *good girl* out of the two of us.'

More laughing in the darkness. A few people whistle.

It is so easy to talk to Dan. It feels incredibly natural. It is not just that he is funny. He makes her funny.

'All right then,' Dan says, and she can tell he is feeling the same way. 'Let's get this show on the road!'

The audience is with them from the first note. They start clapping to the beat as soon as the music starts. Madde takes a deep breath. Stares at the lines of lyrics on the screen. Waits for them to change colour. She feels like a sprinter in the starting blocks.

Zandra giggles again.

And then it is time to sing.

The last of her nerves fade. Madde can sing. No one can take that from her. She is a sprinter extending her stride. Unleashing her power. And she can feel the energy in the room change.

Whooping and whistling.

And Dan is standing next to the stage, watching her, stunned.

Marianne

Marianne and Göran step out into the hallway, leaving Charisma Starlight and the *dansband* music behind. They walk past the casino, the pub, the café. Poseidon is already closed, its tables neatly set for the next day. They continue forward until they are back outside the dark buffet restaurant where they had dinner. They get into a lift next to the stairs and Göran pushes the button for deck five.

A laminated picture of a woman wrapped in a bathrobe is posted on one of the mirrors. She has cucumber slices on her eyes. A bright-green drink is within easy reach. *Treat yourself to luxury at the Charisma Spa & Beauty*, the romantic font urges. Marianne sees herself in a mirror and is shocked. She is shiny; her face is flushed, her hair is wild. She starts running her fingers through it.

'You look good just the way you are,' Göran says.

She lets her hand fall. He bends down and kisses her gently. The stubble on his top lip scratches a little against her mouth. A muffled exclamation of surprise escapes her and she can feel his lips stretch into a smile before they leave hers.

She already misses them.

The lift stops; she looks down at the floor and realises the tips of her shoes are in a puddle of sick. She glances up again. Göran takes her by the arm; he hasn't noticed. They step out on the fifth floor. Straight ahead is the steel door they boarded through earlier tonight. Göran leads her left, but Marianne stops when she spots a young woman passed out on the floor next to the lift. A strand of her blonde hair is stuck to her cheek and there can be no doubt that she is the source of the vomit on the tips of Marianne's shoes.

'Are you all right?' Marianne says tentatively, but the woman shows no reaction.

'Come on,' Göran says.

'Shouldn't we help her?'

'She's just had a bit too much to drink. She's fast asleep, by the looks of it.'

'But . . .'

'Security will take care of her.'

Marianne nods, unsure, as Göran leads her away. In the long corridor, Marianne tries to drag her feet discreetly, scraping as much of the vomit as possible off on the carpet.

They walk past row upon row of cabin doors. Music can be heard from behind several of them, hooting and laughing, unmistakeable moaning. At the end of the corridor is a large glass door. When Göran opens it, an icy gust of wind hits Marianne, immediately chilling her damp blouse. At least it has stopped raining, for now.

She follows him onto the large bow deck, walking through a toxic cloud emanating from a group of smokers. They walk to the railing by the prow. Göran cups his hands around a cigarette. The wind tousles Marianne's hair and she takes a few deep breaths, grateful for the fresh air. When Göran takes a clearly gratifying drag and holds the pack out to her, she just shakes her head. Lights glitter in the distance. The white foam rushing along the hull of the ship almost hypnotises her; the enormous power of the movement, the lulling roar. Somewhere beneath the surface is her windowless cabin, where she changed her clothes before dinner. She shivers in the wind. Göran pulls her closer.

The drone of the engines changes. The vibrations under her feet intensify.

'Can you feel us slowing down?' he says, pointing to the lights ahead of them. 'We'll be docking in Åland soon.'

'But the cruise is for Åbo,' she says. 'Isn't Åbo in Finland?' She bites her lip. She sounds like an idiot.

'Stopping for a bit in Åland is what lets them sell things tax-free. Something to do with the EU and all their red tape, I'd wager,' Göran says. He pulls so hard on his cigarette it crackles. 'Though it's good business for the islanders. They make obscene amounts of money off it, since thousands of ships dock every year. And lots of the locals work on the ships as well. I think there's hardly a person on the island who's unemployed.'

Marianne is quiet for a moment, realising how little she knows about Åland. She has barely ever had a single thought about the island before. It has always seemed a little bit made-up.

'Isn't it strange,' she says after a while, 'that there always seem to be loopholes to avoid rules, if you look hard enough?'

'True. But money's not the only thing the ships bring with them. If people get up to shenanigans on board they're dumped on the Åland police, so they get some of the drawbacks too.' He chuckles. 'A mate of mine was thrown off here a year or two after the *Estonia* sank. He thought it'd be funny to joke around . . . so he got in the shower with his clothes on. Then he ran into one of the night clubs, soaked to the bone, shouting that the bow visor was open. People were terrified.'

He chuckles again and shakes his head. Marianne can only stare at him, feeling suddenly much more sober than she would like to be.

'That's one of the most tasteless things I've ever heard,' she says.

'He was drunk,' Göran replies, as if that is explanation enough.

Disappointment rises inside Marianne like a bitter taste at the back of her throat. The spell has been broken. And she can tell from the way he is standing that he can feel it too.

She goes back to watching the foam in silence. She's grateful she doesn't know exactly where in the sea the *Estonia* and her passengers were lost and if the *Charisma* passes directly above them on her way. Once again, she thinks that this enormous metal structure should be unable to float, and has a childish feeling that the ship itself might realise this at any moment and sink like a stone. Marianne notices that she is thinking of the *Charisma* as a living being, not an inanimate thing manned by ordinary people. It seems impossible they can control all the thousands upon thousands of tonnes, no matter how many instruments the captain has to aid him.

'Are you okay?' Göran asks.

'I don't find jokes about the *Estonia* funny.'

'I know. It was incredibly daft of him. I shouldn't have told you.' He sounds like he genuinely regrets it.

'No, you shouldn't have – or at least you shouldn't have laughed, because it's really not funny. It's disrespectful.'

Göran flicks his cigarette overboard. Marianne watches the glowing dot disappear.

'It's easy to become thoughtless when you're like me,' he says. 'Me and the lads, we're kind of . . . we're not always so polished. I don't usually meet women like you.' He is quiet for so long she is just about to ask what he means when he clears his throat. 'You're classy, Marianne. I like that you put your foot down. I'm sorry.'

And she forgives him. What he says is touching, and she doesn't want to be left hanging, alone, in paralysing disappointment that confirms that this whole trip was a mistake. She wants her adventure.

'I'm sorry too. Maybe I overreacted,' Marianne offers. 'It's probably because I had a friend who died on the *Estonia*.' The lie slips out before she has even noticed it being formulated in her mind, and she instantly regrets it.

She avoids meeting his eyes. The upper decks of the *Charisma* loom behind them. She can see several people by a railing on the top one, above what she assumes is the bridge.

'I'm so sorry,' he says. 'Were you very close?'

'I don't want to talk about it. I . . . I think I'll have that cigarette now.'

Göran lets go of her and her heart pounds like mad. She can hear the click of the lighter inside his cupped hand.

'I feel awful about this. I properly put my foot in it,' he says, handing her the cigarette. 'Me and my big mouth.'

She inhales, tentatively breathing the smoke in, and is surprised by how good it still tastes. She hasn't smoked since – yes, when? Some point in the eighties. She didn't even fall off the wagon during the divorce.

'Forget it,' she says. 'I don't want to think about it tonight. It's been a long time since I had this much fun.'

'So you're having fun at least? With me?'

Marianne nods and finally looks at him.

'Good,' he says. 'Because the night has just begun.'

The *Baltic Charisma*

A few hundred feet away, also on deck five, Bosse is sitting in his office. He's drinking coffee from a white porcelain mug that reads WORLD'S BEST GRANDPA and grinning at the screens in front of him. A young couple are pressed against the wall in one of the short sternward hallways two floors up, unaware of the CCTV camera. The girl's skirt is hiked up around her hips. Every once in a while, she takes a sip from her bottle. On occasion, the thrusting makes her miss the bottle, which in turn makes her laugh. In the grainy image on the screen, her eyes glisten vacantly.

Bosse drinks his coffee. So far, he's the only one who has spotted them, from his godlike, all-seeing vantage point.

The guy is thrusting harder and harder – the girl drops her bottle – and then it is over. The girl pulls her skirt down. The guy does his trousers up and gives her a peck on the cheek. She stays where she is while he disappears down the hallway. Then she turns around and goes into one of the cabins.

Bosse chuckles and shakes his head, scans the other screens and spots a blonde girl who has fallen asleep next to the lifts right here on deck five. A dark-haired woman is squatting next to her with her back to the camera, lightly shaking the girl's shoulder. Bosse looks closer to see what happens. The girl wakes up, seems to struggle to focus on the woman talking to her. The girl nods, fumbles around in her purse for something. Pulls out a key card. The dark-haired woman grabs her firmly by the arms and helps her up. Bosse catches a glimpse of her face. She is wearing a lot of makeup. Something about her makes him uneasy. He hesitates, checks the phone on his desk, then glances back at the figures on the screen. They are walking down the long portside hallway. He switches camera, continuing to watch them. He shrugs off the feeling, figuring there are more serious things for the security staff to focus on.

The young woman is called Elvira. She is drunker than she has ever been and the woman holding her upright smells weird, like mint and something sweet and musty. Elvira thinks to herself that at least the woman is nice. She is talking soothingly and softly and archaically. Elvira wishes she could manage to articulate a thank-you. She wants to explain how she ended up like this, tell her that *I knew I was drinking too much, but I was so tired of always being the boring one, the one who doesn't know how to let loose. I wanted to be like them, just once. We went to Club Charisma and that's all I remember. It's so unfair. How many times have I helped them when they were trashed? I guess that's why they let me hang out with them. But when I need help, they just abandon me.*

She wants to tell the strange woman all that, but her mouth won't obey her. Only grunts come out. They stop at a door and the woman inserts the key card. There are fingers missing from her hand. Elvira stares at her with one eye shut, trying to focus, but her eye won't obey either. She switches to the other one. *Like at the optician. Which is better? Left or right? No difference.* But she can see well enough to realise the woman is not well. There is something wrong with her face. *And her smell . . .*

Elvira feels sick again. She lets the woman lead her into the cabin. Looks around when the door closes behind them. *We had twin beds . . . why is there a double in here now?* Elvira tries to protest, but she is afraid she might throw up again. She hates throwing up. The woman sits her down gently on the bed. It is not made. There's a big stain on the carpet by the foot of the bed, and a glittering shard of glass. Elvira figures someone might have thrown a party in here; maybe that is why the woman suddenly looks angry. And then Elvira can't bring herself to think any more. She lets her head fall onto her chest. It feels so heavy, as if she will never be able to lift it back up. The woman slowly lays her down on her side, strokes her hair with her three fingers. When Elvira tries to say something, the woman hushes her gently. And Elvira closes her eyes. She is glad she is not alone. *I'm just going to have a rest. Then I'm going to ask what we're doing here.*

The dark-haired woman is afraid. The smell of blood is still wafting from the stain on the carpet. She is baffled her son would take such an enormous risk. He must have been desperate. It took her much too long to find this girl. The woman thinks about the older lady she spotted at the start of the evening, from her table in McCharisma. She radiated such loneliness, but she had friends who came to meet her. The woman is not usually mistaken about these things, and the sudden, flaring hope left a hunger in its wake that was even stronger than before. She looks down at the bloodstain on the carpet again, wondering where the body is now. Where her son is. Did he do this to punish her? She knows how angry he is with her. They had a comfortable situation in

Stockholm, back in the city where it all started so long ago; it's the only real home they have ever had. But they couldn't stay. They can never stay. She thinks about the caravan parked on the car deck. Everything they own fits in it. Such a long life together, and yet so pathetically few possessions. She turns to Elvira, puts a hand around her neck. Her fingers count the vertebrae from the top down. Elvira mumbles something, but doesn't open her eyes.

One of the lorries on the car deck was driven by a man named Olli. He sleeps a deep, dreamless sleep in his cabin under the surface. A half-empty bottle of Russian vodka from the tax-free shop is sitting on the floor next to his bed. When there is a knock on the door, it takes him a while to wake up. He fumbles for the bed-side lamp, squinting against the light. Olli is drunk. He thinks that one day he will get caught driving under the influence, and that might prove to be a relief. He needs the alcohol to sleep off the stress and the chronic pain in his neck and shoulders. He thinks about the many hours he will have to do on the road tomorrow. Far too many. The hauliers break the law. Nothing is above board. Oftentimes, they won't even tell him what his cargo is, and he reckons there are good reasons for that.

Another knock.

'*Minä tulen, minä tulen, ota helvetissä iisisti*,' Olli grunts in Finnish, scratching the thick rug of hair on his chest. Glancing at his phone, he realises he has only slept a couple of hours. It is only when he is already pushing the door handle down that he remembers he is in his underpants. He opens the door a crack. A blond boy of about five is in the hallway, looking at him with big eyes glistening with tears. A heart-shaped face. Straight little nose. He pulls nervously on the strings of his red hoodie.

'I can't find my mummy,' he says.

Olli notices a couple of scars zigzagging up from the neck of his T-shirt. They are shiny and pink, very recently healed. He wonders who might have given the boy those scars. A shiver runs down his back. He opens the door fully.

Marianne

There is no carpet on the narrow stairs leading down to her deck. They pass the doors leading out to the car deck and continue to descend until they reach a steel door. When Marianne pulls it open the stench from a septic tank hits them and the rumble of the engine grows louder.

'I would never have booked a cabin down here if I had known what it actually looked like,' she says, and starts walking down the last set of stairs.

The light in the second deck corridor is cold and revealing, the carpet rougher, more worn. Everything screams lower class, Marianne thinks. Quite literally the lowest caste. It even smells like shit.

She fervently wishes they could have gone back to Göran's cabin instead, but he shares it with three friends and she has no desire to have them come bumbling in mid-act.

Marianne can feel herself blushing from head to toe. No matter how much she tries to pretend that she has no idea what is coming, that she doesn't know what she *wants*, she betrays herself with thoughts like that one.

She becomes increasingly confused as they look for her cabin in the claustrophobic corridors. They came down a different set of stairs to the one she used at the start of the evening and she can't figure out how the numbers work down here. Her nerves do nothing to improve her sense of direction, but in the end they locate door 2015, at the far end of a hallway. She walks in first, sits down on the single bed and turns on the reading light. Kicking her shoes off feels divine. She pulls her legs up under her. The almost imperceptible rolling of the ship is making her feel slightly dizzy. The alcohol plays a part too, of course; she is under no illusion about that, but she is feeling surprisingly sober. Completely present. All her senses are wide awake.

Göran shuts the door behind them and when she sees him standing tall and broad-shouldered in the middle of the cabin, she realises how small it really is.

'Were you supposed to share this cabin with your friend?' he says.

Marianne shakes her head. 'No, of course not. She had the one next door,' she says, and instantly regrets it, because how is she going to explain it if they hear someone in there? 'Or a few doors down; I can't remember what she said.'

The wall at the head of the bed creaks. On the other side, the freezing water of the Baltic is pressing with unfathomable weight against the ship's hull.

Göran sits down next to her. His hair is in a ponytail. She likes it. His head is nicely shaped.

'Are you sure your friends won't mind you ditching them?' she asks.

'They'll be fine,' Göran replies. Peers at her. 'They would have done the same, given the chance.'

Marianne smiles, wondering if he means that his friends would have left with anyone, or that they would have left with her specifically, because they find her attractive too. She catches herself hoping for the latter. It is pathetic how starving she is for validation.

'I meant what I said before . . . That it's been a long time since I had this much fun,' she says. 'I thought I'd forgotten how to do it.'

He chuckles. 'I find that hard to believe.'

Her skirt has slipped up above her knees; she pulls gently at the fabric, shifting until they are covered again.

'You'd be surprised,' she says.

Seconds tick by.

'Notice how quiet it is?' Göran says, and Marianne nods.

Then she realises he is referring to the ship. The vibrations have stopped; there's only a low humming.

'We've reached Åland,' he says.

Marianne nods again, because there isn't much a person can say to that. On the way here, Göran told her about all the shipwrecks scattered around the island. Champagne was salvaged from a French ship headed for Russia that sank in the early nineteenth century. The bottles were sold a couple of years ago for hundreds of thousands of kronor each. 'No champagne can be that good, no matter how rich you are,' she had said. 'People who feel a need to buy things like that must have very paltry inner lives.' That had made Göran laugh.

He likes her. He does. She can see it in his eyes.

'It's been a long time since I did something like this too,' she says.

'What do you mean?' Göran says, but luckily, this time, she realises he is teasing her before she has a chance to humiliate herself by launching into an explanation.

'It's just so strange,' she says. 'We barely know each other, and now . . . now we're here. But I don't know anything about you.'

174

'You know I live alone in a flat in Huddinge. And that the lads and I all used to work for the telecommunications authority once upon a time.'

'That's not exactly a lot.'

'There's not a lot to tell,' he says, and leans back against the wall. 'But if there's something you want to know, just ask.'

He looks so comfortable, with his hands folded across his stomach, his feet firmly planted on the floor and his legs wide apart. So untroubled. There are a lot of things Marianne would like to know, but none of the questions popping into her head seems all that reasonable to ask in this situation.

What do you do when you're alone? Have you ever been truly alone? What were your parents like? Do you believe in God? Have you ever been seriously ill? Do you think this could be the start of something? Could you like me for real? Would you put up with me in the long term?

'I don't even know if you've been married,' she says. 'Or if you have children.'

'Married, yes,' he says. 'Children, no.'

What was your wife like? Did she want children and you didn't? Was that why you got divorced? What happened between you? If this leads to something, if we end up together, what will I have to do not to ruin it?

'Is there nothing you want to know about me?' she asks.

'No,' he says, and puts a hand on her thigh, letting his fingertips play over the fabric of the skirt. 'I like that you're a mystery.'

Marianne surprises herself by laughing. 'I've never felt particularly mysterious.'

She takes a deep breath and decides to give up any attempt at coming up with the one question that would somehow make her feel comfortable with the fact that she is about to go to bed with a stranger.

The moment is too fragile for words. If she wants to make sure not to ruin this, she needs to stop talking now.

Göran lies down on his side, resting his head in one hand. The fingers of the other disappear under her skirt. Wander up along the tights hiding the inside of her thigh. His touch gives her arms goose bumps and sends jolts running up and down her spine.

He doesn't feel like a stranger. She knows everything she needs to about him right now. There will be time for questions later.

'Lie down,' he says.

Marianne obeys. Lies down next to him, reaches for the lamp.

'Leave it on,' he says.

But this time, she doesn't obey. The switch clicks and all the light vanishes as if devoured by the darkness. She imagines seeing shadows and formations moving right in front of her face, black against the black, but it is all in her head. Göran fumbles with her skirt; she lifts her hips up so he can pull both it and her tights off. Her panties. He caresses her, and her skin is so hypersensitive she imagines she can feel the fingerprints he leaves behind when he touches her.

She begins to cry and is grateful for the darkness that lets her disguise her sobs as little excited pants. Göran's belt jingles when he unbuckles it. He kicks off his jeans and lies down on top of her. Presses his lips against her chin, finding his way to her mouth.

They kiss each other in the dark, deep in the belly of the cruise-ferry, and the sea outside no longer scares her.

Madde

Lasse Pig Face is on stage with Stefan, belting Kenny Rogers and Dolly Parton loudly. The bridal veil is on the floor between them, grimy with beer and cigarette ash. The audience is howling along with them, loving it.

But Madde can't watch. When she tries to keep her eyes on the stage, it seems like all the lights are moving up, up, as if the whole world is about to topple. Or as if she herself is about to, and if she did start falling, she would keep tumbling over and over in a never-ending somersault. She has to hold on tight to the edge of her seat cushion. She can't close her eyes either, because that makes it even worse. And it is so hot in here. And yet her face is cold.

She is feeling so fucking sick, but she is afraid she might faint if she tries to stand up. Why did she switch to beer? Her whole mouth tastes bitter, like metal, like she has sucked on an iron pipe.

Zandra doesn't notice; she is too busy sucking face with Peo.

Madde needs to throw up. She needs help. She relinquishes her white-knuckle hold on the seat cushion. Reaches out and puts a hand on Zandra's thigh. Zandra looks up. Glistening saliva all around her mouth.

'Are you all right, sweetie?' she says.

At least Madde thinks that is what she says. She can only see Zandra's wet lips moving. Can't hear anything over the caterwauling.

Madde must have managed to grunt something, or maybe Zandra gets it anyway, because she gets off Peo's lap and takes her hand. And Madde stands up from the armchair, quickly, before she has time to reconsider; that is the only way. Now the nausea is coming on strongly. No time. Something tickles her gag reflex, as if all the salmon and herring she ate tonight have come alive inside her, thrashing about, beating their tailfins against the inside of her throat.

Her face is so cold, and yet sweat is streaming down it.

Zandra leads her through the room, forging a path between all the warm bodies. Madde follows, catching a glimpse of Dan Appelgren by the stage.

The fish thrash about more violently in her throat, swimming around her stomach so fast it churns. Madde looks down at the floor. They exit the karaoke bar and Zandra pulls her to the right; suddenly the carpet is replaced with tiles and then they are in a toilet stall and Madde bends over and flings the toilet lid open while Zandra locks the door behind them.

Madde spots a couple of brown stains on the underside of the seat, focuses on them, and the vomit shoots out of her mouth. At first it is just a lot of beer, then bitter gin and tonic and then half-digested food, thick and mushy; it sticks on its way up, making her cough and choke. Hot tears stream down her cold cheeks.

Zandra holds her hair, strokes her back.

'Bloody hell,' Madde says. 'Bloody hell.'

'Feel better?'

Madde tears off toilet paper and wads it up. Wipes her mouth. Dabs at her eyes.

'Bloody hell,' she says again.

She straightens up. Braces for a second wave of nausea, but it doesn't come. She checks to make sure nothing spattered on her clothes. Throws the ball of tissue in the toilet and flushes.

'Yes,' she says. 'I'm better now.'

But a pounding headache has replaced the nausea. It's as if she is already hungover. When she wipes her finger under her eyes, it turns black with running mascara.

'Good,' Zandra says, and strokes her back again.

She looks at Madde with the same mummy expression she wears when she comforts her daughter. Gentle, caring, sympathetic eyes.

'Is it okay with you if I go with Peo to their cabin?' she says.

It takes a few seconds to really sink in.

'Now?' Madde says. 'But we're partying.'

'He's so fucking wasted,' Zandra says. 'I figure I might be dealing with a whisky dick already. If he keeps drinking, I'm going to have to *poke* it in.'

'But . . . but what am I supposed to do?'

'Why don't you stay with the others?' Zandra suggests. 'That guy, whatshisname, seems to be into you.'

'You suck,' Madde says, and staggers backwards, supporting herself against the tiled wall. 'I thought we were going to have fun tonight. Isn't that what we said?'

'But we *are* having fun,' Zandra says. She laughs, completely unperturbed.

'This is so you. The minute you manage to pull someone, nothing else matters. Especially not me.'

'Come off it. You're just miffed because I found someone first. You would have done the same thing and I would have been fine with it.' Her eyes have hardened.

'Great then,' Madde says as rage fills her with new energy. Lots of it. 'Aren't you the fucking generous one? But have you ever considered that I might find it really fucking sad that you dump me whenever you have a chance to bone?'

Zandra looks at her. And before she even opens her mouth, Madde knows she is going to spout something incredibly god-damn sanctimonious.

'I know you're having a tough time right now, what with your work and everything, but don't take it out on me because I don't deserve it.'

Zandra unlocks the door and storms out of the stall. Madde stares at the door slamming shut between them.

'You should just shut the fuck up!' she shouts, without know-ing if Zandra is still outside. 'You're a self-centred fucking cunt!'

How the fuck did this happen? How did it escalate so quickly?

The headache is like iron claws slowly digging through her skull. She exits the stall. No Zandra.

Madde drinks water from the tap by one of the sinks. She doesn't give a shit that a girl who comes out of one of the other stalls stares at her while she washes her hands. Madde straightens up and looks in the mirror. She looks surprisingly okay. Her eyes are a bit bloodshot, that's all.

She tries to gather her thoughts, understand what got into her.

You would have done the same thing.

Zandra is right.

Madde dashes out of the bathroom and walks back into the moist heat of the karaoke bar. Dan is on stage on his own now, singing 'Like Fever in My Heart', and she pushes past all the people who are on their feet, singing along at the top of their lungs.

Zandra is not at their table. A few pink feathers are the only sign of her. Peo is gone too. But Pig Face lights up when he spots Madde and waves her over. The table is full of shot glasses.

'Come on,' he says, and she sinks down into the armchair next to his because she doesn't know what else to do.

He hands her a shot glass. In the dark, she can't make out the colour of the liquid, but it is slick against the inside of the glass. She sniffs it cautiously. It smells of jelly sweets.

'Bottoms up,' one of the others says.

Madde nods. Get back on the horse: it's the only way to get rid of the headache. If she doesn't start drinking now, she is never going to get back in the game.

The shot slides easily down her throat. She barely needs to swallow. Pig Face pushes over another glass.

'Your friend went back to our cabin with Peo,' he says. 'So you can have hers too.'

Madde glances at Dan on stage. His shirt is tight across his chest. He probably has those thrusting muscles around his groin, the kind that disappear down men's trousers like an arrow pointing to their cock.

She isn't going to bed yet.

After she has downed the second shot, Lasse leans in closer. Starts playing with her hair.

'Your cabin is free,' he says. 'I thought you and I might have a nightcap there.'

She shakes her head, can't even be bothered to reply. His fingers stop moving in her hair.

'Yes. Come on.'

'No,' she says, and fixes him with a level gaze, pleased that her eyes have recovered the ability to focus.

First Zandra and now this. She has had enough crap for one night.

'What do you mean, no?' he says.

'What's tripping you up? Don't you speak Swedish?'

He licks his front teeth. Piggy is angry. Furious.

Madde bursts out laughing.

He pulls his hand back and it feels like pin-pricks in her scalp when a handful of hairs are yanked out. She continues to laugh, but it is not funny any more.

'I knew it,' he says. 'You just wanted to drink free booze and then bail. Are you happy now, fucking booze whore?'

His friends watch them furtively, sensing that something is happening.

'So you think I owe you a fuck now?' she says. 'Well, you can forget it. You're not exactly my type.'

His eyes grow even darker. 'No, I get who your type is. I've seen how you ogle him,' he says, waving his hand in the direction of the stage. 'Appelgren's a fucking loser. Anyone who's anyone in Stockholm knows how he treats his women. He beats them. And that's not the worst of it. But you probably think *bad boys* are super-hot.'

He hisses the last part. What the fuck is he on about? And does he think she would ever believe those kinds of things about Dan? Surely there are rumours like that about every famous guy on the planet? But she is not about to say that out loud, because that would only make him feel vindicated.

'All women are the fucking same,' he says. 'When it gets down to it, you just want guys who treat you like shit. I'm a good guy, but what does that get me? No one wants a good guy, no matter what they claim.'

'Maybe that isn't your problem,' Madde says. 'Maybe the problem is that you're incredibly fucking ugly and feel so incredibly fucking sorry for yourself. It's not exactly sexy.'

'You're not so fucking good-looking yourself,' he snaps. 'But you're never going to get it anyway. All girls have to do is show some tit and hike up their skirt and they can have any guy they want.'

'You almost sound jealous. Maybe you're gay?'

'You're so ugly I almost *wish* I were.'

'Great. So why did you want to go back to my cabin then?'

'Because everyone can tell from a mile away how cheap you and your friend are, and I didn't want to have to put in any effort.'

Her hand flies through the air in a wide arc, but she misses him by at least a foot. He smiles at her smugly. His friends stand up.

'I'm sorry,' Stefan whispers, straightening his veil. 'He always gets like this when he drinks. We'll take care of him.'

She makes no reply. Doesn't even watch them leave.

Up on stage, someone has started crooning an old Swedish folk song.

The *Baltic Charisma*

Captain Berggren is back on the bridge. He has taken a long nap, then eaten leftovers from Charisma Buffet in the officers' mess. He gazes out across Åland Harbour. The few passengers who have left the ship are walking through the illuminated glass gangways extending out from the terminal like tentacles.

Most of the older people and families with children have gone to bed. For others, the party has only just started. The dance floors and bars are packed.

The shop and spa staff have finished their shifts. Some of them are already asleep. Others are in the common room playing cards or watching films. A small group has crowded into a staff cabin. They have changed into civilian clothes. They gossip about passengers and colleagues. Tax-free sales were good today; Antti, the shop manager, handed out free champagne after closing. In the galley, the kitchen staff are cleaning up after the evening's service. Thousands of dirty plates have been washed in just a few hours. Even more glasses. Tonnes of food are binned every week because the passengers take more than they can eat from the buffet.

A woman has fallen asleep in the karaoke bar, alone at her table. There is a shot glass in her hand. A couple of pink feathers on the table swirl slowly in the draught from her deep breathing.

On the lowest deck, an old woman is making love to a man she just met.

Two children, cousins, are lying on a double bed, laughing at the things they are seeing on a TV screen showing the dance floor at Club Charisma.

Lying on another double bed, one floor below them, is Elvira. Her fourth vertebra has been crushed. She is paralysed from the neck down, trapped in a body she can no longer feel. Locked in with the panic that makes the blood rush through her body, making her skin flushed, her scent stronger. The dark-haired woman sitting next to her on the edge of the bed has stuffed her mouth full of cloth. Elvira still tries to plead, form words through the pain. *I want to go home. I want to go home. I want my mummy and daddy. I want to go home. I want to go home.* A tear trickles down her temple into her ear. The light from the terminal falls straight in through the window. The woman's eyes glisten darkly in the heavily made-up face. She runs a rough finger across Elvira's cheek, wipes away the tears. Tilts her head, as though she is sorry about what she is going to do next.

The woman has made her mind up. She can't wait any longer. She can't think clearly until she has fed.

The vibrations in the floor change as the *Charisma* slowly starts pulling out of the Åland harbour. It rouses the man called Tomas from his stupor on a bench on the tenth floor. He has no thoughts left, no self. Only a hunger that aches, makes him burn and shiver with cold. Ice and magma in every cell, every nerve ending. It is the hunger, and the panic that follows in its wake, that makes him stand up despite the pain. His legs are so heavy and numb. He tilts his head. Sniffs the air. His heart is beating again. Slow, arduous contractions distributing his dead blood. Tomas walks towards the open door into the ship. Steps into the light. The smells are warm here. So much stronger.

People stare at him with revulsion as he staggers by. A few offer half-hearted comments. *Some people really can't take their alcohol. Someone should help the poor bastard. It's people like him who give cruiseferries a bad name.* But they have forgotten all about him as soon as they pass. He is just another passenger who has had more than he could handle. And there are so many more interesting things to talk about. So many other people to look at. So many possibilities, so many hopes and fears.

Tomas has to lean against the wall to make it down the wide stairs. He catches a glimpse of himself in the mirrors and it feels like a half-forgotten dream. Deep, pumping bass-lines come from the two dance floors and the karaoke bar. They thump through his flesh and bones, like a pulse from several hearts at once. The scents of the people are so tempting, and the most tempting are the ones whose feelings makes their blood run faster. He tentatively snaps his teeth.

In the cabin on deck five, the dark-haired woman has just finished feeding. She grabs the dead girl's head and breaks her neck, conscientiously making sure the vertebrae separate completely, severing all connections between body and brain. Elvira's blood seeps through the woman, finding its way through the fine web of vessels. Her fingers and calves tingle like pins and needles. She pinches the flesh of her hand. Firmer now. She has no time to enjoy what she's been yearning for. She walks into the bathroom, squeezes out a big dollop of soap from the dispenser bolted to the wall and starts washing her face in the sink. The thick layers of makeup she no longer needs run down the drain along with the soap suds. She tries to tell herself things are going to work out. She has bought a return ticket. Maybe no one will miss the girl until the *Baltic Charisma* is back in Stockholm. When the cleaners discover the body, she and her son will have travelled deep into Finland, hidden away in their new home in the vast forests. The woman studies her reflection. Touches her cheeks. The skin is starting to smooth out. Grow warmer.

She walks towards the door. She must find her son. This instant.

Calle

Calle drags himself up the narrow staircase to the *Charisma*'s staff quarters. Every step is like climbing a small mountain. He clings to the white steel handrail and makes it onto the penultimate landing. A square metal sign with the number nine informs him which floor he is on. He glances behind him. The stairs wind their way down in a tight rectangle.

He swipes the pass he borrowed from Filip through the card reader. There is a beep and he pulls open the door, looking down the hallway flanked by staff cabins. There is a party going on behind one of the closed doors. Loud house music. Laughter and voices. To get to Filip's cabin, he has to go past it. He hesitates. Starts walking. The music dies abruptly. Someone turns on Michael Jackson. Loud protests. Happy squeals. Calle speeds up. Something thuds against the door just as he walks by. More laughter.

And suddenly the door is thrown open and Sophia steps into the hallway. His old colleague from the tax-free shop is wobbling in her high heels, reaching out for the opposite wall for support. Her hair is in the same straight bob as before, but peach-coloured now. She giggles, pushes a strand of hair out of her eyes and glances up.

Aside from the hair colour, Sophia is exactly the same. Her skin is shiny and almost translucent from all the scrubbing and acid treatments she puts it through in the spa. Her eyes brighten when she spots Calle.

'Oh my God, hi!' she says emphatically, and looks him up and down again. 'Antti, look who's here!'

Calle squeezes out a smile when Antti peeks out of the cabin: Antti, who started working in the tax-free shop at the same time as him. Blond with almost-white eyelashes and eyebrows, definitely the number one standard-bearer in the vaguely parodic macho culture on board, with a posture that says the world is his and he is pissed off with it.

'Howdy,' he says. 'Yeah, I did hear there were fancy guests coming.'

Two women and a man Calle has never seen before step out into the corridor. They eye him curiously.

Sophia totters over and gives him a hug, enveloping him in a cloud of citrusy perfume and cigarette smoke. Antti introduces him to the strangers. He calls them 'his employees' to let Calle know he is now the shop manager. Calle is not surprised, though it should have been Sophia.

'Congratulations, sweetie! Pia told me you're getting married!' she says.

Calle smiles until it feels like his face is going to crack.

'Your fiancé came in the shop asking for you just before we closed up,' Antti says. 'He looks like a bloody movie star. How did you ever land him?'

Sophia laughs nervously. 'Stop it. Calle's good-looking too, right?' she says, turning back to Calle. 'I'm so chuffed for you. I just love it when good things happen to good people.'

'So which one of you is wearing the wedding dress then?' Antti says with a grin.

'Antti, come on,' Sophia giggles, giving him a tiny shove in the chest.

Calle wonders what Vincent actually said to him. Does Antti know what happened? Is he poking fun at him? Are the other people looking at him weirdly? But no. He is being paranoid. Why would Vincent have said anything? And besides, if Antti knew what had happened, he wouldn't have been able to bite his tongue.

'Don't you want to go to the club and party with us?' Sophia says. 'They're stricter about mingling with the passengers now, but Andreas is the general manager tonight and he won't make a fuss about it.'

Calle shakes his head. 'It would have been nice, but . . .'

'What are you doing up here anyway?' Antti cuts in.

'I was just picking something up for Filip.'

Sophia opens her mouth to say something.

'But we might swing by later,' Calle quickly adds before she has a chance to offer to wait until he has fetched the *something*, ask what this *something* is.

'Brilliant,' Sophia says. 'You have to have a proper celebration tonight. I'll buy you bubbly. Promise you'll come, promise.'

'I promise,' Calle says.

'Good seeing you,' Antti says without even trying to look like he means it.

Sophia gives Calle a peck on the cheek and he squeezes the last ounce of strength out of the muscles holding his smile in place, somehow managing a polite nod. He moves to Filip's door like a sleepwalker. Closes it behind him as soon as he is inside.

He takes in the familiar scene. The blue vinyl floor. The unmade bed. The wardrobe. The little desk with the mirror above it. The darkness that moves almost imperceptibly outside the window. It has started raining again.

There is a bottle of vodka on the desk. He goes over to it, studies the photographs stuck into the frame of the mirror and spots a younger version of himself. The picture was taken at his leaving do in a conference room on deck ten. Pia is laughing hard in the background. Calle stares at his younger self, touched and surprised that Filip has the picture up. He lets his eyes rove across the other pictures, recognising the girl behind the bar in several of them, and the singer who was performing down at Starlight.

Calle grabs the vodka bottle. Lies down on the bed. Listens to the soft patter of rain against the window. Unscrews the top. He is not leaving this cabin until they are back in Stockholm.

Albin

'Check out that drunken old bat,' Lo says, pointing to the TV screen. 'She's going to pass out any minute now.'

They are on the bed in Lo and Linda's room, watching Club Charisma's dance floor. It is packed, bodies jostling against other bodies. Albin scans the screen until he finds the person Lo is talking about. A blonde woman is being pushed this way and that. Albin can't make out the details of her face, but it is clear she is only semi-conscious.

It is past midnight. Dad still hasn't come by to make sure he and Lo are in bed.

'Her name is Anneli and she is a hairdresser,' he says.

'Right,' Lo says. 'Her salon is called Curl Up and Dye.'

Albin shoves a fistful of liquorice in his mouth to stifle a laugh. Keeping a straight face has become the name of the game.

'Anneli's number one advice is to go on a booze cruise,' he says.

'Number one,' Lo agrees.

It makes him warm inside. He is starting to speak her language now, and it is as though they are creating a bubble around themselves when they use it.

'Anneli never wants to go back home,' he says.

'Right, because she has the most boring husband ever, who eats his own earwax when no one's looking.'

'Heartbreaking,' Albin says, biting his cheek. 'Poor Anneli.'

'Nothing heartbreaking at all about Anneli,' Lo says. 'She's having the time of her life.'

Suddenly, the woman's head disappears. She has finally collapsed. People around her turn. A few kneel next to her, others keep on dancing.

'Anneli's just having a bit of shut-eye,' Albin says. 'The floor is so soft and comfy.'

Two security officers are making their way through the sea of people.

'Can't they just leave Anneli be?' Lo says, pretending to be upset.

The officers pick the woman up. Her body is far too limp, like there are no joints holding her bones together.

'I hope they don't wake her,' Lo says, and fumbles about for the remote control.

She changes the channel to the other dance floor, where a woman in a red dress is singing on stage in front of a red curtain. Albin wonders what she sounds like and if she is beautiful. The stage lighting is so strong her face looks almost scratched out on the screen.

A lot of couples are dancing in front of the stage. Men with women, women with women. He is getting sleepy, but he doesn't want to doze off and miss out on even a minute with Lo.

'Ew, gross!' she shrieks, so suddenly Albin almost drops his plastic tub of liquorice on the floor.

She changes channels again.

'What happened?' he says.

Lo whimpers. 'I saw Mum! With a hideous guy wearing the world's most heartbreaking jacket!'

'Can I see?' Albin asks, reaching for the remote.

'No!' Lo yells, and turns on her side, rolling up to protect the remote with her entire body.

'Please.'

'No way.'

'Come oooon! I want to see your new daddy!'

'Cut it out!' Lo screams.

But there is laughter in her voice too. Albin climbs on top of her. She squeals while he tries to pry her fingers off the remote.

The door to the cabin slams open; panic jolts through Albin. When he turns around, his dad is in the doorway, swaying gently on his feet. The corridor behind him is brightly lit.

Albin climbs off Lo. Sits down cross-legged on the other side of the bed. The room is suddenly too hot.

Leave, he pleads inwardly. *Please, leave.*

'Am I interrupting?' His dad's voice is thick and coming from the back of his throat, as though he is slowly suffocating. Lo sits up on the bed.

'No, of course not,' she says, and runs her fingers through her ponytail.

His dad enters, closing the door behind him. The cabin gets darker. He moves slowly across the floor. Grunts when he collapses on the edge of the bed next to Albin, way too close.

'I just wanted to check on you before turning in myself,' he says.

His tongue sounds thick and numb, as if he has been given a local anaesthetic.

'Where's Mum?' Albin says.

'Still out with Linda.'

Albin thinks about his mum in her wheelchair. What is she doing while Linda is dancing with some bloke in an ugly jacket?

194

Do people talk to her, or is she by herself? Would she be able to get back to their cabin on her own if she wanted to?

He can easily picture her, the way she gets when she is nervous in public. The forced smile. The eyes that dart around without really seeing anything at all, like she wants to signal that she is a part of what is going on, just like everyone else, that she is no different from other people.

His mum, who tells him that she has stopped dreaming that she can fly, the way Albin so often does. Now she dreams that she can run instead. To her, that is just as unattainable. So then how must it feel to be surrounded by dancing people?

Suddenly he wants nothing more than to find her and hug her, hard.

'It's great to see you getting on so well,' his dad says, patting Albin's leg. 'Family's important.'

He turns to Lo. His eyes are shiny in the glare from the telly.

Leave, Albin thinks. *Please, please, Dad. Leave.*

'Linda and I promised one another that our children were never going to feel unloved. Children need to know that they are loved unconditionally.'

He reaches across Albin and strokes Lo's cheek. Albin can tell she wants to pull away. How can his dad not notice?

'I love you too, Lo. Almost as if you were my own child. I want you to know that.'

She gives him a stiff smile. Wraps her arms around her legs.

'Goodnight, Dad,' Albin says, but he doesn't seem to hear.

Even his blinking is in slow motion.

'You should always look out for one another,' he says. 'Promise me.'

'We promise,' Albin says, and Lo nods.

'No!' his dad says, sounding angry all of a sudden. 'You have to goddamn promise so I can tell you mean it! Don't be such fucking sissies! A person needs to know they can rely on their family!'

Lo presses herself against the headboard. Having been pre-occupied with feeling ashamed of his dad, it is only now that it dawns on Albin that Lo is scared.

'We promise,' Albin quickly puts in again, scooching down to the foot of the bed and standing up. 'Now you should go to bed, Dad. You look *tired*.'

If only he was brave enough to tell his dad the truth: that he is a disgusting, messy drunk. The rage inside Albin is so strong something is bound to snap soon.

His dad turns his head towards him. His stubble is like little black dots against his pale skin.

'Yes, I am tired,' he mutters. 'I'm so fucking tired of all this crap. I try and try, but . . . everything turns out wrong, no matter what I do.' He gets to his feet, staggers, almost falls back on the bed. But he rights himself. 'I'll be going so you don't have to be embarrassed,' he says, and looks at Albin.

'That's not what I meant,' Albin replies automatically.

Except it was. It was exactly what he meant. But his dad is on the verge of turning into Crying Daddy now. And that dad *never* wants to leave.

'I thought we were going to spend some real time together – that that was the point of this cruise – but apparently no one's interested. You couldn't pretend for even a lousy twenty-four hours.' He chuckles and shakes his head. 'See you tomorrow,' he says.

But he doesn't move from where he is standing in the middle of the room, breathing heavily through his nose.

'Goodnight, Mårten,' Lo says quietly.

'Goodnight, sweetheart,' his dad replies.

Finally, he walks across to Albin and kisses him on the forehead. His stubble scratches Albin's nose. 'I'm not such a bad dad, am I? Or should we have left you in Vietnam, do you think?'

Albin can tell that Lo is shocked, but it is not the first time his dad has said something like that.

'No, of course not,' Albin says. 'Goodnight.'

They quietly watch as his dad finally leaves. Hear him enter the cabin next door. His shoes thud against the wall when he kicks them off. And then, faint whimpering. His dad is crying on the other side.

What if he comes back?

Albin is standing stock-still, feeling Lo's eyes on him. He doesn't know what to do now. Can't look Lo in the eye. Can't go into the other cabin, where dad is. Can't escape out into the ship, where unaccompanied children are not allowed this late.

'Are you okay?' Lo says.

'Yes,' Albin replies, and sits back down.

He stares fixedly at the TV. His ears are straining.

'You can stay here tonight if you want,' Lo tells him.

'Okay.'

Lo puts a hand on his shoulder. He doesn't want her to feel sorry for him. He just wants Lo to comment on someone on the dance floor, for everything to be like it was before his dad stopped by.

More thudding from next door. The toilet flushes.

'Hey,' Lo says.

'Mm.'

'If I tell you something, will you promise not to tell your parents?'

Albin finally looks at her. Nods.

'Promise,' she says, her eyes narrowing.

'I promise.'

'Mum thinks Mårten is borderline. And that Grandma was too.'

Albin swallows hard. He had been hoping Lo would tell him something about her, something that would get them talking about anything other than his dad.

'What do you mean borderline?' he says. 'What's that?'

'It's like a mental illness.'

Albin freezes. If he doesn't move, maybe time will stop, and the rest of this conversation will never happen.

'She talked to some people at the hospital where she used to work,' Lo continues.

'Dad is not borderline.'

'You don't even know what it is.'

Albin can't think of anything to counter that.

'She looked it up online as well. There were loads of symptoms that matched what Mårten is like.'

Linda talks to people about his dad. She talks about the things Albin has never talked to anyone about, not even his mum.

'I'm sorry,' Lo says. 'Maybe I shouldn't have said anything. I just figured it would be easier to know . . .'

'Dad gets sad sometimes, but there's nothing wrong with him.' Albin cuts her off. 'He's had a hard time since Grandma died.'

'He was weird well before that. It's just that you were too little to get it, or that you don't remember it . . .'

'And you're saying you do?'

'No,' Lo says, 'but Mum's told me he was always the same, even though it seems to be getting worse and worse now.'

She is wrong. She has to be.

'Linda doesn't know anything about Dad. We haven't even seen you in more than a year.'

'It's actually the other way around,' Lo says. 'Mum knows exactly what he's like. That's why we haven't seen you. She can't deal with him any more.'

Albin realises the next-door cabin has gone quiet. What if his dad can hear them? What would he do?

He would barge in here, shouting, accusing Lo of trying to turn Albin against him, the way he accuses Albin's mum of doing exactly that. He would shout and shout and no one would be able to get through to him and Lo would refuse to ever see Albin again.

'Mårten calls our house in the middle of the night when he's been drinking,' Lo says. 'Sometimes he calls to yell at Mum and sometimes he says he's going to kill himself.'

Albin can't speak. There are no words in him.

But I would never do it at home so you or Mum would have to find me, I promise.

It's not your fault if I do it, never think that. You're the best thing in my life. I just can't take it any more.

'Mum doesn't think he's going to do it,' Lo adds quickly, 'but it's really hard for her when he calls. And it must be a thousand times worse for you and Cilla, who live with him.'

Her hand squeezes his shoulder. Her touch feels very distant. He has imploded into a tiny dot deep inside his body.

'That's why we moved to Eskilstuna,' she says. 'So at least all he can do is call. Before, he used to come to our house at night. Sometimes she refused to let him in, but then he would call her friends and tell them she's a fake who doesn't deserve to have friends because she doesn't even care about her own brother. And

Mum is such a fucking coward she's never going to say anything; we moved so she wouldn't have to confront him.'

Lo makes his dad sound completely insane.

Is he insane?

And how long has Lo known?

Nothing makes sense any more. All the pieces are in all the wrong places.

He has to get out of here. He has to get away from this cabin, away from Lo, away from the wall with his dad on the other side.

'You don't know anything,' he says. 'You might think you do just because you and Linda have been gossiping, but you don't know what it's like.'

'Where are you going?' Lo asks when he starts moving towards the door.

'To find Mum,' he says.

'Don't tell Cilla. Please. I promised Mum I wouldn't tell you.'

He doesn't answer, opens the door to the hallway.

'Wait for me,' Lo says.

Madde

Being asleep is so comfy. That hand shaking her shoulder gently, it is being unfair. She tries to ignore it, sink back into the depths of sleep, but the hand is stubborn.

Now she is becoming aware of the music too. Somebody is singing about Sweet Home Alabama. And a voice next to her ear is telling her: 'You have to wake up now.'

Madde grudgingly opens her eyes to see a woman with dark hair pulled into a topknot. And, behind her, a pretty fit guy who is smiling. She vaguely recognises them. They are both wearing uniforms.

'You can't sleep here,' the woman says.

Madde blinks her eyes several times. Glances down at her lap. A shot glass is nestled in her limp hand. Drops of sugary booze have spilled out across her fingers and thighs.

The room is packed, but her table is empty. Everyone has left. And the girl singing on stage is failing to hit every single note.

Everything is so slow in Madde's head. She can only deal with one impression at a time. Her tongue tastes bad, and when she pulls it across her front teeth she can feel the gunk on them, thick as a felt rug.

'I'm not sleeping,' she says. 'I was just resting my eyes.'

'I see,' the woman says, exchanging an amused look with her colleague.

Madde should be angry with her for that look, but she just can't be. The woman looks far too kind.

'Maybe you should go and rest in your cabin instead,' the man says.

'No,' Madde replies, 'it's fine. I'm wide awake now.'

'Come on,' the woman says. 'We'll walk you there and make sure you get into bed properly. Wouldn't it feel good to lie down instead?'

It would, actually. Madde doesn't have it in her to fight them.

'I just wanted to have a good time,' she says. 'Look, I put gold on my tits. Proper party tits. Right?'

The man nods, looking embarrassed. Madde bursts out laughing and the kind woman laughs too.

'Do you think you can make it there?'

'Of course I can,' Madde says, and stands up. She tries to put the shot glass down, but it's stuck to her fingers and she starts laughing again, shaking her hand about until the glass comes off. She almost falls over, but the male security guard is there immediately, holding her upright.

They lead her out of the bar, their grip on her firm yet gentle; it feels like she is floating. She closes her eyes.

'You're so nice to me.'

'Do you think she'll be all right on her own?' the woman says.

Madde smiles. 'You have to say hi to Dan from me. You have to tell him where my cabin is.'

'Only if you tell us first,' the woman says. 'Do you remember the number?'

'It's upstairs and in the middle. We don't have any windows.'

It feels so good to close your eyes like this, held by strong arms. She can hear the woman tell the man to look for a key card in her purse. When Madde realises they have made sure she didn't leave her purse, she almost starts to cry. They are looking after her so well and it is almost like being little when Mum and Dad would throw a party and she would fall asleep on the sofa and they would pick her up ever so gently and carry her all the way to her bed and she can hear screaming and laughing and music everywhere and it is a party and she is there but she doesn't need to *be* there; she can just close her eyes and know that she is safe and that people are having fun and that everything is as it should be.

Marianne

Marianne has almost drifted off in the vibrating, thudding darkness below the waterline. Her head is resting on Göran's shoulder. His skin is soft and warm against hers. And her own skin is trying to trick her, make her believe he is still touching her with his fingers, his lips. The body's memories make the backs of her knees, her chest, her genitals flush.

Göran turns his head, kisses her on the forehead.

'I thought you were asleep,' she says.

'Almost.'

Göran pushes up on one elbow so that she has to move her head. She can hear him scratching his neck, and his jaw creaks when he yawns big. He rolls on top of her. Gives her a soft kiss on the lips.

Then she hears the click of the light switch and is blinded by the light. She puts her hand over her eyes, not just to shield them but to keep him from having to see her squinting and pruny.

'My goodness, it's late,' he says, and yawns again. 'We must have been at it for more than an hour.'

He sounds so pleased she has to giggle.

'Jesus, I'm bloody bursting for a piss,' he continues.

'There's a toilet in the hallway,' she tells him.

He puts one foot on the floor and heaves himself out of bed. Marianne pulls the bedding up, studying his naked body for the first time. His ponytail is hanging down his pale, freckly back. He is so skinny his ribs are clearly visible, but there is still a hint of a paunch. She catches a split-second glimpse of his penis, flaccid like a deflated balloon. There is something touching about it. Marianne covers her face with her hands and stifles a laugh. It is almost exactly twenty-four hours since she decided to take this cruise.

It was so easy. Why has she never done this before?

But if she had, she might never have met him.

Göran looks around, bends over with his bum towards her, snatches up his jeans from the floor and pulls his underwear out of them.

He starts getting dressed.

Marianne rolls onto her side, facing him, smooths the duvet into place around her body, trying to hold her head at an angle that conceals her double chin.

'You're not coming?' he says.

A moment of confusion.

'To the bathroom?' she says. 'No, I don't need to go.'

'But then we're heading back out on the boat, right?' he says, pulling on his shirt and buttoning the top buttons.

Marianne sits up in bed, squeezing the edge of the duvet by her collar bones.

'But . . .' She breaks off, not knowing what to say. 'But why?' she finally manages.

Göran puts his denim waistcoat on and slumps down on the edge of the bed.

'So you're not coming?' he says.

Marianne shakes her head before she has time to actually consider it. 'I'm tired. I thought the night was over.'

'It doesn't have to be,' Göran says with a smile.

But I thought we were going to fall asleep together. Set an alarm so we don't miss the breakfast buffet. Have a calm, lovely day tomorrow; take a walk outside, weather permitting. Get to know each other better. Why do you want to leave? What would you miss out on by staying here?

Why don't you want to stay here with me?

'I don't want to waste the night sleeping now that I'm finally on this trip,' Göran says. 'I was going to try to find the lads and have a few more pints.'

So now the lads are important again? Now that you got what you wanted? You know, it's pretty pathetic to still be calling each other 'lads' when you're almost seventy.

'I see,' she says, and lies back down.

It feels like the walls are closing in. As though they are finally yielding to the enormous pressure from outside.

'You should come with me,' he says, stroking her arm. 'You really want to stay here on your own?'

No, I don't. I want you to stay with me. 'Yes.'

'Come on. You only live once.' He smiles.

'Thank God.'

He chuckles, bends down and puts his shoes on. 'If you change your mind, swing by Starlight, where we were dancing. I'll try and get them over there, if they're not there already.'

She doesn't dare answer, because she knows the bitterness would shine through. She has never been good at pretending to be happy and unperturbed and easy-going. She's never managed to hide her disappointment, no matter how hard she has tried. And Lord knows she has had a lot of practice over the years.

When he gives her a peck on the cheek and stands up, she almost blurts out that she has changed her mind. But the idea of having to head back out into the tumult is inconceivable. It is too late. It is done.

He pulls a pen from his pocket and writes something on one of the tax-free brochures on the desk.

'Here's my mobile number if you want to reach me,' he says. 'But I suppose the phones don't always work out at sea.'

'Makes sense,' she says. 'Have fun.'

'Maybe I'll see you tomorrow then, instead?' he says, and opens the door.

'That would be nice.'

Marianne turns the light out. Göran stays in the doorway, a black silhouette against the brightly lit hallway. He seems to hesitate for a second, and hope rears up inside her.

But then he is gone. The door closes and darkness envelops the cabin once more.

Albin

'Abbe, wait!' Lo calls out behind him. 'I'm sorry I said anything!'

She sounds out of breath. Albin makes no reply. He is trying to push through the crowd of drunk people at Charisma Starlight. They are everywhere, tall and sweaty and clumsy and loud and in the way. A woman trips over him, beer sloshing out of her glass, soaking the shoulder of his hoodie.

'Watch where you're going, brat!' she shouts after him.

'Abbe! Wait!'

Lo sounds further away now; her voice is almost completely drowned out by the music.

'Abbe, seriously!'

He glances back, catching a revolting whiff of beer from the wet patch on his hoodie and immediately spots the uniformed man and woman. People move aside to make room for them, and now he can see Lo. She is walking between the guards, looking pissed off.

'Hey there,' the woman says when they reach him. 'I'm sorry, but it's bedtime for you two. We'll take you back to your cabin now.'

Her shiny brass name tag informs him that her name is PIA.

'We're looking for my mum,' Albin says. 'She's around here somewhere.'

'I already told them,' Lo says.

'Wouldn't it be better if you went to bed?' the man, whose name is JARNO, says.

'I'm not going back to the cabin!'

His voice sounds shrill and desperate. The guards exchange a look.

'How about this,' Pia says, 'we'll come with you and help you look for her.'

'We don't need help,' Lo says.

'Yes,' Pia says, 'you do.'

'Let's crack on, then,' Jarno says, slightly too cheerily.

'Seriously,' Lo says.

But when Pia sets out in the lead, Albin is secretly relieved. She kindly but firmly moves people out of the way. A few of them glare at her until they notice her uniform.

'There they are,' Lo exclaims, pointing.

When Albin looks that way, he spots his mum and Linda behind a mirrored pillar. There's no ugly jacket guy to be seen. Linda is sitting in an armchair that is so low his mum has to lean forward in her wheelchair when they talk. Linda is glistening with sweat from dancing; the hair at her temples has grown a few shades darker. The dance floor lights are flashing different colours around their heads.

At least his mum is not alone, like he'd imagined.

Linda spots them first and says something to his mum, who starts fumbling with the joystick, reversing and turning her chair so she can see them too.

'What are you doing here?' she says loudly to make herself heard above the music when they reach them. She glances at the security guards, smiling nervously.

Pia leans closer to her and Linda. 'They were out looking for you,' she says. 'We don't want children running around on their own at this hour.'

'I had no idea,' Mum shouts up at her face. 'My husband went back to the cabin and . . .' Her voice falters. She turns to Albin. 'Did something happen, sweetie?'

Albin doesn't know how to respond. He can't stand here shouting about what they have never even talked about, especially not with the security guards leaning over them.

'Is everything okay?' Linda says. 'Lo?'

Lo shrugs.

'Thank you for escorting them,' Mum shouts, and looks at the guards. 'We'll bring them back to the cabin now.'

'No! I don't want to go back there!'

His mum looks at him strangely. Albin can feel the guards watching them.

'The café is still open,' Pia says. 'You can talk there if you want.'

His mum nods.

Something crackles and Jarno pulls a radio from his belt.

The crackling voice says something about a man outside the karaoke; Jarno's expression is suddenly grave. 'We have to run,' he says, and glances at Pia.

She bends down to Albin. 'Are you okay if we leave you here?'

He nods.

'If you need us, just go to the information desk and they'll call us. Or ask the guy who works in this bar. His name is Filip and he is super-cool. Okay?'

Albin nods again, even though he knows he is not going to do that. He wishes there was someone who could help him, but this is something he has to deal with himself.

Dan

Dan has just snorted another four lines and instantly realises it was a mistake. His overheated brain is sizzling inside his cranium. Everything is moving too fast and yet he perceives everything with painful clarity. The heat. The flushed faces. A couple of girls in their twenties are up on stage, screaming out the lyrics to 'Total Eclipse of the Heart' with strong Finnish accents.

At least the security guards have taken care of that fat girl who sang the *Grease* song. She stayed at her table when her group left, her eyes glued to him, and it made him feel increasingly uncomfortable. The table where she fell asleep has now been taken by a Russian whore sitting on some guy's lap, occasionally putting her hand on his friend's thigh. Dan buys his coke from her pimp sometimes. She is good-looking; if she had been ten years younger, she could have been a model. He wonders if the guys realise she expects to be paid. She is probably going to let them do whatever they want to her, both of them at the same time. His brain creates a flashing torrent of mental images, one leading to the next, and in his pants, his cock begins to stir.

And then the song is finished. Applause. Whistling. Dan claps until his palms sting, smiles as big as he can manage at the audience. The girls step off the stage and are high-fived by their friends.

'Thanks, girls, for that school dance classic,' Dan says, and a few people in the audience laugh their agreement.

A thin, snub-nosed woman in a sleeveless hot-pink top steps out onto the stage. Her hair is dyed so dark it is almost blueish under the spotlights.

'Hi there,' Dan says. 'And who do we have here?'

'Alexandra.'

When she smiles nervously, a small diamond flashes on her tooth. She is decent-looking. Not too far into her thirties.

'Hi, Alexandra! All right, audience, how about we give Alexandra a really warm round of applause?'

They obey. Someone whistles and Dan puts his arm around her and squeezes her bony shoulder.

'And what will you be singing for us, Alexandra?'

She looks up at him. 'First . . . first I just have to say that . . . that I'm your biggest fan.'

'I'm sure I'm going to be a big fan of yours too.' Dan grins at the audience. 'What will you be singing?'

'I'm doing "Paradiso Tropical",' she says, and Dan's smile turns so stiff it feels like rigor mortis of the lips.

'That's great.'

It was the same year he tried to make his Eurovision comeback with 'Walking Against the Wind', a ballad he'd written the lyrics for himself. It was about the death of his father. He went in front of the whole of Sweden naked and exposed, but didn't even make it to the second round. Millan and Miranda won his semi-final with 'Paradiso Tropical', a brain-dead faux calypso that was a fucking joke. Exactly what Sweden wanted. The song that crushed what remained of his illusions was played everywhere that summer.

The temperature seems to have been dialled up another notch. He is suddenly aware of how low the ceiling is. And of how loudly his brain is sizzling. His heart is racing.

Is this some bloody test? Are they filming him for some new fucking TV show whose only purpose is to humiliate people? How many views would he get on YouTube if he bashed Alexandra's face in with the mic, hitting her again and again?

Dan licks his lips. His top lip tastes salty; he quickly wipes it and checks his fingers, anxious he might see a revealing nosebleed, but it is just sweat.

Is the audience dead silent? How much time has passed?

'Let's get this party started!' he says, and hands Alexandra the microphone. 'Break a leg!'

'Thank you,' she replies.

Johan turns on the hateful steel pan intro and Alexandra closes her eyes, starts singing with feeling and vibrato. She makes the song sound evangelical, as though it is about a Christian paradise and not some gay disco at whatever charter resort. Dan smiles broadly while his heart thumps and thumps and thumps and hatred flows through his veins, hissing like carbonation, roaring in his skull.

Someone shrieks in the dark room. A glass breaks. Alexandra falters, trips over her words and carries on, her voice trembling for a different reason now.

The energy of the entire room changes. People turn their heads. A couple of muscle guys in tight tank-tops laugh loudly. The bartender has picked up the wall-mounted phone behind the bar.

Dan follows his gaze and spots the man moving through the room, making people back away. The muscle guys laugh even harder.

The man is in his forties. His eyes are flat; he is talking to himself. His jacket is covered in vomit. His strawberry-blond hair is standing on end. There is something that could be dried blood inside his shirt collar. Alexandra falls silent, but the music continues.

'What the fuck?' Dan blurts out, and it is picked up by the microphone.

The man sniffs the air.

His mind must have gone, drowned in booze. Nothing but reptile brain left.

But he turns his head toward Dan and something in those empty eyes seems into spark to life. Focus. He is not talking to himself, Dan realises. His jaw is working, as if he is chewing something.

What a fucking nut job. It's fucked up that they don't keep people like him locked up.

An older lady unwittingly blocks the man's path. He shoves her aside so hard her glasses go flying. People get up out of their armchairs, start making their way towards the exit. The nut job reaches the edge of the stage; his eyes are bottomless pits of madness.

Come on then, Dan thinks to himself, the coke surging through him. *Just try me.*

He raises his guard when the man climbs onto the stage. Alexandra screams and drops the mic. It sounds like a cannon firing when it hits the floor, and then feedback screeches out through the speakers.

The man hurls himself at Dan without warning and the air is knocked out of Dan when he hits the floor. The nut job snaps his teeth shut, again and again, like a rabid dog. Trying to *bite* him.

The speakers are finally turned off. A few audience members scream. Others hold up their mobile phones. Shutters click in the dark.

Dan is barely able to keep the man's teeth away from him. His mouth reeks and there is something about the stench that finally makes Dan scared. He tries to push the man off him, but the bastard holds on.

'For fuck's sake, help me!' Dan shouts.

But no one comes. He can feel the fear and hesitation in the darkness beyond the illuminated stage. Everyone is waiting for someone else to go first.

'You fucking bastards!' he shouts, drawing new strength from his rage.

Dan drives a fist into the man's face. Pain radiates through his arm and blood spatters from his knuckles. He has cut them on the man's teeth, as though he'd shoved his hand into a pile of razor blades. The man smacks his lips; his eyes are firmly focused on Dan and yet they seem not to see him. Dan aims another blow, but the man quickly catches the balled fist in his hand, clamps his lips onto it, tensing them around the wound as if he is trying to suction onto it, and Dan feels a slippery tongue dance across his knuckles.

The revulsion that explodes inside Dan is so strong he roars out loud. He tears and yanks at his hand. The contact with that suckling mouth is the centre of his universe, so sickening everything else pales in comparison.

And then, suddenly, the weight on top of him is gone. It happens so quickly he is disoriented. Two security officers, Henke and that old milksop Pär, who should have retired long ago, have picked the man up from behind, but he refuses to let go of Dan's hand; it feels like his arm is about to be wrenched out of its socket.

The guards finally manage to wrest the lunatic off him. Dan struggles onto his elbows, sits up at the edge of the stage, staring at his hand. New blood is seeping out of the little wounds, turning pink and transparent where it mixes with the man's saliva. Dan looks up.

The nut job is writhing in the security officers' firm grip, kicking, his teeth snapping in mid-air. Pia and Jarno have arrived now as well. The man tries to take a bite out of Pia's cheek; she only just manages to turn her head away.

'Are you okay?' Pär calls to Dan.

He becomes aware of everyone's eyes on him: all the fucking cowards who just stood there gawking.

'You better lock that guy up,' he says. 'He must be off his tits on some kind of super-smack. Bloody hell.'

He glances down at the saliva-soaked lacerations. He has no desire to catch AIDS from some doped-up head case.

When he looks up again, the guards have managed to cuff the man's hands behind his back. Dan can hear their laboured breathing, the sound of the man's teeth snapping shut so hard you would think they would shatter.

'Do you want us to take you to the infirmary so Raili can have a look at that?' Jarno says.

'I'll head there on my own,' Dan says. 'You just get that one behind bars. Or throw him overboard. Nut jobs like that don't deserve to fucking live.'

Albin

Linda and Lo have gone to the till to buy drinks. Albin and his mum have sat down at one of the tables at the back of the Charisma Café. They are practically the only ones there. The staff seem bored; you can tell they are eager to close.

'What happened?' his mum says.

'Dad came by the cabin. I think he's gone to bed now.'

'Yes, he was feeling a bit tired,' his mum says. 'He wanted to go to bed now so he would have more energy tomorrow instead.'

Albin looks down at the table, pushes scattered biscuit crumbs into a pile. 'He was tired last night too,' he says.

He can't look at her. He doesn't know what to say next.

'Abbe,' his mum says. 'Did something happen?'

He shrugs.

It is so difficult to find the words. When he tries, it is as though a circuit-breaker switches off in his head and everything goes dark.

'I'm sorry, Cilla, but I can't remember if you take milk in your coffee,' Linda says, and puts a tray of clattering glasses and mugs down on the table.

'Either way is fine,' Mum says.

'Are you sure? Because I can go get you milk if you . . .'

'Black is great.'

Linda stays standing, hesitating for a second before sitting down next to Lo. People are often like that around his mother, even her carers: always wondering if they are doing things right. And since they have to do so *many* things for his mum, a lot of time is spent answering their questions. Obviously, it is ultimately because people are well-meaning, but Albin wonders how she puts up with it. His dad is the only one who doesn't do that. Maybe that is why she won't leave him.

He knows children are not supposed to want their parents to get divorced, but Albin wants nothing more. He could help his mum. She doesn't need his dad. And maybe what Lo told him is the excuse he needs to finally be able to talk about his dad for real, about what he's really like.

In the middle of the sea, far from home, with a big, dark nothingness outside the windows, it suddenly seems possible.

'Is Dad sick?' Albin says, and pinches the pile of crumbs into a soft mass.

'What do you mean, honey?' his mum replies.

'Is he sick?' Albin looks up. 'Lo says Linda thinks so.'

His mum blinks. At least he has said it now. No going back. Lo sinks deeper into her chair, as if she has been holding her breath for a long time and is now letting all the air out in one go.

'Lo,' Linda says, turning to her, 'what did you say to Abbe?'

'He just told you.'

'That was something we discussed in confidence.'

'It's his dad,' Lo says, 'and maybe he needed to know.'

'That's not up to you to decide.'

'But it's up to you, is it? Always up to you. Real big shock you don't want to talk about it. We never say it like it is in this stupid family. But maybe Albin and I don't want to be like you.' Lo has crossed her arms and is looking straight at Albin, sending him her strength.

'I'm so sorry, Cilla,' Linda says. 'Lo overheard me talking to a friend and . . . I tried to explain . . . I thought I could trust her.'

'It's okay,' his mum says dully.

'I love how you think I should *lie* to my cousin to prove I'm *trustworthy*,' Lo says slowly, turning back to Linda. 'You really don't see any problems with that logic?'

For a moment, it seems like Linda might slap her. 'Look who suddenly cares about her cousin,' she says instead.

Lo's eyes narrow into slits.

'Abbe,' Linda says quietly, leaning forward, 'it's hard for you to understand this; it's hard for us too . . . But your mum and I are trying to help—'

'Linda,' his mum says, and Linda breaks off abruptly.

Then his mum takes a deep breath. She has folded her hands in her lap. Her coffee sits untouched on the table in front of her. 'We will talk about this when we get home,' she says.

'No,' Albin says, 'we will talk about it now.'

'Abbe, please,' his mum says. He can tell from her voice that there are tears lurking just beneath the surface.

He almost changes his mind. But he knows if they don't talk about it now, they never will. He will never be able to bring this up again once they are back home. And she will never do it of her own accord.

'We have to,' he says. 'Lo's right. We never talk about *anything*. You always tell me Dad is tired, for example, but he's *drunk*. Why can't you just say that?'

His mum's head has tilted forward. Silent tears fall into her lap. She wipes her eyes with her whole hand. 'It's hard for Dad,' she says. 'You can tell from looking at me that I'm sick, but it's not always so obvious from the outside . . .' Her voice fades away.

'So he is sick?' Albin says. 'You think so too?'

'I don't know,' his mum replies. 'But when he feels bad, he drinks.'

'It never makes him feel better,' Albin counters.

'No,' his mum admits, wiping her eyes again. 'It's hard for him. It becomes a vicious circle.'

Albin looks at Lo, draws more strength. 'But why do you pretend with me?' he says. 'Don't you think I get it?'

His mum opens her mouth and closes it again. 'Sometimes I forget how big you've become,' she says.

'The important thing to remember is that it's not Mårten's fault that he's sick,' Linda says. 'It's just like having a broken leg, or like Cilla with her illness.'

'I know,' Albin says impatiently, wishing she would just stop talking, that she would let his mum speak.

Finally speak.

But his mum says nothing.

'Though in fairness, it's not like anyone's lying to Albin about Cilla, pretending she's not really in a wheelchair at all,' Lo says. 'So it clearly is different somehow.' She looks at Linda triumphantly, and Albin is happy she is here. He would never have thought to say that. At least not until he got into bed and replayed everything again and again, like a scene from a film, when it is already far too late.

His mum chortles and Albin looks at her, stunned, because she isn't crying but laughing. 'Oh my, Abbe, what a couple of lemons you've been given for parents.'

He doesn't quite know what 'lemon' is supposed to mean, but he understands her point. And it sounds much too similar to the things his dad likes to tell him.

'Don't say that.'

'No, I'm sorry.' His mum wipes her eyes. 'I just feel so . . .' She shakes her head and tries to stifle a sob.

'Cilla hasn't wanted to worry you,' Linda says.

Albin stares at them. Do they honestly believe he hasn't been worried? Don't they get that this is much easier? If his dad is sick, if there is a name for what his dad is, then maybe there are people who know what to do about it.

'Can't we make him go see a doctor?' he says.

'First Mårten needs to realise he needs help,' Linda says, 'or it won't work.'

'But we're going to make him realise it,' his mum adds quickly, shooting her a look.

She clearly doesn't want Albin to think there is the slightest doubt that they are going to sort everything out. She is still lying and sweeping things under the rug.

Silence falls. Linda hasn't touched her coffee either. She has milk in hers. Grease patches have formed on the surface.

'Can't you get divorced first?' Albin says quietly. 'Then at least we don't have to live with him until he's better.'

His mum shakes her head. 'We're not getting divorced. We love each other. You know that. And you can't tell him about this. Then he'll be upset that we talked to you, and that will make it even harder to get through to him. Lo is right; it's not good to lie and pretend like nothing's wrong. But you have to for a little while longer. For his sake.'

The more she talks, the more Albin feels like he is about to explode. It is so *unfair*. Everyone has to tiptoe around his dad. But Albin doesn't get a say in anything, even though it is his life too.

'But I don't want to live with Dad,' Albin says, and now he is close to tears himself. '*I* don't love him. I hate him.'

'No, you don't,' his mum says. 'And we're going to help him, and everything will be better.'

Albin won't be able to hold back the tears for much longer. 'I hate you too,' he says, and then he gets up from the table and runs away before they have a chance to stop him.

He doesn't know if anyone is coming after him. He runs without turning around.

The *Baltic Charisma*

The man at the heart of the discussions in the café is asleep in his bed. Sweat makes his shirt cling to his body. In his dream, he is running up a flight of stairs.

'Mårten! Mårten! Mårten!' The voice sounds abandoned and scared and angry all at once and it cuts right through him. He looks at the paintings hanging side by side on the walls of the staircase. The woman crying out for him painted them. Thick layers of oil paint have hardened in uneven clumps on the canvasses. A door stands ajar at the top of the stairs. Darkness and the smell of cigarette smoke are seeping out through the crack.

'Mårten!'

He enters. His mother is propped up against a mountain of pillows in her bed. She puffs on her cigarette, emerging more clearly from the gloom as the glow intensifies. Her naked breasts sag over the edge of the duvet into her armpits.

'Hey, sweetie,' she says. Her cigarette crunches when she stubs it out in the ashtray. 'Do you like staying home from school?'

He nods automatically. His mum has called him in sick. She didn't want to be home alone today. His sister Linda is jealous. Linda doesn't know that Mårten is jealous of her too. He wants to go to school. He wants to get out of here.

'Why don't you come here and lie down for a bit so I can cuddle you?' his mum says, and pushes the duvet aside.

Mårten obeys and she pulls the duvet over both of them. It is warm.

'What would I do without you?' she says.

He pokes at the bubbles on the textured wallpaper next to the bed. There is a bare patch there.

'You love me, don't you?' she says, and he promises. 'Because you know we have to do everything right this time. Otherwise it all just starts again in the next life, until we're done with each other.'

Mårten nods and his mother tells him again about all their previous lives. Sometimes they are married, sometimes Mårten is the parent. Sometimes they are friends, sometimes soldiers in the same army.

'It's always been us against the world,' his mum says. 'If not for you, I wouldn't have wanted to live this life. I would have jumped straight into the next one.'

Grown-up Mårten, who is in bed in his cabin, is struggling to breathe. The dream always ends the same way. He wants to break out of it, but he can't.

'We should move on to the next life together,' his mum says. 'Like in *The Brothers Lionheart*.'

The bed is soaked. The mattress is dripping.

'Mårten, I'm waiting for you, you know.'

He turns over. Droplets of water glitter in his mum's hair. Her skin is faintly green. Bits of her face are missing where the eels and crayfish have fed on her. Her eyes are covered by a milky film, but he knows she is looking straight at him. He tries to get out of bed, but he is stuck to the sodden mattress. Murky water pours out of her mouth when she smiles at him.

'It's you and me, Mårten.'

Her breasts are resting on her belly, which is protruding as though she is pregnant. He knows there are eels in there. It has been years since she walked into Lake Mälaren.

It's only a dream, he thinks. *I got away.* A shadow drifts past behind the milky eyes, something wet and slippery moving about. He can feel her fury. In his dreams, he never gets away.

'You promised,' she says. 'You said it would always be the two of us.'

There is a hard knock on the door of a cabin on the ninth floor. Fourteen-year-old Lyra turns off the film on her laptop and removes her headphones, straightens the black Alice band keeping the fringe she is growing out from falling in her eyes. There is another loud rap on the door. Impatient. She figures her mum or dad must have forgotten their key card and wonders if they have been knocking for long, because she had the volume turned up high in her headphones. The legs of her white silk pyjamas are so long she can't see her feet when she gets out of bed. She hopes Mum and Dad won't say anything about how she should be asleep. It is going to be an early start, driving all the way to Grandma in Kaarina. Lyra pushes the handle down, but suddenly hesitates. *What if it's not Mum and Dad? What if it's someone dangerous?* She lets go of the handle.

'Hello?' she calls.

'Hello,' a small child's voice replies.

Lyra pulls the door open. In the hallway outside is a boy in a T-shirt and red hoodie. His blue eyes look up at her from under an ash-blond mop of hair. He looks happy, almost excited.

'Hi,' he says. 'What's your name?'

She warily replies that her name is Lyra. She peers up and down the corridor, but there is no one to be seen. Distant voices from the lower decks are drifting up the stairs further down the hall.

'What a strange name,' the boy says, his voice tinkling with laughter.

She sighs inwardly. Sometimes she hates her name, even though she likes the Lyra she was named after. 'It's from a book my dad read when Mum was pregnant with me,' she says.

'What's it about?' the boy asks.

And she replies the way she always does, 'Magic and different kinds of creatures and things like that. It's hard to explain.'

The boy's brow furrows. 'Are there vampires that sparkle in the sun?' he says, and Lyra laughs.

'No.'

He nods resolutely. 'Good. I think vampires should be dangerous.'

She laughs again, because the boy is cute but so precocious. *Even more than that*, she thinks to herself. *He's kind of old-fashioned, like a little old man.* She asks where his parents are, and he shrugs. Asks if he can come inside to use the loo.

'I don't know,' she says.

The boy presses his thighs together, as if he is suddenly worried. 'Please. I don't want to have an accident.'

So she lets him in. When the cabin door closes, the boy positions himself with his back to it. And when he smiles at her she notices his teeth are yellow.

The deep jarring ring of the internal telephone on the desk wakes Mårten from his nightmare. He sits up, feeling the vibrations of the engines through the bed, and peers around, bewildered,

226

before remembering where he is. The sheets are soggy; he reflexively reaches down between his legs. He has not wet himself. When the phone rings again, he jumps out of bed and picks up the receiver. The anxiety from his dream lingers. He hears voices and laughter in the background when his wife tells him about the children, that they are missing. She has called Lo and Linda's cabin several times but had no reply.

'I'll call you again in a bit,' she says. 'Stay there in case they come back.'

Mårten can tell she is panicking. She hangs up before he can get a word in. Mårten pulls off his sopping shirt, shivers. His eyes fall on the wall the room shares with the cabin next door. He pulls out a bottle of cognac from the tax-free bag sitting by the door.

At the information desk, Mika has grabbed the microphone. Speakers all over the ship come to life with a gentle sound effect. 'Personal message for Albin and Lo Sandén,' he intones, his voice echoing down the hallways. 'Would Albin and Lo Sandén report to the information desk, please? Would Albin and Lo Sandén report to the information desk, please?'

The blond boy glares at the speakers on deck nine. The scars by his collarbones are almost gone now, but he feels sick. It is hard to stop feeding in time. There is too much blood in his tiny body and he needs to find someplace to hide, wait for what is coming. For what is going to change everything. He smiles, hardly able to contain himself.

Dan

'All done,' Raili says, pulling off her white, powdery latex gloves with a snap. 'Now you have to make sure to keep the wound clean. And once there's a scab, let it breathe at night.'

Dan holds up his right hand. Only the very tips of his fingers stick out of the gauze. There is a dull throbbing inside. The muscles in his upper arm are sore where Raili gave him a tetanus shot.

She spins around in her chair and bins the gloves. 'Such bad luck, ending up in that lunatic's crosshairs,' she says as she turns back to him.

He looks at her round unmade-up face. 'It wasn't bad luck,' Dan says slowly. 'He was coming for me; there's a big fucking difference.'

'That's true.'

'I just hope no one tips off the tabloids. I could hear several people taking pictures with their mobiles.' He touches his hand. That head case might have done him a service.

'I'm sure you don't have to worry,' Raili says. 'They probably have other things to write about.'

As if she would know. As if she would have any idea whatsoever.

He is going to get off the ship as soon as they dock in Stockholm; go and see a doctor. How can they get away with not having a real doctor on board? Any troglodyte can become a nurse.

The phone on Raili's desk rings and she answers, speaking to someone in Finnish. Her voice changes when she speaks her mother tongue. Even her facial expressions alter around those strange sing-song sounds. How can a language that looks on paper like it is all consonants sound like that? She stops speaking, nodding gravely as she listens to the person at the other end.

'Well, that was Jarno calling,' she says. 'They've locked that man up.'

She sounds immeasurably proud of her husband for doing his job.

Dan's head is starting to pound, a different rhythm to the throbbing in his hand. The pain intensifies a little with every heartbeat, like a volume dial being turned up, slowly but surely. 'Do you have any painkillers?' he says.

'Of course,' Raili says. 'I have paracetamol here, and ibuprofen . . .'

He cuts her off impatiently. 'Nothing stronger?' Jolts of pain are throbbing all the way down into his gums now.

'These will do just fine,' she says, and hands him a blister pack.

Annoyed, he snatches it from her hand, punches out three pills and washes them down with water straight from the tap.

When Dan straightens up, he feels like the water is going to come right back up again. He takes a deep breath, nods goodbye to Raili without looking at her and exits the infirmary.

That woman is waiting for him in the hallway: Little Miss 'Paradiso Tropical'. His biggest fan. Alexandra. She lights up when she sees him. The diamond on her front tooth twinkles. He realises he is relieved. He doesn't want to be alone tonight, but he also doesn't want to have to go out hunting.

And now the prey has come to him instead.

'I just wanted to make sure you're okay. It looked so scary. How's your hand?'

Dan holds it up and wiggles the tips of his fingers.

'At least it's still attached,' he says with a smile.

Her giggle is over the top, too eager. 'Are you going back on stage?' she says.

'I think I've had enough audience interaction for one night.'

More giggling. 'So what are you doing for the rest of the night then?' she asks.

He looks at her. Smiles. 'I'm going to fuck you,' he says without much feeling. 'And then I'm going to fuck you again. And if you're sharing a cabin with a friend, you're going to either kick her out or ask her to join in. Your choice.'

Alexandra glares at him with outrage, as though it wasn't exactly what she was after. She glances down at a ring on her left ring finger.

He is getting hard: yet another body part throbbing, and powerfully enough to make him forget the others. His foreskin has slid back and when the head brushes against the fabric of his pants, it is so sensitive it almost burns.

'She's not there,' Alexandra says. 'She's at the club.'

'All right then,' Dan says. 'Is there anything to drink in your cabin?'

She nods.

'Lead the way,' he says.

Pia

Pia studies the ginger man through the window in the door. He's sitting on the floor with his back to them, completely motionless.

She squeezes out another dollop of hand sanitiser, rubs it over the scratch on her wrist that she got in the altercation in the karaoke bar. She notices her hand trembling.

Well then, babe, it's a good thing you didn't become a police officer if you're going to be this shaky.

The voice belongs to her ex-husband. Divorcing him didn't help. He always seems to be there at the back of her mind, ready to speak up.

'Dan was right. He must be high on some shit,' Jarno says.

'Or just completely bloody out of his mind,' Pia retorts.

According to the ID in his wallet, his name is Tomas Thunman. He is looking straight into the camera in the picture, a hint of a smile on his lips. He looks nice in a harmless sort of way.

'Should we call the police?' Jarno asks.

She wants to say yes, get this Tomas Thunman off the *Charisma*, but she shakes her head. 'He's not worth calling the helicopter out for,' she says. 'Let's just leave him here. Pär and Henke will have to help us check on him from time to time.'

They really ought to hand him over to the Finnish police when they dock in Åbo, but instead, they will keep him until they get back to Stockholm. Tomas Thunman is a Swedish citizen. Passing him on to the Finnish authorities only makes life harder for everyone.

Pia and Jarno step into the small security staff office and study the four screens on the wall, one for each drunk tank. The two old men who were fighting at Starlight are sound asleep on the beds in their respective cells. The third houses the woman Pär and Henke saved from being trampled on the dance floor. By way of thanks, she tried to kick them both in the nuts, and she has already vomited twice.

Tomas Thunman is sitting where they left him on the floor of cell number four. On the grainy black-and-white screen he is still completely motionless. Hands on his eyes, as though he wants to protect them from the bright light. Pia is standing so close to the screen she can feel the heat coming off it. Static electricity is making the fine hairs on her arms stand on end.

'Do you think we should get Raili down here to take a look at him?' Jarno says.

'He seems calm enough now,' Pia says. 'I don't want her going in there.'

Jarno looks incredibly relieved.

'I don't know how you feel, but I wouldn't mind a break right about now,' she says.

'Yes, please,' he says without taking his eyes off the screen. 'I'm happy to stay here and have a cup of coffee if you want to head up and talk to Calle.'

Pia gives him a grateful pat on the shoulder. Thinks about how happy Calle looked up on the bridge. She can't stand thinking of him alone in Filip's cabin now.

'Radio me if anything happens,' she says. 'If not, I'll see you in about half an hour.'

She looks back at the screens: every drunk tank spoken for. If the two old men have slept off the worst of it, they can let them out soon. But if anything else happens before then, they are going to have to resort to the plan B she dislikes so heartily: handcuffing their inebriated passengers to the railings in the staff stairwell.

She sends up a quick prayer for a calm night on board the *Charisma*, but she has worked here long enough to trust her gut. And her gut is telling her she might as well face it. It is going to be a long night.

Marianne

The mood on board has changed completely. She walks along the edge of the Club Charisma dance floor, spots an open door in the tall glass wall at the far end of the room and sets her course for it. She needs to get out of here.

The deranged music is so loud she has to cover her ears. Drunken faces are everywhere. There is aggression in the air, like an invisible but distinctly palpable fog. She just saw two bare-chested teenage boys trying to wrestle free of their friends' grip to keep fighting. Their eyes looked like animals'. A security guard came running with his hand ready on his nightstick. Marianne moved on so she wouldn't have to witness the mayhem. But the ones whooping and laughing manically frighten her as well. It is like they could turn at any moment. A misunderstanding, one misinterpreted look, could be the spark landing in kerosene.

Marianne does her best to avoid meeting anyone's eyes, but it is difficult when she is also looking around for Göran.

She couldn't fall asleep after he left. In the end, she got out of bed, freshened up with a handful of wet wipes and pulled on the blue-and-white striped jumper she had meant to save for the next day. She put on fresh lipstick, brushed her hair sufficiently into place, the whole time hoping for a timid knock on the cabin door: Göran, having changed his mind.

But he hasn't changed his mind. She has.

Marianne throws her arms up for protection when a man trips and falls right in front of her feet. She resolutely steps over him and feels the first waft of fresh air from the open door.

People are standing about in droves in front of it; she realises this is not the time for politeness. She pushes forward, hears someone say, 'Take it easy, Grandma,' forges on until she exits onto the afterdeck. It is crowded here too, but at least the air is fresh and the music less loud. She walks to the railing, watches the wide, foamy trail the *Baltic Charisma* leaves in its wake. As she takes a few deep breaths she spots another cruise ship on the horizon. It is unfathomable that there are as many people on board that one too. As many dreams and dramas.

She should go to bed, instead of standing here in the freezing drizzle like an idiot.

There is still a sliver of a chance he might come back to her.

Marianne pushes on through the crowd to the deck running along one of the ship's sides. Considerably fewer people here. And a roof.

She ambles forward, running her hand along the wet metal of the railing. There are a couple of benches along the wall, but one is occupied by a man in a thin tank-top and there is a dark puddle of vomit next to the other. Something like little white pebbles glisten in the dim light. Marianne shakes her head and wraps her arms around herself in the wind. Staying where she is, she gazes out across the water.

She is trying to recall exactly what she told Göran when he left, trying to consider the scene objectively. Was she so busy pretending she didn't need him that she came across as cold and dismissive? Or was the reverse true: was she as easy to read as ever? Did she scare him off with her desperate loneliness? The way her son had once told her she scared him off. *You need to get a life, Mum.*

But Göran had given her his number. He didn't have to do that. Would he have stayed if she had just asked him?

Marianne is so sick of herself. She is exactly the same. She hasn't grown one bit during all her years of solitude. Nothing is ever going to get better. *She* is never going to get better.

She was foolish to think she could escape herself. Stupid, cowardly Marianne. It can't have taken Göran long to figure her out. He probably sussed it out even before they slept together, but didn't want to sound the retreat before bedding her.

Why is she dragging this black cloud of hopelessness around? What is the enormous void inside her that no one seems able to fill? And the worst part is that people seem to sense it from afar. No wonder they keep their distance.

Marianne watches the water rushing along the ship's hull far below: so cold, so deep.

Who would miss her if she disappeared tonight? When they return to Stockholm tomorrow, the cleaning staff would probably report that there were still personal belongings in one of the cabins. But if she went down to her cabin now, packed all her things in her suitcase and then threw it overboard before she climbed over the railings herself? No one would miss her for weeks, not until Christmas was approaching. Eventually, there would be an investigation and someone would glean from her bank statements that the last thing she ever bought was two pints of lager on a booze cruise to Finland.

Marianne backs away from the railing, embarrassed by her morbid fantasies and the shameful pleasure they give her. She has indulged them far too often recently. She should take up Sudoku instead.

There is a movement at the edge of her vision and Marianne jumps. The man on the bench has stood up and is walking towards her.

'I'm sorry if I scared you,' he says. 'I was just wondering if you're okay.'

His voice is deep and melodic. He sounds young. And he is: when he steps into the light she sees that he can't be much older than thirty. He must be even colder than her, sitting out here in just a tank-top.

'Thank you, I'm fine,' she says, and wipes her eyes hard. 'It's just been a weird night.'

Is she imagining it or does he look sad?

'I've turned down a proposal,' he says. 'What about you?'

Dan

Dan is standing next to the bed, feeding his cock to Alexandra. When it feels like he can't get any deeper, he pauses for a few seconds, feeling her gag and then relax her throat so he can push all the way in. Stays there. He has been fucking her for a good long while now and she has taken it, virtually incapacitated by sickly-sweet pear liqueur from one of her tax-free bags and a Xanax he talked her into washing down. He didn't take anything, but he didn't need it. He is higher than ever. It is almost time for the finale, but he wants to make it last; he feels like he could go on for ever, until he drops dead, like his dick is a rocket about to blast him straight into eternity.

What is going on?

From time to time, he checks himself out in the mirror above the desk, turning to get the best possible angle.

He playfully slaps her cheeks with his unharmed left hand. He strokes her face, pretends to hold her nose. He wants to suffocate her with his cock.

His head hurts so bad he can hear it. Something is cracking and creaking in there, somewhere above the roof of his mouth. His heart is beating so fast it is bound to explode at any moment. The euphoria he is feeling is unlike anything he has ever experienced. This is where he is supposed to be, this is the time.

Everything is right. Everything makes sense. Even the pain in his head gives him pleasure. His nerve endings no longer distinguish between different kinds of stimuli. They merge, amplifying one another. His entire fucking body is like a giant sparkler, as though every cell wants to cum.

He slides out of her mouth; thick ropes of saliva stick to him and her panting sounds wet and laboured.

'Can you taste your own pussy?' he whispers. 'Do you like it?'

She mumbles something as he bends over her, pinning her arms above her head; it hurts his injured hand when he squeezes her wrists, and it feels so *good*. He nibbles her earlobe.

His front teeth give way: they swing back like hatches and fall out, disappearing into her hair.

Dan lets go of her and digs around her black curls. Alexandra looks at him in confusion. He disentangles the teeth and holds them up to the light. One of them has split from top to bottom. Pain jolts through his head again; he can taste blood. His heart pounds and pounds.

Running to the mirror, he has to pull his trousers up not to trip. He opens his mouth, barely recognising his own face without his front teeth. And several of the other teeth are shifting in their sockets. He shuts his mouth, letting it fill with blood before swallowing, and almost orgasms as the hot blood slides down his throat.

'What are you doing?' Alexandra slurs from the bed.

The pain is almost unbearable now. Shivers break over him like waves. The line between euphoria and panic is so fine.

Has he ever *felt* as much as he does in this moment?

Alexandra has staggered out of bed behind him. He sticks his left index finger into his mouth and gingerly touches his teeth.

They come loose, fall onto his tongue. He sucks them clean of blood, cups his hand around his mouth and spits them out. Alexandra says something but he can't make out the words. The noises in his head are too loud.

But something else has gone quiet. A sound he has never thought about before, because it was always there.

His heart has stopped beating. Has given up, finally.

Dan closes his eyes and prepares for the vast darkness that is about to devour him.

'What is happening?' Alexandra whines.

Dan opens his eyes. She is standing next to him. Her eyes are clearer now, shifting towards his cupped hand and then back up to his face.

And she screams.

Who would have thought she would be the last thing I ever see?

But no darkness seems forthcoming.

'Did you hurt yourself . . . ? You need help—'

She puts her panties on, pulls her hot-pink top over her head. 'We need to go and get someone,' she says.

He tries to reply, *It's too late. My heart has already stopped beating.* But without teeth only vowels and *sh* sounds come out.

He starts laughing. His face looks bizarre in the mirror. The lower half of it has collapsed.

There are new noises in his head. Something white flashes in the fleshy mess that is his mouth. He leans closer to the glass.

New teeth.

Alexandra's confused fear has warmed up her body. It radiates heat onto his back like the sun on the first day of spring. He eyes her in the mirror.

What he feels is no longer lust. It is something else entirely.

240

Mårten

Mårten is sitting on the bed, watching the tinny old telly, switching between the two dance floors in the hope of spotting Albin. His ears are straining. Every now and then, he thinks he can hear a woman screaming somewhere nearby.

He drinks cognac out of one of the plastic cups from the bathroom, but the numbness won't come. The curtains are drawn. He couldn't stop glancing at the window, afraid of seeing her face there, pressed against the glass.

Mummy.

That damn dream won't leave him alone. Anxiety is purring darkly, deeply in his chest.

And Albin is missing.

Mårten takes another swig. A few drops fall onto his stomach; annoyed, he wipes them off and stares at the glass. There's a thin, straight crack in the plastic.

What has got into Abbe?

He shouldn't be allowed to spend time alone with Lo.

Mårten is sure they have talked about him. Lo obviously believes everything Linda tells her. And Abbe is so impressed with his cousin he will take anything she says on faith.

It goes without saying Mårten won't be allowed a chance to defend himself.

All the things he has tried to keep under control have grown too big. Soon, he won't be able to contain them. How long will he be able to hold on? When is it time to give up? He can trust no one but himself. Do Cilla and Linda really believe he doesn't notice all the knowing looks they exchange? They have probably spent all night bitching about him. Complaining to the kids. It is not like he hasn't noticed Albin pulling away more and more.

He turns the glass to make the crack face away from him, takes another sip. He would do anything for Abbe, but they are trying to turn his son against him.

Mårten finally allows the tears to come. He sounds like a wailing animal. He is so tired of trying and trying and it never being good enough.

Everyone feels so sorry for Cilla for being in a wheelchair, but what about him? No one asks how it makes him feel. No one ever says, *Hey, you're a bloody good bloke, Mårten. Hanging in there. Staying, even though Cilla is no longer the woman you married.*

He is trapped. If he left her, it would unequivocally confirm what a bastard he is.

Mårten glances furtively at the curtains, hanging there so still. He listens to the patter of rain behind them. The screams, if they were ever really there, have stopped.

But he can hear something else on the other side of the wall: a door opening.

He steps out into the corridor. The door to the next cabin is open a crack. He empties his glass and walks across.

Lo is kneeling next to the bed, looking like she is searching for something under it. Mårten clears his throat; her body starts.

'Where's Abbe, then?' he says when she peeks out.

'Shit,' Lo says, and tries to smile. 'You scared me.'

Maybe she can trick Abbe into thinking she is all grown up now, but she is still just a child: a child who was never given proper boundaries.

'Where's Abbe?' he says again.

'I don't know.'

'I think you do,' Mårten says, and takes another step into the room.

Lo's eyes narrow. 'Even if I did, I wouldn't tell you. Maybe he doesn't want to see you right now.'

Mårten tosses the empty cup aside and walks over to her, grabs her by the shoulders and hoists her up off the floor.

Her impertinent attitude falls apart almost immediately.

'Why wouldn't he want that?' Mårten says, and starts shaking her. 'What lies have you been telling him?'

'Nothing,' Lo says, and wriggles out of his grasp.

'I don't believe you.'

'Fine. So don't.'

He blocks her way when she tries to push past him. 'I could tell something was going on when I came in here earlier tonight.'

'Is there anything in particular you're worried about him knowing?' This time the disdain in her voice is unmistakeable.

'Bloody hell,' he says, tears burning in the corners of his eyes. 'I knew it.'

He wipes his eyes so he can see Lo clearly again. She is staring at him, looking uneasy.

'Aren't I lucky to be surrounded by such flawless people? What would happen if I weren't around, I wonder? Then who would you blame?'

Lo shakes her head and pushes past him, pulls something off a hanger by the door and turns to him in the doorway. 'No one has to lie to Abbe, you know,' she says. 'The truth is bad enough. You don't even understand that we had to move to get away from you.'

Rage wells up inside him, pushing out new tears. 'What the fuck are you talking about?'

'Get help,' she says.

'Maybe I should have done what your dad did instead,' he roars. 'Just abandon my child.'

'Yeah!' Lo screams. 'I would pick no dad at all over a dad like you every time!'

She slams the door shut and he feels the sound in every part of his body. It's as though she has shot him.

Dan

Dan hears a door slam shut nearby. The shouting has stopped. He is on all fours in Alexandra's cabin, stroking the carpet. He can feel every fibre beneath his fingertips. Every once in a while he moves his bandaged hand to Alexandra's pallid body and digs around in it, licks blood from his fingers. But there is nothing he wants in it any more. If anything, it sickens him. The blood no longer has any power, any life in it.

Dan stops moving. His hand is itchy under the bandage, which is sodden with Alexandra's fluids. He is breathing heavily, even though he no longer needs to. Just a reflex lingering in the muscles of his ribcage. He can feel Alexandra's blood spreading through his body with each contraction of his heart. She is part of him now. They have become one, the way he was never able to become one with anyone before. This is what he was searching for but never found. It was so simple. The instincts were already in him, telling him to rip out her throat to silence her.

It must have started with the man who bit him. He wanted blood as well, but this new power was too much for him. He was too weak, unable to handle it. He wasn't like Dan.

Dan rips the bandage from his hand, licks the crusts from his knuckles. The cuts from the man's teeth have healed. Nothing is left but smooth pink bumps. He smiles.

He is invincible. Maybe immortal.

He is more than human now. He is something better.

Dan studies the raindrops on the window. They are so beautiful he has to walk over for a closer look. He reaches out to touch the glass. Cold against his fingertips. He puts an ear to the window, listens to the rhythmical patter, but he can also refocus his ears, listen to each individual drop, in the same way that he can see them trickle along separate courses down the glass. Even the vibrations of the ship, which he used to hate so intensely, are singing through him now, as if they have become one.

He turns around, immensely curious to find out what his new senses can do. A couple of his old teeth crunch under the soles of his shoes when he walks towards the door, ground deeper into the blood-soaked carpet.

Dan leaves the cabin, blinking in the sharp light. *The smells. The sounds.* The sixth-deck hallway is one of the *Charisma*'s longest. The air is heavy with the scents of all the people who have passed by; his senses get mixed up so that he can almost see the smells billowing like sheets of vapour in the air. And in one of them, there is a hint of someone young. A girl. She was here just a moment ago.

He follows her trail. New smells waft from the carpet with each step he takes. He can hear a man sobbing in one of the cabins. Music behind a closed door further down. An old person's laughter turning into a coughing fit. *So many lives.*

A couple of suits appear around the corner. They give Dan funny looks when they pass. He is tempted to lunge at them, but he can wait. Their blood is too stagnant, thick and viscous from dehydration. He continues down the hallway, turning the same corner they came from.

His right hand is itching and burning. He stares at it. The scars are almost completely gone.

A loud gaggle of teenagers pass him on the stairs. They smell of fresh air and cigarette smoke. Just like with the drops of rain on the window, he can tell them apart if he focuses. He can feel what they have drunk. What they have eaten. They smell so *different*. So many different things are going on inside them: nervousness, joy, horniness. The feelings permeate their muscles, ooze out of their pores, cover their skin. The smells remind him of vinegar, soap, wet moss, honey, yeast.

He reaches deck seven and is greeted by fresh smells of sex and spilt beer somewhere in the hallways behind him. The tax-free shop is dark and quiet. The synthetic perfume scents seep through the glass, stinging his nostrils, and he loses the young girl's trail. He curses loudly. The arcade game screens flash and he pauses for a minute in the corridor, watching them, hypnotised by the colours.

A middle-aged couple walk past. She is shouting something in Finnish, apparently furious. The man is calm and unperturbed on the surface, but his blood is pumping harder than hers.

A woman in a wheelchair is parked by the information desk. Mika is on the phone, putting on important airs. Dan can feel the woman's fear all the way to where he is. And he understands why the man in the karaoke bar singled him out. It had nothing to do with him being Dan Appelgren. It was his hatred, his frustration, the coke making his veins froth. The smell of him must have been irresistible.

So many feelings everywhere, and Dan wants them. Wants to devour them, make them his. This hunger he has, it can never be satisfied. He feels bottomless. And yet he is more content than he has ever been.

Dan has realised where he is going. Ahead of him, the hallway ends in the double doors leading to the karaoke bar.

The *Baltic Charisma*

The man at the information desk is exceedingly tired of the woman in the wheelchair. He tells her again that he has alerted the on-board security officers, that CCTV cameras are being used to look for them. 'That really is all we can do,' he says.

Henke and Pär are searching the karaoke bar, but the children they are looking for aren't there. But Dan Appelgren is. He is standing in a dark nook by one of the windows. He closes his eyes. Beer is flowing out of the taps at the bar. Glasses are clinking against one another. The faint, constant rocking of the floor. The smell of perfume and breath and ammonia and sweat, salt, leather, wine, inflamed tissue. Oil and powder and sweet milk. Dan is intoxicated by the sensations, by the incomprehensible thing that has happened to him.

One of the lifts stops on the seventh floor. The boy who is not a boy cautiously peeks out before stepping off. He doesn't want to be seen. Doesn't want anyone asking questions about what a child is doing out in the hallways on his own. But he has mastered the art of making himself invisible, and it helps that most of the people still awake are drunk.

Everything about the ship disgusts him: the synthetic smells; the artificial music; the imitation wood and leather and marble.

He muses that the only real thing on board is the gluttony: the greed, the insatiability. Humans are destroying the planet, sucking it dry like parasites. They are killing themselves and each other in a hundred different ways, for a thousand pathetic reasons. Yet they would call him a monster, if they knew. If they believed.

He will make them believe. *It has already begun.* Expectation makes his face look even more childish. He steps out into the hallway, noting the doors to the karaoke bar before letting his eyes rove on. They linger on the small, glass-walled room with rows of benches. People who haven't reserved a cabin are sleeping there. He sneaks in and lies down under one of the benches. A perfect hiding place. If someone were to discover him, he can always tell them he was playing hide and seek with a friend and fell asleep. He listens to a few muffled snores, wonders if his mother has been back to their cabin yet. If she has figured it out.

The dark-haired woman is looking for him on deck two. She can smell the blood and death. She has figured it out, been forced to realise that nothing bad has happened to her son. Quite the opposite. He has crossed every boundary. She is afraid of what this could lead to, of the fury of the Old Ones. She has to avert this disaster. She can feel it coming in every part of her body. It is everywhere on board. *All these people, still so oblivious . . .* She is responsible for them now. She has to save them, and by so doing, herself and her son. The Old Ones will mete out terrible punishment if she doesn't. And she will no longer be able to protect him.

Olli the lorry driver is sprawled on the floor of one of the cabins she passes. He is burning with pain from head to toe. He is locked inside the pain. Only blood can quench his thirst.

Albin

Albin is sitting pressed against the wall under the steel staircase leading up to the observation platform. The wind can't get to him here, but the air is full of tiny droplets. His hoodie is damp, and even though he has tugged his sleeves down over his hands, they are speckled with red spots from the cold. He has pulled up his hood as well, dragging the drawstrings so tight only his face is peeping out.

Albin ponders how long he can stand to stay here. Where he might go next.

He hopes they are worried. He hopes they think he is dead. He hopes they are sorry.

'Good thing it's so warm outside.'

He looks up.

'Can I sit down or what?'

Lo holds out a black jumper. Albin has never been so happy to see anyone. In his heart of hearts he was hoping Lo would figure out he'd gone back here. He just nods.

'You look like that guy in *South Park*,' she says, and giggles.

She quickly glances around before crouching down and crawling in next to him. Albin pulls the jumper on over his hoodie. It smells strongly of Lo's perfume, but is baggy enough on him that you can't tell it is a girl's jumper.

251

Lo conjures another mini-bottle of booze from the sleeve of her jacket. 'Still don't want any?' she says, and unscrews the top. 'It's the last one.'

'No.'

Lo leans back against the wall, takes a sip and shakes her head with a disgusted look on her face. Her tongue very nearly reaches her chin.

'Good thing that's delicious,' Albin says.

She giggles, wipes her mouth.

They sit in silence, watching people moving about the sun deck. A man is walking his little furball of a dog, talking to it in a baby voice. Albin is surprised Lo doesn't have anything mean to say about him.

'Your dad came into the cabin when I was there just now,' she says instead.

It feels like a cannonball is sinking into his stomach in slow motion. Lo hesitates. She pushes away a strand of hair that has come loose from her ponytail and blown into her eyes.

'Was he weird?' Albin asks. 'The way he gets?' It's so strange talking about it openly.

'I think so,' she says. 'Well, yeah, I suppose he was. I think he could sense something had happened. But he didn't know. So you don't have let on if he asks. I mean, if you don't want to. It's all the same to me.'

Albin looks at her. He thinks about his dad. About his mum and Linda. It is too late for lies now. Having said it once makes it impossible to keep pretending. His mum will never be able to say that his dad is tired again without knowing what Albin knows.

Whatever happens, something has to change now.

The dark sky is visible through the gaps between the steps. He squints against the drizzle.

'Is it true you want to be an actress when you grow up?'

Lo groans. 'Did Mum tell you that? I love how good she is at keeping her mouth shut.'

'So it's true?'

'Yes. But I know what it sounds like when *she* says it. Like I'm being a complete child for thinking it can happen. Just because she never had the guts to do anything with her life.'

'Why do you want that?' he says. 'I mean, to be an actress?'

'Why not?'

Albin shrugs. It would be his worst nightmare to be on stage or in front of a camera, with lots of people watching, registering his every move.

'Is it because you want to be famous?'

Lo takes another sip. 'No. It just seems great not to have to be yourself all the time.'

She looks at him solemnly and he nods, but he doesn't understand why Lo would want to be someone else, because there is no one else like her.

'Either way, I'm not going to be like my mum,' Lo says after a while. 'She is such a fucking coward. She's, like, afraid to live. At least for real. She just *exists*. Know what I mean?'

'I think so.'

'It's like she never does anything. Things happen, obviously, but she never makes them happen. I don't even think she's ever been in love properly, she's more like, *Oh well, what do you know, someone likes me so I guess we'd better go out*, and then after a while he dumps her and she's just like, *Oh well, what do you know*, and carries on existing.'

Lo looks utterly bizarre when she's imitating Linda. She juts her chin out to make an underbite and her eyes go completely flat. Albin isn't sure if he is allowed to giggle, but he also isn't sure he can stop himself.

'I assume it was the same when she had me,' Lo says. 'She was, like, *Oh well, what do you know, my belly seems to be getting big, maybe there's a baby in there, oh well, I'll just keep on existing then.* I am so never ever going to be like her. I might as well kill myself. She's not really living, you know. She doesn't even seem to have feelings.' Lo takes another sip and moves closer to him, so their upper arms touch. 'If it weren't for Soran, I'd run away to Los Angeles.'

She is so determined, he believes her. Lo would be able to make it all the way to the USA on her own and not be afraid.

'Can't you bring me with you if you go?' he says. 'I don't want to stay here either.'

Not without you. But of course he can't say that out loud.

'All right,' Lo says.

'But are you sure that's where you want to go? I hear it's not at all as cold there.'

Lo laughs. 'I know. What a shame.'

'Yep. Darkness and cold is my number one advice.'

'Imagine if we went and did it,' she says. 'Imagine if we just left, for real. I wonder what Mum would say?'

'*Oh well, what do you know,*' Albin says, and Lo bursts out laughing.

Dan

Dan is still standing by the windows in the karaoke bar. No one has spotted him yet, not even Pär and Henke, who were in here, clearly looking for someone. Maybe it was him they were after. Maybe Alexandra's friend came back to their cabin, discovered the body. Maybe they have figured out he did it, seen CCTV footage of him leaving her cabin just a short while ago. The thought doesn't make him scared in the slightest, just excited. He is trying to keep calm, but his body doesn't want to stand still. Every muscle is humming with energy.

Johan is filling in as host in Dan's absence. He is on stage in his grungy T-shirt, clearly uncomfortable, asking a fake-tanned booze hag what her name is. Fredrika. She is from Sala. Yes, she is having a lovely cruise. The food is so good. And the sea is so lovely. And she is singing her favourite Whitney Houston song.

Johan steps off the stage and Dan goes to meet him at the technician's booth.

'You're back?' Johan says, looking relieved.

'Yep,' Dan replies.

'Is everything okay?'

'Never been better.'

Johan nods and turns on 'I Wanna Dance with Somebody'. The woman on stage spins and wiggles her flat bum.

Dan notices Johan looking at his hand, his smooth knuckles.

The woman starts singing, if you can call it that. Dan closes his eyes and sinks deeper into the sensory impressions. So many feelings in here, undiluted in the cramped space. They seem to bounce off one another, causing each other to shrink or grow.

'Dan?'

He opens his eyes and meets Johan's searching gaze.

'Are you on something?'

Dan grins. Johan must have suspected, of course, after all their nights in here. But he has never asked straight out before.

'I don't think I need that any more,' Dan says, and walks off towards the stage.

The audience is clapping to the beat as Dan makes his way forward. He has despised them for so long. Depended on them. Whatever it is that has happened to him, at least he is finally free of them now.

Dan steps out into the spotlight; his eyes sting as if he is staring straight into the sun. But he smiles, and for the first time on this stage his smile is one hundred per cent genuine.

Fredrika keeps singing, smiling shyly at him.

He tears the microphone out of her hand. 'Really, Fredrika, I think we should let Whitney rest in peace.'

A few members of the audience gasp; others rouse themselves from their half-sleep. The muscle guys in tight tank-tops laugh raucously. Fredrika looks at him uncertainly.

'See this hand?' Dan says, holding it up and making a fist. 'Get it?'

No one answers. The clicking of mobile phone cameras echoes in the darkness beyond the spotlight.

'No,' Dan says, 'of course you don't. You have no idea what's going on here. Even I don't.' He feels as if he is several feet taller in the bright light. His thoughts are racing through his head. He can't seem to catch them.

'I would like to kill all of you,' he says, 'every last one. You are so fucking stupid, and there are so many of you . . . I would be doing the world a service . . . It would be much better off without you. You have no power over me any more. Do you know what it's like to—'

The speakers fall silent. Johan has turned off the mic. But Dan doesn't need it. His voice is clearer than ever before; it makes his chest vibrate.

'—to be dependent on people you despise? To rely on idiots like you? You are so fucking pathetic, with your terrible taste, your self-centred little lives, your paltry dreams . . .'

Several people in the audience boo him. Dan smiles at them.

'Come on, Dan,' Johan says. 'That's enough now.'

'And you know it, deep down,' he continues. 'That's why you come here, to make yourselves even stupider, drinking until you turn into cavemen . . .'

'Shut the fuck up,' shouts a man who has got to his feet at the far end of the room, 'or you're going to get a bloody good drubbing. I'll make bloody sure of it! Real bloody sure!'

With his new senses, Dan can make out the man's outline, even with the spotlights blinding him. The smell of him. The way the air in the room moves around him.

'No one is going to remember you,' Dan says, pointing at him. 'Your grandchildren or great-grandchildren will find an old photograph of you and ask who you are, but there will be no one left who can answer.'

A beer bottle comes flying at him and he casually ducks; it breaks against the wall behind him.

'You are trying to find the meaning of your meaningless lives, but you have missed the crucial point, that there is no point . . .'

Dan trails off when something in the room changes. He holds his hand up to shield his eyes and spots a white-blond boy in the darkness by the entrance. The boy is studying him, fascinated. And Dan knows instantly that there is something special about him.

He recognises himself.

Calle

Calle is sprawled on Filip's bed, fully clothed, staring at the ceiling. He could drink his own weight in alcohol and it would still do nothing to silence his thoughts. They are far too loud when he is left alone with them; they outnumber and overpower him. He has nothing to distract himself with. Filip doesn't even have an old newspaper lying around. Every now and then he glances at the internal telephone on Filip's desk. It would be so easy to call the suite. Just dial the four numbers: 9318.

But what would he say if Vincent picked up?

He takes a slug of vodka straight from the bottle. The white-gold ring is heavy on his finger. Warm against his skin. He thinks about when he slipped it into his bag this morning. How nervous he was.

Was that just normal? Something that comes with the territory? Or did he already know that Vincent was going to say no? That something had crept in between them? Was that why he had decided to make such a big deal of the proposal, in front of an audience, in a context where Vincent didn't feel at all at home?

'*What was I supposed to do, in front of all those people? What was I supposed to say?*'

A cavalcade of memories of everything that has happened since midsummer rushes over him in a jumble, through apparently disjointed chains of associations. He scrutinises them all, turning them over and over in this new light, trying to find a point where everything went wrong: the reason why Vincent is on the fence. He has to find it and come up with a solution, and then tell Vincent what it is. He is going to fix this, for both of them.

His thoughts spin faster and faster and Calle wonders if this is what it feels like, the first few steps towards losing your mind.

There is a knock on the door. Has Filip told Vincent where he is after all? But no, it is probably Sophia. *What are you doing here? Come and celebrate with us already! We need to toast you!*

Calle lies stock-still.

'It's me,' a familiar voice says on the other side of the door.

He puts the bottle down on the floor, almost knocks it over but then manages to catch the neck at the last second. He opens the door. Pia is standing outside in her uniform. He can tell straight away that she knows what has happened.

Pia puts her arms around him, and even though she is smaller than him, he feels completely enveloped.

'What happened?' she says.

'I don't know.'

They sit down on the bed. Pia looks haggard in the light from the bedside lamp. She is pale; the circles under her eyes have darkened since they were standing together on the bridge. When he had just proposed to Vincent. And she hugged him and cried and said she was happy for him.

If only he could cry. If only his thoughts would shut up so there would be room for feelings.

'How are you?' he asks.

'I think I'm coming down with the flu,' Pia says, and presses her fingers against her temples, moving her jaw slowly from side to side. 'Hopefully it's just a tension headache.'

'Tough night?'

'Not as tough as yours,' Pia replies.

Calle attempts to shoot her a grin, but it doesn't really come off. He picks the vodka bottle up off the floor and takes another swig. 'Tell me,' he says.

'Wouldn't it be better to talk about you instead?'

He shakes his head. 'I would like to think about anything other than me.'

'All right,' Pia says. 'Well, for example, some lunatic attacked Dan Appelgren on stage. He *bit* him. On the hand.'

'Jesus,' Calle says. 'What did you do?'

'We put the guy in the drunk tank. It was all four of us against him and we still only just managed to get him under control.'

Pia shakes herself. He can tell what happened affected her more than she would ever let on. Unlike him, Pia rarely exposes any weakness. Now, knowing a bit more about the world and having gained some measure of critical distance from the *Charisma*, he realises that she could hardly afford to, being a woman in a work-place like this.

'Jesus,' he says again, because he can't think of anything else.

'Appelgren will be fine,' she says. 'He's been to see Raili. She patched his hand up.'

'I'm having a hard time sympathising with him,' Calle says. 'At least if all the stories are true.'

'I know,' Pia says. 'We've had our fair share of distraught girls, but none of them wanted to press charges. It sucks the big one, but in a way, I understand them.'

He studies her face, wondering what she is thinking. He knows almost nothing about Pia's ex-husband, apart from random details that have leaked out here and there. What little he has been able to puzzle together has been drawn more from her total avoidance of the subject.

'He was bloody unpleasant to Jenny at one of the staff parties,' she continues.

'Jenny?'

'The girl who sings down at Starlight. In the end, Filip had to step in. We tried to persuade her to speak to the managers, but she was afraid of losing her job.'

Calle takes another sip, making the vodka slosh around inside its bottle.

'Are you sure you want to drink more?'

'Yes. I'm trying to get drunk.'

'Seems to me you're drunk enough as it is.'

'Not even close.'

'I can hardly blame you,' she says.

They look at each other in silence. Pia absent-mindedly pats a cut on her wrist.

'I should never have proposed here,' Calle says. 'I should never have proposed at all.'

'Don't you think you can work it out? Maybe he just needs time to mull it over?'

Calle rubs his eyes. 'I don't even know if we're together any more. And I don't know what the fuck to do now.'

'You'll figure something out,' she says. 'Maybe not tonight, maybe not tomorrow, but you'll figure it out.'

'I wish I believed you.'

'Me too.' She puts her arm around him, and he suddenly feels grief flickering to life inside him.

'I'm happy you came by,' he says. 'I was just starting to wonder if I was losing my mind up here.'

'Of course I came by.'

'Yes,' he says, and his voice is thick now, a breath away from the tears that could set him free. 'Of course you did.'

Her belt crackles. Whoever is trying to reach Pia right now, he loathes that person.

'Now what?' she mutters, reaches for her radio and pushes the button. 'Pia, over!'

'We have trouble down at the gaming machines on seven,' Mika's voice says, much too loudly in the cramped, quiet cabin. 'Jarno is already on his way. Are you coming?'

'I'm coming,' Pia says, and shoots Calle a resigned look.

'And keep an eye out for Dan Appelgren,' Mika says. 'He flipped his lid on stage just now. He might be in shock after what happened, but to be honest, I reckon he's high. The captain wants to see him.'

Pia squeezes Calle a little harder with the arm that is still around his back.

'Just another day on the *Baltic Charisma*?' he says.

'True story. And the drunk tanks are all full. Don't you miss working here?'

Pia

Pia jogs down the hallway and opens the steel door to the staff stairwell, hoping fervently that Calle will manage to sleep until morning. He is going to wake up with a hell of a hangover on top of everything else, but at least she can be there for him tomorrow.

Unless she is passed out herself by then. Her head is aching dully – even the roof of her mouth is taut – and she is feeling dizzy.

Pia pauses in the doorway. She is so tired. Breaking up yet another fight, even walking down the stairs to get to it, feels impossibly difficult. She clutches the door handle, suddenly afraid. She knows this tiredness and it has nothing to do with the flu. It is a tiredness that makes everything pointless. She has always managed to keep it at bay on board; it's when she is at home, alone, that it catches up with her. Inside her, there is a dark space she thinks of as a basement. It's where she shoves all her forbidden thoughts and locks them in. Nails the door shut and prays it will hold. And it does, for the most part. But sometimes the door opens a crack, and at those times she can't make it out of bed on her days off.

She shakes herself, runs down two flights of stairs and spots Dan Appelgren on his way into the goods lift. He is carrying a boy in a red hoodie in his arms. Dan starts, but the child eyes her calmly and curiously. He is almost unbelievably adorable, like something out of an old-fashioned soap ad.

'Hello,' he says. 'Do you work here?'

'I do,' Pia says. 'I'm the one who makes sure people don't misbehave.'

She looks at Dan. His pupils are big and black. 'What are you doing here?' she says.

'My nephew is visiting,' Dan replies. 'I'm just giving him a bit of a tour.'

'I'm going to work on a boat too when I grow up,' the boy says precociously, 'but I'm going to be the captain.'

'That's great. You can never have too many good captains,' Pia says, her eyes still on Dan. She is pondering how to proceed without scaring the child.

'How are you feeling after . . . after what happened?' she says.

'Dandy,' Dan replies. 'Never better, actually.'

He holds his hand up for her to see and she stares at it in bewilderment. No wounds. Not even any scars.

'Fast healer,' he says, anticipating her.

She glances at the boy. For a split second she thinks she glimpses a hint of something in his smile: something that doesn't belong in a child's face.

As if he is mocking her, as if he knows something she doesn't.

She suddenly becomes aware of the pounding in her head again. It has grown roots in her sinuses.

'Captain Berggren wants to talk to you,' she says. 'I think it would be good if you went up to the bridge as soon as possible.'

'In a minute,' Dan says.

'I need to get back to Mummy soon,' the boy says.

'Of course,' Pia says, and tousles his hair.

But it feels wrong. The boy looks at her searchingly, an almost imperceptible smile curling the outermost corners of his mouth. She pulls her hand back.

'Pia?'

She jumps when Mika's voice comes on the radio. 'Here,' she says, after pushing the button.

'I think you should hurry. Jarno is already there. It's about to turn properly lively.'

'On my way. I just ran into Dan.'

'Tell him to go see Berggren immediately.'

'He will. He's just showing his nephew around. Then he'll head straight there.' She turns to Dan. 'Right?'

Dan nods impatiently, but the boy smiles politely and waves. 'Be careful,' he says.

Göran

Göran holds on to the banister as he walks down the steep stairs past the car deck. He has no particular desire to fall and break his neck.

He pulls the door to deck two open and notes with a grimace that the septic-tank smell has grown more intense. He continues downwards, breathing through his mouth as he turns right and finds the short hallway where Marianne's cabin is. Thankfully, he made a point of memorising her cabin number. One of the doors at the start of the hallway is ajar. It is dark inside and he ponders whether he ought to pull it shut. Someone might be asleep in there, or might have left and forgotten to lock their door. But he quickly dismisses the thought. This is not his problem.

He walks up to Marianne's door at the far end of the hallway and taps it lightly. Fixing his ponytail, he realises that he is shifting from one foot to the other like a nervous schoolboy.

'Marianne?' he calls. 'It's me, Göran.'

He waits, straining his ears, but there are no sounds coming from cabin 2015. He vacillates for a minute. Does he really want to wake her? Yes, he does. He wants to see Marianne again. He wants to lie down next to her, between the sheets in the bed where they made love. He knocks again, harder this time.

Is she awake? Is she angry with him? She looked so disappointed when he said he was leaving, but he had thought she would be coming with him, that it was a given. And when he realised he had messed it up, it was already too late: she looked like she'd wanted him gone as soon as possible. Maybe she doesn't want to see him now.

He knocks a third time and hears a shuffling sound, but it is not coming from Marianne's cabin.

Göran turns around and can't see anyone in the hallway. But the gaping door seems to have opened further.

Suddenly he is convinced someone is lurking in the dark behind it, watching him, and Göran is acutely aware that he is in a dead end and that there is no one else around.

He turns back to Marianne's door and pounds it hard.

The decks above him are full of people, all hustle and bustle. Music and fresh air. He tries to remind himself of that, but down here it is hard to believe.

The darkness behind the crack in the door seems to be spreading out into the hallway. He listens hard.

This is ridiculous. Just some curious person staring at him from inside their cabin. So what? He should yank that door open and stare back.

Instead, he starts walking back down the hallway, not taking his eyes off the open door for a second. His heart skips a beat when he thinks he sees something moving inside.

He feels relieved when he turns the corner and spots a staircase nearby, closer than the one he came down. It doesn't matter; he just needs to get out of here. He resists the impulse to run.

He hasn't felt like this since he was a little boy afraid of the dark and his mother asked him to fetch something from the basement. It was like this different world within their house: a dark world with strange smells. He always ran up the stairs like a maniac once he found what he'd been sent there to get, certain a mummy's hand would appear behind the steps, that sharp werewolf claws would rip open his back . . .

Göran puts a foot on the first step and hears the door in Marianne's corridor slide open.

No, of course it's not a monster, but there are plenty of humans to be scared of, and this could be a bloody madman. Who knows?

He glances back behind him. A man in his fifties is standing there in nothing but his underpants, glaring at him balefully. His body is hefty, shapeless. Furry belly, wild tufts of hair on his shoulders. Bloody vomit is caked in his chest hair. But the most frightening part of him is his eyes.

It's as if all the things Göran was afraid of as a child have suddenly found him: here, of all places.

He bolts up the stairs.

The man follows.

An arm shoots out, taking Göran's feet out from under him. He falls. Lands heavily on his back, tries to kick out at the man, but his ponderous heft slams down on top of him, pinning him down. Göran can hear his ribs breaking on the sharp edges of the steps. He doesn't have enough air in him to scream.

The man's teeth snap above his face, then comes burning pain, and Göran sees the man spitting something out.

He realises it's his nose.

My nose is gone.

The man licks the crater in the middle of Göran's face and bites him again, and in one horrible moment of clarity, Göran can feel the man's teeth slide effortlessly through skin and tissue. He is afraid to move, afraid his face will come off. Blood is rushing down his throat, making him splutter. It feels like he is drowning in it. The man's teeth scrape against his cheekbone. His broken ribs jab at everything they are meant to protect inside him.

Göran's field of vision is blurring. The lamps in the ceiling are distant stars. The teeth sink into his throat.

But that too is far away now. Göran is no longer there. His flesh and his self are no longer one and the same. The two halves glide apart. He notes that his suffering body is being dragged back down the steps, into the dark cabin, but he himself doesn't need to go with it. He is no longer trapped in his body; everything he is is on its way somewhere else, far away from here.

Dan

Dan has brought the boy into the goods lift and pushed the emergency button between two floors. It is rarely in use at this time of night, when both the tax-free shop and kitchen are closed. It was the only place he could think of where they would be able to talk in private for a while, without people overhearing, without CCTV cameras. The smell of blood from at least three different people wafts from the boy. And other smells: rotting flowers, liniment.

'You are so new,' the boy says, looking up at him, 'and already so finished. I have never beheld anyone like you.'

The little boy is fascinating to look at, with his round cheeks, hair the kind of white-blond you only see in very young children, and yet such an ancient look in his bright eyes. And his way of speaking: like a character in one of the black-and-white films they run on TV in the afternoons.

'You're the man on the posters,' the boy says.

Dan nods.

'You have already fed,' the boy says, and leans in closer. 'A woman. Your own age. You turned while you were . . . with her.'

His eyes are definitely not those of a child now. Dan can only nod again.

'And you liked it,' the boy continues. 'You liked it more than anything else and you already want more.'

271

'Yes,' Dan says. He can hear that he sounds breathless. Reverent. 'Who are you?' he asks.

'My name is Adam. At least, that is what I'm calling myself now. It felt appropriate.' He fires off a crooked smile. Yellow teeth can be glimpsed between the lips of his tiny rosebud mouth.

Dan can't help feeling revolted.

'Your body is permanently transformed . . . It is dead,' Adam tells him, 'but *you* are more alive than ever. You can feel it, can you not? You feel more than you ever have before. Your senses have been flung open. You can harbour pain and pleasure at a pitch you have never experienced before.'

Dan nods: yes, that is exactly right.

'What am I?' Dan asks. 'What are we?'

'We have gone by many names. There have been stories about creatures who drink blood for as long as humans have been able to speak. Today we are called vampires.'

There it is: the word. As soon as Dan hears it he realises he has been waiting for it.

'We have become myth. Fairy tales. Something to laugh at. The modern world has swept us away. And our own kind have let it happen, because it has been said that it is safer for us.' The boy crosses his arms. His teeth flash again, too big for his mouth.

Dan sinks down on the floor so that he and the boy are level.

There are so many questions he wants to ask, but there is one he needs answered first.

'Am I immortal?' he says. 'I feel immortal.'

'No, but you will not grow old for a very, very long time. And you are practically invulnerable.'

Dan doesn't like that word, *practically.*

'You don't have to worry about turning to ash in sunlight,' Adam says with a smile. 'You can cross thresholds even if no one invites you. You have no reason to fear crosses or holy water or any other superstition. Hundreds upon hundreds of years from now you will look as you do in this moment, more or less, anyway. And you will be as strong, as hungry for life, your own and others'.' Adam's eyes take on a religious sheen. 'You have been given an extraordinary gift,' he says.

Dan looks down at his hands: the strong hands of a man. The bulging veins, filled with Alexandra's blood. He thinks about his dad's hands, how they looked at the end, covered in age spots, fingers curled into talons. And then he looks at Adam's hands: childishly chubby with little indentations like dimples at each knuckle.

'How old are you?' he asks.

A shadow passes across the boy's face. 'I was born around the turn of the last century. I have been locked in this body ever since.'

It is so absurd Dan almost bursts out laughing.

'I lived in Stockholm then,' Adam says gravely. 'Me and my mother, we have been travelling around Europe and North Africa for more than a hundred years, constantly on the move so as not to arouse suspicion. Not that anyone would be able to fathom it . . . but they might ask questions. A child who never grows up, who never seems to develop. We have kept on the periphery, to ourselves, always been so *careful*. Only fed once or twice a month, when we absolutely had to. It has not been a life worth living. It has been a protracted punishment. Much longer than life imprisonment.' He leans back against the orange metal of the lift door.

His smile is bitter. Nothing like a child's. 'My mother thought she was saving me. I was afflicted with what was once called consumption. You call it TB. I do not remember it myself any more, but I have often wished she had let me die. What is the point of a long life, of becoming a superior being, if you have to live like a frightened animal?'

Dan knows something about being forced into an undignified existence. He knows something about wanting redress.

'All because of ancient rules put in place when the world was utterly different,' Adam continues. 'It has been said that we have to be careful, because if our contagion spread across the world we would soon run out of humans. There would no longer be anything for us to eat. But look at them: it is only a matter of time before they destroy themselves and this world. They don't deserve it.'

'No,' Dan says, with a level of feeling that almost moves him to tears.

'I am not going to adhere to the Old Ones' rules any longer. I am going to make my own. And I would rather die tonight than live for hundreds, maybe thousands of years in fear.'

'Better to burn out than to fade away,' Dan says, and feels rapture rear up inside him like a big and mighty stallion.

'The whole world will be talking about us tomorrow,' Adam says. 'They will fear and respect us again.'

A shiver runs through Dan. 'How?'

'I have created more of us here on board tonight. I believe the first one was the one who bit you.'

'Yeah. I thought he was some kind of fucking psycho.'

The boy looks at him as though he has said something unforgivable, but then his features soften slightly. 'It has already started

274

spreading. Did you not notice something peculiar about the security officer we just met?'

Pia. Dan pictures her: her searching eyes on him and Adam.

'Aside from her not leaving us the fuck alone?' Dan says.

It is an attempt at a joke, but Adam doesn't smile. Dan pulls himself together. Tries to figure out what Adam is getting at. He hadn't been particularly focused on that butch old bitch. But there had been something about her.

'She was afraid,' he says.

'Yes,' the boy replies. 'She is becoming one of us, but she has not understood it yet. It has not progressed very far. It may have been a superficial wound. All she knows is that something is wrong and she is trying to fight that realisation.'

'He must have bitten her too,' Dan says. 'The guy who bit me.' He thinks back to when the security officers dragged the man out of the karaoke bar and a peal of laughter threatens to bubble up inside him. Does this make Pia and him some kind of vampire siblings or what?

'That may be. There are more like him on board,' Adam says. 'At the moment, they are like newborn infants: nothing but emotions and instincts. They are hungry. They need blood. It can take anything from hours to months before they become sentient creatures again.'

Dan looks at him, lets his words sink in. 'It's going to be bedlam,' he says, picturing it. Hundreds of them. The screaming. The panic. The snapping teeth.

'Exactly,' Adam says, and smiles, wider and wider. Delighted. Excited. 'But you, on the other hand, you have already left the infant stage. You were made for this.'

Dan nods. He knows in his heart, which is no longer beating, why he got through it.

Unlike Pia and the bloke who bit him, he *welcomed* the change. He wasn't afraid. He didn't fight it. He simply rode the wave.

'I could never have hoped for someone like you,' Adam says. 'If you help me, we can establish a new world order tonight. We can become a proud race again: walk with our backs straight and our heads held high through the ruins.'

'What do you want me to do?' Dan says without a moment's hesitation.

'You know how this boat works. I want it to take us all the way to port. Like when the *Demeter* reached England . . . It would be poetic, don't you think? To have life surpass art?'

Adam laughs, displaying the teeth that are more than a hundred years old, and Dan tries to look as though he knows what he is talking about.

'Then chaos will engulf the whole world in a matter of weeks,' Adam says.

Dan lines them up in his mind, all the people he hates on board. Filip. Jenny. Captain Berggren. Birgitta from Grycksbo. The security staff. All those goddamn old hags in their white-and-blue striped jumpers.

An army of newborns. The living dead. Afraid, desperate, hungry.

He and this boy who is not a boy will lead them.

A new world order.

All his life he has known he was meant for something special. And here it is.

Dan has gone through the same safety drills as everyone else who works aboard the *Charisma*. He knows the emergency routines. If something goes badly wrong, the captain sends a distress call to port demanding a rescue.

There is no time to lose if they want to remain undisturbed and glide into in Åbo Harbour like a big fucking bomb.

I saw a ship a-sailing.

Adam looks at him with his big eyes.

'I know what we need to do first,' Dan says.

The *Baltic Charisma*

In a cabin on deck nine, a young girl named Lyra is leaning on the bathroom sink, squeezing her hands against the porcelain. Crying without tears. She spits, and a handful of bloody molars land, roots and all, on top of her other teeth. She gingerly tongues the white shards emerging from her gums. They are so sharp they cut the tip of her tongue. Her blood tastes sweet and metallic and she knows she should feel disgusted, but she doesn't. *It tastes like life*, she thinks, and panic swells inside her. *Who was that boy?* What *was he?* She tries to cling to consciousness, link one thought to another, but it is difficult to hold on. *He came in. He was cute. So cute. Those eyes. He was a child, but not. He took my hand and bit me. Not too hard, not as hard as he could have. He could have bit straight through but he didn't.*

Her heart is beating ever slower. She feels like she is on a roller-coaster. Down in the deepest dips between each beat. *He didn't want to kill me. But what did he want? This. He wanted this.*

She drops to her knees and rests her head against the cool sink. It feels nice. Her headache has faded to almost nothing. Lyra waits for her next heartbeat, but it never comes. Her body is still. Quiet. The cabin door opens. *Mum. Dad.* Lyra can smell their scents; they intermingle. *Like when you mix all the colours and it just turns brown.* She wants them to hold her. She wants them to leave. *Something terrible is about to happen.*

Must. Warn. Them.

Lyra's mum opens the bathroom door and starts screaming when she sees the blood, the teeth in the sink, her pale daughter on the floor.

Not far from there, Dan closes a door behind himself and Adam and walks down the corridor to the bridge. The little boy's arms are wrapped tightly around Dan's neck. His frail body is virtually weightless, but Dan has just witnessed what Adam is capable of. Every drop of blood spattered on the walls of the engine room is proof of it. The screams are still ringing in Dan's ears; they are singing in his blood, their blood, which belongs to him now, filling him and making him stronger. Every time his heart contracts, he can feel the blood shifting, waves of life being pushed through his body.

Adam tells him his mother is going to try to stop them when she figures it out.

'Then we will stop her,' Dan whispers, lifting him up higher on his hip.

'You mustn't hurt her,' Adam says.

Dan makes no reply. He walks up the narrow staircase. The officers turn around when they hear them. Adam takes in all the screens, flashing lights and blinking buttons of the bridge.

'Berggren wanted to see me,' Dan says. 'I can talk to him now, if someone would go get him.'

On deck two, Olli the lorry driver is lying motionless in his cabin. Göran is sprawled next to him, an almost imperceptible twitching of one of his hands the only movement. His eyes, which Marianne liked so much, are closed.

Marianne

He is no longer studying her with that searching gaze, so she dares to glance at him from time to time. He is handsome, almost too handsome: he cuts a figure that would not look out of place in a classic film. Aside from the tattoos, of course. She wonders what they will look like when his skin starts wrinkling. On the other hand, men age more gracefully. Yet another example of life's little injustices.

They have sat down in McCharisma. It is relatively quiet here; the real carousers have made their way to the dance floors. Outside the pub doors there is a steady flow of people going to and from Charisma Starlight.

'What were you really doing out on deck?' he says.

She swallows and tries to think of something to say.

'You seemed to . . . to have a lot on your mind,' he continues. 'I almost thought you . . . that you were going to do something stupid.'

And it suddenly becomes clear to her why he insisted on having a drink with her. Shame makes her cheeks glow.

It takes considerable effort to appear unperturbed. She has longed to break out of her invisibility, but had forgotten how unpleasant it can be to look at yourself through the eyes of others.

'I wasn't about to jump, if that's what you're asking,' she says curtly.

But she had been toying with the idea. What does that say about her? Enough for her to know she had better keep her mouth shut. 'I was just trying to think about some things more clearly,' she goes on. 'Myself mostly.'

'Me too, I suppose,' he says with a sad smile.

She takes a sip of her Rioja.

'Any luck?' she asks. 'Because I have no idea what I'm doing.'

His smile widens. Had she been thirty, forty years younger, that smile would have set her heart a-fluttering.

'I thought age brought wisdom,' he says.

'The only thing that age brings you is more decisions to regret.'

The force of his laughter surprises her and she catches herself smiling back.

'Vincent,' he says, extending his hand.

'Marianne,' she says, and takes it.

She notes the ring on his left index finger. Hammered silver or white gold, she can't tell the difference. It is thick. Must have been expensive.

Vincent notices her glance, because he holds his hand up and studies it. 'I said yes at first, because I didn't know how to say no.'

She takes another sip and waits.

'There were so many people there, and I didn't want to be hurtful. But of course I was.'

'At the end of the day, it's probably more hurtful to marry someone just to be nice,' she says. 'And you don't get a medal of valour for self-sacrifice either. That I can vouch for.'

She checks herself, wondering what compelled her to give voice to that bitter remark, but Vincent just nods thoughtfully.

'I should have asked for some time to think about it before saying anything . . . I was just so taken aback.'

'I get that,' Marianne says, hesitating before pressing on. 'I'm probably being old-fashioned, but I actually think it's the man's job to propose.'

Vincent looks at her in bewilderment. She must have sounded ancient. Of course, the young people have different rules nowadays, even if she doesn't understand them.

'But I know things are more equal nowadays,' she hurries to add.

'It *was* a man proposing,' Vincent says.

She hesitates, unsure whether she has understood him right. 'To you?'

'Yes.'

It takes an even bigger effort to sound unperturbed this time. When Sisyphus heaved that boulder of his up the hill, it was a nice little stroll compared to this.

'And you . . . you are special friends?' She can find no better word for it.

Vincent's smile is reply enough.

She clears her throat. Her cheeks are glowing again. Pulsating. She doesn't want to think about what two men might do to each other in bed; she's not even sure she has rightly understood how it works. Now she looks at Vincent and her stupid brain is trying to picture it, but it seems so outlandish. 'I'm sorry,' she says. 'I was just so surprised. You don't look like one . . . of them.'

'Like one of them? Like I'm gay, you mean?'

'Yes,' Marianne says, uncertainly. 'Or whatever word we're allowed to use nowadays. It's not easy to keep up, you know . . .'

'It's okay.'

'I just don't want you to think I'm prejudiced,' she insists. 'I have no opinion on how other people live their lives. God knows I have no cause to get on any sort of high horse.'

'It's okay,' he says again.

She exhales, raises her glass for another sip and accidentally downs the rest of her wine.

Silence falls between them, but somehow it doesn't feel as awkward as maybe it should.

'I just made love to a new man for the first time in . . . Well, I wonder if you were even born,' she hears herself say, and then a thought strikes her. 'I don't even know his surname. What do you say to that?'

Why doesn't she have a filter any more? Why is she saying whatever comes to mind to this poor young man?

'In this case, I reckon *I'm* the one who shouldn't get on any sort of high horse,' Vincent says. 'Would you like another round?'

Marianne catches herself nodding.

'Where is he now then?' Vincent asks when he returns to their table. 'The man with no surname?'

'I don't know.'

And then she tells him the whole story, obviously not sharing lewd details about what happened when the lights were out, but what she does tell him feels almost as revealing. Vincent just looks at her, doesn't seem to think she is out of her mind, and maybe that is why she concludes by telling him the most embarrassing part.

'I've been so lonely. Sometimes, I don't even feel entirely real. I never thought I would be one of those lonely old people you hear about, but . . .'

She spreads her hands. 'Turns out ending up alone is easier than you think,' she concludes.

'Maybe I should have said yes after all,' Vincent says, trying to smile.

She shakes her head forcefully. 'Not because you think it's a safe investment,' she says. 'I was married, wasn't I? No, I think friends is the way to go. I just let them drift away over the years. I always put family first. And one day my husband was gone and the children had moved away.'

She silences herself with a big gulp of wine. She has never thought about this before. Maybe the geographical distance is helping her see things more clearly.

'Why did you say no?' she asks. 'To the proposal?'

Vincent sighs and presses his fingertips against his forehead. She notices that he has barely touched his wine and forces herself to leave off her own glass while it is still half full.

'I don't know,' he says, in a way that makes it clear to her that he does know, he just needs a moment to admit it to himself.

She waits, fiddling with the foot of her glass.

'I might have said yes if . . . if there had been a part of me, or of us, in how . . . how he did it. I love him, I do. But ever since we moved in together I've felt like . . . there's no space for me in our relationship. He kind of . . . does everything. Sorts everything out. Thinks of everything. Makes sure we talk about everything. And I feel so . . .'

He groans and rubs his eyes. 'I'm not explaining this very well. He's perfect. He is. As you can tell. I'm complaining about things I should be grateful for. But it's as if I'm always struggling to keep up. I'm just so . . . emotionally slow. I need time to digest things, think them through. Once I know how I feel about something, it's always kind of too late. He's already decided and moved on. And . . . maybe this proposal was the last straw. It was amazing but . . . but I had to pull the emergency brake. I just wanted time to think about something properly for once. I can't get married without being completely sure about what I want.'

Marianne can't stop herself any longer. She sips her wine. 'Maybe you should tell him those things. I'm sure he would understand.'

'I've looked for him everywhere. And phones don't work here. But he probably wouldn't pick up anyway.'

He looks miserable; Marianne wishes there was something, anything, she could do for him. It has been a long time since she felt this strongly about anyone, and it takes her a minute to find the words for what has been awakened in her: maternal feelings.

They watch the stream of people moving through the corridor outside the pub.

Both searching for one particular face among all the strangers.

Dan

'Dan,' Captain Berggren says. 'It's good you stopped by.'

He looks drowsy and smells of sleep. He hasn't had time to put on his uniform jacket with all the fancy insignia, and Dan can see the string vest under his shirt.

He wonders what Berggren's quarters are like on board. The officers' cabins are said to be much swankier than the rest of the staff's, and the captain's must surely be the poshest of all.

Berggren turns to Adam, who is still sitting on Dan's hip with his arms around his neck.

'And who is this then?' he says.

'My nephew, Adam.'

Adam fixes the captain with his big blue eyes: a cherub in his red hoodie, innocence incarnate with his chubby cheeks, once again declaring that he is going to be a sea captain when he grows up. When he is acting his part, it is impossible to imagine that he is older than Berggren.

'You wanted to see me?' Dan says.

'Yes, I heard there was some trouble down at the karaoke today. But I would prefer to speak to you privately. Maybe you can come back when the boy has—'

'We can talk now,' Dan says.

'I don't think that's appropriate. And the boy should be in bed.'

Berggren gives Dan an appraising look, and Dan smiles. He wonders if the captain can sense the reek of blood and death coming from the two of them. Wonders if Berggren has realised, on some subconscious level, that he is about to die.

'I'm a bit concerned about what happened tonight,' the captain says.

'You should be,' Dan says, and sets Adam down on the floor.

The *Baltic Charisma*

Bosse's fingers dance across the keyboard, pressing buttons, jumping between camera angles. The internal telephone on the desk gives a plastic ring. He hopes it is Mika, calling to tell him the little ones have been found. He thinks about how sick he is of parents who fail to look after their children properly and then go hysterical when they disappear.

'We've had calls from deck six,' Mika tells him. 'Cabins 6502 and 6507 are reporting some kind of commotion in the hallway, knocking and thudding against their doors. Can you see anyone who might have flipped their lid over there?'

Bosse pushes a few buttons, expertly scans the screens. The sternward hallway on the portside is empty, aside from a man with a towel around his hips peeking out of cabin 6507.

'Nothing yet,' Bosse says. 'Or ... Well, what do we have here?'

His fingers hover in mid-air as he peers at the screen showing the central hallway. On it is a woman with dark hair hanging down her back in sticky tangles. Her name is Alexandra, but Bosse doesn't know that. He switches cameras to have a look at the woman from the front. He pushes his steel-rimmed glasses higher up his nose, but even so, he squints at the black-and-white screen.

'Here we go,' he says. 'There's a half-dressed little harlot running around, knocking on doors. It looks like she's vomited a whole box of red wine all over herself.'

Mika asks Bosse to spare him the more colourful details, tells him he will send security. Bosse lifts his mug to his lips, eyes still glued to the screen, and realises it looks like the woman is spattered with blood. He tries to tell himself that it is just his imagination playing tricks on him; after all, he's seen thousands of girls like this over the years. *Nothing special about this one.* One of the doors the girl has knocked on opens. 6805. An older man pops his head out. Bosse can't see the details of his features, but his body language is clear: it goes from drowsy to shaken in a split second. Unease creeps up Bosse's spine. When there is a knock on the door right behind him he jumps; lukewarm coffee spills over the edge of his mug, soaking the thighs of his uniform trousers. A few drops end up on his cross-word puzzle, dissolving his scrawled capitals. He spins around in his chair; opens the door without getting up. Dan Appelgren is standing outside. *That pathetic little faggot.* Bosse notices that he looks swollen, figures it must be all the alcohol he guzzles. *Other things too, if the rumours are to be believed.* Dan is holding a little kid by the hand. The boy reminds Bosse of his grandchildren back on Åland.

'Look,' the kid says to Dan, and points to the screens.

Bosse turns around, sees what is happening. He throws himself at the buttons. *A child should not have to see things like that. No one should have to see things like that.* Behind him, Dan and the child step into the office and close the door behind them.

In cabin 6805, Ros-Marie wakes up with an open crime novel straddling her nose. Something has roused her; dazed, she blinks at the darkness. Her body feels heavy and cosy; she smiles and stretches, thinking about the massage in the spa and the wine she had with dinner and how she and Lennart made love until past midnight. She puts the book down on the nightstand and turns on the light. The other bed is empty. The duvet has slipped halfway down to the floor and the pillows are in disarray.

'Lennart?' she calls out, and knocks on the toilet door. Her voice sounds much too loud in her head, as though her ears have popped. Then she remembers why and takes out the bright yellow earplugs. Knocks again. Pushes the handle down. Opens. Fumbles for the light switch while thinking about all the cholesterol in the buffet. *I hope Lennart isn't feeling poorly. Or that he's had a heart atta—* She cuts the thought short. A familiar anxiety is slithering about in the pit of her stomach. The light comes on. The bathroom is empty. No Lennart. *Neither dead nor alive. No, be quiet now, Ros-Marie. Every time you have a bit of fun, you think there will be hell to pay for it. That's not how it works. There wouldn't be a single lottery winner still alive. Lennart would laugh at you if he knew you'd worked yourself into a tizzy just because he went for a stroll; he probably couldn't sleep.*

Ros-Marie tries, but she can't shake the feeling of impending disaster. And then she spots Lennart's brown boots on the floor outside the bathroom. *He wouldn't have left the cabin in nothing but his stocking feet. But then again, he's not here either.* The muscles in her back and neck, soft as butter after her massage, are stiffening again. *Someone might have knocked, some madman out to rob him, stab him, throw him overboard, and I didn't hear anything because of those damned earplugs . . .* She tries to laugh at herself the way Lennart would. *You'd better stop reading crime stories at bedtime, Ros-Marie.* She straightens her nightgown, which has slipped off one shoulder, and opens the door to the hallway.

She appears on one of the screens in Bosse's office. Bosse is slumped back in his chair. His eyes are open but unseeing. Dan and Adam are gone.

Ros-Marie looks both ways down the short central corridor, wondering which way she should go, and curses her poor sense of direction. But then she hears a wet grunting somewhere to her right. *Lennart.*

The carpet outside the door is wet and spongy. Blood is seeping up between her naked toes. Out of the corner of her eye, she can see red spatters across their door, but she refuses to take it in. She runs towards the sound, forcing down the scream trying to push up through her throat. *Lennart is going to make me laugh about this. Ros-Marie and her lively imagination, always such a worry-wart, always convinced the sky is falling. Yes, we are going to laugh at this. I just have to find him first.*

She reaches the T-intersection at the stern, hears a new sound on her right and runs that way, comes out in the long corridor that stretches all the way to the bow. One of the nearest doors is open. Ros-Marie draws nearer like she's sleepwalking. She hears a gurgling from inside. *This is a nightmare, the most vivid nightmare I've ever had, and I'm going to tell Lennart about it . . .*

When she knocks on the door, it slides open. There is blood in there. So much blood. Covering Alexandra's teeth, her soiled top, Lennart's ashen face. The gurgling is coming from his throat, which is nothing but a fleshy mangled mess. And Alexandra looks up at her, drawing her lips back so Ros-Marie can see even more of her crimson teeth. Ros-Marie's scream finally finds its way out of her body, *like a genie in a bottle,* and it just goes on and on, filling the cabin, pushing out into the hallway; it is never going to return to its prison.

Pia

'You can't fucking do this,' slurs the man Pia has handcuffed to the white metal railing.

'We'll stop by to check on you,' Pia says. 'I promise you will be just fine here.'

'But what if . . . there's a fire . . . ?'

The rest of the half-hearted protests turn into an incomprehensible stream of vowels and *nnnnghhh* sounds. He yanks at the handcuffs and the rattling reverberates through the staff stairwell, stabbing at her eardrums.

She straightens up, trying to ignore the headache. Part of her agrees with his objections. It does not feel good putting them here. But she also knows she has no choice. Otherwise they would be back out on the ship in minutes and causing trouble, staggering around one of the weather decks, maybe falling overboard.

Never allow anyone to become a danger to themselves or others. This is the only rule that can't be bent. And all the drunk tanks are occupied. The guys fighting at Club Charisma have taken over the cells the old men from Charisma Starlight were in.

'Are you all right up there?' she calls.

It feels like the roof of her mouth is about to split open. She pushes her tongue against her palate. It almost seems like something is moving in there.

Jarno comes down the steps. His boots are thumping; the steel construction vibrates and clanks. He sounds like a herd of elephants. She tries to force down her irritation. It is not his fault her head hurts.

'My guy's going to pass out any moment,' he says. 'And I can see yours is already well on his way.'

Pia looks at the man at her feet. His chin has fallen onto his shoulder. A saliva stain is spreading across his scarlet jumper. He is still muttering aggressively.

Let them drink themselves to death, she thinks before she can stop herself. *Let them kill each other, the lot of them. I will go back to Calle. Or, even better, my own cabin. I don't give a flying fuck about this. I'll pull the duvet over my head and disappear.*

She is never going to be enough for all these paltry human dramas, night after night. Four security guards to look after what amounts to a small town, cut off from the rest of the world, where the inhabitants have marinated themselves in alcohol and over-the-top expectations.

'I wish tonight would be done already,' she says. 'I'm getting too old for this shit.'

Jarno grins. He has heard her say that before. But she has never meant it more than she does now. She glances up the stairs and hears snoring. Good. Then maybe they will keep calm for a while at least.

Their belts crackle.

'Pia? Jarno?' Mika says. 'We have a woman covered in vomit, dark hair, wandering around deck six near the stern.'

Pia rolls her eyes, but that only aggravates the pain in her head and she immediately regrets it. 'Can't Henke and Pär get this one?' she says.

'No. They're busy elsewhere.' Mika's voice sounds strange. But then again, he usually sounds strange.

'Did something happen?'

'I . . . I wasn't going to mention it until I knew more. I'm sure it's nothing, but . . .' Mika's voice is choking with tightly restrained panic.

'What?' she says sharply.

'I'm not getting a response from the bridge,' Mika says.

'What do you mean? How the fuck is it possible that no one's picking up on the bridge?'

'I don't know. Pär and Henke are on their way to check it out.'

Pia thanks him reflexively as she puts her radio back in her belt. She exchanges a look with Jarno. Sees her own concern mirrored in his face.

Albin

Lo's head is on his shoulder. Her breathing is slow and regular. He thinks she has fallen asleep, but there is no way of checking without risking waking her.

They have talked and talked about all the things they are going to do in Los Angeles and Albin knows they aren't going to go, at least not now, but that is okay. Just fantasising about it has been almost as good as being there for real. In fact, it is better. When it is just make-believe, he doesn't have to think about how it would be for his mum, and how he doesn't want to leave her behind alone with Dad, or that he would miss her way too much and worry all the time.

'Abbe,' Lo mumbles drowsily, 'it's not cold enough for us to freeze to death here, is it? Because I'm going to sleep now. Don't you fall asleep before you freeze to death?'

'Yes,' he says, 'but you're okay.'

'You're not going to leave me here, are you?'

'Of course I won't.'

'I think I'm a little bit tipsy.'

A gust of wind finds its way in under the stairs. He pulls the cords of his hoodie tighter, giggling as he imagines himself as the one who always dies in *South Park*.

'Abbe?' Lo says again. 'I'm sorry I didn't get in touch for so long.'

'You've probably been busy with school.'

She shakes her head. Sniffles. 'I've been a really crappy cousin,' she says. 'Things were just so bad with Mårten and Mum and everything, but that's no excuse.'

'It's okay,' he says. He is happy they are not looking at each other right now.

'Promise we won't ever be like them,' she says.

'I promise.'

'At least you don't have their genes. What if I become like Grandma and Mårten?' She suddenly sounds frightened. 'What if it's hereditary? You have to tell me. We're going to be honest with each other. You have to promise.'

'I promise,' he says again. 'For real.'

Because, here and now, he feels that is a promise he can keep. They will be grown-ups in six years. It sounds like an eternity. It is half of the life he has lived so far. But for a moment it is as if he is looking into a wormhole in space, seeing them in the future, where they can do things their own way. They are more than family; they are friends.

The *Baltic Charisma*

The staff captain is standing on the bridge, staring at the door. The security officers are pounding on it from the outside, shouting, but he has promised not to let anyone in. He has sealed the door from the inside and smashed the handle. That was what Dan and Adam demanded in return for letting him live. Behind him, the bridge is trashed. The bloody corpses of his colleagues are scattered across the floor. He can't look at them.

The two children hiding on the sun deck have fallen asleep. They don't notice Dan and Adam, who are almost done with their preparations. They are going to destroy the radio equipment in the lifeboats and rafts and throw the flares overboard. Once that is done, there is no way off the ship and no way to contact land. The *Charisma* is going to run on autopilot all the way into Åbo Harbour. By the time she gets there, all the people on board will be dead or newborn, and no one outside the ship will suspect a thing until it is too late. Dan breathes in the smell of sea and oil and wet metal as he thinks about Captain Berggren and the others on the bridge, how they must have regretted not respecting him more. The wind tears at his hair. He wonders if it is going to keep on growing. *Don't hair and nails keep growing after death?* He looks at his hands and smiles. Before the night is through, hundreds of mobile phones and cameras will be full of photos and videos. He will make sure they spread around the world. *The revolution will be televised.*

Pia and Jarno step into the public area of deck six, amidships. They exchange a nod before splitting up. Pia takes the portside hallway, Jarno the starboard one. They see nothing unusual and start walking sternwards.

On the bridge, the staff captain hears something moving behind him. He turns around and notices that Berggren has opened his eyes. He runs to the captain, kneels down next to him. And Berggren blinks his eyes, reaches a hand out towards his face, pulls his lips back. Groans with pain. It hurts to be born anew.

Pia

Curious faces peek out of a couple of cabins in the long hallway.

'It's been bloody loud out here,' a man with an enormous moustache tells her.

'So I've been told,' Pia says over her shoulder. 'We're looking into it.'

Sometimes she is surprised by how self-assured she can come across.

She looks down one of the short side passages as she passes it, glancing down at her radio every now and then. She just wants Mika to contact her, to tell her that . . . Yes, tell her *what*, exactly? That everyone on the bridge happened to go on a coffee break at the same time?

Pia reaches yet another side corridor. This one is bigger, widening in the middle to make room for one of the *Charisma*'s two largest staircases. From here, she has a straight shot through the ship to the starboard hallway, which is identical to the one she is in. She waits until Jarno appears on the other side. He waves at her and disappears from view once more. They continue sternwards on their respective sides.

Her headache is getting worse. It is the worst pain she has ever had in her sinuses. She refuses to think about strokes and tumours.

A door flies open without warning right next to her. The woman who steps out into the hallway is dark-haired, pretty, the same age as Pia's oldest daughter. She is naked aside from a pair of turquoise lace knickers. A Minnie Mouse tattoo decorates her upper arm. Little droplets of vomit sit in her hair.

'I need a cleaner in here,' she slurs. 'Someone has gone into my cabin and barfed all over it.'

Pia can't help but smile. 'Is that right? Well, that's not very considerate, going into someone else's cabin to throw up.'

'What, are you saying it was me?' the girl says, raising her thin, felt-tip eyebrows combatively.

'I honestly don't care either way,' Pia says. 'I just want to—'

'Don't think you're better than me just because you're wearing some cheap fucking uniform.'

Out of the corner of her eye, Pia spots Jarno at the end of the corridor; she waves for him to come over.

'I can make sure a cleaner stops by,' she says, 'but first I need to know if you're the one who's been walking around here knocking on doors, because we've had a number of complaints.'

'*We've had a number of complaints,*' the girl mimics in an obnoxious voice. 'Not on my account anyway. I haven't done anything.'

'Just like you haven't thrown up, you mean?'

The girl's eyes narrow. 'What the fuck's wrong with you? Gone too long without getting laid, or what? Is that why you're walking around here acting like you're everyone's fucking mother?'

It is as if the basement inside Pia has a trapdoor she didn't know about – a chasm, a darker darkness hidden in the dark – and she plummets straight into it.

She imagines herself killing this girl. Tearing her to pieces. Turning that taunting, pretty face to pulp. Her head is roaring, as though all her blood has rushed there, filling it until it is about to *explode* . . .

Pia wobbles. Everything goes dark. When the attack passes, she realises the girl has backed into her cabin and is looking at her with fear in her eyes.

'What's wrong with you?' she says.

I don't know.

'Pia!' Jarno shouts. 'Pi-i-a-a!' There is panic in his voice.

And when she checks the corridor, he is nowhere to be seen.

The skin of her neck contracts. She calls his name into the radio, but hears nothing but the rustle of static in response.

'What the fuck's going on?' the girl says.

Pia shakes her head. 'Go back inside and lock the door.'

The girl hesitates. 'But it stinks in there,' she whines.

'Close the door and lock it. Now.'

Pia starts jogging towards the stern, her footsteps thudding softly against the carpet, the keys on her belt rattling loudly. A few doors open. Sleepy faces peer out.

'So bloody loud out here!' the moustachioed man yells, far behind her now.

'Go back inside your cabins!' Pia shouts. 'Lock the doors behind you!'

Her hand is sweaty and slippery, frantically clutching the radio to keep from dropping it when she pushes the button. 'Mika,' she hisses, 'has Bosse seen anything?'

No reply. She calls Mika's name again, her frightened voice sounding like the last bit of air leaking from a balloon.

She starts when the radio crackles much too loudly. She turns the volume down and looks around.

'Yes, I can hear you,' Mika says. 'Bosse hasn't responded for several minutes. And I still haven't been able to reach the bridge.'

What the fuck's going on? She tries to keep her mind from careening off wildly. It is not the first time Bosse has vanished without a trace, after all.

Useless git, she thinks to herself. *He's probably taking a dump with one of his fucking crosswords on his lap. Or beating off over something he saw on one of his screens. Doesn't he realise he's putting our lives at risk?*

Her fury with Bosse, his sluggish eyes behind the invariably greasy glasses, is so fierce she can cling to it. It gives her strength. It silences the familiar voice inside her telling her she is worthless, that putting her in charge of other people's safety is a bloody joke.

'I don't know what's happened to Jarno, but I heard him screaming just now,' she whispers. 'He was near the stern, portside, and now he's gone. I'm on my way.'

'Should I send Henke or Pär?' Mika says.

Pia slows down. She has almost reached the end of the hallway. Just ten, twelve yards, then it turns left at the stern. This is where she last saw Jarno.

Door number 6518 is ajar.

'No,' she says quietly. 'We need to know what the deal is with the bridge.'

'Okay,' Mika says. 'Give me a shout if you need backup.'

Pia's eyes bounce between the cracked door and the sharp bend of the hallway. She hesitates for just a fraction of a second, but that is enough to let the voice back in.

You're so fucking useless. Bloody good thing you didn't become a police officer.

She pushes the button on her radio and calls Jarno's name. Her own voice echoes back at her, crackling and breaking from just inside the slightly open door.

Pia steps closer. She believes she can smell something inside 6518 that both revolts and attracts.

It is so quiet. She looks back down the corridor behind her; everyone seems to have obeyed her instructions.

'Pii-i-a-aahhh . . . Donnn . . . nnnn't . . . commmme . . . iiinnnnn.' The wet moan is coming from 6518. It echoes out of her radio.

Pia. Don't come in.

And suddenly the fear dissipates and all the critical voices in her head fall silent, because something has happened to Jarno. He needs her.

She pushes the door open.

Dan

The music in Club Charisma is thumping through Dan's body. The baseline vibrates in his bones, in his new teeth. The lights are flashing around him, making the humans' movements jerky. He notices a few of them staring at him, whispering.

They think they know who he is, but they have no idea. Not yet.

His euphoria grows, making it feel like someone has filled his body with helium, as though there is, in fact, some truth to the myth that vampires can fly. In this moment it feels like all he would have to do is spread his arms, get a running start and jump.

He is finally free. All the desperate urges pulling him this way and that are gone. There is only one urge left, brilliantly clear and pure. One need, at the heart of everything from now on.

This is what he has waited for his entire life. This is *right*. This is *him*. Everything up until now has just been marking time. Something he had to get through. Everything that has happened to him, every decision, every act of chance, has led him to this point. It is almost touching to think that he believed he could achieve immortality through some pathetic Eurovision songs that were doomed to fade into oblivion. But what they are about to do, *here and now*, won't fail to leave a mark on this world.

Pia

Jarno is on his back, looking straight at her with eyes that are shining brightly in his bloody face. His mouth is opening and closing, but no more sounds are coming out. His uniform jacket is open, his shirt ripped to shreds.

A woman in a soiled hot-pink top is squatting next to him. Her black hair hangs in sticky tangles over his chest, hiding her face. Behind the woman are two more bodies, one flung on top of the other. An older man and woman. At least that is Pia's impression, but she can't say for sure.

So much blood everywhere. Spattered across the bed. Forming continents on the carpet. Her mouth fills with saliva; she can't tell whether it is because she is about to throw up or because she wants to

fall on my knees across from the woman, put my mouth to Jarno's throat.

No. She tries to fight the craving, tries to be disgusted by it.

Lick the blood off the walls.

Jarno's staring eyes blink a few times.

Pia takes a step into the cabin, stands on something soft and lifts her foot up, revolted. She has to force herself to look.

A clump of used bandages is stuck to the sole of her boot. She scrapes her foot against the floor until it comes off.

When Pia looks back up, the woman's eyes meet hers. Her gaze isn't human but that of a hungry, desperate animal. A few wet strands of hair fall heavily from her shoulder when she tilts her head. Her fingers are buried deep inside Jarno's ribcage.

Her lips draw back. Pia recognises her.

From where, from where, from where?

She has seen this woman before, earlier tonight.

At the karaoke bar. When Dan Appelgren was attacked by the ginger bloke who is locked in one of the drunk tanks now.

The one who sucked the blood from Dan's hand.

The blood.

The man called Tomas Thunman, according to his ID.

The snapping teeth. The burning eyes. No thought behind them. Just

hunger

instincts.

Like an animal, him too.

Injured starving thirsty mad rabies.

And he tried to bite me.

She checks her wrist. There's a small red cut in the soft skin below her thumb. It's barely visible. When she touches it, it is not even tender any more. She washed it straight away, used hand sanitiser.

But it was after that I started feeling sick.

She looks at the clump of bloody bandages on the floor and knows that they belonged to Dan Appelgren.

The woman sniffs the air, appears to decide that Pia doesn't interest her; there is nothing about her that can tempt her.

Because I am like her – any moment now that will be me.

The woman frightens Pia, but nothing is as frightening as the thing she can't think about, absolutely mustn't think about.

The thing that would explain the inexplicable.

And what it would mean.

She quickly goes to the woman and hits her on the head with her nightstick, so hard the impact reverberates all the way up her arm into her shoulder. The woman pulls her lips back further, gurgling wetly at the back of her throat.

Pia brings her nightstick down again, and this time the woman throws her arms up to cover her head. The nightstick lands on her wrist, something breaks and the woman hisses, struggling onto unsteady feet. She steps over Jarno's body, wobbles. Pia notices that she has big, smooth scars across one thigh. They look like long-since-healed bite marks.

Bite marks the size of a human mouth.

Jarno's lips try to form a word. The muscles around his mouth are working uselessly. Pia thinks she knows what he wants to say; she can see it in his eyes. *Run. Run. Run.* But she can no longer fight the realisation. She is already lost. And so is he.

Before she has a chance to raise the nightstick a third time, the woman's hand shoots out, wrestles it from her grasp and tosses it aside. There's a flash of pure hatred in the empty eyes: a crazy animal in its lair, guarding its prey, not wanting to share it with a rival. She snaps her teeth, closing in.

Pia can't move. Terror has drained her muscles of strength.

What is the point of fighting it? What difference would it make?

The woman's bloody fingertips dig into her hair and smash Pia's head against the inside of the door, again and again, and everything goes dark, black holes merging in front of her eyes, devouring everything for a moment.

With her other hand, the woman claws at Pia's collar. A tearing sound. One of the buttons goes flying. The collar is immediately looser. The woman grunts, rips at the shirt more violently. Yet another button comes off, exposing Pia's neck.

She can hear Jarno inhaling. It's faint. Rattling. Gasping. And she realises she has to fight. She has to make sure this doesn't happen to anyone else.

She tries to keep the woman away from her, but her arms are trembling with the effort. She doesn't have a lot of strength left and the woman has noticed. Her teeth snap. Her twisted face with its burning eyes bows low.

As Pia feels lips graze her throat she gropes across the woman's face, finds her eyes, braces herself. Pushes her thumbs in.

The gently curved eyeballs are surprisingly resilient. They try to slip away from the pressure, but there is nowhere for them to hide in their sockets.

Don't think about what you're doing, don't think, don't think, just do, just . . .

She presses harder and her thumbs slide through

eggs breaking, just warm yolk running down my wrists

and continue into her skull.

The woman howls, falls to her knees, holding on to Pia's collar. Pia is almost pulled off her feet before she manages to wrench free. Her thumbs leave the woman's eye sockets with a sucking sound she knows she will never forget, if she survives this.

She glances at Jarno. His eyes are still open, but they are unseeing now.

The woman has grabbed hold of Pia's trousers by the hips and is trying to get back on her feet. Pia knees her in the chin, making her jaw snap shut with a crack. She manages to land a kick square in her chest, sending the woman toppling backwards and landing with her head on Jarno's shoulder.

But the woman whose eyes are running down her cheeks tries to get back up again. She is never going to stop.

Just an injured animal. Don't think of her as human. What is the most humane thing to do to an injured animal? Kill it.

Pia looks around the cabin. Almost everything is bolted down. The lamps have cords. Would she be able to yank one out and use it to strangle the woman? But she hasn't breathed

she hasn't breathed

this whole time.

Not once.

The realisation makes Pia dizzy.

She considers the chair by the desk. It is far too light to cause any real damage, but she could use it to break the mirror and try to stab the woman with a shard.

But no, she can't do it. Not after what she has already done. It is too personal, too intimate.

You are such a fucking coward. So fucking weak. You can't even finish what you started.

The woman takes a tottering step towards her, whimpering again. Her arms are extended, her hands feeling the air in front of her. She sniffs and turns straight to Pia, as if she can see through her empty eye sockets, following when Pia moves towards the corner with the old-style TV.

Pia yanks and tugs at the steel wall mount, then hangs from it with all her weight. The wall buckles and the big bolts give way with a deafening crack. She catches the TV as it falls and holds it in her arms, mount and all.

It is heavy. Her arms shake when she lifts it above her head. She is using the last of her strength now; she is aware of that.

One chance. One chance only.

The *Baltic Charisma*

The thumping from Club Charisma's dance floor seeps out to the afterdeck. People are smoking, laughing, kissing, taking pictures with their phones. No one notices the little boy in a red hoodie hiding further down the promenade deck. He is waiting patiently, ready to take care of as many people as possible trying to escape that way from the dance floor. Any time now. He can feel it in every part of his body.

His mother senses it too. Disaster is upon them. She is standing at the prow with her back to the sea, watching the *Baltic Charisma* loom over her. The radar spins on top of its mast, round and round, a whisper in the wind. She removes her locket and pushes her thumbnail into the crack; it opens with a hollow click. Two grave faces look back at her, stiffly holding their poses so the long exposure time back then wouldn't blur their faces. A man with high cheekbones and penetrating eyes. A boy with blond, neatly combed hair. Her son is still the same, but she has lost him for ever. She lost him a long time ago, even though they haven't left each other's side in all these years. She looks at the man, remembering the shock on his face when their son ripped his throat open. She has closed her eyes to the truth about her son ever since. The Old Ones warned her he was too young to undergo the change, that he would forget what it is like to be human, but she ignored them. Once she realised she should have heeded them, it was too late and now she must pay the price.

Rivers of blood will flow tonight. And every last drop is on her hands.

The other woman looking for her missing son is still sitting in her wheelchair by the information desk. She too is blaming herself for what has happened, for not realising sooner that it was inevitable. The man behind the counter has disappeared into the back office with two of the security officers. They looked frightened. They asked her to return to her cabin. They claimed they would keep looking for Albin, but she doesn't trust them. She knows something is going on and that whatever it is has a higher priority to them than her beloved son.

The red-haired man in the drunk tank can't bear the hunger any longer. He puts his mouth to his wrist. His teeth tear at flesh and sinew. His dead blood has started congealing in his veins, but at least it fills his stomach.

Pia

'Don't come in here,' she says into her radio, barely recognising her own raspy voice. 'I won't let you in anyway.'

Pia has managed to barricade the door with the desk chair. She is sitting on one of the beds watching the drizzle fall against the window. She has turned off all the lights in the cabin. It feels good. Restful for the eyes.

She needs to rest. Soon.

'What's going on?' Mika says. 'Pia, you have to tell me what's going on. I don't know what to do.'

He is talking fast, much too fast. She presses the hand holding the radio against her forehead, trying to figure out a way to explain. To think through the pain.

She glances at the dark shadows on the bed opposite. She has laid them out there: Jarno, the elderly couple, the woman who killed them. Victims and perpetrators. Or are all four of them victims?

The TV with its smashed screen is sitting on the floor, blood and hair on the broken glass that gleams faintly in the dark.

She has noticed the old man's fingers moving, even though he was dead a moment ago. Even though his throat has been ripped out.

The best thing she can do, for everyone's sake, is to stay here and guard them so no one gets back up. She'll take care of it if they do. She has fetched a heavy fire extinguisher from the hall-way and used it to finish the job with the woman with no eyes. She almost threw up when she saw the result, but the woman has been motionless ever since.

'There's some kind of contagion on board,' she says. 'It makes people violent. Extremely violent.'

It turns them into monsters.

'They bite. That's how the contagion spreads. They may look dead at first, but they're not.' A chill runs through her. 'Or maybe they are. But they wake up anyway.'

'Pia, are you hurt? You're delirious. Pär and Henke are here. I can send—'

'No.'

'Why not?'

'I've been bitten. I'm going to become one of them. I'll try to hold on for as long as I can, but I don't know how much time I have left.'

A new wave of pain in her mouth, then it fills with saliva that tastes like blood. She catches herself sucking her teeth to draw more out. A canine comes loose. She spits it out into her hand and puts it on the nightstand between the beds.

'Pia . . .'

The radio hisses. Mika might as well be hundreds of miles away, thousands. It makes no difference. Everything outside this cabin is lost to her now.

'What?' she says.

'What am I supposed to do? The engine room's not responding. The bridge is not responding. Pär and Henke couldn't get in. And Bosse is dead. Pia, they say he was completely butchered . . .'

A rivulet of blood trickles from the hole where her canine used to be. She is well aware she used to find the taste of blood revolting, but not any more. She is aching with a thirst for more, for someone else's.

'Pia?' Mika says, sounding close to tears. 'I need you.'

'I can't help you. I think I'm dangerous.'

'No, you're not!' Mika yells.

'You have to find Dan Appelgren – and the little boy he was with when I saw him before . . .' She understands the child's look now: recognition, not curiosity. He wasn't wondering who she was. He knew exactly. 'The child is one of them.'

'This sounds completely fucking insane, Pia. All of it.'

'I know. But you have to believe me. You are responsible for the lives of twelve hundred people now.' She is cold. Her teeth are chattering and more of them are falling out. 'And don't let Tomas Thunman out of the drunk tank under any circumstances. I think it all started with him. If we're lucky, that's all of them . . .'

A guttural groan rises from the pile of bodies on the other bed. She closes her eyes and casts about for anything she might have missed.

'I found a purse. There is an ID in the wallet. The girl who's staying here is called Alexandra Karlsson. Check who her roommate is. It's a woman, judging from her belongings. She might be infected.'

'Pia, this is—'

'And Raili was alone with Dan,' she suddenly realises. 'Talk to her, make sure she wasn't bitten. And . . .' *Don't start crying. Don't.* '. . . and someone has to tell her about Jarno. Don't have Pär do it. Andreas, maybe. But I don't want her coming here. Promise me you won't tell her where Jarno is. If he wakes up . . .'

She can't finish the thought. Another chill makes her shiver

315

and she knows she doesn't have long left. She pulls the bed throw over her head.

'I have to go now,' she says, 'but you're going to see this through. Announce over the speakers that people have to go back to their cabins. Call the club and Starlight and tell them to close. And then you have to get as many of the staff into the mess or, I don't know, somewhere you can lock yourselves in properly while you figure out what to do . . .'

She has to force herself to breathe. 'And tell them about the contagion. They need to know. You have to believe me: it *must* be contained. Think about Bosse. Think about what happened to him.'

The pile on the other bed moves.

The elderly woman's body rolls down onto the floor with a heavy thud. Pia stares at it, waiting for it to stand up.

But it is the old man: he has shoved her aside to get out. He grunts from the exertion.

'Good luck,' she says, and turns the radio off.

She gets up and backs over to the desk as he struggles to a sitting position. She reaches for the internal telephone. Turning around, keeping an eye on him through the mirror above the desk, she dials the number to Filip's cabin.

One ring.

Two rings.

The man is sitting up now, emitting a loud, plaintive moaning.

Three rings.

'Hello?' Calle says drowsily.

Pia's eyes tear up. 'Calle,' she says. 'Calle, it's me.'

Jolts of pain from the roof of her mouth, red-hot steel rods straight into her skull.

'Pia? Are you okay? You sound weird.'

She studies the dark shape getting to its feet next to the bed, nudging the body on the floor with its foot.

'I'm sick,' she says. 'You have to promise me something . . . You have to . . .'

'Pia? Pia, what's going on?'

She inhales, but her lungs are too weak; she can't get enough oxygen.

'Pia? Where are you? Tell me and I'll come and get you.'

'I'm on six, but I can't . . . It's . . . It's too . . . late . . .'

She has started hyperventilating. Dots of light dance in the darkness, like dazzling solar systems, stars connected by faintly luminescent threads.

She can hear Calle get out of bed. 'Promise me . . .' she says.

Gathering her thoughts is difficult now; she has to focus to be able to start again. 'Something is seriously wrong on board, and if you see me . . .'

In the mirror, she watches the man take a step towards her. Her fingers stroke the fire extinguisher.

'If you see me, run as far away from me as you can,' she says.

'What are you talking about?'

Her consciousness is struggling to claw its way out of the dark, like when a drowning person is only just able to get their nose above water.

'I love you, Calle. *Promise me.*'

She hangs up.

The *Baltic Charisma*

Lyra's pyjamas are covered in her parents' blood. She is slinking along the walls of the lower floor of Club Charisma. She's no longer hungry, but she still wants more. She's drawn to this place where the bodies are warm and in plentiful supply. It is dark and crowded. She stops next to the dance floor, sensing another of her kind. She scans the crowd and finds Dan straight away. She knows he is a leader. But something else catches her attention. Lyra turns to the mezzanine: someone up there smells warmer than the others.

On the upper floor of Club Charisma, a woman named Victoria hands her credit card to the bartender. She smiles at Simeone, who says, 'We came to Sweden because we heard about the Swedish love boats,' and she thinks to herself that she loves his Italian accent. She laughs and asks if they are what he hoped they would be, and he replies, 'I hope so.' His hand is around her waist; his fingertips burn through her thin dress.

'The reception's been messed up for a while now,' the bartender says, and Victoria looks at his weather-beaten old face in confusion before realising he is talking about the card reader.

She rummages around her wallet, pulls out a couple of crumpled notes. Simeone's hand comes to rest on her stomach, spreading its warmth there. Victoria puts her hand on his, intertwines their fingers. The blood pumps through her harder. She is starting to perspire, sweat settling like a thin film over the skin on her back.

'Do you wanna go back to my place?' she says. 'It's very close, you know. That's the best thing about the love boats.'

He nods. She takes a sip of her new beer and hopes her breath smells okay. 'Let's go tell our friends we're leaving,' she says.

Hand in hand, they walk towards the stairs that lead down to the dance floor. People have gathered by the brass and smoked glass railing. A middle-aged man in a Hawaiian shirt sprints past, shouting something to the bartender. Victoria only catches a few snatched words.

'. . . call . . . in a bad way . . .'

Simeone asks what is going on and she shakes her head, then spots a girl in bloody pyjamas coming up the stairs. Her lips are covered in caked blood.

Someone must have beaten her mouth to a pulp.

The girl reaches the upper level, backlit by the strobing lights.

She needs help. Victoria lets go of Simeone's hand and rushes over to the girl. For a split second, Victoria sees the girl's face up close, then she lands on her back. Lyra has knocked her over. Her hair tickles Victoria's nose. The bass notes from below vibrate up through the floor, making her body quiver. And then—the pain of Lyra's teeth digging through the skin. Teeth meet inside her throat and rip out a large chunk.

Victoria tries to scream, but her voice is gone. Out of the corner of her eye she notices something spurting through the air like oil from a new-found well: it is blood, *her* blood. People are screaming all around them, but Victoria can't get out so much as a sound as the girl's teeth rip through her throat a second time.

*

Down on the dance floor, Dan catches the smell of hot blood meeting air and looks up at the mezzanine. He hears screaming from up there, but no one down here reacts; they just keep dancing while the reek of fear grows stronger. There are so many scared people upstairs. Their hearts are beating fast and every second he manages to resist is sweet agony. He sees a woman's body in a thin dress crash into the railing. Her face, pressed up against the inside of the glass, looks misshapen and flat. Only one of her eyes is visible. It stares unseeing into the dance-floor lights, the white of her eye reflecting the changing colours. And now he sees a girl in silk pyjamas up by the railing. A man is trying to restrain her from behind, but the girl squirms so violently in his firm grip that one of her arms is wrenched out of its socket. She arches her tense body, snapping her teeth in every direction. The woman in the thin dress is still filled with blood; it trickles over the edge and drips onto the dance floor. Sticky spatter lands on the cheek of a girl in a beige lace dress a few feet from Dan, but she doesn't notice, just keeps dancing with her arms above her head. *The blood.* He *needs* it, can't wait any longer. He goes to stand beneath the edge of the mezzanine and tilts his head back, mouth open. Warm, thick drops land on his cheek, on his tongue, straight down his throat.

The girl in the lace dress stares at Dan, not understanding what is happening. She glances up at the mezzanine floor. Spotting the body lying there she screams, clutching at the people closest to her. Someone calls out, 'It's Victoria, it's Victoria, it's my friend, oh my God, Victoria—'

People are pointing at Dan. There's thudding steps on the stairs as others try to escape from the mezzanine. A body drops onto the dance floor, in the middle of a circle of gyrating girls. There's the sound of bones breaking and the screaming spreads, blending with the cries of pain coming from upstairs.

Dan can't resist. He closes his eyes, sniffs the air and grabs one of the warm bodies running past him.

Filip

Over at Starlight, Filip hangs up the phone. He stares at it for half a second, trying to understand. Mika sounded like he was on the verge of a nervous breakdown. What he said had barely been coherent.

'There's some kind of contagion on board,' he says quietly to Marisol. 'We have to get everyone to go back to their cabins and then there's a meeting in the mess.'

When he hears himself say it out loud, it suddenly feels more real.

'What kind of contagion?' she asks.

She doesn't look particularly worried, which calms him a little. If anything is contagious here, it is Mika's overreaction. Nothing else. Maybe.

'I don't know,' he says. 'I'm sure it's nothing, but we have to stop serving immediately.'

'Oh, that's going to be popular.'

Filip leaves the bar. A few people waiting for their turn shout angrily after him, but he sidesteps the hands reaching for him. Deciding not to push through the crowd on the dance floor, he walks the long way around instead, avoiding touching the brass railing. He looks at all the glasses on the tables. Are there sick people in here? How does it spread? Marisol and he have handled money and cards, their hands brushing against the customers' hands. A woman's naked, sweaty shoulder rubs hard against his upper arm, leaving a patch of damp on his shirt.

He reaches the side of the stage and walks up the steps. It must be obvious from his expression that something has happened because Jenny stops singing immediately. The bass player's fingers come to rest on the strings. The drumbeat slows and falls silent. There's booing from the room. Jenny walks across to Filip, handing him her microphone before he has a chance to ask for it.

Without the music blanketing it, the din in the room suddenly sounds deafening.

'I'm sorry to interrupt the party, but we're experiencing some technical difficulties on board,' he says. 'I've been assured by the management that there is no cause for concern.'

He becomes aware of screaming and shouting from somewhere outside Starlight. He shields his eyes against the spotlights, notices people shifting uneasily. A murmur is filling the room.

'I've been asked to tell you to calmly return to your cabins. There is nothing to worry about. More information will be given to you as it becomes available.'

'What the fuck?' a man by the bar bellows. 'I just bought a pint!'

'Me too!' calls out one of the girls from the group that has been singing along to every song. 'Are we allowed to take them with us or what?'

'If not, I want my money back!' the man by the bar shouts, and is rewarded with shouts of agreement. Filip doesn't know what to say. According to the rules, the answer is no, but he has a feeling that would lead to a riot.

'What's going on?' a woman standing right next to the stage shouts.

'Just a routine check,' Filip says. 'There is nothing to worry about.'

He was never a good liar and the hot spotlights do nothing to help.

A woman somewhere outside the entrance screams. There is a tangible shift in the atmosphere when everyone turns their attention that way. Filip dashes down from the stage and, this time, people obligingly step aside for him. He notices many of them are quickly downing their drinks to make sure the contents will leave with them.

There's more screaming by the doors. Out of the corner of his eye he sees that Marisol has climbed over the bar and started running with him.

'Help me!' the woman screams. 'For God's sake, help! They're right behind me!'

And now he can see her coming in: a woman with short hair, dyed red and black. The right side of her tank-top is dripping with blood. A large chunk of flesh is missing from her arm, near her armpit. Her face is shiny with sweat and tears. She falls onto all fours, sobbing.

People are screaming, and some rush towards the exit while others back further into the room. Yet more move in closer, wanting to see what is going on.

Panic surges through Filip when he sees Marisol squatting down next to the woman.

'They're right behind me!' she pants.

'Who?' Marisol asks, while Filip runs towards the grille.

'There's something wrong with them, something seriously fucking wrong!' the Green Party supporter with the blond dreads shouts.

'Fuck,' the woman holding his arm says.

She points and her hand is shaking so hard her wine spills from her glass.

Cilla

'... is no reason to panic. We are working as fast as we can to solve the problem ...'

The volume makes the plastic rattle in the speaker above Cilla's head. She recognises the voice: the man from the information desk. She can tell he is scared.

The lift dings as it comes to a stop on the sixth floor. Cilla glares impatiently at the doors, trying to open them through sheer force of will.

Abbe and Lo might be back in the cabin, watching a film, eating sweets. Maybe Linda found them.

Good God, let that be the case.

The doors finally open. The voice echoing from the speakers in the hallway has switched to Finnish now. Cilla pushes the joystick forward and the wheelchair rolls out through the lift doors with a soft whirring sound. She needs to get to the portside corridor, but people are streaming down the wide staircase in front of her, jostling towards the two hallways, stumbling into one another. The doors close behind her. There is barely enough room for her to turn her wheelchair. She backs up a foot or so, pulls the joystick, moves forward another foot at an angle, pulls the joystick the other way, reverses again, repeats the process several times.

A series of nightmare scenarios flash through her mind: Abbe falling overboard, disappearing into the freezing water, being pulled into the currents around the ship, drawn towards the propellers . . .

How is she supposed to protect Abbe if something happens?

She wasn't even able to protect him at home. And now he is missing. How could she think Abbe didn't notice, wasn't harmed, didn't understand? This is what Linda has been trying to warn her about for years. And now she can't ignore it any longer. Of course he understands, her clever, lovely boy. But how is she going to explain to him that she can't leave Mårten? He has threatened in no uncertain terms that he would take Abbe from her, because anyone can see she is unable to look after a child on her own. She can't even look after herself. And her condition is getting worse. Sooner or later she is going to end up in a home.

The joystick slips in her hand as she struggles to manoeuvre the lumbering beast into the right position. No one looks her in the eye, afraid she might ask them for help.

At long last, the wheelchair is pointing in the right direction. She impatiently waits for someone to let her through. Most of the people look bored and annoyed, their night of partying interrupted. Some talk and laugh unconcernedly together. But Cilla also glimpses panic in a couple of faces; those people are straining to hear the speakers, hushing people to no avail. In the end, Cilla pushes the button marked with a stylised horn and the wheelchair emits a pitiful honking. A woman in a plaid dress halts on the last step and lets Cilla pass. Cilla thanks her, manages to make her way to the right hallway and turn left without too much trouble.

She honks her horn again. People slowly, unhurriedly move aside; she wants to scream at them as she starts and stops, starts and stops. A trio of obese men walking side by side finally notice her when she is just behind them. They line up against one of the walls; she pushes the joystick to the max. The wheelchair shoots off. The wide tyres whisper against the carpet.

Abbe. Abbe. Abbe.

Please, God, let him be in our cabin or Linda's.

She can see the doors up ahead now, near the end of the corridor. 6510 and 6512.

The man on the speakers is now doing his announcement in English, but is drowned out by the sound of running feet and screaming behind her.

A chill spreads through Cilla when she hears it. For the first time, she is scared for herself. She wouldn't stand a chance if she ended up in the water. She can't even swim any more. People ahead of her in the hallway turn around and up their pace. She tries to twist her head, but her neck refuses to obey.

'What's happening back there?' she calls out. 'Can someone tell me what's happening?'

But no one answers.

A cabin door opens ahead of her and a man with a wide neck and shaved head takes a small step into the hallway. The Rolling Stones mouth on his T-shirt is stretched across his big gut. He could be anything from twenty-five to fifty-five.

'What's going on?' Cilla says. 'I can't turn my chair around in this corridor . . . What's happening behind me?'

The man hesitates for a moment. 'My wife wanted to stay out dancing,' he offers in a thick regional dialect, and laughs. 'As usual.'

'Do you know what's going on?' she says, desperately trying to keep her voice steady.

'You don't?'

She shakes her head. *No, I don't know, I don't know where my son is, I don't know if anyone other than Linda is looking for him, I DON'T KNOW WHAT'S GOING ON and I don't know why we're on this ship at all, why we thought it was a good idea.*

'I saw it on the TV,' he says. 'You know, they have cameras on the dance floors . . . At first, I thought it was a horror film . . .' He falters.

They are the only people left at this end of the hallway. The people who were in front of Cilla have disappeared into their cabins. She hears doors slamming shut.

'What?' she says. 'What did you see?'

He doesn't appear to have heard her. 'It must be gas or something. They transport nuclear waste on these ships, did you know that? What's to say they don't transport other things as well without telling us?'

'Tell me what you saw,' Cilla says. 'Please. My son is missing.'

He blinks as if seeing her properly for the first time. His eyes fill with pity, which scares her more than anything else.

'There's nothing you can do for him,' the man says. 'They're killing each other over there.'

'What?'

Far behind her she can hear a man shouting, '*Hurry, hurry up, hurry.*' More doors slamming.

'Maybe it's a military weapon,' the man says. 'They don't look human, the ones who have lost their minds.'

Cilla shakes her head and grabs the joystick.

'I don't know if I should go and look for her,' he says. 'Do you think I'll ever be able to forgive myself if I don't?'

She looks up at him again, sees the pleading in his eyes and doesn't know if she should tell him the truth: that if she had been able to walk, if she had been able to help, she would have run up and down this ship until she found Abbe, regardless of what was happening. And she would never have been able to forgive herself if she had done anything less.

There is a loud crash as a cabin door is flung open from the inside, thirty feet in front of her. The man starts and turns toward it.

A woman comes staggering out into the corridor. It is the security officer who accompanied Abbe and Lo at Starlight earlier tonight. And yet . . .

'They're here too,' the man gasps.

It is not her, not at all.

The woman's eyes, which had been so warm, so kind, are completely empty. Blood is splattered across her face, staining the white shirt that is torn to shreds around the collar. Almost all her hair has come loose from her tight topknot and is falling across her shoulders in tangles. Her dark, pressed trousers are sticky with something. Her thumbs are a reddish-brown, as if she has dipped them in paint.

The woman opens her mouth and closes it again.

'I'm sorry,' the man says. 'I'm sorry, I'm sorry, I can't, I wish I could but I can't . . .'

His voice breaks off abruptly when he slams his cabin door shut.

The woman comes a step closer. Her grimy name tag gleams, drawing Cilla's eyes.

Pia? Fia? What does it matter? That's not her, not her, that's something else.

The door to her and Mårten's cabin is halfway between her and the security officer. But even if she could reach the door and get her key card out . . . would she be able to get through the narrow opening in time?

She can't risk it. She has to get out of here.

Cilla fumbles with the joystick, reverses and turns. Her wheelchair hits the wall behind her.

She pushes the joystick forward. Turns.

'Mårten!' she screams as she reverses again. 'Mårten, help me!'

Is he one of them now too?

The thought is crystal clear and panic erupts inside her like a mushroom cloud.

An older woman has stepped into the hallway behind the security officer. Her ponderous body sways under her nightgown as she approaches. Her teeth snap in the air.

Snip, snip, snip.

Cilla pushes the joystick as far up and right as she can. Her wheelchair whizzes off in a tight curve and the metal footrest hits the cabin door opposite. She reverses and turns left. Hears footsteps, heavy boots against the carpet behind her; something rattling and wet, like breathing, but not quite. Every cell in her neck is expecting to feel fingers any second, fumbling . . .

She finally manages to point the wheelchair in the direction she came from. She pushes the joystick just as she hears fingernails scrape against the coarse fabric of the wheelchair's backrest, right next to her head. The wheelchair rolls forward. The fingers are there again, trying to grab her short hair, but the wheelchair gathers pace with a whining sound.

Cilla leans forward on the thick seat cushion that was tailor-made to her specifications as door after door flies past, caught out of the corners of her eyes.

A bit further down the corridor people scream in panic when they see what is chasing her. Some people fumble with their key cards and disappear through doorways. Others dash back towards the stairwell or vanish down side corridors, pushing and shoving. But regardless of their response, they all have one thing in common: none of them tries to help her.

And she understands that. She would have thought the same thing they are. *Better her than me.*

Snip, snip, snip.

Cilla screams, because it is the only thing she can do.

Soon the hallway will end in the glass wall of the spa. She hesitates with her hand on the joystick for no more than a split second before zooming past the side corridor with the stairs and lifts. It is full of people staring at her with terrified eyes. She wouldn't stand a chance of zigzagging her way through there again.

Just a few more yards. The text CHARISMA SPA & BEAUTY rushes towards her. Just before it, the corridor makes a ninety-degree turn to the right. She won't make it at this speed.

But she can't just stop and wait for death either.

She is going to do everything in her power to survive. For Abbe.

Filip

The grille. The goddamn fucking bullshit grille from hell. It has stuck in the usual place, three feet from the floor. People are screaming and crying everywhere, but if they had seen what Filip has just seen, the panic would be even worse.

'Don't say anything,' he pleads to the people nearest him while he tugs at the grille.

They shake their heads. A couple of them were part of the group who tried to get past the blokes in the hallway.

They are no more than thirty feet away now: slow, but determined, bloody. They can't be far out of their teens. Two of them are in good shape, their muscles bulging under their tight T-shirts. The third is short and pudgy, sporting a black T-shirt with some idiotic racist slogan on it. Every time Filip tugs at the grille, they tilt their heads, listening to the sound. On the floor behind them are four people who tried to escape.

Filip still can't believe what he saw, but he knows all too well what is going to happen if those guys manage to get into Starlight.

He lifts the grille up a few inches and jiggles it back and forth before trying to roll it all the way down, but it sticks again.

Far-away screams are coming from the next floor up. Something must have happened at Club Charisma.

The guys keep moving their blood-smeared mouths like they're biting the air in front of them in order to pull themselves forward faster. He wonders which one of them tore a chunk out of the woman's arm. If they have bitten more people.

He tugs at the grille. More rattling. The three of them tilt their heads, moving like one, while at the same time appearing to be unaware of one another.

Mika had said something about the infected being violent. Is this the contagion?

They are so close now. Just a few feet. Their eyes are completely flat.

'*Fuuuuuck!*' Filip roars, tugging on the grille – and it finally unsticks, smacking into the floor with a crash that must be the most beautiful sound he has ever heard. He backs away, realising he is panting.

The next second, the metal rattles again as fingers find their way through the holes, curling like talons; their faces press against it.

Sniffing sounds. Teeth snapping.

He turns to face the room, trying to block out the sound from the grille.

The woman is lying on her back by the bar. Her breathing is rapid and shallow. He wonders if it is shock. Marisol is kneeling beside her with a first-aid kit. Open packets of antiseptic wipes and bloody, balled-up napkins are strewn on the floor around her.

'It hurts so bad,' the woman says. 'So bad . . .'

Is the woman infected too? Is Marisol?

He can barely bring himself to meet her eyes in case she might guess what he is thinking.

'I've cleaned the wound as well as I can,' Marisol tells the woman, 'but we should pour alcohol on it too, just to be sure we've killed all the germs.'

'Do you really have to?' the woman says, and shakes her head, like an unconscious plea.

'Just to be on the safe side. Is that okay?'

Filip runs to the bar, leans across it and grabs a bottle of Koskenkorva.

'It's going to hurt,' Marisol tells the woman when he reaches them, 'but I think it's for the best.'

'Can I have a sip of it first?' the woman says. 'Just like a bit of an anaesthetic.'

Filip puts the silver-coloured pourer to her lips and tips the bottle to get the alcohol out. It's like bottle-feeding an infant.

The woman nods to him to show that she is ready. He removes the bottle and she swallows what is left in her mouth, coughs. 'Do it,' she says.

Marisol takes the woman's arm in a gentle but firm grip and turns the wound upwards. A thin, transparent stream pours out of the bottle, splashes against the wound and rinses away the new blood seeping out.

'Bloody heeeeell,' the woman screams loudly, and snatches up Filip's hand, squeezing it like a vice.

The grille rattles loudly again and the woman stares at it with fear in her eyes.

'They can't get in here,' Filip says.

Marisol puts the bottle down and tells the woman everything is going to be just fine, not to worry, that help will be here soon.

Filip says nothing. He takes the compresses from the first-aid kit and carefully dresses the woman's wound; Marisol wraps the gauze around her arm. There is a gurgling sound from the woman's throat. She swallows, clears her throat and swallows again. When she winces with pain, her teeth are covered in blood.

'Did you hurt your mouth?' Marisol asks. 'Did you bite your tongue?'

The woman shakes her head, winces again. 'It hurts so bad,' she gasps.

'They're leaving!' someone calls out from the entrance.

Filip looks towards the grille: no fingers clutching it from the outside, but that does nothing to ease his mind.

He stands up, walks over and watches the guys' backs disappear down the hallway. He wonders where they are going now.

He suddenly feels so disconnected from reality it gives him vertigo.

'I want to get out of here!' a woman shouts.

'Not until we know more about what the fuck's going on,' a man with a boomingly deep voice counters. 'What was with those lads?'

'I need to get back to my cabin. They've told us to go back to our cabins.'

'For fuck's sake! We're safe in here. Can't you hear the screaming out there?'

'I can. And my children are out there. They won't make it on—'

'Then maybe you shouldn't have left them alone to go out boozing!'

'How was I supposed to know this would happen?'

Suddenly, everyone is yelling at once. The voices rise like a tidal wave as everyone tries to talk over everyone else.

The woman has rolled onto her side. She is spitting blood. Her whimpering is getting fainter.

Marisol looks straight into Filip's eyes. Her fear is shining through, so strongly he has to turn away. Out of the corner of his eye, he sees that she has started stroking the woman's hair.

The telephone behind the bar rings. He runs to snatch up the receiver.

'Hello?' he says. 'Mika, is that you?'

'No, it's me.'

'Calle! Is everything okay?'

He can feel everyone's eyes on him as the idiocy of his question sinks in.

'What the fuck's going on?' Calle says. 'People have started gathering in the mess, but I don't think anyone knows what's happening. Mika said something about a contagion, but that . . . that sounds insane.'

'It *is* insane,' Filip says quietly, sticking a finger in his ear to shut out the loud discussions. 'We have a woman here who's been bitten, Calle.'

'Bitten?'

'It's like they have rabies or something.'

Calle doesn't respond. There is a rushing sound on the line, like a chorus of whispers from somewhere far, far away.

Filip swallows. 'We've pulled the grille down. We should be okay, for now.'

'Good,' Calle says. 'Fucking ace. Can you stay there until help arrives from the mainland?'

'I hope so.'

'Is Vincent with you?'

'No. I haven't seen him since you left.'

Calle is quiet again. Filip gets it. 'Stay where you are,' he says. 'It's your best option.'

'Pia called me,' Calle says. 'She said . . . she said that if I saw her, I should run as far away as I could.'

Filip shuts his eyes and pictures Pia, how happy she was when they were hanging the streamers in the suite. Where is she now?

What is she now?

'If that's what she said,' he says, turning around to look at the woman on the floor, 'then I think you'd better do just that.'

Calle

Calle dials the number for the suite. The phone rings, again and again. Vincent clearly isn't going to answer, but he can't bring himself to hang up.

Mika is speaking over the PA system, a message going out only to the staff quarters, repeating that everyone has to report to the mess as soon as possible.

If there is a fire on board, or if the *Charisma* is at risk of sinking, the staff are supposed to gather in smaller groups at their assigned muster stations. There are lifeboats and rafts for every passenger, with plenty of extra capacity, just to be safe. But what do you do when there is an outbreak on board? As far as Calle knows, there are no routines for that.

The phone keeps ringing.

Where could Vincent be, if he is not in the suite?

Marianne

Marianne and Vincent have left their table at McCharisma. The bartender has told them everyone has to return to their cabins. Tens of people have run past the pub. They seemed to be coming from that awful club upstairs. Several of them were screaming, sounding completely panicked, but what does Marianne know? She has never understood the need some people have of making a *racket* as soon as they have had a sip or two of alcohol. Fear is fluttering inside her, but she doesn't want to make a fool of herself, to be the one who overreacts.

She notices a dark-haired woman standing stock-still in the hallway. She has closed her eyes, appears to be trying to hear something. There is something familiar about her. She is beautiful; her hair is healthy and curly, her cheeks naturally rosy. Among all the cheap fast fashion and heavy makeup Marianne has observed on board, this woman stands out as strangely timeless. She doesn't seem to belong here. Marianne almost wants to ask Vincent if he can see her too, but decides against it. Mustn't come across as a complete lunatic.

'Do you think there's something going on?' Vincent says.

'I don't know,' Marianne replies. 'That "technical difficulties" thing is hardly what you want to hear in the middle of the sea.'

'Bloody hell, just calm down,' says an old man sitting alone by one of the tables close to the hallway. 'I've been on hundreds of cruises and nothing has ever happened to me. You're in more danger getting in a car.'

'But what about the screaming?' Vincent retorts.

'Bah,' the old man sneers. 'Just people working themselves into a tizzy.'

'I'm sorry,' the man behind the bar says. 'I have to ask you to return to your cabins. There is no need to worry, but I do have to insist.'

Marianne turns to him. When their eyes meet, he looks away far too quickly.

Whatever happens, she can't go back to her sub-surface cabin. If the ship is sinking, she'd be trapped down there. She glances at Vincent and knows he is thinking about his friend. She wonders if it would be right for her to ask.

'I don't want to be alone,' she says.

'Me neither,' he replies, and stands up. 'Come on.'

The woman in the hallway is gone when Marianne looks out again.

The *Baltic Charisma*

'Ladies and gentlemen. We would like to ask all passengers to return to their cabins . . .' Mika's voice is back in the public spaces. The people who went to bed early are wide awake now and listening intently. '. . . ask you to calmly return to your cabin . . . the staff thank you for your cooperation . . .'

The dark-haired woman walks down the hallway towards Charisma Starlight and stops next to the bodies on the floor. A man in a blue shirt stops her, begging, 'Please, please, please help. I can't take it, I can't do it.' Blood fills his mouth.

She looks at the grille at the end of the hallway and sees people moving behind it, but no one is looking her way just now. She grabs the man's chin, puts her other hand behind his neck, says everything is going to be okay, then gently pushes his chin towards the floor. Hushing him, she pulls his neck the other way in a quick motion. The tissue connecting his vertebrae snaps. She closes his eyes. He won't open them again.

The woman continues to the other bodies. While she works, she can hear screams and the sound of running feet from the floor above her. There are so many of them. Too many. The smell of terror is wafting down the aft stairs. And she is suddenly struck by the unequivocal realisation that this is the catastrophe the Old Ones always warned her about. It could have unimaginable consequences.

The woman squats next to the last of the bodies, a pretty young girl with curly hair. The bite marks on her neck have already healed. The transformation has begun. The woman glances at the grille again, then breaks the girl's neck. She thinks of the bodies in the hallway as a disease. They are not just infected, they are the contagion. They will multiply indiscriminately if given the chance. She has to stop this. Somehow, she has to stop it, without harming her son. And she has to resist the temptation herself. Because all the running, the screaming, the blood have awakened her own hunger, even though she just fed.

The music has stopped at Club Charisma, but the lights are still flashing across the dance floor, which is dark and slick with blood and human innards. By the main entrance, people are pushing and tugging at each other, trying to get out through the compact wall of bodies, climbing over the backs of the people in front. But there are some who want to climb in rather than out. They are as desperate as the humans, but it is insatiable appetite that has driven them here. They left the grille at Starlight when they caught the scents. They push into the crowd, the bodies slick with sweat, tearing open flesh, filling their mouths with blood, but the hunger rages on. The hot bodies escape in the tumult, slip away and are shoved aside or trampled onto the floor.

A few of the people who have reached the doors realise what is happening, even if they don't understand how or why, and try to run back into the club, but those further back are pushing forward with increasing force. On the other side of the dance floor, people are trying to escape onto the afterdeck. A little boy in a red hoodie is walking back and forth through the chaos out there. Every now and then he lets his teeth glide through exposed skin, slicing open hands and arms in the commotion. Most people don't even notice.

Dan Appelgren has found a young couple trying to hide in the DJ booth. They cling to each other, tears streaming down both their faces. He pulls the girl out; she shakes her head, says *no, no, no,* her eyes glowing with fear. Every part of Dan's body responds. Adam has warned him against drinking too much and he tries to refrain, but it is difficult. Everyone is unique. Their feelings feed his intoxication. He doesn't want to let them go until he has extinguished them utterly. His heart contracts to imitate heartbeats. His body is swollen. His rings dig into the flesh of his fingers. He pulls the girl into his arms like an embrace, rips her cleavage open and squeezes one of her breasts hard. He wants her boyfriend to see it. She tries to strike at him, but he bites through the meaty muscle above her collarbone and her arm stops waving about, goes limp. He throws her aside, looks at the boyfriend who did nothing to help her, just squirmed further into the booth, rolled up and shut his eyes, as though hoping Dan wouldn't want him. But Dan does. He smiles at the young man, thinking about what awaits him. What an incredible, historical event he is part of. Behind Dan, a few bodies fall from the mezzanine.

The glass wall of the Charisma Spa has been shattered. An electric wheelchair is lying on its side just beyond it. In the faint light, the shattered glass gleams like blood-spattered diamonds. Pia has curled up behind the reception counter a few feet away. Her cheek rests against the cool floor. She can feel the vibrations, familiar, soothing. The blood she has drunk is spreading through her body and she is at peace. All her thoughts have gone silent. No voices can get to her here.

344

Calle

He decides to go the long way around, past the mess. He pops his head in. It looks the same: the coffee-stained Thermos; the chequered tablecloths; the plastic potted plants; the fruit bowl; the basket of leftover bread from the restaurants, even the same old breadknife with its bright yellow handle is there. But the atmosphere is different from anything he has ever experienced on board before. The air is heavy with fear. The few people who are talking are doing so in low voices. Antti is standing just inside the door with the general manager, Andreas. They give him a vague nod. Calle wonders where Sophia is, but says nothing. None of the security officers are present, no one from the bridge.

'All personnel to the mess immediately,' Mika's voice says over the PA system again.

Calle thinks he can hear screaming in the background through the crackling and rustling.

'We will start in a few minutes. General Manager Andreas Dahlgren is the highest-ranking crew member present and will therefore lead the meeting, which will, I repeat, begin in a few minutes.' The speakers click and fall silent.

His thoughts racing, Calle hurries past the empty common room, where the television is emitting a spectral blue light, and continues towards the stairwell. If Andreas holds the highest rank at that meeting, it means neither the captain nor the staff captain nor the chief engineer will be there, and that makes him even more worried, but also more determined. He has to find Vincent. Somehow. Right now.

He opens the door to the stairwell. While he runs down the steps, he realises he doesn't know where he is going. Where should he start?

'Is the boat sinking?' someone shouts when he gets down to the landing, and Calle jumps, as if lifted off the floor by a tightly wound internal spring.

A pitiful figure is curled up on the floor a bit further down the railing, looking up at him. 'For Pete's sake, you have to let us go. You have to unlock these goddamn fucking . . .'

There's a metallic rattling when the man yanks at the handcuffs chaining him to the railing, and Calle swallows and takes a step back, until his back hits the big metal door of the goods lift.

'I don't have a key,' he says, holding his hands out in an apologetic gesture.

'Bloody find someone who does then!'

'I'll see what I can do,' Calle says.

It is so obviously an empty promise. The man glowers at him with silent loathing.

'Help us!' someone calls out further down the stairwell, and there's more metallic rattling from down there.

Are these the men Pia had to leave him to go apprehend? Are they the ones who infected her?

'I'm sorry,' Calle replies. He looks at the steel door leading out to the public areas. He is on the ninth floor now. He realises what he has to do when he gets out there: he needs to get up to the sun deck, start there and work his way down the *Charisma*.

He needs some kind of system, and he needs to stick to it. He needs to stay in control.

Calle pushes the door release button; it makes a hollow clicking sound, then he thrusts the door open before he has time to reconsider.

It is like looking out into a war zone.

People are flooding down the stairs; they must have come from the promenade deck. Some of them have torn and bloody clothes. Some are holding each other, others ruthlessly shoving everyone within reach to move forward faster. Some are desperately trying to make calls on their phones; others are using theirs to film and take pictures. They never look up, as though they want to distance themselves from the chaos by watching it on a screen. A man is standing by the stairs, crying quietly.

Calle needs to get a grip. He needs to focus. Somewhere in this ten-storey mayhem is Vincent.

The *Baltic Charisma*

The young security officer is climbing towards the bridge on the narrow service ladder on the outside of the *Charisma*. He is holding a fire-axe in one hand. The wind and rain are beating against his face, making his polyester uniform cold and wet. The windows of the bridge are only a little more than an arm's length away. Henke glances over his shoulder. Five storeys down, his colleague Pär is standing on the bow deck, trying to assist a handful of passengers who have found their way outside. Their sobbing and screaming is carried to Henke on the wind, blending with the shouting from the sun deck above him. He places his foot on the next rung, slips on the wet metal, pulls himself up and squints at the tinted windows of the bridge. He imagines bodies riddled with bullets, terrorists with semi-automatic rifles inside. *There's so much bloody talk about 9/11 but ain't no one fucking going through the passengers' bags when they board. Any goddamn madman could easily drive onto the ship with a homemade bomb.*

He grasps the axe more firmly, takes a few deep breaths and climbs another rung. Another. Peering in over the edge of the window. There are things moving in the gloom behind it. He almost doesn't recognise Captain Berggren without his uniform. His hair is standing on end, his shirt is torn and under his string vest his body is flabby and out of shape. *Robbed of all dignity.*

They shuffle back and forth, ignoring one another. *What are they doing?*

Henke wishes he could brush his wet hair from his forehead, but it is all he can do to hold on to both axe and ladder. He looks at the broken screens and loose wires. One of his feet slips with a squeak against the wet metal rung; he almost drops the axe. He finds his footing again, his heart pounding, and turns to the darkness beyond the *Charisma*. No other ships in sight. Only the black night. *As though we've vanished, like that ghost plane . . .*

There is a thud on the other side of the window; he starts and turns around. Berggren is staring back at him. His eyes are like something out of Henke's nightmares. There is another thud as Berggren rams his forehead against the glass. He never looks away from Henke, doesn't blink, even though blood is gushing from his forehead. Henke resists the impulse to let go of the ladder, let himself fall to get away from here as soon as possible. He starts climbing back down. There is only one thing in his head now: *I'm going to get out of here somehow, no matter what the fucking cost.*

Mika has locked himself in the general manager's office. He puts the microphone down. It is time for him to join the others in the mess. He tries to ignore the burning pain in his chest and makes sure all the buttons on his uniform jacket are buttoned. For a moment he hesitates: he just wants to hide, to fall asleep and not wake up until it is all over. The code-lock on the door beeps. Mika backs away, but is relieved to see that it is just one of the cleaners coming in. She is pale and shaken and has brought a woman Mika doesn't recognise – a passenger. It is against regulations, but he doesn't have time to argue about it. The woman is beautiful, dark-haired, wearing a black dress and a baggy cardigan.

349

The cabins are full of people who have locked their doors. Some of them are in pain. They bleed from their mouths in front of mirrors or they lie on their beds, screaming into pillows. Some of them are alone. Others are crying with friends, hugging their children, being comforted by husbands and wives locked in with them. In a handful of cabins there are passengers who haven't noticed anything unusual. One of them is the woman sleeping soundly on deck nine on sheets covered in gold glitter. Her rigid curls rustle faintly against the pillow every time she shifts.

Inside Charisma Starlight, Marisol is trying to hide from the guests the fact that she has started crying. Filip looks at the woman on the floor between them and wonders who she is. If anyone is missing her. Looking for her. He forces down his fear of the contagion and squats next to the woman to give her mouth-to-mouth. The sweet, sickening smell of blood is coming from between her lips.

'Filip . . .' Jenny says, 'don't do it. It's too late already. Don't you see?'

He pauses. 'I have to try,' he says.

But she shakes her head. 'Haven't you ever seen a zombie flick?' She tries to smile, but it turns into a grimace. She holds his gaze until Filip straightens back up. The voices around them are getting louder. Demanding they open the grille. Demanding they keep it shut.

Albin

The screaming woke him.

Lo had grabbed his hand and it was as if he'd woken up all over again when he saw how terrified she was.

'Abbe,' she said, and her voice sounded thin and small.

People are running past on the deck outside their hiding place, alone or in small groups. Most of them are dressed up, but some are in their underwear.

'... *the fuck are we going to go ...? Did you see the blood ...?*'

'Are we sinking?' he whispers, and his stomach drops.

Lo shakes her head. 'I don't think so,' she replies. 'It's something else.'

But he isn't convinced. He can almost feel the ship listing. His hands fumble for something to hold on to. He looks at the sky, the raindrops forming a ceaseless pattern against a black backdrop, and thinks about his mum. She won't be able to use her wheelchair if there's water in the hallways; that's far too easy to imagine. He wishes he'd never seen that old film.

I'm the king of the world!

You realise the Titanic *sank, don't you?*

Lo squeezes his hand so hard his knuckles hurt when they spot the man dressed in nothing but underpants and a T-shirt. Hunched over, he passes the staircase they're hiding under. His arms are folded across his stomach as if he is carrying something heavy. His long hair hides his face.

There is something about that man. He mustn't see them. Albin wishes they could back away, but there is nothing but cold steel behind them.

The man leans over the railing, breathing heavily, sobbing, staring out into the darkness as if he is looking for something in it. The wind catches his hair, blows it free of his face.

But his face is almost gone: there's a big hole where the cheek should be. They can see his tongue move inside as the man mutters to himself.

Albin claps his hands to his mouth. Lo presses herself harder against him. The hair falls across the man's face once more and Albin doesn't care what happens next, so long as he never has to see that again.

He tries not to scream – he really does try to push the scream back into his body – but a strange yelp erupts from his throat.

The man turns his head their way.

Holds up a bloody hand.

Raises his index finger.

Puts it to his lips.

Shhhhhh.

Then he puts his hand back on his stomach.

Time seems to have stopped.

Screaming comes from somewhere else on deck, but Albin can't stop looking at the man, who is standing motionless, trying as hard as they are to be quiet. And he is no longer afraid of the man. He is afraid *for* him.

An old woman in a nightgown comes shuffling towards them. She is barely lifting her feet. Her thin socks have rolled down, bunching around her ankles. Her mouth is making horrible snapping sounds and the man is shouting for help. But he doesn't look Albin and Lo's way. He doesn't give them away.

The woman tears and rips at him; he loses his grip on the thing he is carrying. A big bundle unravels from under his T-shirt. Red snakes landing on the green floor with a splashing sound. He slips in them, gets entangled. The woman drags him away towards one of the stairs down to the promenade deck. The red snakes trail behind him, leaving slimy tracks.

More sounds try to escape Albin. He is going to explode if he keeps them inside.

But he has to. He has to stay strong in front of Lo.

And eventually the sobbing stops, abruptly, as though someone has flicked a switch, and his head goes empty. Like he is no longer here. The only things that feel real are the cold raindrops occasionally falling on his cheeks.

The red, sticky tracks left by the man's innards are already being washed away by the rain.

Filip

Filip stares at the television screen showing the dance floor at Club Charisma, unable to wrap his head around the fact that it really is happening right now, upstairs. It's like when he saw the twin towers collapse on live TV: too like a movie he had seen a thousand times before, too unlike anything he has ever seen in real life. Impossible to believe.

'You have to let me out,' a woman pleads. 'My children are alone in our cabin. What if they wake up?'

She is talking quickly, taking big, gulping breaths.

'Our kids are alone too,' says the dad of the family Filip noticed earlier tonight, and he thinks about the children who were climbing on the sofas, the girl with the glasses.

He looks at the grille, hears the screaming coming down the stairs on the other side, turns to Marisol. Her face is pale and ghostlike in the light from the screen. Her lips are moving quietly, quickly, her fingers clutching the gold crucifix she wears around her neck.

'Not until we know more,' he says. 'They're going to call any minute now and—'

'You don't have children, do you?' the man says accusingly. 'If you did, you'd understand.'

'You're safer here,' Filip offers.

'Safe?' an old man with a white beard hisses. 'That's a poor fucking joke.'

Shouts and muttering of agreement.

Filip wishes he knew the right thing to do. The staff run through safety drills at least every other week, hammering into every employee who is responsible for what. He has often wondered how the people working on board would do if disaster struck, how he would do. No one knows how they will react until it happens. He has agonised about what would happen if there was a fire, or if the ship started sinking. Those scenarios seem like tiny little trivialities now.

'At least they can't come in,' he says. 'And you serve your children better by surviving.'

'But what if my kids decide to go looking for me?' the woman with the gulping breaths wants to know. She sounds close to hyperventilating.

'Anyone with children can call them from here,' Jenny says, looking at Filip, and he gives her a grateful nod. Obviously he should have thought of that himself. Surprisingly, there are no fights about who gets to call first. Jenny steps in behind the counter, bringing the woman with her to the wall-mounted phone.

'We have to get out of here,' a man says. 'We have to get to the lifeboats.'

'You won't be able to lower them while the ship is still moving,' Marisol replies.

'Then why aren't they stopping the fucking ferry? Is there no one driving it?'

For a moment, all is silent. The humming in the floor and the faint clinking of glass against glass becomes very noticeable.

'Help will be here any minute,' Filip says, trying to look convincing. 'They will definitely have sent out a distress call by now.'

'I need to get off the ship,' the band's drummer mumbles, and sits down on a table with his head in his hands. 'I have to get out of here. I'd rather drown. I have to get off the ship. I have to get . . .'

'How is anyone going to help us?' the man with the white beard asks. 'If we can't even get the lifeboats down into the water, how are they going to get us?'

'Helicopters,' Marisol says with conviction. 'The best thing we can do is to stay calm and not panic.'

The man shakes his head, but at least he doesn't object.

The dreadlocked Green Party supporter gets up from one of the armchairs and walks in behind the bar. He is so skinny his legs look like an insect's in his tight black jeans.

Marisol watches him. 'Excuse me, can I help you with something?' she says.

'Don't worry about it, I'll sort myself out,' the guy says, and takes a bottle of Famous Grouse down from the shelf. 'I'm going to get properly hammered, and the way I see it the shipping company might as well pay for it.'

A few people laugh, and Filip is surprised to realise he is one of them. The woman talking to her children on the phone hushes them irritably.

Suddenly there is a loud crash above them. The laughter dies abruptly and when Filip looks at the TV screen, he can see chairs have been thrown down onto the Club Charisma dance floor.

The Green Party supporter pulls the pourer out of the bottle and starts drinking.

'She's alive!' a woman shrieks next to Filip. 'Look!'

Confused, he turns and stares at the woman lying on the floor. Her eyes are wide open. Her mouth is opening and closing.

'Come on, help her up!' someone shouts.

Filip goes to the woman, who blinks her eyes a couple of times and tries to focus on him.

'No, don't move her,' someone else puts in. 'If she's hurt her head—'

'She didn't hit her head, moron.'

'Like we know anything about what happened to her before she came here!'

Filip tunes out their squabbling and squats down. 'How are you feeling?' he asks.

The woman blinks several more times.

'Watch out,' Jenny says. 'She might be one of them now.'

Filip looks at her. Fear is making his stomach turn somersaults.

'We can't just wash our hands of her,' Marisol says, and falls to her knees next to him. 'She's our responsibility.' She takes the woman's hand and feels her wrist with her fingertips. Her brow furrows as she gently touches the woman's throat.

The woman's lips draw back. Her teeth are so gleamingly white in her mouth.

Were they that white before?

'Jenny's right,' he says. 'Be careful.'

To his surprise, Marisol backs away a little.

'I can't find her pulse,' she says quietly. 'Would you mind trying Raili again? And ask someone to bring a glass of water.'

Filip stands up so quickly he almost faints. He presses his hand against his forehead, waits for it to pass. 'Could someone get her a glass of water?' he says to no one in particular.

Some of the people by the bar look at each other, and in the end it is the Green Party supporter who walks to the tap and fills a glass. It spills when he puts it down on the bar.

'I'm not going any closer,' he says.

Suddenly someone behind Filip screams, and the scream becomes one of many, a chaotic chorus from hell.

Marisol.

He turns around and sees the woman's fingers curled like talons, entangled in Marisol's hair, trying to pull her close.

The woman opens her mouth and

she is just like the ones on the dance floor upstairs.

She was bitten and now she's one of them.

'Help me!' Marisol screams. 'Come on, *help me!*'

Just like the woman was screaming when she came in here.

After she was bitten.

The woman's teeth snap shut with a cold, clicking sound. Her neck is straining so hard that a tendon protrudes like a rope.

Filip runs to the bar, grabs the magnum of sparkling wine on display there.

He notices a few women turning away. They know what he is going to do.

'Watch out,' he tells Marisol, and gets down on the floor next to them, holding the neck of the bottle with both hands. The empty, staring gaze of the woman shifts to him. He shuts his eyes, hears the snapping sound and brings the bottle down, bottom first.

The impact reverberates up his arm and something warm spatters his face.

'Oh my God, oh my God, oh my God,' someone breathes.

A droplet trickles down across Filip's lips. If he stuck his tongue out now, he would taste blood. Her blood.

Contagion. Contagion.

He opens his eyes.

The woman's mouth is a gaping red hole. Her jaw is loose, resting against her chest. Her tongue writhes this way and that for a couple of seconds before it stops moving. At the back of her throat is something like white pebbles. Her top lip has been split all the way to the nose, but her teeth look completely undamaged in the midst of the bloody ruin around them.

Filip chucks the bottle aside, snatches the rag out of his apron pocket and wipes at his mouth frantically. The rag turns bright red. It feels as if her blood is seeping in through his pores, into his own system.

Marisol's breathing is rapid and shallow. She is struggling with the woman's limp fingers, trying to extricate them from her hair. Filip shudders when he grabs one of the woman's hands. It feels like a dead animal in a tangled nest. He spreads the fingers wide, trying to coax them out.

'Cut it off,' Marisol whispers. 'I don't care if it all goes, so long as I'm not stuck here.'

Filip glimpses the woman's face again and his stomach lurches. He focuses on Marisol's hair until both the dead hands have relinquished their grip.

'Come on,' he says, grabbing Marisol's arm.

They stand up together and only now does he realise how quiet everyone is.

'I need a big fucking drink now too,' Marisol mumbles, sniffing.

Filip walks in behind the bar, scrubs his face and hands with detergent and the scratchy side of a scouring pad. Marisol accepts the Famous Grouse bottle from the Green Party supporter and takes a big gulp. She has no bite marks, not as far as Filip can see. She puts the bottle down on the bar, wipes her mouth and puts her hair back up. Jenny sits down on the barstool next to her and strokes her back.

The scrubbing is making Filip's lips and skin tingle and burn. He pours vodka on a fresh sponge. When he dabs his face it feels like ten thousand red-hot needles.

He takes a deep swig from the bottle.

'Has anyone else in here been bitten tonight?' he asks, and is met by nothing but silence. People are shifting uneasily, glancing askance at those next to them.

'Do you really think anyone would admit to it if they had?' the Green Party supporter says. 'And end up like the one on the floor?'

'I had to,' Filip says. 'You get that, right? I had to. You've seen for yourselves what happens . . .'

He swallows and makes a sweeping gesture towards the TV screen, which is still showing Club Charisma's dance floor and the horrors under the flashing lights.

How is he supposed to sound convincing when he doesn't know shit? How is he supposed to look at the woman's battered face and know he did the right thing?

Jenny gives him an almost imperceptible nod; his next breath comes a little more easily.

'If anyone has been bitten, we will try to help them,' Marisol says. 'If this is a disease, there might be a cure . . .'

'Not for her,' the Green Party supporter says, and chuckles.

'. . . but we have to lock them up, for everyone's safety. There's a staff room behind the bar . . .'

'Shouldn't we stick him in there, then?' the Green Party supporter says, pointing at Filip. 'He's got blood on him. How can we know he's not infected?'

The burning on his face turns to freezing cold. It is all Filip can do not to look around for signs of tacit agreement. 'I'm not,' he says.

'How do you know?'

'Yeah, how do you know?' says the woman who has hung up the phone behind the bar. 'Anyone here could be infected, right? Anyone. Oh my God, oh my God, what are we going to do?' Her breathing is becoming laboured again.

Filip notices a movement at the edge of his vision and his eyes automatically follow it.

The woman on the floor has rolled over on her front and is getting up onto all fours. The white lumps are falling out of her mouth. Her back arches. One of her dark-pink pumps has come off her foot. She sniffs the air. Her tongue writhes above her sagging jaw as though she is trying to taste the air to find what she is looking for.

People start running towards the exit. The grille rattles loudly when they try to open it.

The woman crawls across the floor, shaking her head, making her loose jaw swing back and forth. Her split top lip draws back, parting like a red curtain, revealing her teeth.

There is a loud jangle when the grille gets stuck in its tracks in the usual spot; the crawling woman turns towards the sound, tilting her head.

Filip reflexively reaches for the alarm button, and instantly realises how meaningless it is, because who would come?

Not Pia. Pia is gone.

There's more screaming as the woman crawls away across the floor. The group of singing girls try to leap out of her way, but the woman's hand shoots out and grabs an ankle. One of the girls topples, landing face-first. The woman pulls her closer. Her upper teeth sink into the girl's bare calf, ploughing deep bloody furrows. Filip sees a hint of her tongue lapping.

Jenny slides off her stool and runs over, aims a kick at the woman's head and makes contact just below the temple. The woman falls heavily onto her side without letting go of the girl's ankle. Pressing her face to the wounds again, the wet, slurping noises sound almost sexual. There's a hollow clicking from her mandible. Her upper teeth scrape against bone; the girl's screams rise in pitch.

The protective film inside Filip is shredded. The film has afforded him the luxury of not entirely believing what is happening. Now rage floods into him, giving him strength.

He grabs a knife from the cutting board and runs around the bar. His heart is pounding so fast it could break free of its tether any second.

When he gets there, Marisol has already brought the magnum down on the woman's head. The woman looks up at it. A sticky rope of blood dribbles from her tongue.

Marisol strikes again, again, again. The crunching sounds grow more muffled with each hit. A big crater has opened up in the woman's skull.

The young girl who has been bitten cries ever more hysterically, reaching out to her friends, who back away.

Marisol drops the bottle on the floor with a dull thud.

Filip suddenly realises the Green Party supporter is standing strangely still. Then he opens his mouth and blood pours out of it.

Fresh panic spreads like a shockwave through the room.

'Come on,' Filip says to Marisol and Jenny. 'We have to get people out of here, then head to the mess.'

Albin

Lo squeezes his hand and silently nods to a group of people gathered by the railing. They have opened one of the cylindrical containers. A life raft is dangling from one of the davits, an orange tent with a black base, swaying in the wind.

The man leading the group is wearing a security officer's uniform.

'Should we go to them?' Lo whispers.

'I don't know.'

But he does know. He doesn't want to leave their hiding place, even if it is a very poor hiding place. He is too scared.

'There's a security guy there,' she says, 'so they must have a plan.'

He wonders where his mum and dad are now. 'Shouldn't we wait?'

'How long for? We need to get off the ship, Abbe.'

He can tell from looking at her that she has made up her mind. And nothing is more terrifying than being left behind, all alone here.

'Mum and Cilla and Mårten will find help too,' Lo says. 'They would want us to help ourselves.'

Lo pulls on him and he has no fight left in him. He knows she is right. He stands up on numb legs; he has to lean against the wall to stop himself falling.

Lo takes the lead, stepping out into the lamplight.

Madde

Dazed, Madde sits up in her bed, unsure what has woken her. If she was dreaming, she doesn't remember what it was about. Her head is pounding and her mouth is so dry it hurts to breathe. The lights are all on and she looks around the cabin at her clothes and tax-free bags and Zandra's pink speaker on the floor. The beer bottles and catalogues on the table. She vaguely recalls a thudding sound. Maybe she did dream it after all. Sleep pulls her back down, down . . .

Something slams into the door, hard.

Madde struggles free of the duvet, tripping over her own shoes as she gets up. She is still wearing her dress; the thin fabric is damp with sweat.

As she watches the door, the handle is pushed down from the outside and then snaps back up again with a clang. There's a new thud against the door. Madde walks right up to it, while the fog in her head clears a little.

'Hello?' she calls. 'Zandra? Is that you?'

Her voice bounces back, sounding trapped. It seems impossible that anyone on the other side would hear it. She puts her mouth to the tiny gap between the door and the doorpost.

'Zandra?'

The thud that follows makes her jump.

It feels like an icy gust of wind is caressing the perspiration on her back, but there is no draught in this cramped, windowless cube.

She hears a drawn-out, guttural groan and grins, recognising that sound. Zandra must have lost her key card, or maybe she's too wasted to use it.

Madde reaches for the handle, but just then the door bursts open with a bang and Zandra stumbles into the cabin.

'Fuck me gently with a chainsaw!' Madde shrieks. 'What the hell are you doing?'

Zandra is swaying back and forth as if the only things holding her upright are her heels, digging deep into the carpet. The eyes are vacant, the mouth is open, slack. Her hair is hanging loose, dishevelled.

Madde looks at the doorjamb, which has shattered where the lock used to be, and sighs. Zandra is too off her tits to be scolded right now. She steps aside so her best friend can get past, reaching out to support her when Zandra wobbles.

'Back already?' she says. 'Did you even take the time to wipe between your legs?'

Zandra's eyebrows draw closer together as she stares uncomprehendingly at Madde.

'Are you okay? Do you need to throw up?'

She shuts the door behind Zandra, but it won't stay closed. Goddamn it. The lock is completely busted.

Zandra blinks and moans something incomprehensible, but the smell coming from her mouth speaks volumes. She has already thrown up. Madde decides to risk it and leads her to the bed instead of the bathroom.

'You have breath like a garbage truck,' she says, kicking aside a bottle of hairspray.

They sit down next to each other on the bed. Madde bends down and pulls off Zandra's shoes. A pink feather is stuck under one of her heels, but there is no sign of the boa. Madde straightens up and looks at Zandra again, at her bottomless, vacant eyes.

'Seriously, are you all right? You don't look all right.'

Zandra tilts her head to the side. A thin string of saliva trickles out of the corner of her mouth, faintly pink in the light from the sconces.

Madde feels that icy phantom wind again.

'Did you take something?' she asks, snapping her fingers in front of Zandra's eyes. 'Did that fuckwit put something in your drink? *Hello?*'

She puts her arm around Zandra and quickly retracts it when she notices it getting sticky.

Sticky and bright red.

Full gale-force winds inside Madde now. 'Let me look at your back,' she says.

Zandra doesn't react, but obediently leans forward when Madde pushes at her gently. Her clothes are torn, her back streaked with blood that has made the fabric cling and stiffen against her skin.

'What happened to you? What did they do? You have to tell me!'

Zandra is still hunched over, but she turns her head. The muscles in her face have contracted into an expression Madde has never seen on Zandra. On anyone.

She digs around the sheets and finds her phone. Her fingers are so wet with perspiration the screen doesn't respond. She wipes her hands on the duvet and manages to unlock the phone. No reception.

She reluctantly leaves Zandra's side and walks to the desk. Picking up the internal telephone receiver, she says, 'I'm going to call someone who can help you.'

She rifles through the brochures and tax-free catalogues scattered across the desk, pausing when she hears what sounds like screaming somewhere outside the cabin. She chooses the thickest catalogue and starts flipping through it from the end. It has to say somewhere what number to call to get through to information, or straight to the infirmary, because surely she saw green signs with a white cross on them?

But she can't find any numbers, only advertisements for the restaurants and perfume ads with movie stars.

'We'll figure this out,' she says, and she starts dialling numbers at random: zero, nine, zero again. 'We'll figure this out, I'll just have to go get someone who . . .'

She trails off when she hears a wet rattling behind her and turns around. Zandra is on her feet, taking a few steps towards her, wincing in pain.

Madde rushes forward through the jumble littering the floor and carefully puts her arms around Zandra for support.

I should never have fought with her when I was drunk. Then this wouldn't have happened.

'If they did this to you, I'm going to fucking kill them,' she says.

Zandra's hands, disconcertingly limp, paw at Madde's sides. She sniffs under Madde's ear, tickling her.

'I promise,' Madde says. 'Do you hear me?'

She takes a step back, examines Zandra and has the air knocked out of her.

Zandra's eyes have regained their focus. She is staring at her hands, sliding up Madde's arms. Her lips draw back, baring her teeth.

368

But they're not her teeth.

One of her front teeth is supposed to overlap the other; I've been looking at those teeth since middle school and I know, I know exactly what they're supposed to look like and that's not them.

Zandra's hands wander across Madde's shoulders. Fingertips climb up her face like giant spider's legs.

'Cut it out!' Madde says, batting them away.

Zandra doesn't even blink.

'What did they do to you?' Madde says again, in a voice that cracks on every syllable.

Zandra lifts her hands up again and touches the big gold hoop in Madde's ear. She studies it, fascinated, hooks a curled finger around it, and Madde feels her earlobe stretching.

'Stop it,' she says, and tries to grab Zandra's wrist. 'Don't pull, don't pull—'

Her ear suddenly burns as though someone has set it on fire.

'Motherfucker!' she roars.

Zandra pulls her hand back. The earring slides off her finger and falls to the floor without a sound.

Madde's ear is burning. Warm blood is trickling down the side of her neck.

Zandra opens her mouth.

Marianne

Marianne is shoved this way and that in the torrent of bodies pouring through the narrow corridor. Vincent and she had hoped the flood of people would thin out, but more kept coming. increasingly battered. Running, tripping, getting injured.

And then they heard the rattling of a grille by Charisma Starlight and a whole new wave of people broke over them.

She squeezes Vincent's hand tighter as strangers stumble into her. She catches brief glimpses of terrified faces; everywhere, people are calling out for their loved ones.

How much further? Somewhere up ahead are the main stairs by the buffet restaurant. From there, they need to get to the ninth floor, where Vincent's cabin is. Marianne is shoved aside by a woman with blood spatter in her hair, then she's pressed up against the back of a tall man whose jacket smells of smoke and spilt beer. Someone pushes past her, and suddenly Vincent's hand is gone.

She looks around, but he is nowhere to be seen.

There is screaming behind her, and the pressure is building. People are pressing in on her from every direction, making it hard to breathe. In the midst of the chaos, as she is swept out of the narrow corridor, she catches a glimpse of the buffet restaurant sign. Now she can see the stairs, but although there is more space here, the confusion is even worse, with people heading in different directions, all running into one another. She hears a dinging sound, again and again, like someone doggedly ringing a doorbell, and sees the lift doors opening and closing halfway, opening and closing halfway again.

More screaming behind Marianne as panic spreads among the bodies, spreads through her own, as though they share the same adrenalin. She is surprised how badly she wants to live, how strong her desire for more life is. Something slams into her from the side with considerable force and she loses her footing. Suddenly on the floor, she wraps her arms around her head and curls up into a ball. Feet trample the floor around her; a knee hits her shoulder; someone trips over her; the heel of a boot grazes her ear. She tries to get up, but something clobbers her hard across the back of her neck.

A body falls to the floor right next to her: a man her age, with a big, white beard and bushy eyebrows with bristles thick as wires. His wide-open eyes stare uncomprehendingly at her. A young man with blond dreadlocks throws himself onto the man's back, grinding his face into the carpet and ripping a chunk of flesh out of his neck. Then he spits it out and clamps onto the wound. It only takes half a second.

Someone hoists her up by the arms.

Vincent.

Marianne feels her feet land on the floor and then he is dragging her through the mayhem, holding her close.

They have reached the stairs. The dinging continues behind them. A red-haired woman comes stumbling down with a bloody sheet wrapped around her. She is holding it firmly closed over her breasts and stomach. She stares at Marianne as they pass each other, shouting something in Finnish.

'It's the next floor up,' Vincent says, urging her onwards, upwards.

People going down shove her, but – *ding* – Vincent keeps his hands on her – *ding* – shoulders. She turns towards the – *ding* – lift.

Lying between the lift doors is a small, brightly coloured bundle. Something like a child's arm sticks out. But it can't be an arm. Not at that angle.

Marianne looks away, noticing all the people lining the hallway, pressed up against the windows. They are standing dead still, flesh-and-blood statues. A couple of them are looking around, as if waiting for someone to come over and tell them what to do.

But no one is coming.

They reach the landing between the eighth and ninth floors. Vincent is walking behind her as they move against the current; people apparently running from something upstairs. She thinks about the Finnish woman in the bloody sheet. What if she had been trying to warn them about something?

'Where is everyone going?' Marianne says.

'There aren't a lot of cabins on the ninth floor,' Vincent says. 'Most people stay further down the ship.'

She thinks about her own cramped cabin below the waterline, the reeking hallway. Her legs filled with renewed determination, as she and Vincent climb to the ninth floor. She hears glass doors opening and shutting on the floor above them and realises the people running down the stairs are on their way from the promenade deck.

Vincent leads her around the stairwell, past a glass wall, the lone, dark conference room on the other side of it.

'Our cabin is down there,' Vincent says, pointing at the maze of hallways in front of them. 'Straight ahead, at the end. See?'

She nods. It is not a particularly long hallway and there is no one in sight. At the end of it is a door that looks like all the others.

A door they can lock behind them.

Madde

Zandra snuffles loudly, her eyes fixed on Madde's torn earlobe. Madde summons the last of her strength and shoves Zandra as hard as she can.

Zandra staggers backwards. Her feet are too slow; they trip over each other. She lands on the edge of the bed and tumbles to the floor.

'I'm sorry,' Madde says. 'I'm sorry, I didn't know what to do.'

Her best friend is trying to get back up.

'Zandra, please. I don't know what's wrong with you, but I'm going to get help, okay? Everything will be all right again.' She imitates the gentle, soothing tone of voice Zandra uses when she talks to her daughter.

Zandra has made it onto all fours and is crawling towards Madde, reaching for her. Madde stares at the bloody streaks across her back.

What the fuck did they give her?

Zandra gasps, arching her back. A red torrent shoots out of her mouth, across the carpet and scattered clothes, splashing Madde's bare feet and legs.

Then her back relaxes.

She drags her fingers through the red gloop, sticks them in her mouth.

Madde backs away in the direction of the door. She steps on the can of hairspray and loses her footing as it skids away; there is nothing to hold on to. Zandra looks up when she hits the floor. Her mouth is still working eagerly around her fingers.

'Zandra, please,' Madde says. '*Please.*'

Zandra's fingers slip out of her mouth, glistening with saliva and blood. She crawls towards Madde, who kicks out at Zandra. Her foot hits her shoulder, but Zandra keeps advancing. Her slick fingers slither up Madde's glittery calves, tickling her above her right kneecap.

Madde's groping hand closes around the can of hairspray. She is panting, and somewhere at the edge of her awareness is the realisation that she is the only one breathing in the cabin. She aims the nozzle at Zandra's face, now level with her waist.

'I'm sorry,' she whispers.

The cloud that comes out with a hiss has a sickly-sweet floral smell.

Zandra yelps shrilly and loudly, rubbing her eyes hard, sounding like a child in pain.

'I'm sorry,' Madde says again, and backs away without getting up, moving like a crab among the scattered clothes.

Zandra lowers her hands, tears streaming from her eyes. Her face is so twisted it is almost unrecognisable. Her lips are drawn back over her teeth, those new teeth . . .

That's not Zandra, that's not Zandra any more.

Madde sprays her again, but this time Zandra is ready: she shuts her eyes tight and turns her face away. The smell of hairspray fills the cabin, making Madde cough.

She keeps moving and finally feels the door against her back. She tries to get up, but Zandra grabs her foot and pulls it towards her.

Madde snatches up the hairdryer and slams it into Zandra's face, gashing her forehead. She whacks her with the dryer again; it cracks with a plastic creaking. Zandra hisses. Madde gets to her feet, grabs the pink speaker and hurls it at Zandra.

Zandra gets up too: she is clearly not going to back down. Whatever happened to her, whatever she has become, she will not rest until the same thing has happened to Madde.

'Please, please, please,' Madde breathes, but panic closes her throat. She gets the door open, finally escapes the cabin and pulls the door shut behind her. The door that no longer closes properly.

Marianne

They are so close to the end of the hallway. There's just thirty feet of carpet left.

But Marianne freezes mid-step when she hears a door slam. There are quick footsteps somewhere nearby. The sound bounces off the walls of the maze, making it impossible to locate the source. The muscles behind Marianne's ears are so tense they ache.

Vincent has stopped next to her.

More running feet: someone who is badly out of breath.

She turns around when the footsteps come into the hallway right behind her and discovers a fat, blonde woman in a see-through piece of fabric that barely covers her privates. The woman stares at them, wild-eyed.

'Help me,' she whispers, and runs up to them on blood-spattered feet.

One of her earlobes is torn in two; blood is still trickling from it. When Marianne notices the big gold hoop in her other ear and realises what has happened, a shudder runs through her. She has seen worse in the past few minutes – much worse; unfathomable things – but the pain of this torn earlobe is something she can imagine. It feels real, which is what makes it worse than all the other things. She shakes her head.

'I'm sorry, my name is Madde, I . . . you have to help me find someone,' the woman whispers, tugging at Marianne's jumper. 'My best friend needs help – she must have been drugged or . . . or . . .'

'No one can help her,' Vincent says quietly. 'Not now. Come with us.'

Marianne gives him a look. Doesn't he understand that this Madde could be one of *them*?

'No, I need to find someone who can help Zandra,' Madde whimpers.

Heavy steps sound in one of the adjacent hallways. Dread makes Marianne's stomach contract. 'The ship is full of people like her,' she snaps. 'You either come with us right now or you take your hands off me.'

Zandra comes out of the same side corridor and glares at them with bloodshot eyes.

Vincent pulls Marianne away. The creature behind them emits a scream that rattles every bone in her body and Marianne runs, ignoring her aching hips and knees. Madde is still clinging to her jumper. Time and space seem to have ceased existing; the hallway grows longer and longer in front of her, like in a nightmare, and now she can hear more feet behind them, more of *them*, attracted by the ruckus. Vincent has reached the door and is fumbling with his key card, stabbing in frustration at the narrow slot. Finally, it slides in, but nothing happens. He jiggles the door handle. Still locked.

Madde pulls the card out and flips it. She gets it in on her first try, the lock beeps and they tumble into the cabin.

Marianne hears the door shut behind them and everything goes dark.

Albin

The raft has been raised up and swung out past the edge of the deck. No one notices him and Lo when they join the semi-circle that has formed by the railing. The security guard is pulling on a rope, shouting instructions to a passenger holding the other end. Albin wonders how many people will fit on the raft. Most of those waiting are wearing life vests, but not all. There is talk of blood and death and not believing what is happening, about mentally ill people and drugs and monsters.

He doesn't want to hear it. He just wants to get off the ship, now, *immediately*. Lo was right: they have to hurry. The water is rushing past far below. Somewhere on the lower floors are his mum and dad, but he mustn't think about them now, not about where they are, or that they might die.

Lo is with him.

'There's no strap to put between your legs,' complains a man who has just pulled on a life vest. 'It's going to slip off as soon as I get in the water. I need another one!'

'Get in if you're coming,' the security guard bellows. 'No more than twenty-five people.'

Lo grabs hold of Albin and they push forward towards the raft. As someone hands them a life vest each a woman steps in under the bright orange dome, the raft rocks and then she is gone.

'What's this fucking strap you're talking about?' someone shouts. 'You have to help me with this shit!'

No one answers. Albin pulls his life vest on, trying to figure out how it works. The security officer helps more people climb into the life raft, and each time it rocks like a cocoon full of larvae ready to burst. Albin wipes raindrops from his eyelashes. The vibrations from the floor spread through his body and turn into a shiver along his spine.

Lo has cut into the line and is waving impatiently for him to follow her.

'Make sure you get these kids on there!' a man shouts behind Albin, and a few people do actually move when the man firmly grabs Albin's shoulders and pushes him forward.

Lo shows him how to fasten that strap between his legs and he wonders where she learned to do that. They are almost at the raft now. The security guard is instructing people on how to sit, alternating right and left. Albin counts the people ahead of him. He and Lo are going to fit, but he wants to sit next to her. He looks at the guard when it is their turn. His name tag says HENRIK.

'Can we count as one?' Albin says, grabbing Lo's arm. 'So we can sit together?'

Henrik just stares at him. Albin can tell from his eyes that the man's as scared as he is.

'Just hurry up,' he says.

'Hey!' someone yells. 'Hey, you can't launch that raft!'

The security guard turns towards the sound, squinting against the rain and the lights. 'And why the hell not, exactly?' he says.

'I used to work here. If I know, you must know too. That raft is going to flip over as soon as it hits the water.'

Albin turns around and studies the guy who has joined them. His head is shaved and he has a dark beard.

'I'm not staying here,' the security officer says. 'No fucking way.'

'Are you not getting that you're going to die?' the guy counters.

Albin looks at Lo.

The security officer pulls a winch handle from the davit. It shimmers like silver in the lamplight.

'Then so be it,' he says. 'I'd prefer that.'

The guy curses and glances at the raft. The people waiting inside are huddled close together for warmth.

'Get off the raft!' He shouts to make himself heard over the wind. 'Right now! You have to go to your cabins and stay there!'

No one answers.

'Lo,' Albin says, 'let's stay.'

She shakes her head.

'It's for your own safety!' the guy shouts.

'Watch out!' Lo suddenly screams, and Albin sees a gleaming arc, like liquid silver flying through the air. The guy barely has time to turn before the heavy winch handle rams into his face with a sound that makes Albin cover his ears.

But it is too late. He has already heard it and he will never be able to unhear it. Blood gushes from the guy's nose and he staggers backwards, falls, tries to get back up.

The security officer walks to where he is lying. Albin can see only his broad, uniformed back. He raises the handle and brings it down hard. When he walks away, the guy is still on the ground with blood all over his face. He looks dead.

'Fucking stellar, you fucking douchebag!' Lo screams.

The officer turns to her, and Albin stops breathing. But he doesn't raise the winch handle again. 'Are you coming?' he says.

Albin and Lo shake their heads. The security officer waves the last few people on board the raft before climbing in himself. It sways on its ropes as it's slowly lowered down towards the water.

Lo runs to the guy, but Albin can't take his eyes off the heavy cocoon. He walks up to the railing, clutches it hard when he is overwhelmed by vertigo. He wonders if the people are talking to each other or if they are quiet, waiting. How many of them heard that guy? Have any of them changed their minds and want to get out? Too late now.

The ropes creak.

The raft is winched lower, lower, lower. It starts skidding on the foam rushing around the ferry and then the ropes are cut with a loud snap. The raft smashes into the hull, then flies into backwards somersaults as if it weighs nothing. Albin thinks he can make out screaming from down there, but it must be his imagination. He leans as far out over the railing as he dares; he has to see how it ends. Far behind them he can glimpse the black underside of the raft through the foam. And then it's gone.

Lo and he could have been on it.

He holds on tighter to the railing and vomits.

Madde

Something heavy slams into the door from the outside. Zandra. Zandra who isn't Zandra any more. She wants to get in.

She's not going to give up.

There's another thud. Madde covers her ears and starts bawling, 'What the fuck's going on here?'

The old lady pats her arm awkwardly and Madde lowers her hands. She feels the next thud against the door in every part of her body.

The lights come on. All Madde can see through her tears is glitter.

'Come on,' the guy says, moving further into the cabin to turn on more lights.

Madde wipes her eyes and blinks. Her fingertips are streaked with black mascara.

She follows them into a big room. The first thing she notices are the pink streamers hanging in bunches from a banister. The cabin has an upper level: this is the suite where she thought Dan Appelgren lived, but it is even posher than she imagined. It's only a few feet away from the cabin she shared with Zandra, but this is worlds apart from the *Charisma* Madde knows so well.

Shrivelled rose petals have been ground into the carpet under her bare feet.

She walks to the windows and studies the gently rounded point of the railing at the prow, sharply illuminated against the compact darkness beyond it. People are running down there. Two young girls have attacked an old man; his face is upturned, gaping, his eyes wide. Only a few feet away, an older woman has climbed up on the railing. She is shaking her head; it looks like she is crying. The wind tears at her blouse as she climbs down onto the gunwale. A semi-circle of young men are converging on her; Madde feels like she recognises them from Club Charisma. And then the woman lets go of the railing, hides her face in her hands and kind of leans back. In the next moment, the night has swallowed her.

She jumped willingly, even though she must have known she would die.

Another wave of tears is burning in Madde's eyes, but she can't look away. A woman is tottering through the mayhem on her own. She turns around and Madde recognises her instantly. Instead of her usual uniform, she is wearing a wet dress that is clinging to her thin body and the rain has made her hair frizzy. Her normally flawless mask of makeup has been washed away. Madde knows her name because she has seen her name tag so many times. It is the woman who works in the tax-free shop: Sophia.

A girl who can't be more than ten years old sprints past. Sophia grabs hold of her, picks up the writhing body and buries her face in her neck. The girl goes limp, like a toy from which someone has removed the batteries.

There are so many of them. They are like Zandra.

'Come and sit on the sofa instead,' the old lady says, leading her that way.

'What's going on?' Madde brings herself to ask again.

'We don't know,' the guy says. 'They're biting people . . . that seems to be how it spreads.'

Madde stares at a bowl of jelly hearts on the coffee table, then gingerly touches her torn earlobe. Even the lightest touch stings.

'Their teeth,' she says. 'Zandra had new teeth.'

She notices the guy and his mum exchanging a look as she sits down.

'How are you feeling, dear?' the old lady says, taking a seat next to her. 'Did she hurt you?'

The old lady looks nice. How old is she? Her hair is straight and dyed red. When did all of those old-lady hairdos with curly grey hair disappear?

'Did she bite you?'

'No,' Madde says.

There's a new thud against the door. Madde stares at the steps leading to the upper level. Where should she run to if Zandra gets in?

'I'm sorry, but we have to ask,' the guy says. 'There's a cut in your ear that . . .'

'She tore out my earring,' Madde says. 'I've not been bitten.' She has a sudden realisation. 'And what about you? How am I supposed to know you and your mum won't turn into them all of a sudden?'

They exchange another look.

'We haven't been bitten either,' the old lady says. 'And I'm not his mother.'

Madde examines her and decides to trust them. What other choice is there? 'I want to get out of here,' she says. 'I want to go home. I don't want to be here.'

'I know,' Vincent says, 'but at least we're safe here.'

She doesn't ask how he knows that, or how any of them could possibly know anything at all about that.

Calle

He touches his forehead. When his fingers get close to the edges of the wound near his hairline, the pain grows roots all the way down to the soles of his feet.

The two children are standing in front of him. They look about twelve. Both have childlike eyes, both are scared, but the girl has learned to conceal it. To try to conceal it, at any rate.

Calle struggles to sit up. He can't breathe through his nose; it feels numb, like a brick in the middle of his face, and his whole mouth tastes of blood. He looks up at the davit. The raft is gone.

'What happened?' he says. His voice sounds thick and sticky. He clears his throat and spits.

'They disappeared,' the boy says. 'They ... they all disappeared. Into the water.'

Calle tries to get up, but the dizziness makes the whole ship list. He gazes into the darkness beyond the railing. The water is over fifteen hundred feet deep in places and it can't be many degrees above freezing.

He thinks about the people who climbed into the life raft and wonders what is left of them now, if they were crushed against the hull, tangled inside the raft. The only thing he knows for sure is that they are dead.

If he had arrived sooner, if he had dodged the blow, if he had managed to stop that security officer they might still be alive.

For a while longer, at least. But does anyone on board really stand a fighting chance?

He pushes his fear away, tries to compose himself and turns to the children.

'Do you know what's going on?' the girl asks.

Calle glances at two staggering figures further down the deck. Are they hurt? Infected? He wishes he had something soothing to say, something they would believe. The boy needs it. But he looks at the girl and knows she would see through it, and she wouldn't trust him again.

'No,' he says, 'not really. They're saying there's some kind of disease on board that makes people . . . weird.'

There's screaming, somewhere abaft, like a confirmation.

'What are you doing here?' Calle asks. 'Where are your parents? Do you know?'

The boy shakes his head.

'Where's your cabin?'

'The sixth floor,' the boy says. 'I think my dad's there. But our mums might be looking for us. We were kind of . . . hiding from them.'

Sixth floor: that's where Pia called from. Calle has no idea what things might be like down there now.

'My mum's in a wheelchair. She can't get by on her own.' The boy tries to look brave.

Calle has to turn away to keep from crying. He forces himself back on his feet, attempting to think through the pain. He is going to find Vincent: he has to focus on that. And he has seen the statistics. The people who survive disasters are the ones who will literally step over dead bodies. The ones who stop to help others don't make it.

The girl has just opened her mouth to say something when they hear screaming coming from one of the stairs down to the promenade deck. A whole pack of infected have backed a couple of middle-aged men up against the railing. The men vanish from sight. The screams are abruptly cut short.

'Don't look,' Calle says, and the boy quickly turns away, but the girl keeps staring.

He is overcome with shame. He can't just leave the children here, but he won't be able to help anyone if he can't think clearly. And to do that, he has to switch off his feelings.

He needs to get from one moment to the next, so one thing at a time. Don't look at the big picture, or his strength will fail him.

'Come on,' Calle says, 'we need to get away from here.'

'Where are we going?' the girl asks. 'They're everywhere.'

Calle's head is throbbing rhythmically, but it feels like the pounding is getting duller, starting to subside. And he realises what he needs to do, then he can head out to look for Vincent again.

'Not everywhere,' he says. 'I'll bring you to the staff quarters. They can't get in there.' He hopes he is telling the truth. Regardless, it is the best he has to offer.

The girl's eyes narrow. 'How do we know you're not one of them? Maybe you're just planning on taking us someplace where you can gobble us up in peace and quiet.'

The boy looks at her, then at him.

The girl is clearly the one he needs to convince. 'They don't seem that good at planning, do they?'

She looks at Calle, wavering. 'Okay,' she says.

'Good.' He looks across at the stairs on the other side of the sun deck. No infected to be seen there, but they have to hurry. He grabs their hands, so small in his.

Filip

The last customers have left Starlight and Filip opens the door to the staffroom behind the bar. Everything still looks normal in there: the hard wooden chairs and the wax tablecloth. The Duralex glass he drank his coffee out of when they left Stockholm is in the dish rack. Marisol and the guys in the band take the lead, pushing open the door on the other side of the room, which leads further into the *Charisma*'s staff quarters.

Jenny is gone. The others haven't seen her either. He can't remember when he saw her last. Could she have run on ahead?

Please, he thinks, *let her be in the mess already.*

For a moment, he is jealous of Marisol's faith. She has someone to turn to with her prayers.

He stops in the doorway and looks back at the empty room. Has a feeling this is the last time he will ever see Starlight.

'Excuse me,' someone says just as he is about to close the door behind him, making Filip start.

A man in a blue shirt has entered the bar. Large strips of skin have been peeled from his face, hanging in tatters across one of his eyes and from one of his cheeks. But he seems completely composed, as though he hasn't even noticed.

Filip swallows hard. 'Yes?' he says, and is shocked by how neutral he sounds.

'Would you happen to know if this is going to cause a delay?' the man asks.

Filip stares at him.

'I have an important meeting in Åbo tomorrow morning. My schedule was tight even before, so I hope this won't make us late.'

Filip shakes his head. 'I don't know,' he says. 'I'm sorry. I . . . I have to go now, but . . .'

He studies the man's face. He can't be saved. There is nothing Filip can do for him, no matter how much he might want to.

But after closing the door behind him and following the others, he can't shake the feeling that he is responsible for everything that happens to the man from now on: as if he personally has signed his death warrant.

The *Baltic Charisma*

The man who worked on board several years ago crosses the sun deck with the two children. The stairs to the promenade deck are too narrow for them to run side by side, so he lets go of their hands and walks down ahead of them, surveying the chaos. He tries to identify the infected, but it is impossible. Suddenly there is tumult behind him; he turns around, sees bodies knocking into one another at the top of the stairs, takes the children's hands and they jump the last few steps. He pulls them close, starts walking towards the door leading into the ship.

'Hold on tight to me,' he says.

The hallways of the *Charisma* are full of running people. There are bodies everywhere, dead, dying, in the process of waking up. Some of the newborns have eaten far too much; they lie motionless while their bodies try to process all the blood they have consumed.

Hundreds upon hundreds of people have locked themselves in their cabins, where they sit listening to the sounds from the corridors outside. One of them is the man called Mårten. Alone in his cabin, he is sitting on the edge of the bed. His wife's cries for help from the hallway still reverberate inside him. The curtains remain drawn. From time to time, he stands up, walks to the telephone and calls the cabin next door. He hears the phone ring through the wall, but no one picks up.

Calle

The glass door is just thirty feet away, and once they reach it, there are only a few more steps to the unmarked door leading to the staff quarters. Calle has bowed his head and is holding the children's hands once more. He keeps an eye out for Vincent while being careful not to meet anyone's gaze.

On the sun deck above their heads, there are loud screams. He catches a glimpse of something fluttering by on the other side of the railing and realises someone probably jumped. There's more screaming behind them and he whispers, 'Don't look,' as much for his benefit as theirs.

He can't bear to see the screamers. He doesn't even want to think of them as human. That would make it all far too real, far too obvious that it might as well have been him or the children; that they might be next. That it may be too late for Vincent.

Calle focuses on the light coming from inside the ship. Fifteen feet left. Ten.

When they reach the glass door they push into the warm glow. Calle spots bodies further down the stairs, a few of them moving. He reluctantly lets go of the girl and boy, pulls out Filip's pass and swipes it, yanks the door open and ushers the children in ahead of him, terrified someone might grab him from behind at any moment. He pulls the door shut behind him, relief washing over him when the lock clicks.

The girl glances around the grey corridor. It is so calm in here, and so hard to imagine the bedlam out there.

Calle wonders whether he should have brought more people in here; if he might have been able to save someone else. But he can't be sure who is infected.

There is no point dwelling on it now. At least, that is what he tries to tell himself.

He squats down and looks the children in the eye. 'There are people here who can look after you. People who work on board.'

'Like that security guard who beat you up?' the girl says. 'I bet the people he *helped* are real fucking grateful right now.'

'Can't you stay with us?' the boy asks.

Calle takes a deep breath, trying to assume the role of resourceful adult. He shakes his head firmly. 'I have someone I need to go look for.'

'Who?' the girl wants to know.

'My boyfriend.'

If he even still is.

'But we can go with you,' the boy says. 'We can help you. And you can help us find our parents.'

'It's better if you wait here. I can't take you with me – you've seen what it's like out there. We can call your cabins. Maybe they're already there.'

'But what if they're not?' the boy says desperately.

'Then I promise to keep an eye out for them.'

They look at each other.

'Let's take it one step at a time,' he adds.

Dan

He is standing on the afterdeck, gazing out across a sea of blackest ink under a bottomless tar sky. There are a thousand nuances of black, gradations Dan had never been able to see before.

There is a burning in his veins, in the capillaries of his finger-tips; his heart muscles are seizing up. *Too much blood*. He's unable to control himself. All this floating tissue has made his body heavy, sluggish; it's soaked his brain, flooded his seizing heart, filled out his cock. He is prickling as if from a thousand needles.

Behind him, sighing and moaning is coming from inside Club Charisma. Someone keeps repeating, 'I'm going to die, aren't I? God help me, I'm really going to die.'

There are other sounds too: the first tottering steps of new-borns, their anguished screams, hungry and afraid.

He turns around.

The deck is littered with bodies. One of the glass doors to the lower floor of the club is shattered. A woman is lying on her front, face down. The broken glass is red with her blood. She is still breathing. Dan steps over a few bodies and stops next to her, puts the tip of his shoe under her chin, lifts her head with his foot and studies her profile. There are pockmarks under her thick makeup. Her eye stares up at him, squinting against the rain as her breathing grows shallower and more rapid.

And then she dies. She simply stops breathing. Life is extinguished in her, without a sound. Her eye stares back at him, unseeing, as raindrops land on her eyeball.

It is time to go. Dan strides across more bodies. A hand reaches out to grab his trouser leg; it belongs to a man with the same chin-length hairstyle he used to have in the nineties. His mouth opens wide as he looks at Dan. Several of his teeth have already fallen out. His fingers squeeze Dan's trouser leg. Dan kicks his foot to shake him off.

For a split-second, Dan is filled with intense unease. The drifts of bodies are a taste of what awaits the unsuspecting world. All this dead flesh, rubbed in lotions, painted bright colours, perfumed, dressed in cheap fabrics: soon, it will rise again.

There is no going back. He comprehends it fully for the first time, and it is like when a car hydroplanes or an airplane flies through severe turbulence: like free-falling, knowing there is nothing you can do.

And then it is gone as quickly as it came, leaving only the dull ache in his chest, the veins burning beneath his skin. But all that will pass.

Dan curses himself. He has been cowed by life for so long he is afraid of his new-found power, but he is a different Dan now: he is as good as invincible, the one who will stand strong while the rest of the world falls. And he is going to enjoy every second of it.

The wind drops abruptly when he steps into the lee of the superstructure on the portside promenade deck. The smell of blood is stronger when not dispersed by the wind. More bodies are strewn about here, all the way to the stairs that lead up to the next floor, where the promenade deck stretches on towards the prow. A woman is draped over the railing. Her spine has been bent backwards and snapped, turning her body into an L. She has just woken up and the tips of her court shoes are sliding back and forth across the slippery floor as she tries to find traction, to get back on her feet despite the incongruous shape of her body.

A tanned man in a neon-yellow football shirt is being chased down the stairs by a couple of newborns. He calls out for help, running straight for Dan as if he is some kind of white knight. His shouts turn into a stream of vowels when the newborns catch him, tugging at his arms as they fight over their prey. The man manages to break free and looks at Dan as if still expecting help. But there is no help to be had.

And suddenly the man has jumped over the railing, disappeared into the night. One of the newborns clumsily climbs after him, throwing himself off the edge, but the other one stays where he is, watching Dan as he walks away.

The glass door leading into the ship is wide open. Dan can hear the newborn following him. Inside, the air is thick, almost quivering with discharges from the still-warm bodies scattered about the entrance of Club Charisma.

He walks down the stairs. One of the newborns, an old man Dan recognises from the karaoke, is on all fours. The body he is straddling is still breathing, the khaki-clad legs twitching, but he is about to die any moment. The newborn looks up, blood pouring over his lips. He slowly turns his head as Dan walks past.

Dan descends to the eighth-floor hallway to find even more bodies littering the corridor in front of Starlight. When he turns around, the old man and the newborn from the promenade deck are standing there, eyeing him warily.

Euphoria stirs in him again. It is just as Adam told him it would be: he needs only to *be* for them to follow him. To the newborns,

Adam and he are the indisputable alpha males. The *Charisma* is their Hamelin and they are the Pied Pipers.

He can hear the sounds of people trying not to make a sound: two people breathing as one in the casino. There's the scent of old people, old flesh, sour sweat and urine.

One of them smells familiar from earlier tonight and he can't resist the opportunity.

He peers into the gloom to see a pair of fat calves in practical walking shoes sticking out from under the blackjack table.

Dan walks across, squats down and pulls aside the croupier's stool.

The old bat's tight outfit is sopping with perspiration. The old man is no longer wearing his sweater-vest; his shirt is loose over his emaciated body. His rheumatic hand looks so pitiful in her meaty paw; she must surely have crushed every bone in it.

They squint at him in terror in the dim light, but he can see them perfectly clearly. 'Well, well, if it isn't Birgitta from Grycksbo,' Dan says with a big smile. 'This probably wasn't the ruby wedding you were hoping for.'

It is a brilliant parody of the Dan Appelgren who was on stage earlier tonight. He can almost feel their relief.

'Oh my dear God, Jesus Christ in heaven,' Birgitta whispers in her sing-song dialect, and sobs. 'We thought you were one of them.'

'Shhh,' Dan says, and holds his hand out. 'Come on out and I'll help you get to your cabin.'

Birgitta shakes her head. 'They're everywhere,' she breathes.

'Don't worry,' Dan says. 'Everything is under control.'

The newborns are shifting excitedly in the corridor. Birgitta looks at her husband, who shakes his head at her.

'Everything is going to be okay,' Dan says. 'Help is on its way and we've locked up all the sick people.'

'But we heard some . . .' Birgitta starts saying.

'It's finished. Come on now. You can't just sit here.'

'Are you really sure?' the old man says, and his accent is, if possible, even thicker than Birgitta's. 'Is it really over?'

'We have seen such things as you would never believe,' Birgitta says with another sob.

'Me too,' Dan says. 'Me too, but you're safe now.'

It is all he can do not to burst out laughing. One of the newborns snaps his teeth: the piles of meat outside Starlight are moving, but Birgitta clearly can't hear them. She has decided to trust Dan.

He waves for them to come out, smiling so big his swollen cheeks almost force his eyes closed. Birgitta takes his hand and he helps her up. When he puts his arms around her short, fat body Birgitta begins to cry, hiding her face in her hands and leaning into him, sobbing harshly behind her fingers.

The old man struggles out from under the table. Every part of his wizened body creaks and cracks when he gets to his feet, supporting himself on the table.

'I don't understand what happened,' Birgitta says. 'One moment we were having a wonderful time, and then everything was like a nightmare . . . We were so afraid . . .'

'I understand,' Dan says in his most purring voice. 'It must have been awful. But at least you had each other.'

Birgitta nods, her sobs now racking her whole body.

'I don't know what I would have done if anything had happened to Birgitta,' her husband says, wiping his eyes.

'I understand,' Dan says, 'although I haven't had the privilege experiencing that kind of great, everlasting love. Not everyone gets to these days.'

Dan hugs the squat body in his arms tighter.

Birgitta falters in the middle of a sob.

'I suppose you'd do just about anything for Birgitta, wouldn't you?' Dan says, fixing the old man with his eyes.

'Yes, of course.'

Birgitta squirms in Dan's grasp; she's grown warmer in his embrace and a new waft of pungent sweat emanates from her.

'Yeah, people like you always say that, but would you *really* give up your life for her?'

'Please let me go,' Birgitta croaks.

'I'm going to give you a chance to prove it now,' Dan says to the old man. 'If you really love her that much, I will let her go and kill you instead.'

'You're . . . hurting . . . me . . .'

He squeezes her harder, the last of the air rushing out of her lungs with a guttural groan. She is not going anywhere.

'What do you say? What's it going to be?'

'Let her go,' the old man says, fresh tears pouring down his cheeks.

'I'm not hungry any more,' Dan say, while Birgitta writhes in his arms. 'It's not going to be quick, and it's going to hurt, more than you can imagine. But I'm giving you an out: all you have to do is say the word and I'll have little Birgitta here instead.'

The old man hesitates.

Say it, Dan thinks to himself. *Say it, you old twit, and make it the last thing Birgitta hears in this life.*

400

The old man shakes his head. 'Then take me,' he says, 'you blasted devil.'

Dan hates him for lying to himself, even now.

It is time to end this, but he doesn't want her; he doesn't even want the taste of her on his lips. He puts his hands around her neck and squeezes as hard as he can. It is warm and doughy and Birgitta's eyes are big and round, bulging from their sockets. His face is going to be the last thing she sees.

The old man's feeble hands pound against Dan's head, a hail of punches he can hardly feel, like a swarm of tiny birds. Dan takes no notice of them. This is about him and Birgitta. He lays her down on the green felt of the blackjack table. It's now: the moment when she realises it is all over, that she is going to die, and that it is because of him. He makes sure he commits every movement of her face to memory, knowing that he is going to enjoy reminiscing about it time and again.

He lets the newborn from the promenade deck take care of Birgitta's husband. It is over quickly.

When he comes back out, more newborns get to their feet in the hallway and follow him: his hungry army, his pliable children. His subjects.

Adam is waiting for him outside Charisma Buffet. Looking unbearably smug, he gestures towards the throng of newborns following him. A pang of irritation needles Dan. Granted, everything may have started with Adam, but he would never have done this well without Dan, he admitted as much himself. Adam wouldn't have known how to cut the *Charisma* off from the rest of the world, to make sure they remain undisturbed. He wouldn't have known what they have to do next.

'You've overeaten,' Adam says. 'I warned you. You're going to make yourself sick.'

Dan can sense the two groups of newborns watching them. He wonders how much they comprehend.

Does he need Adam? Does he have more to learn? It doesn't feel like it; it feels like he is never going to need anyone ever again.

'Don't worry about me,' he says, 'but I appreciate your concern.'

'My concern is for the plan. Can you do it on your own?'

'Why wouldn't I be able to?'

'Good then,' Adam says. 'Meanwhile, I will attempt to locate Mother.'

'You do that.'

You little mama's boy. Not as easy to cut the apron strings as you thought, is it?

He pulls out his pass, but his hand stops in mid-air above the reader next to the door to the staff quarters. A scent has reached him. He can't believe how familiar it is. Of course that's what she smells like. He just hadn't been able to tell before.

A contraction in his chest pushes more blood out into his body, making his skin flush. He looks back at Adam. 'There's just one thing I have to do first.'

The boy's smooth forehead furrows. 'What?'

Never you fucking mind. He doesn't need to explain himself to this brat. If they are going to work together, he is not going to assume a subordinate role from the start. If you agree to be fucked up the arse once, you have to keep putting up with it again and again.

'You go and look for your mummy,' he says, putting his pass back into his pocket.

He walks to the men's room and calmly pushes open the swing-ing door. The synthetic smells almost overpower him: cleaner and cheap soap and the stink of the citrus urinal cakes. But the smell of *her* is strong too.

The soles of his shoes slap hard against the floor; he knows she can hear them.

The newborns file in behind him, eagerly sniffing the air. Several of them haven't eaten yet; there's not a lot of food left in the public spaces. Most people who have avoided being bitten have escaped to their cabins. But Dan will lead them to food, and in here is a little appetiser to start.

He catches a glimpse of himself in the mirrors above the sinks. The bloated blood vessels in his eyes have burst, turning them so red they look like lesions in his face.

He stops at the flimsy door of one of the stalls, where he can hear her trying to hold her breath. She knows she is trapped in there, helpless. Her smell is becoming more like a hunted animal's with every heartbeat.

He walks to the stall, close enough for her to see his shoes under the door. There's a muffled sound: a gasp. He relishes the moment.

This is divine justice. And he is his own god.

Albin

They have just reached the grey steel door at the end of the hallway when a screeching, grating sound erupts in the stairwell.
Albin can't stop himself from looking down.

A man is handcuffed to the railing on the landing below. Albin
can make out a shiny, bald head, a broad back.

'Come on,' Calle says, pulling on his hand.

'Is he one of them?'

'No. I talked to him a little while ago.'

'All the ones outside were normal before too,' Lo retorts, and
moves next to Albin. 'And why would someone have handcuffed
him if he was completely harmless?'

'They do that sometimes when there's no more room in the
drunk tanks.'

'Is that really allowed?' Lo says. 'That's messed-up.'

'It's for their own good,' Calle says, but Albin can tell he doesn't
really agree with it.

'If they get in here, it's gonna be "Bye and bon appetit",' Lo says.

Albin looks downstairs again. And the man tilts his head back
and stares straight at them.

'There you are!' he shouts. The handcuffs clatter and rattle as
he pulls them against the railing again. 'Have you found a key yet
or what?'

404

'No, I haven't found one,' Calle says.

The man stops moving and his shoulders sag. 'You fucking suck,' he says. 'Am I just supposed to sit here and drown when the ship sinks, huh? The newspapers are going to hear about this, how you treat your passengers. Or is that why you want me to drown, yeah? So they don't find out that—'

'I'll try to find someone with keys,' Calle calls to him, 'but we're not sinking.'

'Something's going on, though. I heard over the speakers that there's an emergency meeting upstairs.'

'There's no need to worry,' Calle says.

Lo glances at Albin. They all know what an enormous lie that is.

'Come on,' Calle says, and puts his hands on their shoulders, but Albin can't tear himself away.

The man downstairs has started crying. 'Lillemor told me not to go,' he says, so quietly Albin can barely make out the words. 'She's always hated the sea. She's never been on a ship her whole life. But now I wish she were here with me . . . How selfish is that?'

Albin looks away. It feels like the ship is closing in around them and soon it will crush them alive.

'We're not going to sink,' Calle says again. 'Don't worry.'

This time, Albin and Lo move away from the railing with him. He opens the steel door and a din of loud voices spills out from inside.

Dan

'There's something I'd like to show you,' Dan says.

Jenny tried to run when he kicked open the door to the stall. It was a pathetic attempt. He fills practically the entire opening, but she still tried to squeeze past, so he slammed her head into the wall behind the toilet until her eyes rolled back into her head.

He waited, gave her a few slaps. Now her eyes are clearing once more.

She has to see. She has to *understand*. That's the whole point.

The newborns who have followed him in are crowding around them, silent, waiting.

Dan lifts up his hand and sinks his teeth into it, then bites until the sound of fragile bones being crushed echoes against the tiles. Blood fills his mouth and runs down his chin. He sucks his hand, hard, licks the edges without looking away from Jenny for so much as a moment. He's giving her a show.

'Hang on, you'll see,' he says, wiping his chin.

Jenny has started crying softly. Each streaked tear is proof that he has defeated her.

'I could have made you virtually immortal,' he says, 'but I'm not going to.'

He grabs her chin and forces her to look at his hand, where the wound is already closing. There is a faint crunching from bones knitting themselves together inside his flesh.

She doesn't get it. She never gets anything. Stupid fucking cow.

'See?' Dan says. 'You could've been something else, something better, just like me, if only you had been a bit nicer.'

Now who's a has-been? Now who has the power to say no?

He is going to kill her; he is going to kill her so she never wakes up again. Adam has shown him how.

Filip

The general manager is standing at the front of the mess, talking so quickly he is tripping over his tongue. Filip feels sorry for him. Most of the people in the room know Andreas well. He supervises all customer-facing staff on board, but no one thinks of him as a leader and, clearly, Andreas doesn't either. Now he is suddenly the highest-ranking officer on the ship.

And no one knows what has happened up on the bridge or down in the engine room.

The ship's signal booster has been disabled, the radio destroyed, they can't reach the satellites and DSC and VHF have been sabotaged, even in the lifeboats and life rafts. They have no way of contacting anyone. They don't even have flares. They are completely cut off.

On the Baltic, no one can hear you scream, Filip thinks, and almost lets out a chuckle, a laugh of desperation he can't afford. Not now, not here.

As long as the autopilot keeps the *Charisma* on her pre-programmed route, no one outside the ship will suspect there is anything amiss. If there is enough fuel in the tanks, the autopilot can take them all the way to Åbo. Once they reach the final input-ted waypoint, the autopilot will continue on its last set course and the *Charisma* will likely ram into the pier or run aground.

'Once we get close enough to Finland, we can use the regular mobile network,' Andreas says. 'We can call the Finnish police for help, or the army . . .'

'But that's *hours* away,' someone says. 'What do we do until then?'

Filip looks around. All the familiar faces look so different, naked with fear, but he is feeling strangely calm. It is worse than he thought, much worse, but at least now he knows what he has to deal with.

The mess is warm and damp with so many bodies crammed into it. He tries not to think about who is missing, about what might have happened to them, but he can't hold down the thought of Pia, or the knowledge that neither she nor Jarno are here. Raili's face is ashen and her eyes are red. Marisol is holding her, but she doesn't even seem to have noticed; she just keeps twisting her wedding ring.

Jenny still hasn't turned up.

Calle is missing too. The vodka bottle was almost empty; other than that, there was no sign that he'd even been there. He's probably gone back out into the ship to look for his boyfriend. It is an idiotic decision, and Filip totally gets it.

He lets his eyes rove across the room. Mika has sat down on a chair by a table at the front. He is pale; his thin hair is slicked to his scalp.

There is a handful of strangers here too: one-night stands or relatives. He realises one of the strangers is the woman he saw hovering near the dance floor at Starlight. She has rammed her hands deep into the pockets of her baggy cardigan. She looks younger, healthier. It must have been the flashing lights of the dance floor casting unfortunate shadows, creating illusions. She is the only one in here who doesn't seem to be sweating, despite her cardigan. Her eyes are alert, watchful, but she hasn't lost her head.

Lizette gets up from a chair in the middle of the room. She's the new chief housekeeper, head of the cleaning staff, and Filip has never seen her out of uniform before. Now she runs her hand through her tousled hair and looks around. 'We're safe here,' she says. 'I and a bunch of others are planning to stay here until help comes from outside. You can't make us—'

'But what about the passengers?' one of the cooks puts in. 'Are we just going to leave them to their fate?'

'Exactly,' a girl who works as a croupier in the casino says. 'It's our job to do everything we can to—'

'There's nothing we can do for them now,' Lizette declares, and spreads her arms like a conductor trying to make her orchestra play more softly. 'We don't even know what's happened to all those people.'

People look at each other uncertainly. No one wants to be the first to agree.

'If you want to head back out there, be my guest,' Lizette tells the croupier. 'But no one can force us to go on some kind of suicide mission. Or am I wrong, huh, am I?'

She turns to Andreas, raising her eyebrows dramatically. This time, there is a murmur of agreement.

They still don't get it. Many of them haven't been out there yet.

'There is no guarantee that we're safe in here either,' Filip says, exchanging a look with Marisol. 'People in here could already be infected. They may not even know it themselves yet.'

More furtive glances criss-cross the room, an entirely new kind of fear in them.

His own words sink in for him too. Sweat trickles down his back and drips from his armpits underneath the nylon of his shirt. His mouth is dry; he wonders if that could be a symptom. He studies his colleagues. He has lived on board with many of them for years.

If I'm infected, will I attack them?

For a moment, there is dead silence. He realises the woman from Starlight is watching him. Does she know something? Can she tell from looking at him that he is infected?

He doesn't dare meet her eyes.

'There's one thing I would really like to know,' someone starts. 'What kind of illness turns people into psychopaths?'

'Pia talked about Dan Appelgren,' Mika says. 'She thought he was infected . . . and he has an all-access pass, he knows how everything works . . .'

'Don't you get it yet?' Pär the security officer puts in. 'This isn't some over-the-hill Eurovision star. This is *terrorism*. This is fucking Isis. They've cut us off from the rest of the world and put some fucking super-anthrax in the water tanks or something. They're behind this.'

'Let's just calm down,' Andreas says, wiping his forehead with his sleeve. 'No one is helped by us working ourselves into a panic.'

'I think it might be too late for that,' Lizette mutters.

Someone puts a hand on Filip's shoulder, and when he turns around Calle is standing there with a big gash in his forehead and a swollen nose, but very much alive.

Filip throws his arms around him. 'I'm so fucking glad to see you. I needed some good news.'

'Me too,' Calle says.

Then Filip realises that Calle has brought two children with him. He recognises them: the boy and the girl from earlier tonight at Starlight. Damp has turned the girl's hair a few shades darker. They watch him silently. Both of them look several years older than just a few hours ago.

That is what almost makes Filip fall apart. He hides his face in Calle's shoulder and slaps his back, hard. Wonders what the three of them have been through outdoors. 'Good news is pretty thin on the ground here,' he says, lowering his voice, hoping the children won't hear. 'We can't get in touch with land.'

They let go of each other. Calle looks at him.

'I have to get off the ship,' a woman says. 'I'm not going to die on one of these boats.'

When one of the waiters from Poseidon tries to take her hand, she bats it away.

'As long as the *Charisma* keeps going at this clip, we can't lower the life rafts,' Andreas says. 'We'd have to slow down to ten, twelve knots to launch even an FRB, and we're currently doing at least eighteen, nineteen—'

'What are you talking about?' the woman says. 'What's a fucking FRB?'

'A fast rescue boat,' Andreas replies. 'They—'

'I wouldn't get into a raft with any of the passengers anyway,' Lizette cuts in. 'What if one of them changes while you're out there, bobbing on the waves?'

'It has to work!' the other woman says. 'Can't you just put the rafts down really gently and—'

'You can't,' Calle interrupts. 'Some people already tried. It was full of people. One of your security officers was on it.'

The attention of the room shifts to him, but Filip looks at Pär, the only security officer in the mess. Calle must be talking about Henke.

'Calle tried to stop them,' the girl says, 'but the guard said he would rather die than stay here, and then he beat him up.'

Filip's eyes go to the cut on Calle's forehead. What he just told them is impossible to imagine, but a lot of impossible-to-imagine things have happened on board tonight.

'We have to get up to the bridge,' Pär says, rubbing his eyes. 'And we have to clear the ship of those fucking monsters.'

'They're not monsters,' Raili puts in. 'They're people. They're sick.'

'How can you say that after they killed your husband?' Pär asks.

He seems to regret it instantly, conscious of having crossed a line, but Raili just fixes him with a level gaze.

'I agree,' Antti from the tax-free shop says. 'Let's weed them the fuck out of the *Charisma*. We'll make mincemeat out of the lot of them and get onto the bridge one way or another.'

Filip stares at them.

He wonders if they are experiencing that feeling now, the one that came over him at Starlight: that what is happening is just a film. People like Antti and Pär have probably dreamed of being action heroes their entire lives. But they haven't grasped that they don't have the starring role in this film. No one in here does. It all revolves around the *Charisma*.

Albin

The voices grow louder, more and more joining in. And the room keeps getting warmer. He looks up at Calle, who is whispering something to his bartender friend.

Albin doesn't want Calle to leave them. He understands that Calle has to look for his boyfriend; he just wishes that wasn't the case.

'We should sink the ship,' a woman says. '*That way*, at least it would stop and then we can get the fuck off.'

Calle and his friend turn to her. 'And let all the other people drown?' Calle's friend says.

'Better to have a few survive than none at all.'

Out of the corner of his eye, Albin sees some people nod their agreement. He thinks about his mum's wheelchair in flooded corridors and he hates every one of them.

Somewhere outside the room a heavy steel door slams shut. It sounds like the one he, Lo and Calle entered through moments ago.

'And who gets to choose who we rescue?' someone else says.

'Women and children first, and—'

'Oh, right, so now it's like that. Not so keen on that gender equality nonsense now, are you?' says the old man in the security officer uniform.

And the voices keep growing louder.

'Can't we dump the fuel to stop the boat?'

'Too risky. It's difficult and takes time.'

'We could turn out all the lights, or try to flash them . . . If all the lights went out, another ship might see and realise something was wrong . . .'

'You want to go fumbling around in the dark with those things?'

'But we could go down to the engine room and pour water on the main switchboard. If we do a shutdown—'

'I don't see why we're even talking about this. We have to reach the bridge and we're going to get in there somehow, and on the way there we make mincemeat out of any fucker who walks around biting people, and—'

'Shut up, Antti,' Calle's friend snaps, spreading his hands wide. 'You're as bloodthirsty as they are.'

Albin notices that there are big pit stains under his arms.

'We have no idea what's happened to them,' the friend continues, 'but they're people. They're sick and they need help.'

'Oh yeah, you reckon?' a voice says. 'Because it seems to me you're the ones who need help.'

Several people turn around and someone screams. And even though Albin doesn't want to, his gaze is drawn to the door as well.

Dan Appelgren is standing in the doorway, but he is almost unrecognisable. He is swollen, and his eyes are bright red, shining, crazed.

The doorway is filling up with sick people, sniffing, snapping their teeth. But they stop behind Dan and don't move, as if they are waiting for something.

Albin looks at Lo.

It is like when they used to scare each other at night back in Grisslehamn. Now they have peeked behind that curtain, the curtain whose very existence he could only vaguely sense back then. At last he knows what kind of monsters lurked behind it all along: they are here now.

Chairs crash to the floor, which trembles underneath Albin's feet when the people closest to the door run towards the other end of the room.

Someone has started praying, *ourfatherwhoartinheavenhallowedbethyname*, hurriedly, as though he wants to make sure he gets to *amen* before it is too late.

Marianne

Her heart is pounding rapidly, even though she is sitting quite still on the sofa: a ticking bomb in her chest that could blow up at any moment.

At least no one is throwing themselves at the door any more.

'What if we sink?' asks Madde, who has gone back to stand by the window.

'We won't,' Vincent says, and knocks back a quick slug of whisky.

'How would you know?' Madde says, her voice quavering. 'Maybe no one's even there to drive the boat any more.'

Marianne tries to fight the vertigo that suddenly overcomes her. Here, in a suite that is larger than her flat, she had almost managed to forget that they are not on dry land. A completely irrational fear grabs her. It feels like Madde is going to conjure a new catastrophe simply by talking about it. 'Be quiet,' she hears herself say. 'Just shut up.'

Madde ignores her. Her back sparkles with gold dust. 'What if we're already dead?' she says. 'Maybe we've gone to hell.'

'Please,' Marianne says.

'It certainly looks like hell.'

'Come and sit down,' Vincent says. 'You'll drive yourself crazy, watching that—'

'I think I'll go crazy no matter what I do.'

Vincent nods, even though Madde can't see him. 'Maybe you should step away from there regardless. If one of them spots you, you might attract them.'

The sleeves of Marianne's jumper feel like they're shrinking, squeezing her so tightly they cut off her circulation. The hairs on the back of her neck are standing on end.

'I don't think so,' Madde says. 'I'd say they're keeping themselves pretty busy.'

'Come away from there, anyway,' Marianne snaps.

Vincent stands up and joins Madde by the window. He scans the mayhem down there, looking for his friend.

What would he do if he saw him? Would he leave them? Yes, of course.

'Do you think they . . . do you think they have any idea what they're doing?' Madde says, and looks at him. 'Because Zandra, she was like . . . It was like no one was . . . inside.'

'They must be acting on some kind of instinct,' Vincent replies.

Madde sniffs. 'I wonder why Zandra came back to our cabin,' she says. 'Why she wanted *me*. If it was because she likes me . . . or because she hated me?'

'Why would she hate you? I thought you were friends.'

'But we fought the last time I saw her. It was my fault. I was an idiot . . .' And then she bursts into tears. The glitter on her back twinkles like stars under the black see-through fabric as her body heaves with each sob.

Marianne is close to tears herself. She can tell from looking at them how much it hurts to lose a dear friend, to be worried about someone you love. And yet she is jealous of their pain.

That is a kind of loss too: being forced to realise just how lonely you really are. Whatever fantasies she weaved about Göran, they were just fantasies. She rubs her moist palms against her skirt and wonders if she should write a letter to her children and leave it here, in the suite. Something someone might find when it is all done, in case she doesn't make it. But she rejects the idea; that would feel like giving up. And she wouldn't know what to write anyway.

Marianne gets up from the sofa, goes to Madde and puts her arms around her.

The embrace is accepted without protest. Madde weeps and wails into her sweaty jumper.

'There, there,' Marianne says, and pulls her closer, studiously avoiding looking out of the window. 'There, there now.'

'I just want to go home,' Madde says.

'Me too,' she replies. 'And I hate my flat.'

Vincent snorts; she isn't sure whether he is laughing or crying, or if it matters.

Dan

He leans against the doorpost. He is not feeling good. Not good at all. His veins are vibrating. Jenny's blood came back up as soon as he managed to swallow it. If only there was more time, then he would have saved her for later and relished the anticipation.

But the newborns behind him are still hungry. They're desperate now they have smelled blood up close.

He looks around the mess: this paltry room full of the paltry people working here, all clinging to each other, screaming, trying to press themselves against the back wall, as if *that* will save them. The room is steaming with their smells. This is better than all the applause, all the fucks in the world, even all the drugs he has ever tried. He wishes he could kill them, every single one of them, personally. But watching is the next best thing.

If only he wasn't feeling so sick.

His eyes are drawn to one of the losers in Jenny's band. They laughed at him that time, even though he has had more and better pussy than they ever will. And that pompous Filip from Starlight, acting like some big-man protector? He'd probably hoped to stick it to her himself.

You go ahead. Just go and have at her. Scrape what's left off the bathroom floor.

Next to Filip is a bearded bloke with two kids. Dan recognises the Asian boy who snapped him with his phone. The girl is maybe a few years older, but it's hard to tell.

He sniffs and realises it was her trail he was following through the hallways from Alexandra's cabin: the first smell he experienced with his new senses.

She'd be a real looker if she were allowed to grow up. You can already sense it behind the makeup on her childish face. He hopes she wakes up again after. She would grow older, but that tight little body wouldn't change. He could permit himself to do her in a couple of years.

'Don't do this, I beg of you.'

The voice speaking is soft and melodic, so old-fashioned it is almost eerie: an echo from a bygone era. She speaks just like Adam. He knows instantly who she is.

'The consequences of this are so much greater than you can fathom,' she says, and steps out into the room. She looks like Adam too, despite her dark hair.

Dan leaves the doorway, straightening up to conceal how much pain he is in. 'I understand just fine,' he says. 'That's why I'm doing it.'

She shakes her head. 'At least spare the ones who are here. You already got what you want.'

Dan has to laugh. He *hasn't* got what he wants yet. He has saved the best for last. The cherry on top. 'How noble of you to try to help them,' he says, 'but do you really think any of them would help *you* if they knew what you are?'

Adam's mother glances around; he can see that he has thrown her off balance. *It's so easy.* He takes a step towards her, sniffing dramatically, theatrically, so the wide-eyed audience is sure to understand.

'You've fed since you came aboard. What do you think they would say about that?'

'And what do you think my son is going to do to you once he no longer has any use for you?' she hits back at him.

'We have far-reaching plans, love,' Dan says.

'He has longed for his freedom for so long. Do you really think he will ever submit to anyone again, once he gains it?'

'Why are you fighting this?' he says. 'Why are you torturing yourself?'

'I can resist. I am not an animal.'

Dan looks at her. He would like nothing better than to silence her for ever. Adam would never know. But he is too weak right now.

It doesn't matter, he tells himself. She can't stop him either. There is just one of her, and he has an entire army.

He withdraws and takes up position next to the doorway.

The newborns pour into the mess.

The first one in is a skinny guy with blond dreads. Dan can smell his greasy scalp and something pungently cheese-like when he rushes into the room and grabs the girl who works in the casino. The first gush of blood from her throat lands on the floor but the rest spurts straight into the dreadlocked guy's mouth as his lips close around the wound.

Albin

Time seems to stop; everything is moving far too slowly. Albin stares at the feet rushing into the room: feet in tube socks, high-heeled shoes clicking loudly, naked feet with neon toenails, a pair of boots. A trainer slips in a pool of blood. The woman lying under the man with dreadlocks has turned waxy and pale. She is almost out of blood.

Monsters exist, and they are here now. There is nowhere to run.

A sweet, sickly stench fills the room. There's so much screaming. So many sounds like snapping scissors, like scissors cutting through meat. There's the clatter of tables and chairs being upended or thrown aside, bones breaking, blood splattering the floor and walls, even the ceiling, painting the room red. The old security officer who was talking before is dragging himself across the floor, leaving a wet trail. And in the middle of the room is the woman who was just talking to Dan Appelgren.

Dan is standing by the door, watching everything with his red eyes, an insane smile on his puffy face.

Lo is pulling at Albin; her mouth is moving, saying something about getting out of here. Doesn't she understand?

'There's no point,' he says. 'We can't get out of here.'

She blinks. 'Stop it, Abbe. You can't give up now.'

He is just about to answer when his feet leave the floor and suddenly they are kicking at nothing but air. Hard fingers squeeze his ribs like a vice. He can smell blood and lipstick and catches a glimpse of shiny pink lips, dazzlingly white teeth, like uneven rows of bone fragments, a brightly coloured scarf on the woman's head. She presses her mouth to his neck; he feels her tongue against his skin and screams.

The guy with the blond dreadlocks lunges at Calle just as he reaches out for Albin.

Lo's scream cuts through all the others, *Letmego-letmegoihavetohelphim!*

Calle

Teeth: they are all he can see, snapping against each other milli-metres from his face. A curtain of blood-smeared dreadlocks hangs at the edge of his vision. The body on top of his is so ema-ciated he can feel the bones through the jacket as he strains to keep the man away from him.

Calle manages to roll them both onto their sides. He climbs on top of the man, gets a hand around his throat and squeezes, but the man doesn't react. His teeth continue to snap and the muscles of his neck writhe like snakes under his skin. Panic makes Calle grab a fistful of dreadlocks and slam the man's head into the floor; he does it again and again, losing count. He can't stop. The man doesn't so much as blink, even though blood is pooling under his head.

When Calle lifts his head up again, a grey, glistening mass floats out onto the floor and the man's eyes roll back. His teeth snap one final time and stop moving. Calle lets go, staring at the bloody lumps that used to contain thoughts, memories, opinions.

Trembling, he gets to his feet, retching as his stomach con-tracts painfully, but nothing comes up. He searches for Albin and spots Filip, who has his hands full holding Lo back. She is scream-ing Albin's name; Calle looks to where she is trying to go.

The woman with the scarf around her head is on the floor. The yellow-handled breadknife is sticking out of her throat and blood is pouring out of her, more blood than there should be room for in a human body.

Like a mosquito right after it feeds.

Her mouth is opening and closing. Maybe she is trying to scream. She snatches at the knife, but her hand keeps sliding off the bloody handle; it is stuck

between the vertebrae? Oh my God, between the vertebrae?

There is a woman standing behind her, the woman in black who talked to Dan Appelgren. She is carrying Albin under her arm. Her hand is missing a couple of fingers. She walks towards them. Calle notices that the other infected keep well clear of her, watching her with some kind of reverence.

'Hurry,' she says, 'before she comes after the boy again.'

Calle glances down at the floor behind her. The woman with the scarf is sitting up and staring wildly at Albin.

That is impossible.

But Calle doesn't hesitate. 'Come on,' he says, and looks at Filip.

Lo shakes her head. 'She's one of them,' she objects.

'I just saved his life,' the woman says, and sets Albin down in front of Calle. 'You will have to arm yourselves if you want to protect the children. The heart or the brain must be destroyed.'

He nods mutely, and is suddenly aware that the mayhem in the mess is dying down. There are bodies everywhere.

The bloody knife is still lodged in the woman's throat, but she has managed to grab hold of the handle now. There is a smacking sound when the blade slides out of her flesh.

You will have to arm yourselves.

'We have to go to the galley,' he says.

The woman walks to the doorway, where there is no longer any sign of Dan Appelgren. Calle takes Albin by the hand, and after making sure Filip and Lo are with them, follows her. A couple of the infected creep closer, but they hold back because of the woman.

They're afraid of her. They think we belong to her. Maybe they're right.

Calle pulls Albin closer as he hears Filip call out to Marisol.

'Wait for us!' Mika's familiar voice shouts somewhere behind them.

They step out into the hallway. No Dan Appelgren here either, but yet more dead bodies crowd the floor outside the common room. Calle tries not to look as he steps over one of them; he doesn't want to know if they are friends of his.

When the woman pushes open the door to the stairwell Calle hears screaming from the lower floors.

'Hurry,' the woman urges.

She looks sad, as if she wants to ask for forgiveness, even though she just saved their lives. He wishes he knew why she is helping them, whoever she is, but this is not the time to ask. He throws one last glance down the corridor. Antti and Mika are running towards them from the mess. Behind them are a couple of the infected.

'Let's take the lift,' Filip says in Calle's ear. 'It goes straight down to the galley.'

Calle looks at the orange steel doors about thirty feet away in the stairwell and nods.

He squeezes Albin's hand harder and starts to run. He trips right by the stairs but manages to recover and picks up speed again. Hearing Marisol and Filip and Lo behind him, he throws himself against the lift and jabs frantically at the button. It lights up and the heavy machinery slowly grinds into action. The children are screaming and clinging to each other. He pushes the button again, even though he knows it makes no difference, simply because he has to do *something*.

Antti pushes past the dark-haired woman, almost knocking her down. Mika is just a few steps behind.

'Hurry up!' Filip yells. 'Hurry the fuck up!'

Calle is suddenly aware that the screaming downstairs has stopped. Now he can hear footsteps: slow, but much too close. Ascending.

He looks at the woman again. She is still in the doorway. She draws her lips back and Calle feels like freezing water has just rushed through him when he sees her yellowed teeth. They don't belong in her youthful face.

The lift door rattles open and Calle whips around, afraid there might be infected waiting inside, ready to jump him— But the lift is empty.

He places himself in the way to keep it from closing while Marisol and Filip usher the children to the back of the lift.

Two of the infected are coming up the stairs. Three of them. No, five. Antti has reached full velocity and comes barrelling into the lift, holding his hands up in front of him to avoid crashing head-first into the back wall.

Mika has a few more yards to cover. Why is he so slow? He's almost as slow as the infected coming up the stairs.

'Hurry!' Calle shouts, stabbing at the button for the eighth floor. Lo is jumping up and down, making the lift rock.

'What do you think I'm doing?' Mika replies, panting.

'Go!' the woman shouts. 'Go without him!'

But Mika finally makes it into the lift and Calle backs inside. The doors are motionless for a second, two seconds; he screams with frustration before they finally start sliding closed.

He goes to stand with the others by the back wall.

The doors are almost completely shut when a freckled arm with thick gold bracelets pushes through the crack. The fingers are curled like talons, clawing at the air, trying to reach them. A gaping face is pressed into the opening. The doors shudder and start opening again. The children scream shrilly.

There's a swift movement outside the lift, a glimpse of the baggy black cardigan. The face disappears from the crack between the doors. Anguished noises come from outside and Filip pushes the button again.

Calle's pulse roars in his ears as he stares at the doors sliding shut.

It is only when they are firmly closed and the lift starts moving downwards that he realises he has been holding his breath.

Madde

Madde leaves the window. She can't bear to watch any more of what is happening down on the bow deck.

In fact, she is barely able to stay awake. She has cried so much she feels beyond exhausted: steamrollered. She slumps heavily on the sofa, wanting to lie down flat on the soft cushions and never get up again.

What if Zandra infected me somehow? Is that why I'm so tired?

Thinking about it makes her want to crawl out of her own skin.

Marianne glances at her as if she can read her mind.

What would they do if they thought I was sick? They'd throw me out of here. She stares fixedly at the bowl of jelly hearts. If she dies on this fucking ship, what has she really accomplished? What has she done that means anything to anybody? Her parents are going to miss her, of course. And her brother. But they don't know her. Not the real her.

No one knew her better than Zandra. But Zandra is gone now.

Her tear ducts ache, but no more tears come. Maybe she has run out. Madde snorts up some snot and wipes under her nose with her index finger. She looks at the dining table. There are mirrors on the ceiling above it. She gets the feeling there have been more carnal feasts than food on that table.

She looks at the streamers hanging from the banister. The rose petals on the stairs. Between the balusters on the first-floor landing she can see a big banner above the bed: CONGRATULATIONS.

And she suddenly gets how everything is connected and doesn't know whether to be grossed out or impressed. She looks at the old lady again. She must be rich, and Vincent must be very desperate.

She glances up at the mirrors on the ceiling again. 'Are you guys getting married or something?' she asks.

'No,' the old lady replies quickly, 'no, not at all.'

'Then what are you celebrating?' Madde says.

'Long story,' the guy says, and turns away from the window.

His eyes look darker from a distance. He is actually incredibly fit. Zandra would have loved him.

Zandra.

'Well, it's not like we have someplace to be,' Madde says. 'I wouldn't mind thinking about something else.'

Vincent takes a seat in the armchair across from her. 'I was proposed to,' he says, 'by my boyfriend.'

Madde is relieved not to have to imagine Marianne and Vincent getting it on. 'Where is he?'

'I don't know,' Vincent replies, his voice fading into a whisper. 'He disappeared even before . . . I don't know where he is.'

He looks so devastated she is sorry she asked. She would like to make him feel better, but he has looked out of the window too.

'Congratulations,' she says. 'On getting married, I mean.'

He smiles, but it is the most mirthless smile she has ever seen. 'I said no,' he says.

'How come?' The question just slips out. 'I'm sorry,' she adds quickly. 'It's none of my business. It's just that . . .'

This time she stops herself just in time. *It's just I can tell from looking at you that you love him.*

'Don't worry about it. But, yeah, I don't know. I thought I needed some time to think about it . . .' He chuckles. 'I assumed there was more time.'

'You could hardly be expected to know people would start tearing each other apart with their teeth.'

'Please,' Marianne interjects.

'No, that's true,' Vincent says, and laughs again, putting his head in his hands. 'I should look for him,' he adds. 'He's out there somewhere.'

'No,' Marianne says. 'He will come here if he can.'

'Exactly. *If* he can. What if he needs help?' Vincent says.

'But what if you miss each other?' Marianne says. 'He would want you to stay put.' She looks at Madde as if she wants to be backed up. As though Madde has the faintest idea about what Vincent's boyfriend might want.

'Yeah, he probably would,' Madde says. 'It's what I would want.'

If she loved someone, she would want that person to be as safe as possible, and somewhere where she could find him or her.

Also, she really doesn't want Vincent to leave.

Calle

They watch the doors slide open in silence. Outside the rectangle of light from the lift, the shadows lurk deep. Green and orange dots gleam here and there: tiny lights on enormous kitchen machines.

Calle listens into the dark, but hears nothing but the humming of the ventilation system. He gives Filip a quick look.

Antti heaves an exasperated sigh and steps out of the lift. Walking with his back overly straight, holding his arms away from his sides, he looks like a small dog trying to look big and threatening. The effect is the opposite.

Calle and the children move into the galley, along with Marisol and Filip. Mika is the last to leave the lift.

There is a jangling above them and the fluorescent lights come to life. Antti is standing by the light switches, his face extremely flushed, almost purple. The vast stainless-steel countertops, the big ovens, grills, holding cabinets, deep-fryers all gleam in the bright light. Everything is spotless, meticulously cleaned. On a regular cruise, it would almost be time to start prepping breakfast. On the wall next to the dishwashers there is a noticeboard with schedules and a couple of postcards with girls in bikinis on beaches. And next to the board is a grey wall-mounted phone.

Vincent.

433

If he doesn't call, he can keep telling himself Vincent is in their suite and safe. But if he calls and Vincent doesn't pick up . . .

'We need weapons,' Antti says, opening a few drawers at random and slamming them shut again.

Calle gently lets go of Albin's hand and walks to the prep area: four long counters surrounded by oversized refrigerators. He opens a drawer and sees a neat row of big knives.

'There's loads here,' he says.

Marisol walks to the next counter; she pulls out a couple of cleavers and a meat tenderiser and places them on the worktop. Their eyes meet and Calle instinctively feels he likes her. He lines up a number of blades in front of him and gingerly tests the edges with his finger. They are sharp, clearly well cared for. He wonders whether the big ones are better by default, or if the parers might be nimbler. And should the kids have sharp implements too?

'Can you believe we're doing this?' he says.

Marisol leans against the counter and wipes her brow. 'I beat a woman to death up at Starlight,' she says. 'She was one of them . . . but I . . .' She swallows. 'I don't know if I can do it again.'

'I know. I mean, me neither.'

He pushes aside thoughts of the man with dreadlocks, the thoughts of the things that leaked out of his head, and studies the selection. Suddenly the notion of putting them to use seems ridiculous. He glances around for the children.

Lo comes up to him, holding out a big pair of kitchen scissors with stainless-steel blades. Albin is standing half a step behind her. His gaze is blank, chillingly vacant.

'This should be useful for something,' Lo says.

She looks so childish and yet so grown up at the same time.

434

Calle has to look away when he accepts the scissors. She and Albin shouldn't be here. They should be at home, safe in their beds.

He lets his eyes sweep across the dishwashers, the stacks of dishwasher racks, the high-pressure hoses dangling like slumbering snakes above the sinks. His gaze catches on the phone again. He will call, soon. He just has to gather his wits first.

A loud crash and clattering behind him makes him spin around. Antti has pulled out a couple of drawers and turned them upside down. Whisks and pasta forks and potato pressers lie scattered across the floor.

'Could you maybe keep it the fuck down, yeah?' Filip says.

Antti stares up at him, pulls out another drawer and deliberately empties out the contents onto the floor. 'Just being efficient,' he says. 'Maybe you should try it.'

'You're going to draw them here,' Calle says. 'How hard is that to understand?'

Antti gives him a look of utter contempt. 'Shut the fuck up, faggot!'

'Stellar fucking guy,' Lo mutters to Albin. 'Can they please come and kill him right now?'

Calle barely registers her words. Hate surges through him when he looks at Antti. It is so strong he barely recognises himself.

But then it dawns on him that the opposite is true: he recognises this hatred all too well. He was too much of a chicken to talk back to Antti when they worked together, but now he wants to punch him, beat that blowsy face to a pulp, kick it to shit with his boots.

The hate feels good; the fire of it burns away his fear, temporarily obliterating all thoughts of contagion and Vincent and Pia and the children.

435

'Fuck you, Antti,' Filip says. 'You can take your macho bullshit and shove it up your arse.'

'Shove it up your friend's arse instead,' Antti says. 'I bet he'd like that. Fuck you too, fuck being here with two brats, a bitch and the fucking thought police!'

'I can't take it any more,' Mika says.

Calle had almost forgotten about him. He notices Mika is slumped on the floor with his back against one of the holding cabinets.

'And that one,' Antti sneers.

'I don't want to be here,' Mika says. 'Why is this happening to me?'

'To you?' Calle says. 'At least you're alive, unlike all the people up there in the mess. And Pia and Jarno. And all the passengers who—'

'I just don't understand what I've done to deserve this.'

'No one deserves this!' Filip almost screams.

Mika glares at them sullenly, as though it is highly unfair of them to deny him his self-pity.

'Let's all calm down now,' Marisol says. 'We don't even know what the fuck we're dealing with.'

'I do,' Lo says. 'I know what they are, but you're not going to believe me.'

Calle turns to her.

'They're vampires,' she says.

'Lo . . .'

'But they are. Don't you get it?'

'Bitches and brats,' Antti mutters under his breath.

'I thought they were zombies at first,' Lo continues, 'but zombies can't talk or think. But you saw him, Dan Appelgren; he could do both, but he was one of them. And the woman who helped us too.'

'Can you shut her up?' Antti says. 'I'm not in the mood to listen to a fucking kid who's seen too many horror films.'

Lo's eyes narrow as she rounds on him. 'So why don't you give us a *natural* explanation then?' she says. 'I'm sure that won't be far-fetched at all.'

Vampires.

Maybe it is a sign that he is losing his mind, but the word makes everything fall into place. No matter how insane it sounds, it is the most rational explanation he has heard so far for the irrational things happening all over the *Charisma*.

The teeth. The biting. All the blood, the carnage out there. The mayhem in the mess. The woman with a knife through her throat who fumbled for the handle while blood gushed out of her. The man with the dreadlocks who wouldn't stop moving until there was nothing left of his head.

The images from the mess flood his brain and he almost loses his grip on reality. It's as if he has careened right to the brink of insanity but managed to stop at the last moment. The abyss tugs at him, but he doesn't fall in. Not yet.

But now he knows it is there, waiting for him.

'Pia said Dan was with a little boy,' Mika says. 'She thought the boy was one of them too.'

'That woman said something to Dan about her son,' Lo says eagerly, looking at Calle.

'Oh, right then,' Antti says with a theatrical laugh. 'That confirms it. Great. Well, there should be garlic around here somewhere. Or shall we whittle ourselves some wooden stakes?'

'Maybe we should,' Lo says. 'We have to destroy the heart and the brain, she said.'

'It's terrorists,' Antti says, looking around, 'or am I the only one here who doesn't believe in fairy tales?'

Calle hides his face in his hands and accidentally touches the gash on his forehead; the sweat on his fingertips makes the wound sting.

'I don't know what I believe,' Filip says, 'but it doesn't matter what we call them. The question is what we do now.'

Antti kicks one of the drawers on the floor.

'We have to stop the ship so we can launch the life rafts,' Marisol says.

'Henke and Pär already tried to get to the bridge once and they . . .' Antti's voice trails off.

'All right, then we'll try the engine room. Does anyone know how to do a shutdown?'

Antti sighs. 'It's simple,' he says, sounding almost reluctant. 'You just have to throw a couple of buckets of water on the main switchboard. That makes the pumps stop, which in turn starves the engines of both fuel and coolant.'

They look at each other.

'Good,' Marisol says. 'Then we have a plan.'

Calle looks at the phone next to the noticeboard. If they are going to do this, he has to call now.

I may not get another chance.

The thought is too enormous, too impossible, so he forces it down. He has to keep his wits about him. He walks to the phone, his heart pounding, picks up the receiver, pushes the greasy buttons. 9. 3. 1. 8.

It rings. Again. And again.

'Hello?' Vincent says, breathing heavily.

The plastic receiver creaks as Calle clutches it. 'It's me,' he says.

He has to breathe deeply and slowly not to burst out crying. If he does, he will fall into that abyss and never be able to crawl back out.

'Where are you?' Vincent says in a thick voice.

'I'm in the galley,' Calle says. When Vincent doesn't reply he adds, 'In the kitchen.'

'Are you okay?'

'Yes,' Calle says, 'I'm okay.'

The wires running through the *Charisma* hiss with static as if to remind them that the line could cut out anytime.

'And you?' Calle asks. 'Are you okay? You've not been bitten?'

'No,' Vincent says.

That word makes all the difference. A wave of relief washes over Calle and his eyes well up with tears.

'I wish you were here,' Vincent says.

Calle swallows again and again to get rid of the lump growing in his throat. The *whishing* on the line sounds like the wind rustling through trees, like distant whispers.

'Me too,' he manages.

'What's happening to people? Do you know anything?'

Vampires.

'No.'

'Is it safe where you are?'

Hot tears begin to spill, rolling down Calle's cheeks. 'We're going to try to get down to the engine room to stop the ship. Then we can launch the life rafts . . . and someone from outside is going to notice that something's wrong, sooner or later . . .' He trails off. It suddenly dawns on him that if people come to rescue them, they will be in danger too.

He leans against the wall, trying to calm down, reminding himself not to be overwhelmed by the enormity of the situation. Focusing on one thing at a time is the only way to stay sane.

'Can't you stay where you are?' Vincent says. 'Please. For me.'

'We have to try.'

Vincent doesn't respond. Calle just wants him to say something – anything – so he can hold on to Vincent's voice just a little longer. But Vincent doesn't say anything else.

'Stay in the suite. Promise me you won't leave,' Calle says. 'If we can't stop the ship, I'll get to you as quickly as I can.'

'I'll wait here,' Vincent says.

Do that. I love you. Don't let anything happen to you.

'I'll see you soon,' Calle says.

'Yes. I'll see you soon.'

It sounds like Vincent has started to cry. Calle doesn't want to hang up, but he mumbles goodbye and forces himself to put the phone back on its hook.

'Albin? Lo?' he calls, his voice surprisingly steady. 'Come on, let's try your parents.' He wipes the last of his tears from his eyes and turns back to the others.

Filip has found some plastic buckets, and duct tape, which he uses to attach a steak knife to a long metal stick that might be a mop handle.

'Did you reach him?' he asks.

Calle nods.

'Good,' Filip says, and brandishes his makeshift spear.

He looks so pleased with himself Calle has to smile.

Vincent is safe. It is only now, when he knows, that he realises how dangerously close he came to giving up.

Dan

Adam is waiting for him by the arcade games on deck eight. Dan kicks past the bodies littering the hallway in front of Poseidon, placing his feet carefully. He can hear them slowly moving against each other. Some raise their heads, watching him as he passes.

He is tired.

If only he could have enjoyed what happened in the mess.

But at least they all saw him. Everyone knew he was behind what went down. When they wake up, they will follow him, and when they regain their cognitive functions, they will know he was the one who gave them their new lives.

He stands next to Adam and peers out of the window with him. A paler streak can be detected where the sea meets the sky. He wonders if his human eyes would even have been able to perceive it.

A new dawn. A whole new world. And no one outside the *Charisma* knows yet.

'Did it go well?' Adam asks.

'Yes.'

Their reflections in the window are transparent. Dan's face is puffy. The shirt is straining over his blood-filled body. He looks away. Meeting Adam's gaze in the glass, he thinks about what his mother said: that Adam won't submit to anyone ever again.

And neither will Dan. Maybe he should kill Adam, right here, right now, venture into the new world without him. He'd be commanding an army of newborns by himself.

'I haven't found Mother,' Adam says. 'I haven't even been able to locate her scent.'

'She was there,' Dan says.

Adam turns to him, but Dan continues to look out of the window. The faint light is turning the sea into quicksilver.

'She helped some of them escape,' he says.

'And you let her?' Adam says.

Dan grits his teeth and turns to Adam. That tiny neck looks so easy to snap. But being fooled by Adam's fragile appearance would be a grave mistake. He has to wait until he has recovered.

'Who did she help?' Adam asks.

'Just a handful of losers. No one significant. And some kids.'

The blood moves more effortlessly through Dan when he thinks about the blonde girl. So young. So fresh.

'Children are one of her weaknesses,' Adam says, and his dainty lips tighten. 'Could the ones who escaped present a problem?'

Dan shakes his head. What could a dud from the tax-free shop possibly do? Perfume them to death?

Adam takes a seat on the window bench. His legs dangling, he kicks the heels of his shoes against the wall. His blue eyes bore into Dan. 'Are you certain?' he says.

'They won't make it anyway. One of them is about to turn. He didn't have long. He'll take care of them.'

Dan pictures that hateful face with new teeth in it, the fear and hunger in the eyes, but he can't manage to summon up any feelings.

Behind Dan, one of the newborns grunts.

442

'Maybe you should focus on all the ones who didn't get away,' Dan suggests. He avoids adding *thanks to me*, because he can tell he is sounding whiny, defensive. 'We only have a couple of hours to go. There's nothing your mum can do now.'

'She's going to try,' Adam says, sounding like he is thinking out loud.

'Then you have to make sure you deal with her.'

Dan doesn't want to talk about this any more. When he met Adam's mother in the mess it was abundantly clear she wanted to kill him. He can't have been given all of this just to lose it. He has so much *more* life to lose now. More years, *better* years.

'Man the fuck up,' Dan adds, 'even if you do look like a toddler.'

They lock eyes. Adam is the first to look away. 'Don't worry about Mother,' he says. 'I will take care of everything. You are right. Enjoy what we have achieved. You have done well.'

'Cheers, thanks.' Dan doesn't need Adam's validation, but he can't be bothered to squabble any more.

'You must be very tired,' Adam says.

Dan nods. He is, to the bone.

'I think you should rest until we get there,' Adam says. 'You are going to need all your strength then. Think about what lies ahead. This is only the beginning.'

Yes. Rest. That is what he needs.

And he knows exactly where: he will go to the place that should have been his all along. He is going to have a front-row seat when they arrive in Finland, when the world wakes up to a day unlike any other in all its long history.

Albin

'Abbe,' his dad says, 'Abbe, where are you?'

He is neither angry dad nor crying dad but a dad Albin has never heard before. He sounds so small, as if they have traded places and now Albin is the adult.

And Dad has been drinking so heavily Albin can barely make out what he is saying.

Albin doesn't know why he is disappointed. Had he expected anything else? That his dad would somehow turn into that dad from the stories he used to make up when Albin was little? The dad who was brave and fought monsters and saved everybody?

'I'm with Lo and some people in the galley,' Albin says. 'Where they make the food.' Has it really only been a few hours since they were all having dinner together at the restaurant?

'Where's Mum?' Dad asks. 'And Linda?'

'I don't know,' Albin says with a sidelong glance at Lo. 'Aren't they with you?'

Lo gets it instantly; she tries not to show it, but she droops as though an invisible piece of string holding her up has suddenly been severed.

'I'm all alone here,' his dad says. 'Why did you just run off?'

Albin fiddles with the phone cord, twisting the soft, grey plastic coils around his index finger. 'I had to talk to Mum about something,' he says.

'Why didn't you come to me? I was right next door!'

The cord is so tight his fingertip is turning dark purple. 'I don't know.'

'Yeah, I don't know either,' his dad says. He starts crying, wet and gross on the other end. Now Albin recognises him.

'I would come if I could,' Albin says, 'but I can't.'

As soon as he says it, he knows he isn't even going to try. He is not going to be in that cabin, cooped up with his dad. He would much rather stick with Calle and the others.

'Then tell me how to get to you,' his dad snuffles.

Albin extracts his finger from the plastic cord tunnel. It is slippery with sweat. 'You can't.'

'I'm going to go crazy in here.'

You're already crazy. And I don't want to see you. And I don't want Calle and the others to meet you. You would ruin everything.

'I have to go now. If the ship stops, make your way to the roof if you can. There are life rafts there.'

'Abbe – Abbe, don't hang up! You know I love you more than anything else in the world, I have to . . .'

'I'm sorry, Dad. I love you too.' Albin has to stand on his tiptoes to hang up. He turns around; Lo is looking at him with glistening eyes.

'They're not there,' he says, even though he knows there is no need. 'And I don't want to go back.'

She nods mutely.

'Did you get them?' Calle calls.

Albin looks at him. It suddenly strikes him that Calle and the others might not be too thrilled about having to look after him and Lo. That Antti guy definitely doesn't want to, but at least no one is paying any attention to him. But Calle, Calle did tell them he couldn't . . . But things were different then, weren't they?

'Just Dad,' he says. 'We'd rather stay with you until we find our mums.'

'Shouldn't you—' Calle starts saying, but just then something seems to click for him, because he breaks off and nods.

Marisol comes up to them with one of Filip's improvised knife-spears. She shoots Albin a warm smile. 'Of course we're all sticking together,' she says.

'Where did you actually last see your mums?' Filip asks from where he is standing by one of the counters.

'The café,' Lo says. 'Then they must have gone to the information desk, because there was a message over the speakers . . .'

'Then you must have talked to them, Mika,' Filip says. 'Do you remember them?'

Albin curses himself. Why didn't he think of that? He did recognise Mika, after all. Of course he was the one his mum and Linda spoke to.

'My mum's in a wheelchair,' he says, and moves closer to the man sitting on the floor. 'And Aunt Linda has long blonde hair.'

But Mika doesn't respond.

'Hello?' Calle says. 'Are you deaf or what?'

There's still no reply, and Albin suddenly notices that Mika's eyes are open, as though he is staring out into a big nothingness.

'Mika?' Calle says. He walks up to him, squats down by his side and feels Mika's throat.

'Bloody hell, Calle!' Filip shouts, and comes running, one of the spears over his shoulder. 'Be careful!'

'I can't find a pulse,' Calle says quietly, looking up at Filip.

'Stellar,' Lo mumbles under her breath. 'Really fucking stellar'.

'Get back, Calle,' Albin says. 'Please.'

Calle unbuttons Mika's jacket; the gold buttons flash. When he pulls it open, they see his shirt is torn across his chest. There is a big bloodstain on it. Calle closes his jacket and wipes his hands on his jeans.

'Fucking moron. Why didn't he say something?'

Marisol gently grabs Calle's shoulder and he finally backs away, far enough that Mika's hands can't reach him. He walks to one of the sinks and opens the cupboard under it.

'What are we going to do?' Antti says. 'Is he one of them?'

'He will be,' Lo replies.

'She's right,' Filip says. 'The one in Starlight seemed dead at first too.'

Calle returns, wearing a pair of bright-yellow rubber gloves. He squats down next to Mika again.

It feels like everything in Albin's stomach is slowly tensing, tensing, tighter and tighter, contracting into a ball of the same red snakes that fell out of the long-haired man on the sun deck.

It doesn't matter what colour we are on the outside because we look the same on the inside. His mother always used to tell him that when he was little and started asking questions about why they looked so different. But he never understood what that had to do with anything.

Mum. Where is she now? His mouth fills with saliva. When he swallows it tastes cold and metallic.

Calle gently pushes Mika's chin down. Blood pours out of his mouth when his lips part.

Filip gets in position right behind Calle, holding out his mop handle so the knife points at Mika, square in the face. Albin moves in closer; he can't resist.

'Fucking hell,' Calle says. 'Check this out.'

Mika's teeth are falling out at the lightest touch.

'Enough already,' Filip says. 'Move aside.'

'Wait.' Calle tilts Mika's head back so the light from the ceiling can reach inside his mouth. There are tiny white dots in there moving up through the shredded gums.

'That's how it happens,' Calle says, and stands up.

'He's going to wake up any second,' Marisol says. 'We have to get out of here.'

A memory pops into Albin's head: a photograph from his biology book; he hadn't been able to stop thinking about it for days. It had been an X-ray of a child's head and the adult teeth were neatly lined up deep inside the gums, ready and waiting to break through as soon as the child lost its baby teeth.

Calle puts the gloves down on a counter. 'Come on, let's fill the buckets. Hurry.'

'He's moving!' Lo exclaims.

The man on the floor blinks his eyes, wincing. His hands are twitching so hard they're bouncing up and down against his thighs. His mouth opens as if in surprise.

Albin turns away. He tries to speak, but can't get a sound out. He wants to run, but doesn't know how. Lo is shaking his shoulder, saying his name, but she can't get through to him. No one can. His true self is rolled up somewhere deep inside him, hiding in a fortress of flesh and blood.

448

The others are screaming at each other, gesturing frantically. Lo's face is right next to his, but she is still so far away. Is she trying to tell him to move? *But how?*

His cheek, which is so remote it no longer feels like it belongs to him, suddenly burns, and he realises Lo has slapped him.

'Abbe,' she cries, 'what's *wrong* with you?'

He can't explain. Explaining it might ruin it. He wants to stay where he is, hidden inside himself.

'Abbe, I can't do this without you,' she says. 'You have to come back.'

He looks at her.

'Can you even hear me?' Lo says. 'Please, don't break down now. We can do that later, when it's over.'

He can feel his head nodding mutely, for her, because she seems to need it. But what does she mean by 'over'? This night is never going to end.

Filip

Filip is shaking so violently he almost drops the mop handle. He's staring at Mika, who is trying to stand up, bracing his back against the holding cabinet. His face contracts in pain, turning it into a horrifying mask.

'Kill him,' Antti urges, but Filip shakes his head. How can he?

It doesn't matter what he really thought about Mika. They have worked together for more than fifteen years.

'He'll kill us if you don't,' Lo says.

'I know!' he says, and raises the mop handle so the knife is dancing in front of one of Mika's eyes. 'I know . . .'

He glances at Marisol. Her entire body is tense, as though it consists of a single muscle, ready to spring.

Mika gets on his feet. His hands move up to his mouth and he starts plucking out his teeth, one by one. He sniffs like he is crying, but his eyes are dry.

'Screw this,' Filip hears himself say. 'Let's just go.'

'We have to get water first,' Antti says. 'Just do it.'

'Why don't you do it?' Filip snaps. 'You're the one who wanted to make mincemeat out of all of them! This is your chance!'

Antti doesn't respond. Fucking coward.

Filip glances at the children. The girl is scared, but the boy looks like he isn't even present any more. Filip clutches the handle harder, takes a deep breath and tries to aim the point of the knife. The blade is long and thin.

A gurgle erupts from Mika's throat. Filip thrusts the handle forward.

The knife slides into Mika's eye, all the way, until the point hits the inside of his skull. Mika howls, a single, drawn-out syllable, piercing and atonal. Filip wiggles the mop handle. The knife roots around in there, scrapes against the edges of the eye socket, shredding tissue. When he pulls the blade back out, it is covered in blood and pink bits, and Mika collapses like a pile of dirty laundry.

How do you kill a monster without becoming a monster yourself? The thought comes to him from his subconscious; he wonders if he has read or heard it somewhere.

How is he going to live with what he has seen? With what he has done?

The *Baltic Charisma*

The ship's public spaces have almost been cleared of living bodies. Only a handful remain, having found hiding places on the weather decks, in remote hallways, in the closed restaurants they have broken into. The newborns are growing increasingly desperate. A few of them have started regaining their memories. Not thoughts, exactly, but enough for their instincts to lead them to the corridors where their cabins are. They hurl themselves at the locked doors, rattle the door handles. A few are let in by people who love them, which attracts other newborns who come to fight over the prey. Other cabins fill with the screams of unfortunates who locked themselves in with infected people earlier in the evening.

The dark-haired woman fights to resist the temptation of the enticing smells. She is still shaken by what happened in the mess, but there is no going back now. She has stopped looking for her son; now she is doing her best to steer clear of him instead.

She is making sure the newborns notice her, start following her through the corridors.

In the mess, a few of the bodies have got off the floor. They sniff the air, but there is nothing left here to still their hunger.

*

In a stairwell not too far from there, a man is on all fours. He has a wife called Lillemor, but he has no memory of her now. He pulls on the arm that is cuffed to the railing. He has to break free, has to eat. He bites into his wrist with his new teeth, rips off big chunks of meat and spits them out. He gnaws through the bones until all that connects the arm is flimsy sinew and flaps of skin, then he tugs so hard the metal screeches. He's almost free now. Soon, he can hunt. The blood from his arm trickles across the floor, dripping down onto the man on the landing below. He hasn't woken up yet, but his new teeth have already surfaced in his mouth.

The woman has lured a herd of newborns into the narrow stairwell leading down from the fifth floor. She opens the door to the car deck using the card she took from one of the dead people in the mess. The strong reek of petrol comes as a relief; it hides all the smells she has to hold out against. The vibrations from the ship are strong down here. There's a faint jangling from the chains securing the cars. She looks at her caravan, plays with her locket and reminisces about everything they have done together, all the years, all the time they stole. The boy she loved more than anything is gone for ever. She still doesn't understand how it happened, how he found the man who works here; she figures they must have been planning this for a long time. He worked with determination and skill, but she has realised her son's determination is also a blessing. It gives her a chance to avert the greater disaster without anyone outside the ship finding out what happened here tonight. If her son and his helper had not been so meticulous about cutting the ship off from the rest of the world, videos and photographs from hundreds upon hundreds of phones would already be spreading across the globe like wild-fire. She no longer has any hope of saving her son, or herself, but there is still a way to save everyone outside the *Baltic Charisma*.

She closes the door, trapping the newborns, and heads up the narrow stairs to round up more.

Madde

Madde is sitting on one of the upholstered dining chairs, tapping her nails against the tabletop and gazing out of the window. The sky has lightened outside: shades of darkest grey, deepest blue. The sun is going to start inching out of the sea soon. She wants to shout at it to hurry up. The impenetrable darkness they have been travelling through has felt so eternal, as if time has stood still.

Somewhere ahead of them is Åbo. She has travelled there aboard the *Charisma* so many times without ever actually seeing the harbour. She was always asleep when they arrived.

'Do you mind?' Marianne says. 'Please.'

Madde beats out a few more drumrolls before letting her hand rest. She can feel the faint vibrations in the table: the engines Vincent's boyfriend is going to try to kill.

What happens if they don't succeed?

'I'm sorry,' she says, looking at Marianne. 'I just . . .' She can't think of what to say.

Marianne nods. 'I know.'

Vincent is sitting on the spiral staircase leading to the upper level. He is also gazing out of the window. 'There's practically no one left on the bow deck,' he says. 'No one moving, that is.'

He is sitting stock-still, clearly on edge. She understands. If the engines do stop, he will know his boyfriend made it at least that far.

Madde puts her hands on the edge of the chair. Her sweaty fingertips have left marks on the polished tabletop. They slowly evaporate before her eyes.

Does she even want help to come? What would that mean for the contagion? Will it keep spreading until the whole world is like the *Charisma*?

Suddenly she just wants to get up, leave the suite and let herself be killed. She wouldn't have to wait any longer, or be afraid any more. It would be over.

She stands up. The door is pulling at her, as if it's exerting its own gravity, but she forces herself to go back to the sofa and sits down next to Marianne. She folds her arms, shudders.

Marianne misunderstands, lifts herself off the sofa and pulls a maroon blanket from under her, same shade as the carpet. She wraps the blanket around Madde's shoulders and Madde pulls it tighter, draws her legs up so most of her body is covered by the blanket.

To think that such a simple thing can feel so good. The door loses some of its attraction.

'You haven't said if you have someone out there,' she says to Marianne.

'I came here by myself,' Marianne replies dully.

'Were you having a good night? Before everything happened?'

Marianne makes no reply, but Madde is beginning to feel overcome with sleepiness.

'It certainly turned out eventful,' Marianne says at length.

Madde can't suppress a smile. Her eyelids are so heavy. It would be so nice to fall asleep, duck out for a while. 'I'm glad we found each other,' she murmurs.

Madde opens her eyes when Marianne doesn't respond and watches her wipe a few tears from her cheeks, toss her head slightly.

Something electronic beeps: a familiar sound. Madde's heart leaps into high gear and she sits up straighter, hearing the door opening.

'Calle?' Vincent shouts, and runs down the stairs, making a turn so tight when he reaches the bottom that he would have fallen if he hadn't kept his hand on the banister.

'No,' a tired voice says, and the door closes.

Vincent stops in the middle of the room.

Madde gets up from the sofa, still wrapped in the blanket, staring at the man, trying to piece it together.

Has he come for me?

No, of course not. How would he know I'm here?

'How are you?' she says, brushing her hair from her forehead. 'Are you okay?'

The man who stood next to her on the karaoke stage, laughing at her jokes, is covered in dried blood from head to toe. His beautiful face is swollen, barely recognisable.

He looks at her.

And she gets it.

Calle

Calle watches the water level rise in the grey plastic bucket. Crumbs, specks of dirt and an old plaster are drifting in circles on the surface. He worked aboard the *Charisma* for several years and yet he has only the faintest notion of where the water in the taps comes from. There must be tanks somewhere, and they must be enormous to provide the water needed for drinking, showering and cooking for thousands of people.

Water being shipped back and forth across water.

He hangs the pre-rinse tap back on its hook above the sink and stands motionless, watching as the debris moves ever more slowly across the surface. He's picturing the man with dreadlocks.

He has killed someone. *He has killed.*

'Let's get this thing done,' Filip says.

Calle looks up, bewildered.

Filip is talking to the children, who have climbed up on a counter and are sitting cross-legged side by side. 'And then we make our way to the life rafts, bringing along as many of the non-infected as we can, and get off this boat,' he continues. 'Easy-peasy. The sun's going to come up soon and we're not too far from Finland. Someone will spot us.'

'Sure,' Lo says. 'Easy-peasy.'

Albin says nothing; he just stares vacantly into space.

'What do you say, kiddo?' Filip says.

No response.

He tousles Albin's hair and walks away. Calle can plainly see how tired and scared he is. He wonders how he could have ever forgotten how much he liked Filip. He thinks of the picture of the two of them in Filip's cabin.

Filip comes up to him and grabs hold of the handle of the bucket. They lift it out of the sink together and put it down on the floor. Water sloshes over the edges onto Calle's boot.

Marisol comes as well. She has found a fire-axe somewhere; now she puts it down next to the sink while she fills another bucket.

'I'm glad you managed to get through to Vincent,' Filip says. 'I don't know what happened between you, but he seems like a good guy.'

'He is.'

It suddenly dawns on Calle that he knows almost nothing about what Filip's life is like now; Filip was just thrown headlong into his own private inferno last night. There are so many things Calle wants to ask him. *Afterwards.*

'If you do end up getting married, at least you'll have a solid proposal anecdote,' Filip says, and Calle bursts out laughing.

'Maybe the two of you should consider postponing your sewing bee,' Antti calls to them. 'Hurry the fuck up, will you?'

Calle looks at the lift. It will take them all the way down to the beating heart of the *Charisma*.

And they are going to stop it.

Madde

It is just how she dreamed it would be, except seen through a fun-house mirror. Dan Appelgren is walking towards her in the luxury suite, and he *wants her.*

His teeth are snapping slowly in his swollen face.

'It's you,' he says. 'You're the one who sang the *Grease* song with that other cow.'

His words sink into her body, boring through her bones, and then she realises he just spoke. He is like the sick ones, *but he can talk*. The others don't appear even able to think.

She backs into Vincent, who pulls her towards the stairs. Out of the corner of her eye, she notices that Marianne has left the sofa and is standing with her back pressed against the wall, with the dining table between her and Dan.

Madde and Vincent turn and bolt up the spiral staircase.

The streamers rustle softly when Dan reaches in between the balustrades, groping around for them. He seizes Madde's ankle and pulls and she falls, her elbow slamming into the edge of a step. She screams as a wave of pain breaks over her, but she manages to get back on her feet. She can hear Dan behind her now, at the foot of the stairs.

Vincent shouts at her to duck and a champagne bottle zips past her head. There is a satisfying thud when it hits Dan. Madde reaches the upper level, turns around and discovers him still climbing the stairs, unperturbed.

'Get the fuck out!' she screams.

His lips draw back. His teeth are far too white, so clearly a part of his skeleton.

Brand new.

'You're the ones who don't belong here,' he says, and puts his foot on the floor of the upstairs landing.

Vincent throws the Plexiglas ice bucket at him, but it over-shoots and hits the wall behind Dan with a loud crash. Vincent picks up one of the champagne flutes, breaks it against the banister and holds it up in front of him, a stalk with sharp, glittering petals. When Dan comes closer, Vincent slashes at his face.

But Dan grabs hold of his wrist with one hand and Vincent's tank-top with the other, then stares him straight in the eyes.

'Leave him alone!' Madde screams.

His teeth, his contagious teeth, are so close to Vincent's face.

And then Dan braces himself and pushes Vincent over the banister.

There's a heavy thud below. Madde believes she heard something hard snap.

Marianne shrieks.

What is she seeing down there? What happened?

Madde backs away until she feels the edge of the bed against her legs. Dan turns towards her, and the worst thing about him is the look on his face. He is so bored. He doesn't care about what he did to Vincent in the slightest, or about what he is going to do to her now. She is just a chore to get through: tedious but necessary.

'Just let us go,' she pleads, stepping up onto the bed. 'Please. We won't do anything.'

'You won't *do anything*?' Dan sneers, moving closer. 'Now isn't that just a generous fucking offer? You *can't* do shit. Is that some-how unclear to you?'

'No,' she whispers, because she knows he is right. She is pathetic for pretending otherwise. She has nothing to offer and nothing to threaten him with, and there is no way out of this other than giving up.

He reaches out for her, tugs at the thin fabric of her dress, and she falls to her knees on the bed. He slaps her so hard her ears ring. The starched linen rustles softly when Dan climbs on top of her.

'It is high fucking time for this cow to get slaughtered,' he says. The puffs of air from his mouth smell sweet and fusty but are cool against her face.

She shuts her eyes tight when he presses her upper arms into the mattress, straddling her stomach. She can feel the muscles in his buttocks; his thighs pin her down. He is so heavy her internal organs are being pushed out of the way, and it hurts *so bad* and she can't breathe and she hears his teeth snapping, just like Zandra's.

Darkness materialises in her field of vision and she runs towards it, welcomes it. She doesn't want to be here when he bites her.

Is this how I die? Madde thinks. *Is this how it ends?*

She barely notices when the pressure across her abdomen eases and the hands around her arms disappear, but her body inhales greedily, gasps for breath.

Dan is standing on the floor by the foot of the bed. He shakes himself like a dog.

'I can't take any more.'

Is this a trick? Is he toying with her?

She pushes herself up until she's sitting. Her stomach hurts with every breath. She is afraid of him, but at least as afraid of the hope flaring up inside her.

'I'm tired,' he says. 'I just want to be alone. Someone else will get you anyway.' He leans out over the banister, looking down. 'You hear me?' he bellows. *'I just want to be alone!'*

He stays there, his back to her. Madde climbs off the bed. Her cheek is burning, her stomach is tender. She slowly moves towards the stairs without taking her eyes off Dan, prepared for him to turn at any moment: to come at her, laughing at her.

You really fell for that?

But he doesn't even register her presence now, just gazes out of the window on the lower level.

She walks to the stairs and pauses, studies his profile. His chin is drooping; his jawline is gone.

'Close the door behind you,' he says flatly.

Vincent is lying on his side by the coffee table, his face ashen. Marianne is squatting beside him. It looks like he just came to. Blood is trickling from one of his wrists. Madde glimpses a flash of bone poking through his skin and quickly turns away.

'Come on,' she says. 'Hurry.'

The sound of footsteps from above. When she looks up, Dan is no longer standing by the banister.

She knew it. He was just toying with them, like a cat toys with a mouse: letting them think they have escaped, only to— She hears him sitting down heavily on the bed.

With Marianne's help, Vincent gets to his feet, and Madde leads the way towards the door. She presses her ear to it. The corridor outside is silent.

The life rafts are close by, but who knows who they'll encounter on their way there.

She opens the door a crack and peers out. No one in sight. She opens it fully, eyeing the side passage where the cabin she shared with Zandra is located.

Marianne and Vincent follow her out. Marianne is holding a thin chequered scarf she must have found in the hallway. After pulling the door softly shut behind them, she gingerly grabs Vincent's injured wrist, murmurs soothingly, and then gives it a push. There's a clicking sound and Vincent moans loudly, beads of perspiration on his forehead.

Marianne wraps the scarf around his wrist. 'I used to work as a medical secretary,' she says when she notices Madde staring. 'And before that I was a nurse.'

Madde checks the corridor. Where the fuck are they supposed to go now?

'Calle,' Vincent says. 'If Calle comes here . . .'

Marianne starts rummaging through her purse and pulls out a lipstick. A mail-order brand Madde vaguely remembers from when she was little. She wonders if the old lady might have lost her marbles. Is she going to put on makeup now? But Marianne puts the lipstick to the door, moving it firmly across the wood.

KALLE! DON'T OPEN!

She underlines the word 'don't' so hard her lipstick breaks in half. She discards the rest on the floor. Vincent gives her a grateful look.

'Can we go to your cabin?' Marianne asks Madde.

She shakes her head. 'The door's broken.'

They hear a scream from somewhere, glass breaking in the distance, and every hair on Madde's body stands on end. 'Let's go to the life rafts now,' she says. 'There don't seem to be that many on the outer decks.'

'Not on the bow deck, sure,' Marianne says, 'but we have no idea what things are like up there. And it's far too cold. The two of you are barely dressed.'

'So where's your cabin?' Madde asks.

'On the lowest deck.'

'Deck two?'

She had thought Marianne fancier than that. Madde and Zandra booked the cheapest cabins the first time they went on a cruise without their parents, so she knows exactly what it looks like down there. And what it smells like.

'I can't go back down there,' Marianne says.

Madde agrees. If they get trapped down there, they will have nowhere to run.

'The two of you should get up on the roof,' Vincent says, 'but I'm going down to the car deck.'

Marianne and Madde turn to him as one.

'That's where the engine room is. Calle's there. Or at least I have to believe that. And if there is anything I can do to help him . . .'

'With a broken wrist?' Madde says, and it comes out much harsher than she had intended.

But Vincent just nods. 'I just want to . . . I just want to find him.'

'I'll go with you,' Marianne says. 'I have nowhere else to go.'

'Are you out of your minds?' Madde bursts out. 'You want to go further down when we're so close to the life rafts?'

But she already knows she is going to go with them. It is her best option. She knows the worst thing they can do is to stand here dithering for even one more second.

465

Marianne

Two women are sprawled on the floor at the top of the stairs. Marianne wonders who they were, if they knew each other, which of them died first and if the other had to watch. She looks away, tears filling her eyes; she does nothing to stop them and they fall silently, quickly, as though something inside her has burst.

There are more bodies on the stairs.

Marianne doesn't know if she can do this: moving downwards through the ship goes against her every instinct. It feels like descending straight to the inner circles of hell. But she follows Vincent and Madde and tries not to look at the bodies. She can't take any more death. The carpet is wet in patches, blood-soaked, and Madde whimpers quietly when she steps in it with her bare feet.

Eighth floor. Bodies litter the long hallway where she was almost trampled. She would have been if not for Vincent. The lift doors are closed now.

She hears shouting from the floor below, glass breaking, running. Cheering. That might be the most terrifying sound of all. What could there possibly be to cheer about?

They reach deck seven. The windows of the tax-free shop have been smashed. Dark shapes are moving about inside. Marianne freezes mid-movement.

That is where *they* are holed up.

But then a group of men come dashing out of the shop with their arms full of liquor bottles and cartons of cigarettes, and Marianne recognises one of Göran's friends. She's pretty sure his name is Sonny.

'Marianne, sweet as the mints!' he calls out smarmily. 'What have you done with Göran?'

Her cheeks flush when she feels Vincent and Madde's stares. More people come running by with their loot. Some have grabbed baskets and piled them high with sweets and perfume and booze. Always booze.

'I don't know,' she says. 'I thought he was with you.'

'But he ditched us to go back to yours!'

Marianne looks at him without comprehension. 'He did?'

Sonny smiles maniacally. The front of his shirt is blood-spattered, she realises. Has he been bitten? Have any of the others?

'Tag along,' he says, pointing with his thumb to one of the men Marianne doesn't know. 'We're off to his cabin to drink ourselves into a coma until this shit is over!'

'No,' the man says firmly, and shoots Marianne an apologetic look. 'Nothing personal, but I don't know you. At least I met these guys . . . before.'

'I understand,' Marianne tells him.

She looks at Sonny, wanting to ask about Göran, but she doesn't know how.

A few of the men outside the shop, entangled in a fight over a jumbo pack of *snus*, are tripped up by a couple of the dead bodies and start rolling around on the floor. That quote from Sartre, about hell being other people, comes to Marianne's mind. And she notices a few of the corpses on the floor have started moving: they're waking up.

They need to get out of here. Vincent has noticed too.

'Would you mind giving us a bottle?' he says. 'The stronger, the better.'

'Get your own drink,' one of the strangers tells him, but Sonny hands him a bottle of lemon vodka.

'Thanks,' Vincent says, accepting it with his uninjured hand.

'All right, sweet mint, seems we're going to have to toast each other in separate cabins,' Sonny says.

'We're not drinking this,' Vincent says. 'We're making a Molotov cocktail.'

'Smart,' someone in the other group says with reluctant admiration. 'Bloody smart.'

'You're setting fire to the booze?' Sonny says, and his maniacal smile grows even wider. 'Now that's what I call substance abuse.'

It occurs to Marianne that Göran would probably have laughed at that stupid joke.

'Good luck,' she says.

'You too. And if you find Göran . . . look after him.'

He hesitates. Marianne looks around nervously. The fight is still ongoing. A woman drops a stack of six-packs outside the shop and cans roll in every direction. The ruckus is going to attract more of *them*.

'I will,' she says.

'He's a good 'un, is Göran,' Sonny says.

She nods at him and continues down the stairs.

The *Baltic Charisma*

Dan Appelgren is in the shower. The hot water is making the blood warm again. The red streaks swirling into the drain are growing wispier. He washes himself meticulously. He has vomited and feels less bloated, but the thoughts won't stop churning in his head, racing in circles, chasing their own tails, doing endless somersaults. He presses his lathered-up fingers against his skull, because it feels like the only thing he can do to keep it from exploding. Dan has been through this before, after too much coke. *It's going to pass, you just have to wait it out. Keep cool and stay strong.*

The dark-haired woman is standing inside her caravan, looking at the photographs in her locket. After all these years, the pictures are burnt into her retinas, carved into her heart. She only has to shut her eyes to see them. Even so, she can't bring herself to close the locket. Memories and feelings wash through her and for once she does nothing to stop them, this last time. Her son. Her husband. The time before her son fell ill. Before she used her contacts in spiritualism and found the apostates from the Theosophical Society, who introduced her to two of the Old Ones: the ones who can no longer pass for human, who depend on assistants. Back then she was rich enough to believe money could buy her

469

anything, and she was right. The Old Ones acquiesced, despite their objections, when she offered them all the money she had.

Afterwards, she and her husband brought their son home to their flat in Stockholm. They had taken every possible precaution: they took turns draining themselves with a razor. Those days that turned into weeks disappeared in a haze; she was constantly faint with anaemia, with grief and fear, terror and hope. Their son always wanted more, and he grew strong and healthy, living off what her body could give him, just like when she had nursed him a few years earlier. It felt like a miracle when he seemed to become himself again. His father finally relented and loosened the straps tying him to his bed.

The woman told herself that what happened wasn't her son's fault. She forgave him. She has forgiven him ever since, blamed herself instead. He never asked to be changed. She made that decision for him, and he has never forgiven her. She misses the man in the photograph. She hid his beloved face under a towel before she severed his head from his body.

One night, when the smell in the flat had become unbearable, impossible to hide, she dragged his exsanguinated body to the bathtub. She started by bisecting the body at the waist, then chopped off his arms and legs and cut them into smaller pieces. Back then, she still believed in God, and she agonised about what would happen to her husband's soul after what they had done. But it was in that bathroom she came to understand that hell is not a place apart, separate from the Earth, from life.

She spent the next few nights dragging sacks of meat and rocks to Nybrokajen harbour and throwing them into the water. And, of course, she caught the infection from the boy eventually.

Was it a mistake or did she let it happen? She doesn't know. Her son looked after her during the change, fed her. Men and women would ring their door with his hand in a firm grip, convinced they had helped the poor lost child find his way home. The boy fetched many more than they needed. He enjoyed it far too much, even then. It was just a game to him, and he never tired of it, just like the Old Ones had told her he wouldn't. She had to tame her instincts quickly to be able to keep an eye on him.

The woman closes the locket, walks to the dining area, lifts up one of the bench lids and takes out an ice-axe. She weighs it in her hand. She and her son have cheated death for more than a hundred years. This far, but no further.

She thinks about all the things she used to believe about vampires long ago, in a different life: all the myths that turned out to be lies and superstition. Everything would have been so much easier if she could have relied on the sun that is about to rise. But they can be killed with fire – fire purifies, fire devours – and then water, deep enough to hide the evidence.

That is how it has to happen.

She doesn't look around the caravan before she leaves; this is not where her memories are. The newborns watch her, several hundred pairs of eyes following her silently as she walks between the rows of cars.

As the woman breathes in the petrol fumes she sees signs of life behind the car windows. Half-filled plastic bottles of soft drink. Blankets. Sweet wrappers. She stops by a blue Nissan with decals on the inside of one of the back-seat windows, clutching the ice-axe. She watches one of the newborns, who has stopped in front of a silver car and is staring in through the windscreen at a baby seat. Perhaps he is starting to remember something from his previous life. Perhaps it is his car. His child.

The woman thinks about the boy and girl she tried to save up in the mess. It may have been the last good deed of her life, and it was futile. She has to cause one disaster to prevent a much larger one. This too is unfathomable, what she has to do, but at least she won't have to live with it afterwards. If her plan works, everything will be finished the same moment she puts it in motion. And she is going to take as many newborns with her as she can: the newborns who have put all their instinctive trust in her. The woman aims her ice-axe at the plastic tank under the car, striking it until it punctures. Petrol gushes out onto the floor. There's a clucking sound from the car's insides. She moves on to the next one.

One floor up, in the narrow stairwell outside the car deck, Vincent unwraps the scarf that has been tied around his wrist, tears a strip from it with his teeth and hands it to Madde, who takes a swig from the vodka bottle before folding the strip in half and pushing it inside.

'Is this how you do it?' she asks.

'I think so,' Vincent replies, and hands her a lighter, while Marianne helps him wrap the rest of the scarf back around his wrist.

Dan Appelgren turns the water off and steps out of the shower, wipes the condensation off the mirror and feels instantly better when he notices that his muscles and features are resurfacing. *I'm going to look like myself again, and for a long time too. No more hours at the gym. This is the mould I'm cast in now, just like Adam is never going to be anything other than a toddler with a Napoleon complex.*

He pulls on the clothes he's found in a bag in the suite: jeans, a dark-blue knitted jumper that smells strongly of fabric softener. He fixes his hair, leaves the bathroom and walks to the window. Far away, on the horizon, he can see another cruise ship on its way from Åbo.

The *Baltic Charisma* is only about an hour from the Finnish archipelago.

Albin

Albin's entire body is shaking. He has stuck his tongue between his teeth to keep them from chattering. The vibrations from the engines are strong down here in the control room; he can no longer tell which quivering is his and which belongs to the ship.

A picture of a naked girl has been taped to the wall. She has one hand between her legs, spreading herself open with her fingers so you can see straight up her, almost as though she wants to turn herself inside out. But it is the men on the floor who have been turned inside out. What used to be inside them is now spread out around them. Albin can see the engine room on the other side of a big window. A small group of men in boiler-suits are staring back at him and banging their heads against the glass. They want to get in, so badly they have beaten their foreheads bloody, leaving gory smears on the glass.

Albin turns away, trying to see if the vibrations are visible on the surface of the water in the nearest bucket, but Calle picks it up before Albin can tell.

Calle takes up position in front of the orange metal cabinets full of flashing buttons and windows with various gauges, locked hatches. 'Are you ready?' he says, looking at Filip, who has also picked up a bucket.

Lo glances surreptitiously at Albin. He knows she is worried

474

about him and he wishes he could reassure her, but he is locked inside himself, and the more she looks at him like that, the harder it is to come out. Every glance is a reminder of how weird he is being.

Filip swings his bucket back and forth a few times and then a glittering arc of water splashes into the cabinets. He tosses the bucket aside; it clatters when it bounces on the floor and Albin reflexively glances down at the bodies. They are not moving. Antti picks up his bucket while Calle and Marisol empty theirs. Water sloshes across the floor. The puddle is about to reach Albin's trainers.

And then the room goes dark. The thudding against the window to the engine room increases in frequency, as if the creatures on the other side have suddenly become more eager, or maybe anxious.

The vibrations change in the dark.

'Abbe,' Lo whispers with tears in her voice. 'Abbe?'

He can't answer.

'Are you okay, kids?' Filip asks. 'The emergency lights will come on in a minute. Don't be scared.'

He sounds scared saying it. He thinks he can fool Albin and Lo just because they are children, but he can't even fool himself.

Madde

They stand dead still in the narrow stairwell, waiting for their eyes to adjust to the darkness. The faint light from the emergency exit signs bathes everything in a green glow. Through the door a floor and a half above them, Madde can hear the sound of running feet. She tries to keep completely quiet, but her breathing sounds far too loud in the dark. Before the lights went out, she could see the door to the car deck on the next landing. Beyond that the stairway spiralled out of sight on its way to the lower decks.

She listens to the sound of the *Charisma*'s engines. Have they changed? They have, haven't they? Aren't they a little slower?

'Can you hear it too?' she says softly.

'Calle,' Vincent breathes. 'They did it.'

Without warning, the lights switch back on, fainter than before, flickering. A door opens further down the stairwell and Madde's heart almost stops. She thinks she can make out the sound of feet shuffling against the plastic carpet. How far down are they?

'Can we go up to the sun deck now?' Madde asks. 'I can't bear being down here. I just can't.'

She has to get out of here, up into the fresh air. Anywhere is better than here.

A new shuffling comes from below. It sounds closer this time.

'I'm sure it's locked anyway,' she says, pointing at the door to the car deck.

'I have to try,' Vincent replies. 'Calle must be there right now. But I understand if you want to take off.'

She looks at Vincent's fractured wrist. Looks at Marianne. 'We stick together,' she says. 'But hurry up.'

They start descending again in the flickering light. Madde fiddles with the lighter, nearly dropping it when she spots a shadow on the wall by the foot of the stairs. Someone is coming towards them. She curses.

The creature down there snuffles as he appears around the bend in the stairs. His hair is long, gathered up in a ponytail. Large parts of his face are missing: craters covered by thin, wrinkled scar tissue. His nose is gone; there are just two holes straight into his skull. She can feel Marianne stiffen.

'Let's get out of here,' Madde says. 'Please, okay, let's go. We have to go.'

The man's eyes glint in the light that ebbs and flows, as though the stairwell is *breathing* . . .

'Yeah,' Vincent says, pulling on Marianne with his healthy hand. 'Come on.'

But Marianne isn't moving. She just stares at the man.

Madde's mother was a hunter; they spent a lot of time in the woods together, walking the dogs. She taught Madde which mushrooms were edible, how she could make sure she wasn't walking in circles by observing the sunlight on the trunks of trees, what to do if she came across a bear.

You have to be super-super-quiet. Back away slowly. Don't turn your back. Don't show weakness. Don't look him in the eye. Don't run.

But now, Madde does the complete opposite. She screams, turns on her heel and starts running back up the stairs.

Marianne

Marianne can't take her eyes off the creature that was once Göran. He is standing right in front of the door to the car deck, staring back at her with what appears to be anguish. And a part of her, a very dangerous part, wants to run to him and comfort him, even though she knows it is no longer him, even though she knows he would kill her given half a chance. But he is suffering. She doesn't want him to suffer.

'I'm sorry,' she whispers.

It is her fault he is one of *them* now. He came back down here for her.

'Marianne,' Vincent says, 'we have to get out of here.'

A woman in a blood-soaked hoodie appears behind Göran. The words SEXY BITCH sparkle in rhinestones across her chest. Her teeth snap when she spots them.

Göran puts his foot on the first step. His beautiful eyes are dead now, pale imitations of the eyes that looked at her on the dance floor. When she gazes into them, all her strength evaporates.

'Come on,' Vincent says.

'You run,' she says. 'Do it for me. I'll only slow you down.'

And she means it. Madde did the right thing. Vincent shouldn't risk his life for her again. He should find his friend.

She wants to thank him for everything he has done so far. She wants to tell him she hasn't felt so alive in years. So needed. That that is enough.

She starts walking down the steps towards Göran.

'Marianne, what are you doing?' Vincent says. He grabs her arm again, but she twists free.

'Run,' she hisses. 'I'll hold them off.'

This is how she is going to die. For once, she is going to be strong and brave. And Vincent is going to survive. One person is going to remember her this way, as the strong and brave Marianne, and then it won't have been in vain.

But Vincent wraps his arm around her waist and pulls. Her knees and hips ache when she is forced to jog backwards.

They reach the landing. One more set of stairs to get to the steel door to deck five. It feels impossibly far, but Vincent is pushing her from behind, forcing her to climb on.

'Why are you doing this?' she says. 'It's better if they take me, don't you get that?'

'Shut up and run!' Vincent yells behind her, and she can hear the panic in his voice.

He is not going to let her off so easily; he is risking his life by trying to save her, so she forces herself to find hidden reserves of strength in her thigh muscles and pushes herself up and up and up. She glances behind her. Göran has reached the landing where they were just standing. The woman in the hoodie is hard on his heels. Behind her, two more of *them*: men in sporty-looking sweatshirts.

They are coming closer, closer.

'Let me go,' she whimpers. 'Run, Vincent!'

The steel door opens above them and Marianne knows everything is over now. More of *them* have come; they are trapped in the stairwell. The silhouette of a woman fills the doorway.

'Duck!'

Madde's voice. A flame sails through the air above Marianne's head and disappears behind Vincent. A second later, fire illuminates the stairwell. She sees it spread along the wall of the landing behind Göran and the others. The heat slams into her like a wall; there's a smell of alcohol and lemon and warm plastic.

'I'm sorry,' Madde calls out. 'I'm sorry I just took off!'

Göran and the others have stopped advancing. They are looking at the flames. The woman's hood is on fire and she screams when the flames reach her hair.

It starts raining.

Rain? But we're indoors.

Water is leaking from the ceiling. They are going to drown down here.

Fear sinks its claws into her: being drowned in this stairwell like a rat in a sewer is quite different from being torn apart by *them.*

Her overheating brain registers the hissing sound and finally manages to make a logical connection: the water is coming from a sprinkler system in the ceiling. The fire is already going out. And Göran has shifted his attention back to Marianne and Vincent.

The adrenalin has injected new strength into her legs. She starts running, Vincent right behind her, Madde impatiently jumping up and down on the next landing, one hand on the door, ready to slam it behind them. Just a few more steps . . .

A deafening roar fills the world. It is coming from the ship itself; it is making a sound like a wounded animal.

Marianne reaches the landing, Vincent just one step behind. Behind him is Göran, with his wild eyes, his demented urges, his snapping teeth.

Suddenly she can no longer see Göran. The blaring of the fire alarm is back and this time it mingles with Vincent's scream as his mouth gapes, his eyes open wide. He looks at Marianne and Madde, bewildered, as though he doesn't understand, just like Marianne doesn't understand.

She doesn't *want* to understand.

And then Vincent topples forward, yanked back down the stairs. As he bounces off the edges of the steps, his hands grope at the smooth walls of the stairwell for something to hold on to.

Göran has buried his teeth in Vincent's heel, just above the edge of his shoe. His jaw works as his teeth saw through sock and flesh, severing the Achilles tendon. Vincent screams all the way down to the landing, where the woman in the blood-soaked hoodie throws herself on top of him. They disappear around the bend while the deafening alarm blares plaintively. The fire is completely out now, nothing but acrid smoke rising from the plastic carpet in tiny blue-tinted wisps.

'Vincent!' Marianne screams, and the two men in sweatshirts look at her and start moving up the stairs, surprisingly swiftly.

Madde pulls her through and gives the door a shove. A sweater-clad man's arm reaches in through the crack, fumbling around, seeking to grab them.

Madde puts all her weight against the door. There's the sound of something breaking, an inhuman roar and the arm goes limp. She opens the door an inch or two and the arm disappears. There's a heavy thud as the man crashes down the steps on the other side, and then the door slams shut with a clang.

The alarm stabs at Marianne's ears again. They are back on the carpet on deck five, and she can see more of *them* coming down the wide staircase.

The *Baltic Charisma*

The ship glides ever more slowly through the waters of the Baltic Sea.

The monotonous sound of the fire alarm follows a dying man into the big void. He has been dragged down to one of the narrow corridors under the car deck. He can no longer feel the newborns tearing at him, can't see them fighting each other over his blood. He can only hear the wet noises, and the klaxons, again and again, but fainter each time.

The newborns on the car deck are unsettled by the blaring sirens. The dark-haired woman has felt the vibrations in the floor change and knows time is short now. This was what the staff were discussing at the meeting. Once the ship comes to a stop, they can launch the life rafts. Then the world will notice that something is wrong. She has to finish this before more people arrive and before any of the infected can get away.

The alarm echoes across the dance floor, through the hallways where the emergency lights flicker overhead. It cuts through the wind on the outer decks; it fills the cabins where people are hiding. Some of them open their doors and peek out, trying to figure out what's going on, what they should do. Others stay put and watch the dawn break outside their windows.

The newborn who was once the captain of the ship claws at the inside of the door to the bridge.

The klaxons drill into the newborns in the mess, awakening instincts from their life on board, thoughts they can't formulate in their current state. Nurse Raili has found the breadknife with the bright yellow handle and is stabbing the point into her ear, hacking and twisting until she can no longer hear the blaring. She is barely aware of the pain, because it is nothing compared to the hunger.

The alarm rouses one of the newborns in the spa. She is lying face-down in the hot tub. Her eyes are open in the water. She is in pain, but she is used to that. She struggles to lift her head up above the still surface and peer around for the source of the hateful noise.

Adam, standing further astern on the same deck, studying a deck plan, puts a hand against the faux-mahogany wall of the *Charisma* and feels the silence of the engines. He remembers the engine room is next to the car deck: the only place he hasn't been to look for his mother. She must be the one who stopped the engines. Running his finger along the route to the car deck, he knows she has to understand why he has done what he has done: that this is for her sake too. *She just has to free herself of the old preconceptions.* He pulls a pass from his pocket and starts walking towards the stairs.

*

The first person infected on board is still sitting on the floor of his drunk tank. He has clapped his hands over his ears and is screaming to drown out the klaxons. The humans in the cells next to his are awake too, calling for help, banging on their doors, but no one is coming.

In the suite, the former Eurovision star is walking around smashing lamps. The faint flickering light hurts his eyes. The blaring of the alarm stabs at his ears. The floor is no longer vibrating under his feet. The *Charisma* is not going to reach Åbo. It feels so unfair. He is convinced the people who escaped from the mess did this. *This is not how it was meant to go.* He should have killed Adam's mother. He should have killed them all. The klaxons blare again, shredding any conscious thought.

The air on the car deck is shimmering with fumes. The dark-haired woman is swinging her ice-axe ever faster, ever more resolutely. Petrol splashes her dress and seeps across the floor. Diesel gushes out when she punctures a tank on the side of a lorry. The sound of the blaring klaxons is more than she can endure, but it is almost over. Soon, everything will be over.

Marianne

'I can't breathe,' Marianne gasps. 'I can't breathe.'

She is panting and clinging to Madde's arm, dizzy from lack of oxygen. No matter how hard she tries, she can't force enough air into her lungs. She doesn't know if the lights in the hallway are flickering or if she is about to faint.

'We're almost there,' Madde tells her.

'I need to go outside. I need air.'

Everything is so different, so quiet between the blares of the klaxons. No more humming of engines under their feet. It's as incomprehensible as the Earth itself grinding to a halt, because the *Baltic Charisma* is her whole world now.

Next to her, Madde is crying, big tears rolling down her chubby cheeks, but Marianne can't cry. She looks over her shoulder. No one seems to be following them and the mangled bodies they pass are still motionless.

Every once in a while a door opens and people poke their heads out, ask them if they know what is going on, if they are sinking, if there is a fire. She can see their fear, but she's unable to reassure them. At any time it could be something else opening one of the doors or bursting from a side passage, ready to kill her and Madde, like they killed Vincent. Like they killed Göran, before he became one of *them*.

They finally reach the glass door at the end of the hallway. Madde pushes it open and the first waft of cold, fresh air chills Marianne. She tries not to look at the bodies they have to step over as Madde leads her to the railing; she tries to ignore that the deck is sticky with drying blood.

They go to stand at the prow. Marianne tries to focus on the water, the waves rippling towards her in never-ending patterns. There is just a gentle lapping against the hull now, so different from the rushing and foaming last night. Strands of cloud are moving rapidly across the sky, darker grey against lighter, like a film played at the wrong speed. She finally manages to pull air all the way down when she breathes; the oxygen almost makes her dizzy. She lets it wash through her lungs as the klaxons blare yet again.

Madde shivers in her flimsy, see-through mini-dress. Marianne puts her arms around her and feels the soft body against her own. And Madde puts her head on her shoulder, crying harder.

She is even more scared than Marianne, and that makes Marianne pluck up courage, simply because she has no choice. They can't both fall apart at the same time.

'I'm sure they'll be here from the mainland soon,' she says. 'Someone'll come for us. We'll be home before we know it.'

'I'm sorry,' Madde says, 'I'm sorry I just took off. I was so scared and—'

The rest of what she says is inaudible. Marianne just murmurs soothingly and strokes her back.

'—my fault Vincent is dead!' Madde sobs.

'No,' Marianne says. She shuts her eyes, but that only makes Vincent's face in the stairwell appear all the more clearly. So she opens them again, squinting against the wind. 'No, it's my fault.

486

He tried to make me run away from there much earlier, but I . . .
I couldn't.'

She had been hoping it would feel better if she said it out loud,
but the opposite is true. It is getting harder to breathe again.

'But if I hadn't taken off . . .' Madde sobs against her neck. 'Or
if I had come back sooner . . .'

'It wouldn't have mattered. And you did come back.' Marianne
shouts to make herself heard over another blare of the alarm. 'I'm
not sure I would have been brave enough.'

'I wasn't brave. It was just even worse to be alone.'

'Listen to me. *It wasn't your fault.*'

Madde pulls free of her embrace, wipes her eyes and takes a
deep breath. 'It wasn't yours either,' she says, and turns back
towards the ship, raising her eyes.

She is almost beautiful in the wavering light of the lanterns.

Marianne turns as well, realises what Madde is looking for
and immediately spots the windows of the suite, four floors
up. She feels like she can make out movements behind them,
but the lights are out and the faint light out here is reflected in
the glass.

'It's his fault,' Madde says. 'If we had still been up there, we
would have been safe. *Safer*, anyway.'

Marianne nods.

'And we are getting off this fucking boat,' Madde continues,
turning to Marianne. 'We just have to get up to the life rafts.'

'Yes.'

Marianne thinks she can hear muffled screaming from inside
the ship. A new blaring from the klaxons drowns it out. She looks
at Madde, who is pointing.

'They're here,' she says.

Marianne turns to the glass door they just came out through. Some of *them* are approaching it. There is no mistaking that slow, determined walk.

They run to the other side of the bow deck and peer in through the identical glass door there. There are more of *them* in the corridor on this side too. And they are on their way out.

'*Fuck!*' Madde exclaims. 'Fuck, there's nowhere to go.'

Marianne looks at the bow deck, allows herself to see the bodies strewn everywhere for the first time. There's a pile of them right next to the railing.

The idea is so revolting she immediately dismisses it. But then she glances at Madde and knows she has to try.

The alarm blares again, then abruptly falls silent.

Filip

Marisol and he have finally managed to turn the alarm off. They are standing in the general manager's office staring at the microphone in front of them. Filip is thinking about Mika, wondering how many times he has held it.

'Do you want to do it?' he says.

She shakes her head. 'I wouldn't know what to say,' she says.

'Me neither.'

The truth is that he is afraid his voice is going to betray him. He is so tired. They are so close, and yet it feels insurmountable.

They are going to get in the life rafts. They are going to wait for help. And then what?

I wouldn't get into a raft with any of the passengers anyway. What if one of them changes while you're out there, bobbing on the waves?

And he can't even be sure he isn't infected himself. His left hand reflexively reaches up to his lips. They sting to the touch. He scrubbed so thoroughly, but . . .

'How are you doing?' Marisol says.

He shakes his head. 'I just don't know how I'm supposed to make it sound like . . . like I have any faith in this myself.'

She puts her arm around him. 'You know what?' she says. 'I quit just a few days ago.'

Filip realises that he is not surprised. Wasn't he thinking just that to himself as recently as last night? That she was going to leave the *Charisma* sooner or later?

'I was going to tell you sometime this shift,' she adds, looking downcast.

He tries to smile. 'After tonight, I might want to quit too.'

'About time,' she says with a small laugh. Then she turns serious again and takes his hand. 'I'm pregnant, that's why. I'm going to start working in my aunt's café instead.'

Filip's smile grows wider, and this time it's genuine. 'I should have figured that out already, shouldn't I?' he says.

'Probably.'

'That's why you never come out with us after work any more.'

Marisol shrugs with a grin.

'You're going to be a really great mum,' he says. 'If you're tough enough to handle the clientele at Starlight at three in the morning, you can deal with any toddler tantrum.'

'Now do you see why we have to make it through this? Both of us? Because I was thinking you might be the godfather, actually.' She says it flippantly, but she almost looks embarrassed. 'If anything were to happen to me . . .'

'Nothing's going to happen to you,' he cuts her off.

She lets go of his hand, looking like she has more to say, but then she heaves a sigh and picks up the microphone.

'All right,' she says. 'Let's get this done.'

Calle

It had been his idea that they go here to look for signs of a fire on board. He regretted it as soon as they opened the door, but Albin and Lo barely reacted. He can't help but wonder what all of this is going to do to them.

Bosse is slumped in his chair. Someone has thrown a fleece blanket over him. It is sopping with blood where his face would be. His arms dangle limply by his sides, his curled fingers almost touching the floor.

Calle carefully grabs the backrest from behind, trying not to touch the body as he pushes the chair aside. The chair bumps over a cord, making Bosse's head roll onto his chest. But the blanket stays on. Thankfully.

Antti steps up to the desk and starts pushing buttons at random. Calle looks around the office and spots the phone in a pool of blood on the floor. It's in pieces. He curses.

The different camera perspectives flash by on the screens. In the hallway above them, on deck six, a handful of passengers are peeking out of their cabins. Their faces are spectral in the faintly flickering emergency light. How many are acting like Mika, trying to hide that they've been bitten? How many haven't even realised themselves?

Antti pushes more buttons and the tax-free shop appears on the screens. Its glass doors have been smashed, broken bottles and discarded packaging litter the floor and bodies are scattered across the carpet outside.

Come on, Calle thinks when they see the information desk, the closed door to the general manager's office where Filip and Marisol should be. *Say something already. I need to know you're okay.*

New hallways on the screens. A wide-open door here and there. Blood on the walls around them. On deck five, near Bosse's office, some of the infected are moving towards the prow. In a corridor on deck eight more of them are milling about, apparently aimlessly. In the café a small group of people are hiding behind some upended tables; it looks like they are consoling an injured man. Others are being chased through the maze of short hallways near the stern on deck seven. Blood is spattered on the windows around the ball pit. There's yet more blood on the walls and floor outside the karaoke bar.

But there are fewer infected than he had expected. That does nothing to put him at ease.

Where are they?

The wall of a landing in the stairwell outside the car deck is charred. A smashed vodka bottle is lying on the floor beneath it. Calle exhales. If that's the fire that set off the alarm, it was extinguished a long time ago.

Antti pushes more buttons; more images from the ship flit past. 'No more fire, as far as I can see,' he says. 'Fucking hell, wouldn't that just have been the last bloody straw.'

Calle nods. 'Can you find the hallway outside the suite?'

Antti pushes a few buttons; Calle tries to follow along on the screens. Spots deck nine, starboard side. The door. 9318.

'There!' he says. 'Stop there!'

He leans so close to the screen he can feel the static electricity against his face.

KALLE! DON'T OPEN!

The word 'don't' is thickly underlined. Calle stares at the words, his misspelt name.

Vincent can't have written that.

A melodious signal chimes over the PA system and then he hears Marisol clear her throat. Finally.

'Dear passengers,' she says, 'we have managed to stop the ship, which means that sooner or later someone will discover that something is wrong on board. It should not take long. We are just an hour or so from Finland and this is a busy sea route.'

Calle watches as people begin to congregate in the hallway on deck six. They are listening intently. Some are filming with their mobile phones, holding them up to the speaker or their own faces.

None of them are Vincent. *Where is Vincent?*

'We don't know what has happened here tonight,' Marisol continues. 'We know people get sick if they are bitten, but we don't know what kind of disease it is or why there is an outbreak on board. Some of us are going to try to make it to the sun deck, at the very top of the ship. Now that we have come to a stop, we can launch the life rafts and wait in them until help arrives. Bundle up warm and join us, if you think you can. If not, stay in your cabin or wherever there is a door you can lock.'

She falls silent. Calle can almost hear her wavering. Antti is panting heavily next to him.

'Remember that this contagion can affect *anyone*. If you have family or friends who have been bitten . . . don't try to help them. Don't even go near them. I understand that it's horrible to hear, but . . . it's the only way you can protect yourself from the contagion and be sure you won't infect others.'

Pause. He can see the little group on deck six hesitate, before most of them go back into their cabins.

'Good luck, whatever you decide to do,' Marisol concludes. The speakers click off.

Lo tugs gently on Calle's shirt.

'What's the matter?' he asks.

She doesn't reply, just looks at him in silence, then at the screen showing the entrance to the spa. Some kind of large machine is sitting on the floor just inside the smashed glass wall. And he can see someone moving further in. Jerkily, staggering.

'What's so—' he says.

Lo quietly hushes him and glances pointedly at Albin, who is staring at the floor. And Calle breaks off and takes another look at the screen. Properly this time.

The machine is a wheelchair on its side.

He swallows, understanding who the staggering figure is. He stares at the silhouette of Albin's mother until she is nothing but a conglomeration of pixels in various shades of grey. He reaches out and pushes a few buttons to make the creature on the other side of the broken glass disappear from the screen. Antti shoots him a glance; he has also understood.

'Come on,' Calle says. 'We have to get up to the life rafts now and help anyone who wants to get out of here.'

Albin stares at him. There are no signs that he has realised they are hiding something from him.

They check the screen showing the hallway outside Bosse's office. None of the infected appear to be around at the moment.

Antti opens the door a crack. Calle places himself behind the children, grabs the mop handle with the taped-on knife and turns to the screen, where a black-and-white Antti can be seen popping his head out through the door. Calle's eyes move on to the blanket-covered figure in the office chair. Has Bosse moved? Was that the way his head was hanging?

'Hurry up,' he says. Antti gives him an annoyed look before stepping into the hallway.

Calle puts his hands on the children's shoulders. Lo looks at him, mouths a thank-you.

'It's going to be all right,' he whispers.

Antti hushes them. He has stopped in the middle of the hallway. His face is redder than ever. He seems to be listening for something. The knife is trembling in his hand.

And Calle feels panic seep into every limb when he hears steps approaching from a side corridor.

Someone running.

Madde

She tries to make herself stop shaking, ignore the cold, the wind, the fear and focus on the calm lapping of the waves against the hull. The gentle rocking.

The creatures moving awkwardly about the deck are nothing to her, nothing she needs to trouble herself with. Nor should she think about the fact that the thing pressing against her hipbone is an elbow. That a strange woman's hair is draped across her face, tickling her nose. A heel is digging into her ankle. She should not think about the fact that the heel is part of a shoe, and that inside that shoe is a foot, a foot that belongs to a corpse.

No. She shouldn't think at all. She should just make sure to stay very still.

Play dead.

She and Marianne are hiding in a pile of bodies next to the railing. It was Marianne's idea. She pulled the long-haired woman's body to cover the two of them. Madde is lying face-down, her nose pressed into a knitted jumper that smells like smoke and the bottom of the laundry basket. Marianne is next to her. Her body is warm, despite the wind, and reeks of layer upon layer of anxiety, perspiration, old perfume and hair dye. Madde guesses that she doesn't smell like a bouquet of flowers herself.

She can only hope the wind out here on the bow deck will disperse their scent, or that it is drowned out by the smell of the dead bodies all around them.

She thinks she can make out the sound of footsteps approaching, the snapping of teeth over the howling of the wind. She shuts her eyes tight, tries to not even breathe.

Her heart is pounding hard, and every beat brings a dull pain in her torn earlobe. She wishes she hadn't looked out of the window of the suite and seen what happened here. She knows how these people died. It is all too easy to imagine what is going to happen when *they* find her and Marianne.

Don't think about it, don't think about it.

Sniffing in the air. Still some ways off, but far too close.

That feeling fills her again: she wants to stand up and scream, fight. She could jump into the freezing water and hope for the best. Or allow herself to get bitten. Anything, so long as it is finally over.

But she can't, no matter how tempting it might be. She would risk Marianne's life too. They haven't made it this far just to die when help is on its way.

Fuck no. They are going to make it. They are going to get out of here and get up to the goddamn life rafts on the sun deck. They are going to wait for the help that will come sooner or later. The woman said so over the PA system.

They are going to survive. They are getting off this fucking boat. If not, Vincent's death was completely pointless.

The footsteps behind them fade into the distance. Madde is still holding her breath, not quite daring to believe it.

But yes: they are fading.

Madde exhales slowly and opens her eyes. She has been squeezing them shut so hard the muscles around them ache. The faint grey light of dawn is trickling in through her eyelashes.

Her ears are straining. She can't be sure there aren't more of *them* on the bow deck.

Marianne shifts. Madde turns her head a few degrees, glares at her.

Marianne is staring back at her, wide-eyed.

'Lie still,' she mouths.

'I am,' Madde mouths back.

Something is gently nudging Madde's stomach.

The body underneath them is moving. The man in the unwashed jumper emits a groan that rumbles through the ribcage Madde's nose is pressed against. He has started waking up.

Calle

'Let's go,' Calle whispers, urging the children on. He takes the first few steps up the wide staircase.

Something flutters by at the edge of his vision.

Someone screams.

It happens so quickly that it's done before Calle can even turn around.

A wild-eyed man in a dressing gown has run straight into Antti. The man coughs and tiny droplets of blood mist Antti's face. Antti stumbles backwards, revolted, wiping at his face with his shirt sleeve.

The man's hands slide down to his stomach. The handle of Antti's knife is sticking out of the gap where his dressing gown has fallen open.

'But . . . why?' the man gasps, and falls to his knees, staring at his bloody fingers.

Something is twisted around them: colourful plastic beads on a heavy-duty sewing thread. A necklace, made by a child. Nausea rises in Calle's throat.

'He can talk,' Lo says. 'He's not one of them.'

'I'm sorry,' Antti says. 'I'm sorry, fuck, I'm sorry . . .'

The man looks up again, grabs hold of the knife handle and

tries to yank it out; his whole face contorts in agony. He lets go of the knife and starts sobbing silently.

Calle can tell that every movement is making the pain in his gut worse. 'What the fuck have you done, Antti?' he says. 'What the fuck have you done?'

He squats down, vaguely aware that a number of people have emerged in the surrounding hallways, that they are staring. Some are wearing coats, others are wrapped in blankets.

'He just ran straight at me. You saw it too,' Antti says. 'I thought he was one of them.'

'Stella,' the man whispers, fixing firmly on Calle, as though to make sure he has heard the name. 'Stella . . .'

'Who is that?'

The man's gaze cuts right through Calle.

'We saw them at dinner,' Lo says. 'Stella's your daughter, right? She thought my aunt was in a pram.'

The man nods, wincing with pain again. His face pales, so rapidly Calle can see the colour change. 'She ran out of our cabin ahead of me when . . . my wife . . .'

His mouth opens and closes, but no other sounds come out. He is having trouble holding himself upright, so Calle helps lower him onto his back.

'What about your wife?' Calle says.

The man pulls up the sleeve of his dressing gown.

A large bite mark just below the elbow.

'Bloody hell!' Antti shouts. 'Bloody hell, he's infected, and I have his blood all over me! Fucking twat!'

Calle is practically speechless, then he roars, 'Shut the fuck up!'

'It wasn't my fault,' Antti says. 'He was going to die anyway!'

'But you didn't know that!'

When Calle turns back to the man, he has stopped breathing, and Calle realises he is standing at that precipice again. He is balancing on the brink of insanity, leaning out over the edge. He is staring into the abyss and the abyss is staring back at him.

'I'm telling you, it wasn't my fault,' Antti whimpers.

He turns around and runs back down the hallway, away from them.

Calle closes his eyes. He has to try to hold it together, just a little while longer.

Madde

The man is squirming underneath her, making the whole jumble of bodies move. The heel burrows deeper into her calf, striking a nerve. Madde cautiously lifts her head up.

She almost wets herself.

The man is staring back at her. The look in his watery blue eyes is as animalistic as Zandra's was, both empty and determined. He is straining to get his face closer to hers. His teeth snap.

Madde braces her hands against his chest and pushes up on all fours. The long-haired woman and Marianne roll onto the deck. Madde scrabbles backwards, puts her knee on someone's thigh, finds the floor, freezing cold against her bare toes, and manages to stand up.

Marianne doesn't move but stares at the man with panic in her eyes. They are so close. The man slowly turns his head until they are face to face. He sniffs.

That disgusting fucking sniffing and snapping of the teeth. Madde is so sick of being afraid of them. She hates them so much, so incredibly fucking much.

She gropes around until she hits upon Marianne's elbow and pulls her upright, checking behind her while Marianne finds her balance. A group of *them* have gathered by one of the glass doors. They have apparently abandoned the other side of the bow deck.

The man sits up and reaches out for them, snaps his teeth. The corners of his mouth point straight down. He looks like a spoiled child, sulking in the sweets section because he can't have everything he wants.

Marianne whimpers, but Madde hushes her, gestures in the direction of the huddle, which is bound to notice them any moment now.

They set their course for the other glass door. Madde steps across the woman, slipping when she treads on her hair.

Madde barely manages to force down a yelp when there is a hard tug on her dress.

The man is staring up at her when she whips around. His hand has a vice-like grip on the hem and he tugs and pulls at it. His hairy knuckles rub against her thigh. His round face is a mask of unadulterated urge.

Enough already. Fucking *enough* already.

Hate fills her to the brim. Blows into her on the wind. Roaring and swirling.

She tries to pull free, but he clings on. She almost falls over, but catches herself on the railing.

'Suck my cock, you fucking perv,' she hisses so quietly the words dissolve in the gusts of wind.

The huddle has spotted them now. Empty, burning eyes study them.

Suddenly Marianne is beside her. She kicks the man in the head with the pointy toe of her shoe. She kicks again and this time gets his arm. He loses his grip on Madde's dress.

Marianne kicks him a third time, so hard he topples backwards, rolling over the body underneath him and landing face-first. He tries to get back up, arms flailing.

Madde pounces on him, grabs the hair at the nape of his neck and pulls it so hard it's a wonder it doesn't come out. She slams his head into the lower bar of the railing with such force the metal rings. She screams at the top of her lungs. She can't hold it in. What difference does it make? They've already been seen. This is for Zandra. For Vincent. This is for the conversation she has to have with Zandra's parents. This is for Zandra's daughter, who will never know her mum properly, never know how wonderful she was.

'We have to get out of here,' Marianne says, but Madde isn't listening; she's slamming the man's face into the railing, again and again. The metal becomes slick with blood and something else, which trickles across the deck and into the water. She slams his face down again, as hard as she can, and only when his body goes limp does she let go. His head falls to one side and Madde sees the bloody mass where his face used to be, the profile that is now concave, and she finally backs away.

The wind snatches at her hair and she pushes it away from her face. Triumph roars inside her.

'Come on now,' Marianne says, and the graveness of her tone bores into Madde, who turns around, and is stunned. The woman at the front of the pack is barely three feet away. But Madde isn't scared; she is too high from what she has just done. It feels like she could kill them all, one by one or several at a time. She has to force herself to realise that the most dangerous thing she can do is let herself believe there is no danger.

She takes Marianne's hand and they hurry towards the glass door. Hearing footsteps behind them, she shoves Marianne into the hallway.

Without the wind in her ears, the ship is eerily quiet. The air is warm against Madde's chilled skin. She looks down the side corridor on their right, just inside the door. Some of *them* are standing there. They open their mouths when they notice her and Marianne and begin ambling towards them.

The two women break into a run. There is a small stairwell going up in the next side corridor, but Madde can't recall where it leads and it's too narrow anyway; she doesn't want to risk getting stuck between two bands of *them*. When they pass the corridor, she spots a young man with dishevelled hair. He has already noticed them, so she accelerates, hoping they will have a clear shot up the main stairs. She is practically dragging Marianne along behind her now. She wonders why more people aren't making their way to the sun deck. Maybe they prefer hiding in their cabins. She would probably have done the same.

They come out in the main hallway, and Madde stops mid-step when she sees a man in a bloody dressing gown on the floor right in front of the staircase. A blonde child in nothing but underpants is kneeling next to him. She can count every vertebra in the little spine.

Marianne is gasping with the effort.

'Hello?' Madde says, and holds her hand out to the child, then changes her mind and quickly retracts it.

Not a child that's one of *them*. She wouldn't be able to handle that. She wouldn't be able to hurt that tiny body even if she had to.

The child turns around: it's a girl, looking up at them with eyes red from crying.

'My daddy won't wake up,' she says. 'He has to wake up so we can hide from Mummy.'

Albin

He steals a glance at Lo as they walk through the ship for the last time. It feels like she is hiding something. Before, she kept looking at him; now she won't look at him at all.

Calle is holding his spear at the ready. They reach deck six, where a few groups of frightened people come stumbling in from the hallways; they nod to them before they start making their way towards the sun deck too. One of them is a woman with cropped hair, muttering to herself in Finnish. He recognises two other women from last night, when he was on his way to the cabin to get Lo.

Tonight's going to be amazing, Mum. So fucking amazing!

Now they look like people in news photos from war zones. Albin wonders if he looks like that too. He stares down the corridor where their cabin is. His dad must have heard the announcement. How would he feel about his dad if he could feel anything right now?

'I wonder where Mum is,' Lo says as they continue towards the seventh floor. 'Maybe she was with . . . with Cilla . . .'

Lo's voice sounds thin. It kind of just evaporates towards the end. He glances at her. She suddenly looks so small.

'We were going to get massages tomorrow,' Lo says, 'although I guess that's today now.'

Is she as worried about Linda as he was about his mum before everything went so numb and weird? She must be. Why hasn't she said anything? He probably should have realised anyway. But Lo never gives the impression she needs her mother, or even likes her very much. She never has; not even when they were little did Lo want Linda to comfort her when something happened.

One of the bodies on the landing reaches out for them and Albin notices Calle taking a firmer grip on his spear. 'At least Linda has a better chance than Mum,' he says.

'Not necessarily, just because she can walk. It's like I said before.' Lo looks like she is about to cry. '*Oh well, what do you know. There seems to be someone gnawing on . . .*'

And then Lo stops dead on the stairs and starts crying. She pulls her sleeves down over her hands, hiding her face in them, hunching down as sobs rack her body.

Albin puts a hand between her shoulder blades, unsure what to say.

'Come on,' Calle says. 'Just a few more floors.' His voice sounds thick.

Lo lowers her hands. Her face is flushed, her eyes swollen, but she is not crying any more.

Albin allows himself to slip away again, to the place where nothing can get to him.

Filip

Filip keeps a white-knuckle grip on his makeshift spear, resting it on his shoulder when he and Marisol reach deck ten. He glances at a couple pushing past them. His whole body is tense, ready. Every now and then he meets Marisol's eyes, checking to make sure she hasn't spotted any of the infected either.

A full set of teeth, held together by gleaming braces, sits on the floor by the door to the promenade deck. He looks back over his shoulder. Still no sign of Calle and the children. Two women come up the stairs, so alike they must be sisters, followed by a man in a suit. He recognises a woman with cropped blonde hair from the Finnish conference group who stopped by Starlight early last night. She kept rejecting the advances of one of her colleagues, a baby-faced bald man who was so drunk Filip had considered calling security. Mascara has run down her cheeks. But he doesn't see anyone who appears to have been bitten.

'Where are they?' Marisol says.

Filip knows who she means. Shouldn't all these people attract the infected?

They step out onto the promenade deck on the starboard side. The temperature must have plummeted during the night. The wind quickly cools his damp nylon shirt, makes it cling to his body. The sea is eerily still, unmoved by the things that have happened on board.

They have almost reached the stairs to the sun deck when they hear screams behind them. Filip's hold on the mop handle tightens and he spins around.

'You!' Dan Appelgren bellows, shoving aside anyone who is in his way.

He is less swollen now, and he has changed his clothes. He fixes Filip with those bloodshot eyes and heads straight for him at a run, bellowing, 'You self-righteous arsehole! I fucking hate you!'

Dan

He heard the announcement and instantly knew it was the señorita from Starlight speaking. He came out to make sure no one gets on the fucking life rafts and immediately noticed there are far too few newborns roaming the ship.

Something is wrong.

And now Filip is here, brandishing a pathetic little toy spear, waving it about in front of him. 'Marisol, run,' Filip says, playing the hero to the last.

But Marisol doesn't listen: she comes at Dan with a fire-axe in her hands. Her pulse is beating hard in her throat, every thump making the gold chain of her crucifix gleam in the pale light of dawn. Dan easily dodges the blade of the axe as it sails past his face. She raises it again, but he is too fast; he punches her in the face, hard, feeling her nose break. He wrests the axe from her hands, tosses it aside, hearing the crowd behind him scream.

'You can forget about anyone getting off this ship,' he says, smelling the blood streaming out of her nose, and instantly understands.

He grins at her.

And then a searing pain blossoms above his waist.

He turns around and sees Filip standing there with both hands on his mop handle. The knife has gone all the way in, stopping somewhere behind his lower ribs.

The pain is violent, but it doesn't scare him; on the contrary, it sharpens his senses, makes every contour clearer. Nothing about Filip's attack can hurt him. The wound will heal.

Filip pulls the knife back out and tries to stab him again, aiming for Dan's ribcage, but he lunges and misses by almost a foot. Filip's fear makes him unfocused; he glances at Marisol.

'Fucking run!' he shouts, and stabs at Dan again.

Dan throws his hand up and the blade slices right through it. He closes his fingers around it. The edge digs into his skin. Time to finish this. He grabs the mop handle, yanks the ridiculous spear out of Filip's hands and flings it overboard.

Filip has placed himself between Dan and Marisol, who is too stupid to even try to run.

Getting him on his back is easy. Filip attempts to twist free but quickly realises he can't move. People are screaming behind them. The smell of Filip's fear is growing more acrid by the second.

Finally. Finally, he knows his place.

'I'm glad you made it out of the mess,' Dan says. 'I was too tired to take care of you then. I'm not now.'

Filip screams when Dan rips a big chunk of flesh from his neck. The blood is warm, enticing. Dan spits it out; he won't make the mistake of overeating again.

'Run!' Filip shouts, and tries to look at Marisol. 'I'm done for. You have to help the others, you have to—' But his shouts turn wordless when Dan buries his teeth in his throat once more, encountering the gristly resistance of Filip's Adam's apple.

Dan pries and crunches until Filip's cries are abruptly cut off. His blood gushes like a warm, sweet fountain straight into Dan's mouth. He can hear Marisol crying and the crowd behind them screaming in panic.

He looks deep into Filip's wide-open eyes. He knows he is going to die now.

Dan tears Filip's shirt open and bites a big chunk out of his chest, working his way towards his heart. He is going to annihilate Filip. He is going to erase him.

Calle

Something has happened on the promenade deck. People are congregating outside the glass doors, several crying in terror. Some are trying to push back inside the ship and one man is screaming, 'We have to get back to our cabin. Come on, Kerstin!' Others stay where they are, straining to see what is going on up ahead.

A gust of wind brings in the cold air from outside. Calle is suddenly more afraid than he has been this whole time. All the things he has been trying to push down are catching up with him: everything that has happened; everything that can still happen.

And if they manage to get to the life rafts and Vincent isn't there . . .

A couple of women barrel down the stairs, almost knocking him off his feet. One of them says, 'Did you see him? It was the guy who works in the bar. It was, right?'

The cold wind chills him to the bone.

Albin's eyes look lifeless again. The spark that flared in the stairwell has gone out. But his grip on Calle's hand is surprisingly strong.

'I'm just going to see what's going on,' Calle says. 'Okay? I'll be right back.'

Albin's slender fingers squeeze his hand harder. Calle glances down at Lo.

'Can you wait here?' he says. 'Just for a few seconds.'

She nods.

'I'll be right back,' he says, and frees himself from Albin's grasp. 'Be careful.'

He climbs the last few steps, pushes onto the promenade deck, recognising the woman from the Finnish conference group at Poseidon. So many people are far too lightly dressed: pale faces, lips already turning blue. He walks around a group of people huddling together, hugging.

Albin was holding his hand so tightly he can still feel it, like a phantom.

The crowd is thinning out. He sees Marisol dashing up the steel staircase to the sun deck.

She is alone.

And Calle *knows*.

He pushes to the front and spots Dan Appelgren first. Dan is wearing Vincent's jumper, the one he bought last winter.

The fire-axe Marisol found is discarded on the deck by Calle's feet.

Nothing makes sense. Nothing at all.

Dan Appelgren is on all fours, straddling the body sprawled on the deck. And it occurs to Calle that Filip must be cold in his flimsy work shirt and waistcoat. The deck must be freezing.

But then Calle's brain catches up with itself. Filip can't feel the cold. He can't feel anything any more.

It isn't Filip lying there; it's his body Dan is tearing into. His head is lolling, rolling from side to side, like a flower on a broken stalk. It's his blood. But it is not Filip.

For a moment, everything is clear to Calle. He is suddenly completely calm, inside and out. If there is such a thing as a soul, it is no longer there. What Filip was is something Dan Appelgren can never take.

And then the moment passes. Calle staggers and falls to his knees.

Dan Appelgren looks up. Blood covers his face, drips from his chin. He spots something behind Calle, draws his lips back, baring his teeth. But he is not the Dan who swaggered into the mess.

He is afraid.

Calle turns around, watches her make her way through the crowd. Her shirt is torn and bloody. Her hair has come loose from her tight topknot; the matted strands with their grey roots are fluttering in the wind.

If you see me, run as far away from me as you can.

I love you, Calle. Promise me.

But he can't. He can't move at all.

The *Baltic Charisma*

Most people stay in their cabins, waiting for the help they have been promised. A little more than a hundred unharmed people all told have braved the hallways and are making their way up through the ship.

Antti has launched the ship's fast rescue boat. He looks over his shoulder one last time to see the *Charisma* looming over him. He hears screaming on the promenade deck and sets off, letting the boat's little engine and the wind drown out all sounds. He tries not to think about the children and everyone else still on board, tells himself he is doing them a solid. He will head towards Finland in the hope of getting close enough to land to use his mobile to call for help. *But you could have brought the kids*, a small voice inside him says.

He accelerates.

Albin's father has left his cabin and is running down the long hallway on deck six. He trips over a dead body and is just about to make a turn towards the stairs when he hears screaming coming from that direction. He stops, breathing heavily, spots the shattered glass wall at the end of the hallway and instantly recognises the wheelchair lying on its side just beyond it. The lights next to

516

the joystick are gleaming faintly in the dark, signalling that the battery is running low. But there is no sign of his wife.

On the car deck, the petrol smell is so overwhelming that Adam's head is spinning. It blankets all other smells, hiding her scent. But he can hear her footsteps, thudding and crashing, clucking and splashing. He finds her on the starboard side, near the prow. Hundreds of newborns are gathered in the gloom. They shift anxiously when they notice him, looking back and forth between him and his mother. Her dress and the sleeves of her cardigan are wet. Her hands on the ice-axe glisten with petrol. And he understands what she is planning to do.

'Mother,' he says, 'you can't. You are going to kill them all – the people too. The children.'

She looks at him. The flickering light casts deep shadows across her face. 'It is better,' she says. 'I know that now.'

He shakes his head. 'You're going to kill *me*,' he says, and runs up to her, nuzzles his face into her stomach and wraps his arms around her thigh. 'Don't you love me any more?' He tries to sound like the little boy she loves so fiercely.

The newborns watch them in silence, hanging back, waiting to see who is going to lead them. He is going to take them with him when he leaves, up to the sun deck.

'Don't you see?' he says, and takes a step back. 'We can finally be free. The Old Ones won't even understand what's happening until it is too late. They won't have any power over us any more.'

She just stares at him without responding. But he can see the doubt in her eyes. Her grip on the ice-axe has loosened. Beneath them, the floor rocks almost imperceptibly. He tries to find the right words. 'You don't have to be afraid. This is the start of something new – something much better. The humans are destroying themselves anyway. If we don't decimate them, the world won't survive for long. This way there might still be a chance for them and for us.'

Her features soften. Now, when things have come to a head, it seems he is finally getting through to her.

'Don't you understand I want to experience this with you?' he presses.

She starts crying and it shocks him. He hasn't seen her cry in so long.

'Yes,' she says. 'I understand.'

He nods eagerly and holds up his arms for her to pick him up.

The newborns are a silent horde.

The woman looks at her beloved son. She raises the ice-axe and crushes his skull with a single blow.

Pia

Dan. His name is Dan. She knows him. He is like her. She doesn't like him.

She knows his name, but she doesn't know her own.

Cold. It is cold here. She recognises everything. Home. This is home but it is all wrong. Too quiet. The deck still under her feet. The sea so grey. Everything is grey. She tries to hold on to her thoughts but they scatter in the wind. Still, it is better now. Not like before, when she was hungry. Her insides don't burn now. Her wound is gone.

She is probably waking up. She has been dreaming for a long time. Time that has disappeared.

She kicks him in the head and he falls onto his side. She stares at him. This Dan person. She tries to fight through the fog shrouding her thoughts. He gets up on all fours. She looks at his injured hand. It has been injured before, another time. Something about the hand is important. There is a child as well. Does Dan have a child? No. The child is his father. She can't figure it out. Everything started with him and the child. She will stop it.

She will stop him. It is her job. That is why she is here. She knows that.

She focuses on the body behind Dan. He has killed but not eaten. Things have been ripped apart. Everything has been wasted. Blood covers the floor, cold and dead. She recognises the smells coming from the body and memories flicker inside her. She can't hold on to them, just *Filip*. The name sticks. She knows he is important. She has cared about him.

She kicks Dan in the head again and he falls backwards, lands heavily. He gets back up. He is bigger than her now that he is standing up.

He frightens her. He hates her too. He is afraid too. One of them must die.

He tries to grab her and she slaps his hands away. She knows what she is doing. In another life, she knew. It is enough. Her body remembers.

Her knee comes up between his legs. He bends down and her other knee rises up to meet his face. Something breaks. She hurls herself at him, using all her weight, trying to get him down on the floor.

But he is stronger, he resists, so she tries to bite him. Her teeth shut around his ear, cold in her mouth. She tears it off, spits it out.

He knocks her over. She is on her back now, he on top. Heavy. She tries to break free but can't move.

'You cunt, you fucking cunt.' He slams her head against the floor. It hurts. He hates her. He hates everyone. He slams her head against the floor again. Her skull crunches.

Something is moving through the air, making it whine above her. There's a wet thud. Dan blinks; no strength in his fingers now. Blood. Cold. Dead. Dripping into her face. He keeps blinking.

She pushes him aside and wipes her eyes.

There is a man there with no hair on his head but hair on his face. She recognises him. He is a friend. But he looks at her like he is afraid of her. There's a fire-axe in his hand, blood dripping from it. She turns to Dan. There is a new gaping mouth in his throat, just above his collarbone. He is injured, but still strong.

Hurry up. She leaps on top of him, digs her fingers into his throat and tears open the gaping mouth that wasn't there before.

Dan screams, his teeth snapping and snapping. She finds the hard, slippery column inside, grasps it firmly. He stares at her, trying to say something, but she doesn't want to hear it. She braces her knee against the side of his throat and bends it until the column snaps.

Dan goes limp.

She pulls her hands out. She looks up at the man with hair on his face. There is a gash across his forehead. He is crying. It makes her sad.

They belong together. He is not like her, and yet they belong together. She loves him.

'Pia?' he says.

Yes: that is her name. *Pia.* Her name is Pia. She used to be a person. Someone gave her a name.

Now she knows his name too.

She tries to say it, wants to show him she knows, but her lips won't cooperate. Her tongue is thick and strange. 'Call ... eeeehhh.'

He nods and cries harder.

She touches her neck: no hole. But her skull has fractured and the edges are grinding against each other under her skin. Pain flashes across her vision like lightning.

Two children come running: a boy and a girl. She has seen them before. She tries to remember. The girl was afraid, pretending to be angry. It was so easy to see, to recognise herself in the girl.

There was a woman too: a woman whose blood fills her now. The blood made the pain go away but the hunger remains, and the smell of the children is so tempting.

She has to leave. Get away from them. She doesn't want to harm them.

Has to help others.

She looks at Calle. He will help the children. She points to the staircase; she doesn't recall where it leads. But it is where they are going. Along with everyone else.

'Yes,' he says, 'we are getting out of here.'

Out of here. She tastes the words. He means something beyond the grey light and the water.

She is not getting out of here. She has to help others. It is her job. It is why she is here.

She raises her hand to Calle's face. He starts, still afraid of her. She strokes his cheek. His hair is soft against her fingers. She hopes he finds what he is looking for. There is someone important to him. She sees pink paper streamers. She can hear them rustling in her hands. Calle wasn't there, but he was still with them.

She lets her hand fall to her side.

She has to leave, get away from the children.

There is screaming inside, by the stairs. That is where she is going.

People move aside when she passes.

She must help people get out. She must kill anyone trying to stop them.

Calle

There is no shelter from the wind on the sun deck and the people gathered by the life rafts are shivering. Calle scans their faces as he crosses the deck. There are maybe a hundred of them, all told, and another twenty or thirty in the group coming up behind him.

He can't see Vincent anywhere.

He has picked up Albin; Lo is running next to them. Pia's voice is echoing inside him.

Call . . . eeeehhh.

He has fought the urge to fall apart for so long now. The children are the only thing keeping him from losing his mind; the thought that he has to stay strong for them. Maybe they are saving him, not the other way around.

Marisol is standing by a davit, shouting instructions to a couple of passengers who are pulling on the lines to hoist the raft out over the water, then she runs on to the next one. She is deathly pale, determined; there's dried blood on her upper lip. A couple of girls still wearing their cleaners' uniforms are handing out blankets to anyone who needs one. A waiter from Poseidon is helping people put on life vests.

Calle does a three-sixty in the wind, gazing out across the water beyond the confines of the *Charisma*. There's no land in sight but at least the Baltic is calm. And there is light now. After everything that has happened tonight, the world has, in spite of everything, reached out to them.

He puts Albin down on the deck and grabs blankets for himself and the children, thankful that they are wearing relatively warm clothes.

If they make it, at least he has achieved something.

They have to make it.

A fight has broken out over the life vests. The waiter from Poseidon tries to intervene, nervously assuring everyone that there are plenty to go around, but they ignore him. Calle is unable to suppress the thought that Pia would have resolved the situation in seconds.

Call . . . eeeehhh.

He glimpsed a part of the real Pia in the creature

the vampire

she had become. And Dan Appelgren: he could talk; he could think. He was a monster, but then, he might have been a monster even before he was infected.

They're vampires. But they are. *Don't you get it?*

He wonders if they did the right thing not telling Albin about his mum. Can the infected be helped? Can they become themselves again?

Would the man he killed in the mess have been able to?

'I'm going to help them with the rafts,' he says, wrapping the blanket tighter around Albin. 'And I want you and Lo to get on the first one you see.'

The boy barely reacts.

'Mum!' Lo shouts. 'I can see my mum!'

Albin looks up for the first time as Lo runs towards a group of people who have just come up on the sun deck. Her blanket comes off her shoulders and flaps away in the wind. A woman with blonde hair throws her arms open, starts running towards her, screaming loudly.

Calle takes Albin's hand. They walk towards Lo, who is burrowing further into her mother's embrace. Calle can't see their faces, but through the sound of the wind he can hear they are both crying.

Mårten

Mårten takes a swig from the bottle but can barely taste the alcohol any more. The broken glass crunches underfoot when he steps into the spa. There's a faint smell of chlorine and spicy essential oils. It is dead quiet. In front of him is the reception desk and behind that a glass-brick wall. A pale greyness is seeping through; he realises there must be big windows behind it. A door is standing ajar. He walks forward, passing a sofa and some armchairs, a bowl of water on the coffee table, plastic flowers with fleshy, pink petals floating inside it. Glossy magazines in a rack on the wall show laughing women with their heads thrown back, all pearly white teeth, biting into apples. Their eyes seem to follow him as he walks past the wheelchair.

He hears a splashing sound somewhere up ahead.

He peers in through the door. A green plastic non-slip carpet lines a wide aisle leading to a hot tub. The edge is four tiles high. There are panoramic windows from floor to ceiling behind it. The lanterns outside are glowing faintly against the grey sky. The clouds are moving so quickly; when he looks at them it almost feels like the ship is flying, even though it is no longer moving at all.

'Cilla?' he calls, and takes a swig from the bottle. 'Are you in here?'

He enters, the soles of his shoes squeaking softly against the plastic. He passes the doors to the changing rooms, the sauna, glassed-in treatment rooms with massage benches. Now he can make out the bow deck on the other side of the windows. There are piles of bodies. A man in a cornflower-blue windbreaker is dragging himself forward on his elbows.

Mårten takes another swig. 'Cilla?' he calls. 'Where are you?'

His intoxicated voice echoes back at him. He has never felt more alone.

Water sloshes over the edge of the pool and he notices that it is tinged faintly pink. He forces himself to take a step closer so he can see down into the water. There are red streaks in it, but there is no one in the tub.

'Cilla?'

He hears something wet moving, smacking against the floor.

Mummy. She's here now.

A hand gropes its way into the air on the other side of the hot tub, grabs hold of the edge, and Cilla's profile appears, reflected in and distorted by the water. She turns her head, looking straight at him with empty eyes. Her neck crunches loudly. Water drips from her short hair into her face. She leans against the edge of the tub and pulls herself onto her feet in front of the windows. Her wet jumper clings to her delicate frame. He can't stop staring at her legs, which are clearly visible through her dripping skirt. They are much too thin, after being unused for so long. Her thighs don't touch. Her knees look like enormous growths.

Her skirt squelches when she takes a step towards him. She stumbles, but doesn't fall. She takes another step.

How?

Her face has contracted into a grimace of agony he recognises; he's seen it before. She always tries to hide it, always has to act so bloody stoic, but this time she doesn't even seem aware of it: she doesn't seem to be aware of anything, except him.

What is going on behind those vacant eyes?

'Cilla?' he says.

Another step. Her teeth snap together with a sound like scissors.

Mårten drops his bottle. It bounces against the non-slip carpet, clattering loudly as it rolls over the edge and away across the tiled floor.

Cilla tilts her head, looking at it uncomprehendingly.

The announcement said bites are contagious.

She is infected – sick – but she can walk. How is that possible? Nothing is how it should be, and yet it feels like his whole life has led up to this moment.

Cilla reaches out for him, and he grabs her skinny arms and shakes her. Her head wobbles back and forth, her neck creaks and clicks. He hears himself scream at the top of his lungs as he shoves her as hard as he can. Cilla totters backwards, falls and almost smacks the back of her head against the edge of the pool.

Mårten's body feels light, as if he has thrown off a burden he has carried all his life. He is getting out of here. He is going to find Abbe up by the life rafts.

He is going to have Abbe to himself.

Mårten runs back towards the glass-brick wall and hears *slop*, *slop* behind him as Cilla gets back up. He tears open the door and steps out into the reception area.

528

The gloomy room is teeming with them. The broken glass crunches when they start moving towards him. He can hear the snapping of their teeth. More are filing in from the hallway. There is nowhere to go.

Slop, slop. The lights have gone out on the wheelchair Cilla no longer needs.

She wraps her arms around his neck and presses herself against him, making the back of his T-shirt cold and wet. Her lips brush against the skin of his neck. He can feel the teeth underneath.

Albin

The sea is grey and choppy; it looks like it's made of stone. The first life rafts have been lowered into the water and bob peacefully on the surface.

Linda is still crying, squeezing him and Lo tightly, and yet they are barely touching because their life vests are in the way.

'Come on, Abbe,' Linda says, and stands up. 'It's time.'

He shakes his head. A raft is dangling from the davit in front of them and people are already seated under its orange dome. Some of them are trying to use their phones, but no one can get reception. Marisol asks everyone climbing up if they have been bitten, but how is she supposed to know if they are lying?

'Abbe,' Lo says, 'we have to go.'

It is all far too similar to the last time she tried to persuade him to get on a raft. It hardens his resolve and he stubbornly shakes his head. 'Not without my mum,' he says, 'and not without Calle.'

Calle sinks down onto his haunches next to him and turns him around so they are facing each other. 'I'm going to wait here to see if my boyfriend is coming. Just a little while longer. You have to get on this raft now.'

'And then what?' Albin says. 'What happens after that?'

'If they don't find Cilla and Mårten by tonight, you will come with us to Eskilstuna,' Linda says, 'and we'll wait to hear from them together.'

'What if we don't hear from them?'

'Then you will stay with us,' Linda says. 'We're going to get through this, you know. Please, Abbe, let's go now.'

Abbe presses his lips shut. He notices Calle and Linda exchanging a look, then Calle calls out to Marisol that she can fill the last spots on the life raft and launch it; they'll take the next one.

A red-haired old lady in a striped jumper comes up to them. Albin peers up at her. She looks nice, but she is nervous.

'I'm sorry,' she says, 'but is your name Calle?'

'Yes?' Calle says, and stands up.

'I saw your ring,' the old lady says. 'I . . . I knew it was you.'

Something white moves at the edge of Albin's vision; when he turns to look, he realises it is a seagull. It flaps its wings, opens its beak to let out a screech.

If the gull is here, they can't be far from Finland. At least, he thinks that is right. He has never thought about how beautiful they are: the curved beak, so perfect for catching prey; the pretty lines formed by the darker feathers on its wings.

'Can I tell you something?' he says to Lo. 'In the olden days, they thought seagulls were the souls of dead sailors.'

The gull lands on the railing right next to him, looks straight at him and tilts its head. The wind ruffles its feathers. It opens its beak again.

Calle has started crying behind him, and Albin understands that it is about the man Calle has been looking for all along.

'I'm so sorry,' the old lady tells him, 'I'm so very, very sorry.'

Albin reaches out to touch the gull; it emits a final screech and flies off.

'I'm going to tell you everything,' the old lady says to Calle, 'as soon as we're off this ship.'

Albin turns to Calle.

The old lady is holding his hands and she is crying too. 'He loved you very much,' she says.

Albin wants to tell them that he knows who that seagull must have been, but Calle wouldn't understand right now. He will have to tell him some other time.

It is time to get off the ship.

The *Baltic Charisma*

The dark-haired woman is sitting on the petrol-soaked floor, holding her son's body close. He almost disappears in her arms. He feels so small; he feels like her little boy again. If she closes her eyes and tries to ignore the smells, she can almost imagine that they are back at the turn of the last century, that he has fallen asleep in her arms. Eternal sleep. She reluctantly opens her eyes and looks at the newborns through the shimmering fumes. She pulls the gold lighter out of her cardigan pocket. It clicks loudly when she opens it.

Time is short now, but she is scared of what she has to do, much more scared than she had expected. She tries to tell herself that it doesn't matter if a few people have already made it off the ship, as long as they are not infected, that it doesn't matter that they are bringing videos and photographs with them. The only thing the world will see is a lot of people acting incomprehensibly and violently; no one will believe the truth, not if the bodies that have turned are gone.

Humans are so skilled at finding explanations that fit their world view. They have done so before, and they will do it again, if she succeeds in her task. She can't know for sure what will happen once she ignites the petrol. She can only hope.

The woman hugs the boy tighter still and sniffs the nape of his neck, but he smells only of death. She tries to conjure the good memories: cold nights in Russia before the Great War; the fifties, all those beautiful, impoverished teenagers travelling to the Riviera to chase forbidden adventures; the fireworks marking the new millennium, when she remembered the dawn of a different century. She kisses her son's chubby cheek. Will they meet again on the other side? The Spiritists were convinced there is a life after this one, but she and her son have already crossed death's border once. What will be left after they pass it again?

The tiny wheel on the lighter spins under her thumb, sparks crackle and the flame burns bright and clear. She closes her eyes again, throws the lighter down, hears the fire whisper to life. Feels the heat of it. The newborns scream in panic, but she is not letting go of her son. The fire will melt them into one. It caresses her petrol-soaked clothes, devours her hair in one breath and spreads across her skin. The pain is unbearable, but it will soon be over. The smell of charred flesh is spreading. The voices of the newborns are growing shriller, louder, but her mouth remains closed. Her eyes stay shut.

The fire reaches a lorry with Finnish plates. Its driver was one of Adam's first victims. In the trailer are empty acetylene canisters the hauliers never declared. Olli didn't know, and no one checked his cargo before he rolled aboard.

The explosion shakes the *Baltic Charisma*, can be felt in walls and floors and ceilings. It rips a hole in the poorly maintained hull. The gash extends down below the waterline. The sea can finally make its way in.

The fire spreads through the car deck, melting plastic, shattering windows. It consumes the curtains of a coach; it burns in the wide-open mouths of the newborns. The water from the sprinkler system is powerless against this inferno. The flames spread towards undamaged fuel tanks, the LPG canisters in the dark-haired woman's caravan. The smoke filling the car deck is thick and acrid.

The heat makes the woman's skin crack; the flesh underneath bubbles and sizzles. The rubber soles of her son's shoes have melted.

For a moment after the explosion the sun deck went absolutely quiet. Now everyone is screaming in terror.

The ship is taking on ever more water. It floods deck two, lifting the remains of Vincent's body off the floor.

Having heard and felt the explosion, people flee their cabins, fighting to reach the stairs, trying to keep their balance as the floor starts tilting almost imperceptibly under their feet. The bottles in the bar at Charisma Starlight slide off their shelves. The microphone stand topples off the edge of the stage. Glasses slip from the tables. In the tax-free shop, bottles of perfume and bags of candy fall from the shelves.

The more the *Charisma* lists, the more water she takes on, and the more water she takes on, the more she lists.

People are staggering, bracing themselves against the walls as best they can. Bodies roll across the carpets, across the outer decks and plunge into the water. People cling to the brass banisters of the staircases; some fall and others are knocked down by panicked passengers trying to get past, get up, get out.

Madde

'Hurry!' shouts Marianne, who is already seated in the last life raft on this side of the ship. She is holding on to Stella, whom she has wrapped in several blankets. The bottom of the raft is resting against the *Charisma*'s hull. They are going to have to slide down the steep side of the ship and hope the raft stays upright when it hits the water below.

Madde clings to the railing, looking at the people who have managed to climb out of the ship, only to end up in droves against the railing on the other side of the deck. Some are trying to dash up the slippery uphill slope to their side; others have found life vests and are jumping from the railings into the water. Madde hopes they don't end up under the *Charisma* when the ship finally settles onto her side.

There is barely room for Madde in the raft, but Calle holds out his hand. His ring sparkles faintly. It's identical to the one Vincent wore on his left hand.

She straddles the edge, thrusting her foot under the rope that runs around the outer edge of the raft to keep from falling out and holds on to Calle for dear life.

She nods and the girl who worked in the bar at Starlight cuts the lines. They start sliding. There is not a sound inside the raft. Madde tries to focus on keeping her balance, watching the edge of the hull rush nearer and the steel-grey water below. She can't judge the drop. She closes her eyes when there is nothing but air under the raft. Her stomach flips. The blanket around her shoulders is torn away by the wind.

The raft hits the water and Madde flies off the edge, hurtling through the air. There is a terrible pain in her ankle, then, suddenly, she is in the water and the cold shocks her entire system. Her ears ring. Everything is so dark, and so cold her face is already numb. She shuts her mouth and eyes tight and tries to swim, but she can no longer tell up from down.

And then finally, *finally*, she breaks the surface. She can hear the screaming from the other rafts, hears the *Charisma* sigh and creak behind her. She shoves a suitcase floating towards her aside and spots the life raft bobbing on the water not too far away. Marianne is shouting something at her, but she can't make out the words.

She tries to swim, doing her best despite the pain in her foot, but she can't get anywhere in the gently billowing swell. Someone on the raft has put paddles in the water. She squints. Are they coming for her, or are they going to leave her here?

How many minutes before she freezes to death?

Madde looks around, panicking. The ship is listing even more, exposing its enormous belly to her. She pumps her legs faster, but her head keeps ending up under water and now she is swallowing big gulps of it. She can't get away from the *Charisma*. The ship is pulling her in. She vaguely remembers something about eddies around sinking ships. She's panting heavily. The coldness of the water is numbing her ankle, dulling the throbbing pain. It feels like her lungs are going to explode, but the raft is coming closer.

Calle leans over and holds his paddle out to her.

Her fingers slip on it. She gropes at the air, but she can't reach it again.

Something touches her ankle. Cold fingers brush against her skin.

She kicks out behind her with her uninjured foot and feels silky smooth hair slip between her toes. One of *them*.

She screams, afraid to kick again in case she comes into contact with the teeth that are probably snapping under the surface of the water.

The fingers are there again, closing around her ankle, tugging it, pulling her back down.

Her mouth fills with water when she screams.

They don't breathe, they don't breathe, they don't care that they're under water.

She manages to pull her foot free of the slippery grasp and breaks the surface again, but the hand could grab her at any moment. She splutters and gasps for air.

They don't need air.

And this time the people in the raft reach her, strong hands grab her arms, wiggle in under them and hoist her up. She kicks her legs wildly to help, and there is loud splashing behind her and cold droplets on her back. The edge is so high, so fucking high. The hands in the water graze the sole of her foot and she screams, pulls her knees up, trying to find purchase against the rope with her uninjured foot. And the strong hands keep pulling her up until she falls into the raft, landing on her knees.

'Can you see anything?' she shouts. 'Have I been bitten? I can't feel anything. Have I been bitten?'

The raft starts to tilt when some of the passengers quickly shift to get further away from her, until the girl who works at Starlight yells admonishments.

538

Madde coughs up water while Marianne inspects the back of her legs and feet and assures her there are no bites as far as she can tell.

Madde looks down at the water. She can't see any of *them*, but she knows they are there, under the surface. Would they be able to climb onto the raft?

'They don't need to breathe,' she says. 'They don't need to breathe under water.'

The *Baltic Charisma*

The newborns flail under the surface, kicking their legs, but they can't move fast enough to stay afloat. Their open mouths let in freezing water, making them heavier, pulling them ever further into the depths.

The ship has settled onto its side. The sun has come up, gleaming in the portside windows. They face the sky now. On the starboard side there is nothing but water outside the windows that are now hundreds of feet deep. Bodies float past: some have their eyes open; they stare back at anyone looking out. Walls have turned into floors; floors have become walls. Everything has been overturned, and still a few people are fighting to climb out of their cabins and find ways out.

The dark-haired woman and her son are nothing but ashes and bone fragments now, dissolved in the currents on the car deck.

The water inside the ship is rising fast, filling the hallways.

In the galley, cupboard doors have swung open, spewing out their contents.

In Poseidon, glasses and white linen tablecloths and chairs are floating on the swirling surface.

The long serving tables in Charisma Buffet are on their side, barricading the entrance.

When the water reaches the generators, the emergency power cuts out and all the lights on board go off.

A dressing gown billows gently around the man with a knife in his stomach. He is floating in the water filling the stairwell on deck five. He opens his eyes.

The woman who was always saying she wanted to live aboard the *Charisma* has had her wish fulfilled. She is stuck under an arcade game that has tipped onto its side on the eighth floor. Her teeth snap against the rising water.

In the sea outside the *Charisma*, those who have ended up in the water are yelling desperately. No one aboard the last raft to be launched says anything. They know there is no more room; they would risk everyone's lives if they tried to save even one more.

Madde watches the ship, wondering where Zandra and Vincent are now. She hears screaming and loud splashing from another raft: one of *them* has managed to surface and is clawing at the edge of the raft. His snapping teeth are sharp enough to puncture the rubber. The people on board are striking at him with a paddle, but Madde has to look away.

Marianne is shaking, not just from cold. Now the tension is dissipating, violent convulsions are racking her body. She tries to keep them under control for Stella's sake. The girl has snuggled up in her arms and is sucking her thumb. Marianne watches Calle, who is paddling on the other side of the raft. Their eyes meet and she reminds herself to tell him that Vincent saved her life. That he was a hero.

Calle looks away, gazes at the *Charisma*. Her bow has risen up out of the water. When she sinks, she is going to pull down everything nearby with her. He and Marisol paddle harder; his arms are tired, the gash in his forehead is throbbing, but it feels good to work his body. A young guy vomits down the side without warning.

'I'm not sick,' he says quickly, and wipes his mouth, 'just drunk.'

A woman swears in Russian. Calle studies the young guy, thoughts racing through his mind. They need a plan: they need to get information through to whoever comes to rescue them. He looks at the people around him: Linda, who has her arms around the children, kissing the tops of their heads; the women on another raft who are singing to stay awake. Calle has always been told it's the people who put themselves first who survive a disaster, but maybe that's not entirely true. He glances at Marianne again, seeing her wrap her blanket around Madde, even though she is shaking herself. It is such a simple gesture, yet it contains so much kindness. Calle suddenly realises he is happy Vincent was with her. *Vincent is dead*. He tests out the thought. *Vincent doesn't exist. He is gone.* He can't believe it. It is too absurd to imagine that Vincent, who is the most alive person Calle knows, no longer exists. And even so, he hopes Vincent is dead. That is better than Vincent having turned into one of *them*.

Albin squints at the cold sun. There are fewer and fewer screams from the water as people die. Albin just wants to sleep. He has noticed that Linda is worried about him: the more worried she gets, the more she talks. Now she is telling him that she is sure his mum and dad are fine, that they are probably really worried about him right now, that they will all be reunited soon, but he can't focus on it because what she is saying is meaningless. His eyes close. Tiredness spreads through his body, making it warm.

'Don't fall asleep now, Abbe, okay?' Linda says, and he grudgingly looks up at her. 'You can't fall asleep, Abbe. You're going to freeze to death if you fall asleep.'

And he knows she is right, but sleep is pulling him under. The raft is rocking beneath him. The sound of the oars being dipped into the water is soothing.

Then he feels Lo's breath next to his face. 'I've been thinking about the vampires. Shouldn't they get hammered, drinking the blood of all those drunk people?'

Albin opens his eyes again. What Lo said has made him curious. 'Yes,' he says, 'that's weird.'

He suddenly becomes aware of a thrumming sound in the air: a helicopter. It's still far away. He isn't even sure he has really heard it until he notices other people scanning the sky too. He closes his eyes to hear better, and feels the tiredness making his body heavy again. Heavy and warm. The cold can't get to him any more.

'I don't think it's that weird,' Madde says. 'When you're really wasted, your blood alcohol level is the same as, like, reduced-alcohol beer. And that's hardly enough to get you sozzled.'

Albin remembers her from the terminal. She is shivering and her lips are blue, as if she's eaten blueberries. Her friend who dropped peanuts down her cleavage isn't here.

'Drinking blood is my number one advice to the general public,' Albin says.

The people nearest them on the raft stare at them.

'You eat blood sausage though,' Lo says. 'That's, like, the same as a scab, you know.'

The young guy who threw up before glares at them, and that makes Albin giggle.

'All right,' Linda says, 'that's enough.' But she shoots Lo a grateful look when Albin isn't looking.

The thrumming of the helicopters is getting louder. The first can be seen on the horizon now.

The *Charisma* has risen out of the water like a tower. The prow is pointing straight up and she is sinking steadily, foot by foot, in the pale morning light. The white bird with its pipe and captain's hat is just clear of the waterline.

Marisol rests her aching arms now they have put a safe distance between themselves and the ship. She puts the paddle down in the raft. Her head is throbbing and she wishes she had a water bottle to hand. The pain is radiating up through the roof of her mouth. She licks her lips and tastes the blood that has dried on her upper lip. *Gross.* But she licks it again. It feels like the new life in her belly needs the blood. Wants more.

The eddies rising up through the ship make its walls buckle and break, shatters windows, sucks suitcases and clothes and toothbrushes out of cabins, sweeps up bodies that have fallen down stairwells and corridors.

The last bit of air is squeezed out of the *Charisma* with a rumbling sigh, a terrifying final exhalation.

Pia can't fight it any longer. She is pulled under by the current. It's like free-falling. Cold water fills her nose, mouth, rushes into her stomach. She looks at the sunshine, slanting down through the water above her. *Beautiful.* She doesn't want to sink down into the darkness. She doesn't want to disappear. The hulking shape of the ship looms, a gigantic sea monster. There are bodies beneath her kicking feet. A few of them are like her. They are sinking, sinking, and she is sinking with them into the dark.

The first man infected on board claws at the walls of his water-filled cell. The woman and men in the cells next door have drowned, but he was not so lucky.

Some of the newborns are already crawling across the sea floor. Their eyes are open. Their teeth snap like scissors. Everything is so different down here. It's dark. Sound works differently, smells act different too. But it is enough to guide them. They crawl and drag themselves towards land.

They are slow, but determined.

ACKNOWLEDGEMENTS

They say it takes a village to raise a child. That goes for this book as well. I would like to thank all the friends and strangers who helped me: answered questions, read drafts and gave me feedback from their many different fields of expertise, or cheered me on when I was sure this ferry would sink and take me down with it. Anna Andersson, Kim W. Andersson, Ludvig Andersson, Åsa Avdic, Helena Dahlgren, Gitte Ekdahl, Måns Elenius, Maria Ernestam, Varg Gyllander, Emma Hanfot, Rickard Henley, Karl Johnsson, Jenny Jägerfeld, Ulf Karlsson, Fredrik Karlström, Åsa Larsson, Patrik Lundberg, Jenny Milewski, Elias Palm, Alexander Rönnberg, Mia Skimmerstrand, Gustav Tegby, Maria Turtschaninoff and Elisabeth Östnäs – thank you.

The eighteen months I spent on board the *Baltic Charisma* were, for better or for worse, the most intense time of my life. There are a few people I feel an extra-deep gratitude for. Levan Akin, Sara B. Elfgren and Anna Thunman Sköld – you guys were my life rafts. It would take at least another book just to name all the things I have to thank you for. That also goes for Pär Åhlander, who was the first one to read it, who went with me on a cruise ('Are you the one smelling like sausage?') and who designed the cover to look just like I pictured it, only much better.

Also, thank you, Kim Petersen, a great friend and a great concept artist, for creating the cover illustration of the blood-soaked corridor.

Thank you, Dad, for letting me work on your couch, always with a coffee cup and your excellent food within reach.

And, of course, thank you, Johan Ehn, for putting up with my obsessing over corridors and characters during this eighteen-month cruise. Marrying you was definitely the best decision I ever made.

A lot of amazing people have helped me with my research. They have patiently answered stupid questions, and looked for answers when they didn't already have them. Sometimes, they even gave me answers to questions I knew too little to know that I should ask. They even meticulously combed through my drafts to look for mistakes. Most of these heroes and heroines wish to keep their anonymity, with two exceptions: Matilda Tudor, who gave me a lot of insight into the social structures on board; and Sven-Bertil Carlsson, who helped me with the technical stuff. I would like to add that any factual errors are completely my own, whether they were intentional or not. I would also like to add that if I ever set foot on a ferry again, there are no hands I would feel safer in than those belonging to the wonderful people I've talked to.

Thank you to my publisher, Susanna Romanus, and my editor, Fredrik Andersson, who understood exactly what I wanted to go with *Blood Cruise* and helped me get there.

Thank you to my agent Lena Stjernström and the rest of the crew at Grand Agency, my life vests when the ship is rocking.